Sight Unseen Book One:
Tea Room Tales

By Ellen Anne Eddy

TMS Press

This is a work of fiction. All of the characters, organizations, and events in this novel are either products of the author's imagination or are used fictitiously.

Sight Unseen Book One: Tea Room Tales

By Ellen Anne Eddy ISBN: **9780982290170**

 TMS Press Galesburg, IL

Dedication

To Lauren, who asked for these stories, for Don who had his doubts, and for Chuck, Kathie and Donna, who fought endlessly against my dyslexia and punctuation. Thank you!

Books by Ellen Anne Eddy:

Quilting and Fabric Art

- Thread Magic Garden: Create Enchanted Quilts with Thread Painting & Pattern-Free Appliqué (2012)
- Dragonfly Sky (2009)
- Ellen Anne Eddy's Dye Day Workbook (With Lynn Clayton, 2009)
- Thread Magic: The Enchanted World of Ellen Anne Eddy (1997)
- A Ladybug's Garden (2009)
- Quick and Easy Machine Binding Methods (2009)
- Many Creatures Under Many Skies (2013)

Children's Books

- The Town of Torpor and the Very Vulgar Day Lily (2011)
- Tigrey Leads the Parade (2009)

Fiction

- Sight Unseen Book One: Tearoom Tales (2017)
- Sight Unseen Book Two: The Inverted Cup (2018)
- Sight Unseen Book Three: The World in Reflection (2018)

Join the Tea Room!

You want to know all the crazy things that happen at the tea room. Right? Join our mailing list and you will. You'll also know about new books and new stories coming out, inside information about what it means to be a psychic, insights into the making of the stories and the art for Sight Unseen.

And a free for you sneak peek story from *The World in Reflection*, Book Three of the Sight Unseen Series.

Email us at: Sightunseenseries.2016@gmail.com, and take your space at the tea table.

Or join us at www.sightunseen2016.wordpress.com

Sight Unseen Book One:

Tea Room Tales

by Ellen Anne Eddy

Contents

Introduction

Introduction

Years ago, my good friend Lauren Strach began to insist that I write my memoirs. I was teaching quilting on the road at the time. When you're teaching, there are some things you just can't talk about. Too scary. Too separating. Too much for someone who's come into your classroom to learn free motion. It's not kind. You are there to teach, not tell.

We all have a private life. A place where we can't tell all the secrets. I believe that is a good thing in simple society. Internet media has made us want to know way too much about each other's lunch, health, political opinions, sorrows, and secrets. We are all hanging out in the open. I have had some amazing journeys in my life, and my experiences in the tea room were part of that. I don't believe I am unique as a psychic. Instead, I see it as a part of the human genome that we all share. My personal belief is that it opens up in fear and pain for our protection, and should naturally shut down otherwise, like your eye does, for rest and for cleansing. I hand it to God and I leave it at that.

But I learned so much at the tea room. Not about being psychic particularly, but about living in a world where people were not like me. And the stories, sanitized for our protection, are a whole lot of fun.

I have a history in this. Within the confines of history, I have played loosely with fact because it is fiction.

Within these stories I intend to share this odd journey that I took thirty years ago. I am not inviting your criticism, religious advice or help. Nor am I offering any of that to any of you. My belief is in a personal God. I believe we are all met by God on that road, and no one else can lead us but Him. If you worry for my soul, say a prayer and I will pray for you as well. If you decide to breach this arrangement and come save me, I will be praying for you anyway. But I am willing to follow God where He takes me, and I trust you are willing to trust that.

I don't intend to tell anyone's secrets. I will never read again because I consider it massively unhelpful. There are two great gifts given by not knowing the future: the cushion of shock against pain, and the joy of surprise. I won't rob anyone of either of those.

Sight Unseen is fiction. Never meant to be anything else. I wrote stories that are clearly fantasy in most regards. For those of you looking for a manual as a reader, or for tips and clues, you'll need something else. Don't ask me. I won't tell.

Ellen Anne Eddy

Reader

Reader

I held the folded newspaper under my arm as I crossed the Boston Commons and headed for the door across the street that said Rita's French Tearoom. It had been a short walk from my apartment across the open space that had once been city land for cattle grazing. The Commons was a legendary public area, mostly a park, but a park in the heart of Boston and deeply tied into the history of the city. On one side was the heart of Boston's old town. On the other side was a jumble of small businesses and ramshackle apartments, one of which I had taken as a college student at Boston State. College had ended, but my passion and desire for a psychology degree gave me no job credits with a mere bachelor's. Eventually I would need my masters and doctorate. But that would have to wait for more funds and more energy. So I was looking for a job that was just a job, not something I would pour myself into, or care about after hours. Just a nine to five with some benefits and salary. I'd gather some cash and catch my wind before entering the upper academic whirlwind. After a long round of interviews for shop clerk girls, a set of tests at a temp agency and an offer to be your own boss doing telemarketing, I circled the ad that said, "Are you Psychic? Tea Leaf reader wanted." Almost as a lark, I went past the downstairs wig shop that could have served either cancer patients or working girls or both, from its window into the elevator that took me to the second floor where the tearoom was. I asked for a cup of tea and casually laid down the circled newspaper ad.

The woman who served me was a well cushioned black lady with a smile as warm as Georgia. "Hmm," she said, looking me up and down. "Young lady, Rita going to want to talk to you."

I blinked. "Who is Rita?"

"Child, you looking for a job or not? Trust me, you want to talk to Rita. Come with me."

She returned with my teacup in hand and led me to an office in the back of the room. As I entered, a huge blue macaw in a birdcage lifted one wing and said "Tell me what you see! Tell me what you see!" Then he turned his head at me as if he expected my answer.

"Rita will be here in just a moment," the woman said, leaving me with the bird and my tea.

I almost tipped my teacup over, waiting for the reader. I touched the silver charm at my neck for luck. Nona gave it to me so long ago, I couldn't remember before I had it. It was a silver crafted hand with an evil eye bead center. "For you, Cara mia," Nona had said as she pressed it into my hands. I could feel her with me whenever I touched it. I wore it always at my throat.

The tearoom featured a tiny dining area with Victorian striped wallpaper. The decor was ladylike without being cute in any way. There was nothing French about Rita or the tearoom, or, for that matter, the tea. In the world of psychics, you were who you said you were. But everyone lied or misdirected, just a bit.

Rita entered and sat at the desk across from me. "What do you want me to read for you today?" she said, smiling. Rita should have been ugly, but she had far too much presence for that. Her hair was piled on top.

She wore a plum print dress. Her body and face seemed to be made of round clumps of clay. The animation in her face changed that perception. When she read she was electric.

"Your name?" she asked as she sat by me.

I finished my sandwich and sieved the last of the tea leaves with my teeth. "Marlene. My name is Marlene Calley." I stumbled over my name.

Rita turned my cup over.

"Tell me my past. Tell me my future. Tell me what you see." I was echoing something I'd heard before. I couldn't remember who said it.

"They're not that separate, you know," Rita said. She settled into her chair and my cup. "A journey, but not too far. A man you're with and two men you'll meet. You won't want the first two once you've met the third. The second man hunts where the others seek. The third no longer hunts because he's found who he is. You're at a new passage. A new road but you can't walk it until you know your past. You think the past is gone, but it rides on your throat and sits in your pocket. You'll attend a party that changes everything. Pay attention. Don't let the drink dull your senses.

It's not your friend. The car you're using isn't your car. But be careful. I see a car crash. Beware of fire. It will not burn you but it's the enemy of what you are trying to save. There's a snake in your cup but it will not hurt you. It belongs to a friend you haven't met yet." Rita rattled on. "Do you know any priests?" she asked me. I shook my head no. Her reading was different from my college friends. She read well. She was correct in the details. But I suspected the purpose of Rita's reading primarily served her.

I got a glimpse of the leaves in my cup. I'd been reading tea leaves with college friends since my freshman year in college. I learned some of it from them.

She looked straight at me. "You have a powerful gift."

I hadn't thought about it like that. We drank tea and read cups in college to avoid our homework.

She put down my cup. "I could read more for you. But will you read for me?"

She got us both another cup of tea. We both sipped and talked about the weather. When I held her cup, my hands shook a bit.

Her cup overflowed with images of people and enterprises. Odd buildings. A clothes press. Small people coming to her in streams. I learned later that the tearoom was only a small part of her fiscal empire, which included tenement housing. She also owned a dry cleaners service. But the tearoom was her heart. It was who she was. She'd read for years and had an enviably stable client list. She'd been married, divorced, remarried and widowed. She had become precisely who she pretended to be.

After I'd read she said, "Your gift is strong. Why don't you come and read for me here?" It was surreal. I had a bachelor's degree I'd just earned in psychology. And I'd just learned that it would gain me 85 cents per hour more than a high school diploma at the clothing shop I applied at. "How much do you pay?"

Rita smiled. "It doesn't work like that. We read for tips. But with a gift like yours ... the clients are generous to readers they can trust."

I was twenty-one years old. I'd spent all of that time being safely practical and practically safe. My mother was dead and past being shocked. I had no other prospects. And not much to lose. I felt the pull of my own gift. So I came to read at the tearoom. So much for a low-pressure salaried job with benefits.

What is a gift? The ability to see the past, the future, the now. It's about perception. Readers perceive more than the present. Their sight stretches from past to future. A gift comes and goes. But at the tearoom you needed to be able to read when asked, never mind whether the gift was flaring or dormant. Rita taught me the observation that could fill the gaps. She could have taught my psych professors volumes.

"Look at their eyes first," Rita explained. "It means you see them. See how they hold themselves. Three quarters of the reading is in their posture and eyes. Their clothing shows you who they are physically. If you are wrong and they correct you, nod as if it's what you just said. And always end with something you know they want."

I was dumbfounded. "How do I know what they want?"

"It's not that complicated," she explained. "Everyone wants to be safe. Everyone wants to be loved. Everyone wants their best self to be recognized. Everyone wants to pass down what they've learned. If you end on one of those, they'll come back to you for years."

In fairness, Rita didn't scam people. Some readers frightened clients with the "terrible forces against them" and for a small fee would light candles for your protection, or cleanse you from evil spirits or remove curses. It was a vile scam that tended to make clients into slaves. It also made buckets of money.

Rita's gift was genuine. She was not so honest that she told them everything she saw, not if she thought it would harm them. She wasn't above making up a happy ending. She told them what she thought would help them most. She protected the people she read for. They loved her for it.

I stayed at Rita's tea room and she treated me much as a daughter.

She spent time on my training. My own mother was gone; it was a lot like being under a dragon's wing. I was warm and protected, as long as it was okay with the dragon. To read, you had to detach from the present to see the future and the past. Cards, cups, palms and auras all functioned as a focus.

Rita brought out her best crystal ball. She draped black silk behind it and sat me down. As she spoke I recognized her tone. She worked a mild form of hypnotism on me in training sessions. Her velvet voice shut the door on the outside world. "Focus on the center. Can you see the swirl in the center?"

It was not the crystal that swirled. It made my stomach tip a bit. I looked up from the ball, not so sure. "Stay with it," I heard Rita say. "No thoughts. No problems. At least not any of your own."

I thought I saw movement within the stone structure. But I couldn't put words or pictures to it. It was not enough to read from. Twenty minutes later I was still at a blank spot.

I simply couldn't read a crystal ball. I already knew tarot. At least, I knew the meanings of the cards. But Maggie taught me how cards fit into a whole.

Maggie was a huge-hearted black woman who had a gift like a thunderclap. She was, perhaps, the strongest psychic there. She looked at my tarot deck and sniffed. "Why you gotta read on those old nasty things?" she asked me. "I love to have you read for me, child, but not on those. Rita," she called out, "Have you got a plain deck of cards?" Maggie took the new deck into her hands and shuffled like a poker master.

Maggie taught me that the cards in tarot were the basis for a playing deck, and how to translate tarot into ordinary card decks. If you hit a level of perception, the meanings of the cards separately faded into a whole picture. It was like blending letters into words. The images had meanings as a whole, past separate meanings.

Maggie didn't need a deck. Or a teacup or your palm. She just knew on sight. Maggie couldn't teach anyone how she read. It was pure gift.

Rita taught me reading palms and astrology. I read hands well. I never mastered the math behind the astrology charts.

We had other readers who purely cold read, without any gift of sight. Their gift was observation. Since they told everyone what they wanted to hear, their clients loved them. They seemed faded though. They appeared to be translucent. They had a thin dreamy quality, as if they were already a little bit dead.

Rita also had an accountant, Will, who came in twice a week and reconciled the books. He slid past the readers at their tables, mildly afraid of them, and ensconced himself safely in the office where the numbers knew nothing of psychic powers and would not trouble his sleep. He was a big soft man in his fifties, loyal to Rita, planted firmly in the day-to-day world of accounting.

Most of our clients were middle-aged Bostonian women on their lunch breaks or out of the house for the day. They came to be entertain or stroked. It was a massage session for the ego. They wanted a time in their week that was all about them.

But a few of them wanted something different. A fair number of those worked as psychic practitioners themselves. In the same way you wouldn't do your own psychotherapy or your own tooth extraction, you didn't do your own reading. For about the same reasons.

Readers live within a hierarchy. They swim in a puddle of jealousy over other people's abilities. Most of them acknowledged an energy or entity bigger than they were. Some people confused that with power. I always knew it didn't belong to them personally or to me either. No one owned energy. It's lent, borrowed, stolen, or given, but it never belonged to anyone. Everyone has an electricity around them, but when it's past ordinary levels, it's startling. It's also easy to be become hungry for it, because we all by nature of our bodies crave energy. It often presents itself as a high sex drive or hyper activity, but that's just a physical manifestation. It also shows up with great artists, scientists, musicians, and politicians. Think Marilyn Monroe, or Cary Grant. Or Leonardo Da Vinci. Or John Kennedy. Think of energy as ice cream or coffee. More always sounds good. But it doesn't work that way. Just like coffee, there's a point where it becomes destructive. Psychic energy might feel like yours, but it came from somewhere. I'd begun to be nervous about where.

Most of the time in the tea room that was a moot point. I read as much by observation as by gift. It was the combination that made me sought after as a reader. I often wasn't in contact with much more than my own ability to observe. Reading people who had deep spiritual connections for any reason was much more direct. They're readings would fling off energy and images. You didn't have time to read the bend of their shoulders or their expression. It was all there broadcast in front of you. It was all "what you saw".

My first reading was for one of Rita's regular clients. Betty Rider was in her late forties. She was a plump, colorless woman, as contented as a matronly cat. Her colorless hair was in a slightly overgrown bob, her clothing a bit too tight around the middle. But that did not interfere with her enjoyment of her muffin or her tea.

"Betty, this is our new reader, Mirella," Rita said. "She's really wonderful. Do you mind if she takes your reading today?"

Betty pouted for a second as Rita popped another muffin on her plate. "She's good, right?"

"She's new," Rita admitted. "But she's very gifted."

Betty nodded assent as she pulled the second muffin apart. She drained the last of her tea and placed the cup upside down on her saucer. "Turn it around three times to the left," I said, as Rita had taught me. I held up the teacup and peered inside.

There was a room full of tables with toys all around. "You teach primary school, don't you?" I started.

Betty smiled. "Yes and no." I cocked my head, listening, and continued as if I hadn't heard. "Your car needs new tires." I saw the car itself with one wheel flattened. She nodded. I saw coins rolling away from the car itself. A stream of tea fell out of the cup taking the money with it. "Be careful who you take it to. I don't think the tire guy is honest."

I went on. "You have mice in your classroom." I saw one sitting in her hand. "Are they pets? Do the initials OZ mean anything to you?"

Betty laughed out loud. "She's not only good, Rita, she's precious. Yes, I teach primary after a fashion. I teach art to adults, which means I teach them to play like kids. Yes, my tire went flat and the guy I took it to was a scumbag about fixing it. He way overcharged and didn't tell me he was going to until he handed me the bill. I have a frightened little lady who's my class mouse. Oz is my cat. She can read for me any time, Rita!" Betty slipped me five dollars, a respectable tip, and collected her bags to go. She hugged both Rita and me, and skipped out the door like an eight- year-old.

I read regularly for Betty after that. Almost every Saturday morning saw her at the tearoom waiting for a reading with me.

Usually her concerns were small, everyday things. People in her class. She didn't seem to have a boyfriend or husband, but her cup was full of friends and activities. Her passion for food and cooking also showed in her cups. As did her cat.

Oz the Munificent was a long-haired, Buddha-sized gray cat. She herself was catlike and Oz was the male cat who ruled her world. She finally 'fessed up' that she cooked certain things especially for him. One day she came in and asked me to see if I could see anything about him. His appetite was off, and he was older. I looked into her cup and saw him flat on the rug. He looked dead.

I tried to remember what Rita told me about seeing the hard, bad things for people. I knew Oz was the love of her life. I tried to be gentle.

I started with a huge understatement. "I don't think Oz has been feeling well. You might want to take him to the vet." I said it as mildly as I could, although I knew it was bad.

"He's sick?" she asked, hovering on my answer. "He's not going to die, is he?"

Confronted outright, I said what I was sure of. "He seems to be just lying there."

"Is he going to die?"

What could I say? The answer was yes, sometime. Everyone dies, sometime. I didn't think I could tell her that.

"I don't know," I said. "He doesn't look well."

Betty's face pinched in. She grabbed her purse and ran out the door.

Later that day, Rita got a call from her. "You tell that Mirella I don't ever want her to read for me again!"

Rita was, of course, her conciliatory best. "Did she read poorly for you? Was she in some way impolite?"

"Oz is dead. I had to put him down. Today. She knew. I know she knew. And she didn't tell me." Rita shut the door to her office so I couldn't hear her response. Except when she put down the receiver. I went over to take whatever punishment that was waiting for me.

"What exactly did you say?" she asked me.

"I told her Oz wasn't feeling well."

"Did you know Oz was dying?" Rita tapped her fingers as she scanned my face, looking for some inner explanation.

"Maybe," I answered. I shook my head and looked down at my hands.

"There wasn't a right answer, you know," Rita said. "Had you told her, she still would have been dreadfully upset."

Several weeks went by. Mary Lou was an angular woman dressed in black and gray. Mary Lou spent her days looking after her older mother. Once a month, respite care would give her a morning out. She spent it partially with us. She wore gray that matched her gray hair although sometimes she spiced her color combination with rose beige. Her skin now was almost the same color. I peered into her cup, appalled to see a coffin.

Again, I was so unsure what to say. It seemed unambiguous. Her mother had been hovering over the grave for months. I tried again to soft pedal the news. "Is your mother unwell?" I asked.

Her smile was rueful and terrible. "Mother died three days ago."

I saw her relief and grief, both too strong for me to bear. I stumbled through the rest of the reading. Mary Lou said almost nothing. She just folded things into her purse and left. I sat shaken by her pain, by her loss, by her evident relief and her attending guilt.

Rita came over to my table with a muffin and a teapot. She poured a cup of tea for me, which I drank. Then she picked up my cup. "Let me read for you," she said.

Rita slid gently into trance. "You're going to meet gypsies. There's a fire storm you need to be careful of. Look for a man whose name starts with E.

He'll be your friend, but he's not your lover. He'll ask for something you can't give him. Look for another man whose name starts with R. You don't think so, but he's the person you need. There's a lady whose name begins with B who will bring you all kinds of clients. You will go to a wedding where there are ghosts who need you. You'll meet a mermaid. Be careful of large birds. A shaman will give you three feathers and a dog. You'll meet a nun who will be your mentor. Her best friend is a two-hundred-year old witch. I see you running from a tiger. And from a boy in brown shoes.

"You'll have power in your day. But you can't be confused. You can have power, you can wield power, but you never are a power. No one is. It's a delusion. Beware of being right. Beware of proving you are right."

The images splashed over me. I couldn't hold on to them. As I listened to Rita read, I understood that she was telling me what my life as a reader would be like. It would be full of amazing people, some crazy, some broken, some astonishing. Full of people's stories. Full of the solutions they would have to find for themselves. Full of witness to their lives, their pain, their growth, their triumphs and their losses.

"No matter who opens the door on their pain, whether they do or we do, it is opened," Rita said. "Aired. Allowed to breathe. Kept from festering. That doesn't mean it doesn't hurt terribly. Sometimes they'll shout in their pain. But we give them a space and place to sort it out. We're readers. It's part of what we do."

"Part of what we do?" I asked. I was puzzled. What more could there be?

Rita smiled. "The best of us hold the line between good and evil, living and dead, while we figure out what part of the future we can and can't change. Or maybe just should and shouldn't. And we entertain them. All clients like to be entertained." One of her eyes slid shut. Had Rita winked at me?

I fingered Nona's charm at my throat. I suspected reading was something Nona had done as well at some point.

If Nona could do it, so could I.

Cosmic Lift Off

Cosmic Lift Off

Every fourth Tuesday at 1:45 the tea room was invaded by the Air Force. The Air Force tracked UFO activity through a reporting program called Project Open Skies. Few UFO sighters were willing to go onto a military base, so officials chose more accessible places to report sightings. Our tea room was a registered report center. Every fourth Tuesday, Officer Willis came in for his report. I might have confused his blue uniform with a cop's uniform, except for the clutter of colored ribbons pinned to his left breast. Willis stood head and shoulders over even my partner John. Willis was the picture of a military officer.

At first glance, Willis' uniform confused Jamie, Maggie's nephew, mightily. Jamie slid around the wall of the kitchen to get out of Major Willis' view. I gave him the hairy eyeball. "Get yourself out there and bring the guy his tea and muffin."

"He ain't here to arrest me?" Jamie pressed himself into a corner beyond the stove.

"Jamie, he doesn't know you. He doesn't know you're here." I said, to relieve his panic.

"Neither did the guy with the neighborhood watch." Jamie mumbled.

"Maybe so," I answered, "But this guy's not here for you. He's here for the UFO report."

Jamie had come up from Alabama to live with his great aunt, Maggie, the family's matriarch. When the police found Jamie with the wrong crowd at the wrong place, with a very wrong substance in his pockets, his mother sent Jamie up to Maggie for a locational cure.

Jamie hadn't had a lot of male role models. But he knew men in uniform were trouble. Uniforms scared the crap out of Jamie.

"He's a cop of some kind." Jamie wound himself into a panic. "You can see your face in the shine off his boots. What kind of uniform is that? Is he a state trooper? FBI? Neighborhood watch?" Jamie's neighborhood watch consisted of 5 grandmothers, and a desert storm veteran who had not yet settled back into civilian life. When Jamie got in trouble, the neighborhood watch hadn't gone to the police. They went to Maggie.

"He's Air Force, Jamie," I told him

"Why does he look so pissed off?" Jamie asked me. He peered around the kitchen wall to get a better look at the officer.

"He just is, Jamie. He comes in for the UFO report," I said. "I'm pretty sure it's the worst part of his week."

"The what report?" Jamie was now startled out of being scared.

"UFO. Unidentified Flying Objects. We're a report center.

"We what?" He shook his big head.

"People come here to report their UFO experiences," I told him.

That was not strictly true. No one had ever reported a UFO experience at the tea room. But we were a report center, and Willis came to the tea room to check for reports.

Jamie's face broke into a tiny smile. Then he made a choking sound. "Little green men? My favorite Martian? Mork and Mindy? Dr. Spock?"

"Just go out there, Jamie, and bring the man his tea. He hates visiting us, but he's nicer after he has a muffin. He's a bit of a sugar junkie." Jamie grabbed the tray I'd prepped.

Jamie worked in the tea room four days a week when Maggie read.

Jamie arrived at Maggie's, betrayed, miserable and bored, so we turned his tea room time into a paying job. He wiped tables, cleared dishes and brought water and tea to the customers. We paid him a small salary but he kept the tips from the clients.

Jamie shuffled out with a muffin and tea and escaped to the back.

Willis picked at his muffin. Carolyn sat at his table to give him the report. That was my cue to go hide in the kitchen and do the dishes. Major Willis looked at me like I was some sort of sex worker. Carolyn, in her misplaced hippie days, had been a sex worker, so it didn't offend her. She smiled sweetly as she swirled her blond hair around her finger and explained that no, no one here had seen a UFO this month. Not all month. Not last month either. For real, not ever. No one ever reported a UFO. Willis looked up and said, "When someone does, have them fill out this form in triplicate, and file it for my next inspection here." We snickered ourselves silly over the form. He left us a pad of them.

Blue Book Report Form Document 328-UF
All UFO Reporters Must Fill Out the Following Questionnaire

Reporters name
Reporter's address
Reporters age
Attached doctor/psychiatrist's report
Medical history
Psychological history
Security report about reporter
Siting details
Location of siting
Drug report

- Urine test
  - Street drugs, P/N
  - prescription drugs P/N
- Blood test
  - Street drugs, P/N
  - prescription drugs P/N
- Blood Alcohol test result
- Breathalyzer test result

To be filled out by the siting reporter:

Did you experience:

- Cattle mutilation?
- Bright lights?
- Aliens
- Personal testing
- Disorientation
- Inability to sleep
- Inability to wake up
- Unreasonable terrors

Did you visually see aliens? Were they

- Reptilian?
- Insect like?
- Humanoid?
  Other?

Did they speak to you/ make sounds/ try to communicate?

- In English?
- In some other language?
- In an unknown language?
- With hand/body signals?
- By telepathy?

I solemnly swear or affirm that the above is completely factual to my knowledge. Under penalty of perjury.

Signed by X_____
Witnessed by reporting officer
            X_____
Date of report

            X_____

Willis insisted everyone who came in with a UFO sighting fill this out. It was a hopeless task. No one in the tea room used their legal name for anything except their taxes. Willis' torment continued monthly as he visited our den of female intuition, just to receive blank stares and barely contained hilarity.

So, Willis sat at a table, ramrod straight, with the form and pen in his hand hoping for a straight answer to a question no one was going to answer. Carolyn placed muffins and sandwiches in front of him. The rest of us watched the show from the corners like the Saturday Matinee. We bent over laughing as Carolyn batted her eyes at him.

At the end of each visit Carolyn smiled a gooey smile again and said, "Lovely to see you again, Major. Maybe we'll have a report next month." Then Willis rose stiffly out of his chair, aligned his hat to the center of his forehead and made his way to, one presumed, the next tea room/UFO report center.

Major Willis didn't have words for how much he hated this particular detail. His face told us all, but he never said what he thought. Even we thought it was a silly shit mission. But it was official. Willis was assigned to Operation Open Sky for UFO and he did his duty. Clearly, he'd pissed in someone's Wheaties.

Since no one in the tea room did see UFOs, it was a thankless mission. Occasionally someone might rave about white lights and flying cattle. Those cases resolved once people adjusted their medication on doctors' orders or as a personal experiment.

I was tempted to tell him a fairy tale about cows sucked up by large silver disks in the sky. I don't have enough impulse control. Would that be lying to the government? How long could they stick you in a hole tied to a gurney after that? So, I hid in the kitchen every time he came in. It didn't mean I couldn't see everything or hear what was said. It kept me from cruelly playing with him.

Maggie looked over her shoulder at Major Willis, and said "That boy's pants are on too tight." She sniffed and went back to giving her client the lottery numbers.

Jamie came back out of the kitchen where he'd been hiding. Maggie had a huge heart, but that softness did not extend to Jamie. He came to her to straighten out his life, and he would straighten out. Or else.

Jamie's patience with old ladies (we were all old if we were over twenty-five) didn't extend to Maggie. She snapped at him and you could hear his response even if it wasn't spoken. "Now pull those pants up. I got you a belt. You best wear it. Those fall down around your ankles. The girls won't never forget that. You want to be a legend?"

He did not. He dropped his eyes and mumbled in response. She put both hands on her hips and leaned in towards him. "Get that belt on and get yourself to the tutoring center or I'll use it on you."

When Jamie didn't wait on customers, he practiced being transparent. You could walk in a room, look straight at him and not see him. He was that kind of quiet.

The next month when Major Willis came in, Jamie's panic had worn off enough to be able to do his job around the man. The officer was tough, male, and disciplined. The uniform was cool in a manly man way. Jamie didn't know men with that kind of self-control and self-respect.

Jamie silently placed tea and muffins in front of him, and disappeared. The next month when Major Willis came in, Jamie walked up to Willis's table with shy admiration, and called Willis "sir." Willis went through his non-report with Carolyn, but as Jamie wiped his table, Jamie asked Willis what service he was in. Before the table was clean, they bonded while Willis told the boy stories about fighting airplanes and aircraft carriers, evil sergeants, military foul ups, and honorable men. They sat together telling tales, sunk in a world of testosterone and war.

It was a quiet day. It didn't matter. Jamie listened to stories for at least an hour before Willis remembered that he needed to be moving on.

Jamie was transformed. For the first time in his life, he'd met someone he wanted to emulate. Even Maggie agreed there was no harm in it. Better still, Willis was, like most military men, color blind. He saw Jamie not as a troubled black kid but as a young man with possibilities. It became part of Willis' monthly visit. We even set aside time to make sure he and Jamie would have talking space. Willis didn't bring recruiting fliers, but he did make it clear that a brave young man with discipline and ambition could have a good life in the Air Force. And Jamie decided to figure out how to be that brave young man.

Willis confessed to Jamie how he really felt about project Open Sky. Willis personally believed UFO sightings were a function of street drugs

and schizophrenia. Carolyn was cute, and Willis didn't mind her flirting with him for a half-hour each month. But militarily, Willis saw Project Open Skies as a documentation of decadent drunks and druggies recovering from orgiastic parties.

Jamie found that confusing. He took everything Willis said as gospel. But Jamie couldn't imagine the controlled men of the Air Force wasting their time on hallucinations. Jamie's vision of the future featured a sharp uniform and a position of respect. Surely the military wasn't interested in folk stories and hallucinations.

Maggie's family in Alabama wasn't exactly rural. But they hailed from a small town and lived like many marginal families did in the south. Jamie hadn't been in a town larger than 1000 people. Boston overwhelmed him. The technology and the travel systems left him so lost he was dizzy. Jamie hadn't connected with books before. But now that Jamie saw a reason, he began a stream of weekly library trips. He returned with an armful of WWII stories and military histories. Willis and Jamie spent hours over those books. It was more military lore than we could handle. But Jamie became responsible and respectful in a way we'd prayed for.

Winter arrived and everyone crabbed about the ice and the wind chill. Cabin fever leapt from one person to another in the room. Maggie and Jamie were hard hit, not being northern snow birds. Jamie loved winter until he took his first humiliating fall on an icy sidewalk. Neither of them were ever warm enough. By February he was surly and discolored around the eyes. Maggie had no patience with the boy. She kept up a stream of helpful comments that did everything but help. "Pick your feet up and don't you dare tramp snow in on the rug. Get yourself in the kitchen and make yourself useful. You can't be that wooden-headed." But something was wrong. Jamie went from being disconnected and unhappy to being jambled. His eyes looked bruised from lack of sleep. He almost walked into walls and fell down stair cases. He was a zombified mess.

Jamie lay his head down on the table when no one was watching and dozed for a moment. His eyes twitched. He talked in his sleep. "The lights! Huge! Under the tree. Huge. Willis... sky... lights..."

I wanted to class this as a bad dream. Maggie wouldn't have it. "He did that all morning too. Fool. Nobody believe in UFOs. He was up and

down all night last night clunking around. Can't sleep to save himself." Maggie shook her whole body instead of just her head. His condition was past her knowledge and skill.

"Do you think he saw a UFO?" I asked her.

"I think he saw something. God knows what." Maggie grimaced.

We finally asked him. "Jamie did you see something odd over the last couple days?"

"I dunno," he answered, head down. Maggie folded her arms and leaned back.

"I don't know what you think you dunno! You talk to Marlene like you ain't some jumped-up bumpkin. Did you see something?" You never told Maggie "no."

"You ain't gonna like it," he mumbled.

"I don't give a shilly-shally whether I like it or not. Out with it." Maggie was winding up to a conclusion I hoped wouldn't bruise Jamie worse than usual.

"There's a whole bunch of lights at night, way up in the sky," Jamie said. "I seen them every night for a week. They move all over the sky.

They go on all night long. Scared me green," he said. "I thought it was dream, but they keep coming, night after night. Willis told me that aliens do that. He don't believe himself, but he been asking people about it for years. I thought it might be helicopters, like he told me, but the lights were so far up, and there weren't no noise. I finally put my head under the covers and tried to sleep. I ain't slept in three days."

Maggie and I listened, appalled. Unfortunately, this constituted a UFO sighting. We didn't wait for Willis' regular visit. We called him and Willis came immediately. Jamie grabbed Willis' arm, before Willis could even reach the table. We stayed clear so they could talk.

An hour later Jamie went back to bussing tables and Willis spoke to Maggie. They had nothing in common but their concern for the boy.

That was enough.

"He's terrified, He can't quite tell me why," Willis said. "He's seeing lights in the sky. I'm here to report that kind of thing, but you know I think it's nonsense."

"Will you file a report?" Maggie was suspicious of any public papertrail.

"I'd like to know what we're looking at first." He put both palms up in surrender. It was his job.

Maggie nodded. She didn't believe in UFOs either. Witches, voodoo, hoodoo, druids, ghosts, demons, and psychics, yes. UFOs, no.

"I had the pastor talk to him," she said. "He don't think Jamie's lying, although Jamie has in the past. But not to me. What he's seeing, we don't know."

"Is he on drugs?" Willis ventured. I could see from his face Willis hated the thought. But he had to ask.

"If he is," Maggie said, "he's dead by nightfall. He knows that."

"There's a clinic around the corner that can do a drug test." Willis

wrote down the address. Another woman might have argued that her boy couldn't be on drugs. Not Maggie. She took the square piece of paper with the address, pressed it into her pocket book and promised Willis results forwarded tomorrow.

"Can we wait on your report?" she asked Willis.

"I can't report anything without the tests." Willis acknowledged.

Jamie was crushed. His eyes darted between the two people in the world who cared most for him in the world. They'd just called him a junkie. Or worse. "Why doesn't anyone believe me?" he wailed.

"Nobody believe or disbelieve," Maggie answered. "When you see something no one else sees, they're going to ask."

"No one asks you," Jamie said. "They just take what you say for real." The unfairness of that glowed through Jamie's voice. Everyone took Maggie at her word.

Maggie spoke in a flat voice. "What I say is real. What I see is real." Maggie's gift was undeniable. She could be mistaken or misinterpreted, but she was never wrong.

"How do you know what I see ain't real?" he asked her.

"This is how we tell," Maggie answered. "Get your jacket. We're going for that test now." She pushed him ahead of her solely with her gaze. The elevator took them down.

Willis looked at me, distraught, His face twisted with disappointment.

"Do you really think...?" He could suggest the test, but he couldn't bring himself to ask it.

"I'm sorry, Major. He has a history. But I'd say he was clean while he's been here. Maggie is formidable. She's kept a firm hand on him." "No doubt," he replied. Willis had experience with pissed-off old ladies. Maggie scared him. Willis handed me his personal number. "If he needs something..."

"We'll keep you in the loop," I answered.

Willis marched off, woodenly.

We waited through the dreary afternoon. Late in the day I fixed myself some tea. I drifted into a memory.

"Momma, why don't we see Nona anymore?" I asked. My mother always was angry. But she blazed bright red at the mention of Nona. "Nona left us, Marlene. She just left. She's a stupid old woman. She believes all kinds of stupid things." I jerked awake.

Maggie and Jamie came in right before we closed. We had new supplies in and it was Jamie's job to get them sorted out. Maggie and I though normal rhythm of the task would help settle him. Maggie said, "Can I leave him with you? Will you get him to church after? I've got a choir thing I'm promised for." Maggie sang choir at the Miracle Baptist Church.

"But of course," I answered. Jamie went into the back.

"So, what did they find?" I asked Maggie.

"Clean, they tell me. No grass. No hash, no amphetamines, no barbiturates, nothing. Even the hair test was clean," Maggie said.

"No drinking?"

"No. I'm relieved in one way and scared spitless all in one," Maggie said.

I understood. We all hoped for a clean drug test but none of us liked

what the alternative problems might be. Jamie was young for juvenile schizophrenia, but he was within the age range. He might have lied but I'd have bet my back teeth he hadn't. Not to Major Willis. Not a chance.

Maybe he had a vision of some kind. But Jamie was all boy. The gift rarely ran through the male line. When men read it was through divinatory systems like Tarot or Horoscopes. Women in Maggie's family didn't need any props. They just knew. So what were our options? Mental illness, a desperate lie for attention. Or a hallucination. I flinched when I imagined him with a brain tumor. No. No. I told myself. That's not psychic. That's just panic.

"Will you read for me?" Maggie asked me. "I'm too close."

"I hate to tell you, Maggie, we're all too close. He's our kid by now."

She gave me a smile mixed with pain and pride. "I know that." She reached out and bear-hugged me. It was both sweet and suffocating. "I got to go," she said. "Will you have him to me by 7:30?"

"Sure," I said. "Should I feed him first?"

"You better. Unless you want him to eat the upholstery in your car." She placed her church hat on her head, buttoned her coat and checked her lipstick in the mirror while she waited for the elevator.

I called Major Willis to give him the report. He understood what the options were if it wasn't drugs. I could hear heart-break in his voice.

"I'm taking Jamie out for dinner," I said. "Would you like to join us? I think it would lift his spirits."

Major Wallis said, "Of course. I'll be over in around a half hour." I suggested the little diner near Maggie's church.

Jamie clanged pans and pots in the kitchen. That natural reaction normal enough after being falsely accused. I let him bang away. He could burn his anger off without hurting anybody, especially himself

He came out from back wiping his hands on his jeans. "It's all up and I'm all done." He slumped in a chair and gave me an angry grimace. "Why is it," he said, "Everyone believe anything my aunt says?" His lips turned in a bitter smile. "She say all kinds of things. Sometimes she's right but sometimes she ain't. Why do you all believe her?"

"Your aunt Maggie is for real, Jamie. I don't think she separates what she sees as a psychic from what she sees with her eyes. Sometimes she doesn't understand what she sees. Sometimes we don't either. And sometimes it gets misinterpreted. I've seen her misunderstand, but I've never seen her vision be wrong. We can't always make sense of what we see. But you need to understand. We know Maggie's real because we've known her for a long time. We know who she is. As we get to know you, we'll know who you are too."

"You think I'm a liar?" he said in more bitterness.

"Actually, no." I rubbed my arms. I suddenly felt cold. "Everybody tells untruths sometimes, but I haven't seen you tell the big and hurtful lies, the ones that make a person a liar. We don't know how to interpret what you've seen. Hey, Major Willis is going to join us for dinner. Get your coat."

The elevator opened. Major Willis was there, not in his class A uniform, but in slacks and a sweater and a winter coat. "Did someone say 'dinner'?" he asked, a bit too brightly. "Do you still have the car with the moon roof?"

"Yep." It was ancient, but it ran. It was a very cool car in its heyday. Now it was a very cold car when the moon roof didn't quite close. We walked over to it together.

We drove off to the diner. Jamie and Willis discussed personal combat training, through cheeseburgers and fries. I glazed over, unable to join in that but glad for the comfort it gave them both. The conversation was interrupted only by the french fries Jamie crammed into his mouth. I spaced out for a moment. I heard Nona say, "Just because you don't understand something doesn't mean it's wrong. It means you don't understand." I snapped back to hear Jamie ask Willis about the Bridge at the river Qui.

After ice cream Jamie, went to the heart of his hurt. "Damn," he said. "I've done good here. I don't have any bad friends, cause I don't have any friends. The doctors and Aunt Maggie got up all in my face and you know I ain't touched a thing."

"I know," said Willis. I did too. I almost wished it were drugs. The alternatives were heartbreaking. I passed the ketchup over to him. How do you help a child who sees what isn't there? Who can't see what is? Was this a desperate need to lie? A brain injury? A tumor?

Willis chewed on a toothpick, as I drove out of the parking lot. Jamie leaned back in the passenger seat to take in the night sky. Even though he was fourteen, his knees jutted out from the seat in this tiny old car. He would be a big man someday, if we could get him there. Willis sat in the back, silent. Watching. Worried about the boy.

As we went around the service road to get on to the high way, Jamie pointed straight up and yelled. "There! Right there! Stop the car!" There it was. There were huge lights scraping the sky in patterns. I slammed on the brake. The lights continued their journey across the sky and back again. Jamie's face, lit by the dashboard was a mask of mystery and wonder. "UFO!" he screamed.

I had a moment of clarity. I knew. Willis might have too, but he didn't say.

"UFO! UFO!" Jamie screamed. "It's there. It's real. Can you see it? I'm not making it up. I'm not on drugs and I'm not crazy." Jamie's smile beamed wide. It wasn't safe for a boy of his size to bounce up and down in a car that small. Just as well we had the moon roof open.

"No, Jamie. You're not," I said. I turned down the service road past a roadside full of fast food palaces and car dealerships. Willis's face was quizzical, but he kept his silence. He waited to see where this was going. I found what I was looking for, three blocks down, in front of the Chevrolet lot. Along the rows of stickered cars, a bank of searchlights raked the sky in a syncopated light show.

Jamie dropped his eyes from the sky to the front window. He took a moment to connect the dots, How do you tell a kid he just mistook the light display as a UFO sighting? I didn't. I let him do the math.

"Damn," he said. He looked so embarrassed, I was afraid he was going to cry. Then he made a bubbling noise that turned into raucous laughter. I joined him.

"Do we need to report this sighting, Major Willis?" I asked. Willis was too busy snickering to speak.

"Do you have to report this, Major Willis?" Jamie asked.

"Are you worried about your record?" Willis asked.

"Yes, sir," Jamie said, scrambling for his dignity. Maggie, Willis and I pointed out frequently that records followed you forever. Jamie was keenly aware of records.

"Good," I answered. I put the car into reverse and headed for the church.

The music poured out of the parking lot as we drove up. "Didn't my Lord deliver Daniel? Didn't my Lord deliver Daniel? Oh Lord. Oh Lord."

I parked the car and we walked Jamie in.

The song finished on a crescendo. The choir froze on the last note and then broke ranks. Maggie headed in our direction.

"I hope I don't have to correct anything you said to Marlene or the officer, do I?" She spoke to Jamie, but she'd just asked me.

"I don't think so. Auntie," Jamie answered. "Does she, Marlene?" Jamie had received enough ego hits for the day. I could understand that. "Uh, no," I confirmed. Willis made a gesture that confirmed that.

I'd finally realized how much Maggie scared Willis.

Jamie posed himself like a professor giving a lecture. "Did you know people up north have big-ass lights they use when they want to get your attention?" Jamie's voice was full of sarcasm and bravado. He'd figured it out. This was his joke now.

"Police?" Maggie said in horror.

"Car dealerships," I answered.

Maggie's head lifted even as she crossed her arms. "Well, of course they do. Did you find one?"

Jamie nodded. "Major Willis saw it all. He can tell you all about it." Maggie's jaw dropped. "Oh, dear sweet baby Jesus! I haven't thought about that for thirty years! Jamie, the same thing happened to me when I first moved up North. I saw the lights and I thought it was the Rapture for sure! I like to died when I found out it was nothing but some slimy white guy selling used cars." She grabbed her nephew by the ears and kissed him on each cheek. "I believe you, and I am proud to be your Auntie."

Jamie swallowed hard. "Thank you, Auntie. Officer Willis saw it all.

He can tell you all about it."

Willis confirmed Jamie's statement with a nod and his most officious voice. "Jamie showed us the phenomenon. I don't think we'll need to investigate further.

Willis, confirmed him with a nod and his most officious voice. "Jamie showed us the phenomena. I don't think we'll need to investigate further."

Maggie half shoved both of them towards the table full of desserts the choir had brought.

It was Jamie's lift-off. From then Jamie knew we would not desert him. Nor would we put up with lies or horseshit. He knew he could be mistaken but no one would automatically count him as wrong.

Willis put his arm around the boy. "You know an Air Force officer needs to go to college first, don't you son? We need to start working on that."

"Yes sir," Jamie said.

Without Benefits

Without Benefits

Rita sometimes arranged us to go in as readers for entertainment at parties. That was how I met John. He was one of the waiters, dark and sardonic in his black jeans and shirt. I didn't know how handsome an fternoon shadow could be on a man until I met John. I was too involved in reading really to focus on him during the party. I glanced at him as he wove through the crowd with the canapés. I was aware of him as an erect shadow at the corners of the party holding a tray. But I knew he was watching me.

At the end of the night, I stuffed my cards in their bag. I unwrapped the scarf I'd worn as a turban and draped it around my neck. He had broken off from the pack of other waiters he'd been with. He was behind me as I rose from the table to leave. His smile was crooked and his dark eyes danced. Now he leaned against the wall, almost blocking my exit. "Do you always tell them stories like that?"

I was too tired for this garbage. Tired enough that I couldn't just let it go. I had sagged back in my chair but then squared my shoulders back to prepare for battle with him.

"It's all a scam, isn't it?" he said. "How do you make up what stories to tell them?" He shifted to his other foot, arms crossed, weight on one side. Nonchalant.

"No. I don't make up stories like that. I tell them their own stories."
"Psychics lie like Persian rugs."

"Well, some may. I don't."

I never actively lied to a client. Most of the time, I told them what I saw. Most of the time, what I see is fairly true, except when my sight fails me. For those moments, I don't have to lie because I'm very good at guessing.

I felt my mouth flatten into a hard-straight line. Just because he had a point didn't make me less annoyed at him.

He was obnoxious, but he was decorative if your taste ran to Eastern European types. His hair was coal black and waved slightly. His waiter's blacks made him seem elegant, but I learned in time that he was eye-catching in dirty jeans or sweats. Or naked. We bantered as though we were in grade school.

"I don't need to prove anything to you. Or anyone else. You're afraid let me read for you."

"Whatever." He sniffed at me, as if I were a bad odor.

"Think what you like. But you'll never know unless you try me."

He answered that with a knowing laugh and a smirk. Somehow, I was leaving the building with him. He held the door open for me, almost like an insult.

We walked aimlessly until we came across a coffee shop. "I give up!" he cried in mock exasperation. "Go ahead. Read for me." He pulled out my chair and sat across from me.

I ordered tea for both of us. It arrived with leaves swirling in the bottom of the cup, steaming and too strong. One of the leaves stuck to his front tooth.

I brushed at his face to remove it, but he wouldn't let me. He fished the leaf out of his mouth.

"How do you drink this stuff?" he said, with that crooked smile again.

I looked down into my cup rather than in his eyes. "Sip and you can strain out the leaves. Are you done?"

There was a small puddle of tea in the bottom of his cup.

I lay a folded napkin in front of him on the table. "Turn your cup upside down and turn it three times to the left."

He gave me another you've-got-to-be-kidding stare. "Really." "Really," I insisted.

So he did, smirking all the way.

I picked up his cup and read. All the activity in his cup centered under the handle. That meant everything was about him.

But it wasn't really a reading. It was banter with potential. We outright flirted with each other. I watched his eyes, glimmering full of mischief. He touched my arm a couple of times. I said something as I looked into his cup. "You live by yourself." How could he possibly have a roommate and act this way? "You don't like being a waiter." Duh. He didn't want to serve anyone anything. "You have unknown ambitions and abilities." Every man wants to hear that. Don't ask me what I said after that. I don't remember. I do know he laughed at me. Somehow, I didn't mind. When we walked out together into the dark, he slid his hand under my chin as he pulled me in for a kiss. It was quick and a bit sharp for my taste. It left me stunned and confused on my doorstep

Both my mother and my Nona had lived single lives. They'd preferred not to have the whirlwind of men confusing their day-to-day existence. My mother was attracted to men, although her choices were unfortunate. Her life had a revolving door full of men who were all alike in being wrong. Nona seemed past the age where she included men in her world in any way. So, I hadn't a lot of practice or a good example of what a relationship ought to have looked like.

John turned out to be a great mystery. He poured attention on me when I was reading or acting as a psychic. Outside of that, he was nowhere near as nice as his manners or his charm would have indicated. They were a cheap veneer over a somewhat manipulative heart. He seemed to like me well enough, but displayed that with kisses and hugs only in public. He religiously watched me read. Party after party, reading after reading, he came along, ostensibly to see me safely home. He stood in the background, nonchalantly focused on the reading itself. Eyes on me, ears straining, the same sardonic smile. Somehow, I found myself more alive around him. His interest baffled me. He didn't believe. He certainly didn't believe in me. He largely ignored me when I wasn't reading.

In time, I learned why. His mother really had read cards. His family traveled with some carnival where they told fortunes. He'd grown up night after night outside the shabby trailer they traveled in, listening to her spin her stories to one frightened or desperate woman after another. It was a family business.

I wanted to be in love enough to close my eyes and ignore the cold edge under his skin. He had an eye for appearances. I viewed my reading as a part time party trick I'd learned at college. He saw it as a career. He started with suggestions. It was easier to follow them than to fight. He began to shape me as a psychic. I wore the skirts and scarves he picked out for me. For all his contempt of readers, he wanted to control my career as a reader. I spent some nights with him, some nights in the rooms I rented with my friend Jane from college.

I had always thought spending the night with a man would involve making love with him, but we always seemed to watch old movies all night instead, or do hours of internet research, or even just talk all night, about everything and nothing. We kept separate apartments, because we couldn't quite imagine our lives without that bit of separation.

It meant that I never had to live entirely in his world or let him live in mine. Mostly he resolved my ambivalence. He held me at arm's length sexually. I though he was shy or possibly had some kind of religious conviction, so I let him take his time.

My mother had died during my last year in high school. My father was an ancient mystery she'd refused to illuminate. I was drifting. John anchored me. I couldn't follow my own dream at the time. I drifted through his.

My roommate Jane was appalled. Bright-eyed and brilliant, Jane was a stewardess for a major airline. She had studied marketing, but her dark, lanky looks made her a stunning representative for the friendly skies. It was a stellar career that left her time to wander and goals that she could easily reach. Jane and I had been friends since we were outcasts together in college. Now as a stewardess, she was home one day out of three or four. Our friendship was light but strong, able to carry over through distance and absence. But she disliked John from the beginning.

"He's decorative. But he's cold. I never get the sense he cares about anyone but himself," she told me.

I wasn't sure she was wrong. "He's good company," I answered her. I wasn't fooling her. I was only fooling me.

"Friendly?" she asked. "Helpful? Kind?"

I had to shake my head no at each of these.

"Sexy?" She finally put her finger on it. "That's a ride that doesn't last."

I didn't let on that that it was not a ride that was working, either. But he was useful. By the time I arrived at his place, he'd have dinner waiting. For my part, I got a bookkeeper, a short order cook, and a career analyst, even if he wasn't top notch in any of those regards. But best of all, I got an internet researcher. He could sort pepper from gnat shit online.

Whenever I came upon something I didn't understand or know about, I dropped it into John's lap and he would have the information I needed, usually within an hour or so.

Jane shook her head at the whole mess. "As long as you don't forget you can leave when you need to ...." She had a point. So, I kept my apartment with her and kept some nights alone.

John and I settled into a friendship with odd and unexpected benefits. Two unexpected extras were his ability to gather information, and to make amazing food out of seemingly empty cupboards. He was an astonishment at gleaning information over the internet. All of his spare time was spent searching through online sources for things that interested him.

As a reader, I took information as it came to me. If people come and ask you constantly about daily events, you hardly have to look them up. It wasn't ever really my information. It belonged to the person I was reading for. But it was John who taught me how to confirm what I'd seen.

Jane and I had moved up to a new apartment in Brookline. It was only new to us. It was a solid 1950s building, arranged for soldiers and their families after World War II. There was a neglected courtyard and a somewhat shabby lobby. But the windows were large and set so that the winds blew cool off the nearby park. We moved in our beds and dressers and scraps of furniture still from our college digs. Fresh white curtains and an elderly Persian rug gave it a hippie air of dilapidated comfort and diversity. We'd settled in, bought new towels and pillows, and had a new couch delivered from the secondhand shop when Jane received her doll.

As a stewardess, Jane had the opportunity for many trips to exotic places. The others who worked with her did as well. She had an elegant collection of world dolls. It ranged from European gnomes, troll dolls from Scandinavia, French dolls of the lost royal line, beautiful china dolls with soft leather bodies, elegant Indian dolls riding elephants. She bought them and friends bought them for her. Her birthday present this year came from a pilot friend who had come back from Japan with a doll for her.

In his wandering throughout Japan, the pilot had found a tiny doll of a Japanese woman at a temple at Hiroshima. The doll was nestled in an elegant furishiki wrap of blue printed cotton. Her costume in red and pink silk echoed Jane's red service uniform. Jane made a place for the doll on the shelf as part of the collection.

I knew Jane loved the doll because she kept moving it, presumably to show it off. I found it on the coffee table, then sitting on our elderly piano. One day it was on the mantelpiece. I was more disturbed to find it sitting on my pillow, one morning when I awoke.

That was when I remembered Jane was out on a flight. She hadn't been home since the last time I'd been.

Jane had boyfriends, but none of them had house key privileges. John certainly didn't have our key. We'd changed the locks last month.

There had to be an explanation. But two days later, when Jane arrived off the road, she was clueless.

"I didn't move the doll," she stated for the record. "I was gone. I hope you don't think it's funny?" she asked acidly.

I didn't. She didn't. But we couldn't find an explanation.

I woke up that night with her doll on my nightstand again, moved from her cabinet. I thought I saw a faint smile on its face. When I picked it up, a smear of red brushed off its mouth onto my hand. A blood spot bloomed red on my arm, as if a small mouse had bitten me. I screamed as I dropped the doll to the floor.

Jane insisted it was nonsense, but there was the blood spot on the doll and on my arm. A drop of hydrogen peroxide that bubbled up on the spot and dissolved the stain as we watched confirmed that.

Jane moved the doll to a locked cupboard. I was flummoxed to find it afterward in the bathroom, complete with a wafting of soft Japanese flute music playing from no known source.

That night Jane called her pilot friend. I could hear her side of the conversation as it heated in volume and tone. "You just took the doll?

From a temple? Without asking?"

More soft noises from the receiver. "I don't care if it looked like me.

It's biting people!"

I heard a sound like a phone thrown across the room. That was confirmed when I found her moments later fishing the phone out of the corner where it landed.

I watched her drop the doll into a plastic bag and dump it down the recycling chute.

The next morning it was sitting jauntily on the breakfast table by the flowers. It had another red stain by its mouth. I checked my own arms.

Jane insisted it hadn't gotten her. It was late morning when we noticed a small bite wound on poor Dartanian the cat.

"This has got to stop!" I declared, waving the hydrogen peroxide bottle around for emphasis. Dart was yowling in personal objection. Whether he was angry about being bitten by dolls or medical care afterwards was unclear. But it wasn't fair. Dart was a lover, not a fighter, and this doll had a mean streak.

I picked it up gingerly, placed it in a sandwich bag, stapled the top and took it in to Rita.

"Rita, what do you do about a doll that bites?"

"Do you mean that you don't like it, or that it's ugly? I can't keep up with the daily slang," she confessed. She undid the staple and looked over the doll in the innocuous bag.

"No," I repeated. "Bites. Opens its mouth in the middle of the night and marks people with its teeth."

"Oooh." She looked in the bag. "It doesn't look nasty." Her nose wrinkled as if it did smell bad.

"It is, though," I insisted. "What do we do about it?"

She picked it up with a finger and thumb, carefully placing it on the desk. "Where did it come from?"

"It's Jane's. Someone brought it to her from Japan."

"This is why I hate ethnic décor," Rita said. "You've got no idea what this stuff means or where it's from. Or what it might do when it gets upset. Tell me what's going on." I repeated the tales of my attack and Lotus's and told her about the doll returning even after we threw it away.

"I really don't know," she said. "You need to know the tradition. I don't know any Japanese people to start with. You could start with the ambassador to Japan or to someone who teaches Japanese in a college. You can't burn the doll or break her, though. If there's a curse on her, that might escalate it. Or seal it."

"The doll is cursed?" I asked her to confirm it.

"Use your brain, Marlene. It bites people and comes back after you throw it out. I'd tend to think it's cursed."

I met John for lunch.

"What's in the bag? Is it a present for me?" he asked.

It took me a moment to push down the urge to just give it to him.

Would that have made it strictly his problem? Instead, I told him about it. I pulled out the doll and put it on the table.

"That's cute," he said. He knew I hated things that were cute. "It's straight-up evil," I told him.

"And you brought it to my house. I'm so touched!" he answered. "I'm at a loss. It attacks people. You throw it out and it comes back and bites people."

"Did it bite Jane?" he asked me. "No, but it bit both Dart and me."

"I could understand biting Dart ...." He really didn't have a good relationship with Dart. Too much competition. "But...."

The idea of attacking Dart offended me, as did his attitude. I turned to run. "I don't know how to find out about something like this." I grabbed my purse and keys and started out the door.

He grabbed me. "Wait," he said. Within minutes he was on his laptop, deep in a dozen sites from Japan. The first images he'd pulled up were court dolls. The court dolls were completely unlike Jane's doll, sitting on their knees with a series of thirty silk kimonos one on top of another, heads tilted up to look at the people they were bowing in front of.

They were beautifully formal but not like Jane's. You could see something of the relationship that Jane's doll had with the viewers, just in her stance. The court dolls were just prettily posed people. Then there was a series of baby dolls and girl dolls, lots of round roly-poly smiling babies. Finally, he found a doll poised and formed like Jane's.

"Hani dolls," he read off the screen, "represent someone who had been real at one time." There was a very similar doll on the screen, her face and posture changed a bit, her dress more blues than reds.

"The Japanese believe their dolls have souls," he continued. "You can't throw out a Japanese doll because the doll has a soul and is alive."

"Does that leave the doll with room and board privileges where it gets to hunt people in the house for food?" I asked.

"I'm not sure," he answered. "Was this a tourist item?"

"No, as I understand it. It was a souvenir her friend stole from a Japanese temple in Hiroshima."

"Hani," John read off to me. "Sacrificed dolls signifying the death or loss of a person to their family or loved ones. Given to temples as a living sacrifice of the person lost. It's a doll-like orphan."

I finally got it. We had an abandoned object with a soul who was cast out and furious with its abandonment. Without the benefit of the rituals that would have soothed its soul.

John typed some more. "Let's try the consulate," he suggested. "The consulate has to have a silly questions department. They all do." He typed in my name and contacts, snapped and sent a picture of the doll with his phone, and asked for an appointment.

The next morning, I found myself in a taupe colored room in the Japanese embassy. An elegant young man whisked me into a room with an older official whose English was slow but adequately clear.

"Ms. Calley," he said, looking at the doll. "They sell these as souvenirs all over Japan. Couldn't you just give it away as a gift? It's very charming."

I agreed that it was. How did I tell him that it bit people? The man didn't invite confidences.

There were a number of polite and useless things said and I was shuffled out the door. I stopped at the restroom and left the doll in her open bag on the counter. When I got out of the stall, there was a lovely Japanese girl, perhaps part of the typing pool. She was holding the doll in the palm of her hand.

"Don't touch that!" I snapped, terrified she would be bitten.

She smiled at me gently. "Doll. Hana doll." She squealed happily as if remembering part of her childhood.

"Belong to you?" she asked me.

"No. My friend." I think she understood. "A gift from Japan," I explained.

"Angry. Dolls get angry. She not home. Needs to go home. Take dolls home to heaven. Temple takes dolls home to heaven." Then she shocked me by mimicking a person who was biting someone.

"Could you take this doll home to heaven?" I asked her.

"Take to temple. Temple take her home to heaven. Not your doll?

Not your friend's doll?"

"No. Not really. Doll angry." I showed her the bite mark on my arm.

She nodded in comprehension.

"I take doll home to temple. They release her to heaven. She be happy there.

"The girl left with the brown paper bag and Jane's doll. The next morning the doll was still gone, presumably where she needed to be.

In thinking about it afterward, I recognized that Japanese culture, like our own, had cultural splits between the sexes. Although neither the man or the woman knew anything personal about the doll, I could read enough of their reactions to get the difference. The Japanese man barely knew the dolls existed, because they were strictly part of a Japanese woman's world.

He had seen them, but his part of the culture knew nothing about their care or powers. The doll was completely familiar to the woman. It was a part of woman's culture, not men's.

But I had also learned the miracle of having a research assistant. John was limited in a social sense. He treated me as though I were a girlfriend, but not a lover. It felt like a show put on for someone's benefit, but not mine. But he was the best research assistant I ever had. He knew who to ask and where to ask and what question might open doors. You can't fight something you can't talk to, that you don't understand, and that doesn't understand you. You can't help something you don't understand. You can't make peace with a stranger without breaking down the barriers that make them seem so very strange. You need to know enough about them to even try. John was an informational ace in the hole. And he made a good cup of tea.

Fire Walk

Fire Walk

Do I believe all the stuff I've seen in the tea room? Is it real? Am I real? How much of the future can I see? That's not quite the right question. I may not be the right person to ask.

Don't ask my friend, John. He's a born promoter. He spouts shit like, "The strongest psychic we've seen since ... truly a phenomenon!" It makes my stomach quease. But we built my reputation on his verbiage, and my readings pay for my rent. He says I don't understand promotion. He's right. I don't.

Don't ask Rita, my boss. She'll spout a fair amount of the same nonsense and offer to sign you up for a reading package for the next 2 months at a 10% discount for your tea service.

Don't ask my roommate, Jane, either. She considers reading a party trick.

In spite of that, both of them are somewhat cynical about reading and psychics. I am too.

Maggie might be able to give you a real answer. She's more of a psychic than a reader. "Child, it ain't all that complicated. You just take care of what the good Lord puts in front of you and you say what He wants you to say." Here physical and spiritual intertwine seamlessly for her. For her there is no difference.

I'm not on the same first name basis with God that Maggie is, but I've learned from Rita the ethics a reader needs. I have to do what is kind. Not polite, but responsible and respectful, because clients are often in pain. I say nothing that harm them or keep them from moving on with their lives. I'm no saint. I can feel their pain like a tooth ache. I don't want to add to it.

How does my gift work? It's not linear and it's not always sensible.

Emily's story is a good example.

Laurel called into the tea room, panicked, for an appointment. Laurel was a misplaced mom. She was thirty- eight when she and her husband had separated. She'd found a job as an office assistant. Now she kept track of two children instead of one. Once she got Emily sorted out and on the bus, she looked after the company kingpin as well. She said there was virtually no difference.

She didn't mind. The money was good and it brought independence from her husband. Ben was a bit of a rough hand. He hadn't hit Laurel, but he called her everything but a white woman at their last shouting match. She left when it escalated to door slamming. Ben paid his child support, but not always on time. Ben played Disney dad any time he got to see his princess, Emily. Parties at the Stuff-a-Bear Store. Out of state trips to amusement parks. A class on how to be a model for 11-year-olds, complete with vampy makeup and slinky clothing. Laurel couldn't compete. No one could. Not if you were insisting on homework, eating vegetables, and internet safety. Laurel maintained the connection with Ben for Emily's sake. Emily needed a father even if the jerk couldn't be a good husband.

Of course, Emily preferred to live with her dad. The court took in account his anger issues and decided otherwise. So now guerrilla warfare between Laurel and her daughter seethed beneath the surface at all times. Ben was Emily's knight in armor. The shining knight never let his princess down. Emily's mother officially was her prison warden.

Emily snarked endlessly at her mom. Laurel ignored as much as she could. Some things she couldn't let pass. Laurel couldn't let the unauthorized piercings go without comment. But it blew up solidly the day Ben didn't bring Emily home. When her father didn't deliver her on time from a weekend, Laurel's world ripped apart at the seams. In between waiting for ransom calls and Amber alerts, Laurel called me for a reading. Her voice was a hoarse whisper with tears behind it. She wasn't coherent enough to tell me what was happening. That was okay. She would when she arrived. Laurel pitched out of the elevator like she'd been pushed. When she wasn't in a business suit she was the perfectly groomed soccer mom. She sported pink college sweatshirts, pumps and designer jeans. She was still dressed in her sweatshirt and jeans but the sweatshirt had a coffee spill on it, from the smell. No high heel pumps.

Her normally coiffed hair was caught in an unkempt pigtail. Her eyes were red-rimmed raw. Behind her was a blocky man in a black suit with a look on his face that would have boiled water. He sat at a table across the room. I heard him refuse Jamie's offer of tea.

Laurel rushed into my arms like a lost child, crying. It wasn't like she was able to talk.

I got her to a table and sent out the signal to Jamie that we needed tea and heavy chocolate here, stat. It wasn't anything tea or chocolate could touch. After five minutes of Laurel's tears, head-shaking and incomprehensible language, Jamie placed tea in front of her with careful civility. It brought her back to herself. She held the cup in her hand and let the steam warm her face.

"It's Emily," she said. I knew that. Nothing else could have hurt her like this.

"Is she okay? I asked. "Is she ill? Was there an accident?"

"I don't know. She's lost. Or kidnapped." Laurel was rubbing her hands as if she were terribly cold. "The police are trying to figure out what happened."

"How long has she been gone?" I asked.

"Three days since she left. She and her dad left Friday night. I expected them home for early Sunday dinner."

"What happened, Laurel?"

"More Disney dad shit" she wailed, "Oh god, what if he's taken her?" "I need you to breathe, Laurel. Where do you think he took her?" I asked.

"It was his weekend. A friend has an old farm house that Ben likes to use as a launching pad when he's up there. He rented horses at Dalton for them to ride. They went up the October Mountain trails. The police confirmed that with the stable staff."

Ben was a solid outdoorsman. Laurel, not so much. All Emily cared about was time with her dad. Emily should have been safe with him.

Unless he'd run away with her. Or been hurt. Or got lost. I saw dreadful possibilities branching out in Laurel's head.

Ben responded differently to the divorce. Where Laurel found independence, Ben found unbearable silence. He pined for the loss of Emily in his daily life. He medicated himself with a cycle of alcohol and caffeine. One to wake up. One to sleep. He spiraled downward, month by month. Ben blamed all his misery on Laurel and fed Emily impossible daydreams. It was a combination built for disappointment.

"Why do you think he kidnapped her?" I asked.

"Mirella, they're gone. The rangers can't find a trace of them anywhere in the hills after Saturday. We know where they picked up the horses and the foresters saw them Saturday afternoon. But no one has seen them since. I don't know Ben kidnapped her. But he wanted to. He'd take her just to hurt me."

That was possible. Ben lived in a world of one. No one mattered to him as much as he did.

"Do you think there was an accident?" I said.

"I don't know," she answered with her hands covering her eyes. "I don't know what to think" She waved her hands in panic. "Read my cup. Tell me where my baby is."

She pushed her upside-down tea cup over to me. I picked it up and a stream of left-over tea ran over the saucer and on to the table. "Oh, I'm so sorry. I didn't mean to do that." Her politeness was reasserting itself. I almost preferred the panic or the tears. At least those were real.

"What are the police saying?" I asked her.

"They want me home at the house waiting on the phone. I can't do it. I'm climbing out of my mind. I told them I was going to therapy. Did you know this is therapy?" It was a thin joke. "They're outside in a black town car watching the building. They had a guy in the lobby." I turned to look in the mirror. There was a black-suited man facing our table sipping a cup of tea. He looked like a pit bull at a poodle show.

"I hate to tell you Laurel, they're right here." She followed my gaze to see the man cramped uncomfortably in a tiny chair, with his knees under a too-small table. He held a delicate tea cup in his hand.

"That's okay. He's my ride home." Another, thinner joke. "Is someone searching the trail?"

"The whole community has searched the park. They've had 200 rescuers tromping through there all day. They're trampling the bushes and they've got three choppers up there. Nothing. It's too dark now. Early light, there's another specialized rescue team that will go in hunting for them. But I can't wait. I have to know, is she okay?"

I stared into her cup. A reader knows that it's not the tea leaves that "tell you something". The leaves help you focus to a state of mind where you can see things. But you can't distinguish deep fear from the future. They tend to look the same.

I saw a horse without a rider, running. I saw lightning above it. I saw a man in a huge truck with a gun. I saw what looked like pines. I saw aged railroad tracks. I saw an upside-down car that looked like it was spinning. I could see black wings encircling it. And I heard something like ruffling cellophane and an acrid smell. Like a fireplace. Like burning wood.

If I were reading teenage girls asking about prom dates, I'd just spill what I saw, without reservation. Let them sort out what it meant. Usually that's how reading works.

But that wouldn't work in the effect of bone-deep panic or despair.

In the state Laurel was in, I was much more likely to project her fears rather than any real future path. "I see pines. I see a bridge with water beneath it. There may be a storm. I believe someone was probably hurt but is still there. I see a railroad track. There's wings. Black wings. There's local help. They'll do their best to get them home. Whatever else, I don't think it's a kidnapping. Ben and Emily are in trouble, but they're not on the run."

I stopped there. Anything else was too much for her and no help whatsoever. Her fear was ripping her in half. I couldn't add to that. No matter what happened from here on out, this was a fire walk for her. All we could do was walk it with her.

"She's alive?" Laurel leaned in towards me.

"I don't see her as dead. I don't feel her among the dead." And I probably would have if she were. If nothing else, I suspect she'd have had one last thing to say to her mom.

"So, Ben didn't kidnap her?" Laurel's lips pressed together, her head set motionless.

"I don't believe so. I think they had of an accident of some kind," I said.

She clung to that and to my hands. Her face brightened. "Are you sure?"

"Nothing is ever really sure. But that's what I see." I pulled off my scarf and tucked it around her neck. It covered the coffee stain. She might have been falling apart, but we'd propped her up for what came next. She was composed by the time she left the tea room. The officer in the black suit escorted her into the elevator.

I went through the day with the news running in the background. Rescuers had been sent out to find Emily and Ben, in the assumption they were lost or hurt. I closed the tea room down and went home. John was waiting with a picked-up pizza. It was two AM when the police arrived.

I was dreaming. Nona and I were playing hide and seek. "Find me, cara mia. Follow the thread," she told me. I closed my eyes to see the thread glow against the dark.

I awoke to pounding on the door. The police did knock, I'll give them that. I was in my pajamas. I answered the door.

"Are you Mirella?" the cop in uniform blue barked at me. He was as stiff as his uniform. Behind him stood the detective in the black suit who'd been to the tea room with Laurel. I pulled the neck of my pajama top up to cover more of my front.

"I'm sorry to bother you, ma'am," The detective said. "This is a bit unusual but we hope you can help us. May we come in?" I looked down to avoid looking at him. The detective wore polished brown shoes, with deep creases in them. "I'm Detective Mark Loew. This is Officer Petra." Loew extended his hand to shake mine. I reluctantly met it with my own.

"Is there something wrong, officer?" I asked.

"No. No, but this is terribly irregular. We're on the case looking for Emily and Ben Worth. We just left Laurel Worth's house. She said we had to talk to you." I inwardly rolled my eyes. Cops hate psychics.

"You do know that I read tea leaves, don't you? Most people view what I do as entertainment."

"Do you?" he shot back. There was no safe answer. I didn't try. "Ah, ordinarily we wouldn't bother someone like you," he continued. Meaning a psychic. Probably a fake psychic. He looked past me to avoid the embarrassment. That took a fair amount of training.

Actually, I sort of agreed with them. I had no idea if I'd seen something true or helpful.

"Is Mirella really your name?" Petra shot at me.

"I was born Marlene," I answered him. "Marlene Calley." "That doesn't sound like a gypsy name."

"I never said I was a gypsy. I read tea leaves. I come from Cleveland. My family is part Italian, part Irish and all American. I went to school at Boston State and I settled here after."

"Did you change your name legally?"

A number of the girls at the tea room don't use their real name," I answered by not answering.

"And you don't either?" By now Officer Petra was genuinely snarky, as if we were discussing my gang aliases.

"It's a safety issue, officer. Sometimes people are confused about who readers are and what we're able to do. Have you ever found that true?" It wasn't smart. It wasn't a great idea to taunt him. But it was 2:30 in the morning and I didn't quite have my wits yet.

"What did you study?" Loew asked.

"Psychology. At Boston State." I shrugged at the uselessness of my degree.

"Do you practice psychology?" Loew asked me.

"I don't have the training, sir, or a license to do that. I have a bachelor's degree. I hope to go back to college at some time." I let that drift off.

It was a dead end for that line of questions. Detective Loew started again. "We're here because of Laurel. She came to see you this afternoon?"

"She did." Always stick with the truth with police and keep it simple, I reminded myself. I'd watched enough cop shows for that.

"Did you counsel her?" Officer Petra asked. His smirk told me what he thought of counseling.

"I'm not a counselor," I said. "I just read tea leaves."

"But you told her what you saw?" Detective Loew's eyes narrowed.

He was looking for a deception of some kind on my part. It wasn't there, but he had to look.

Loew went on, "We wouldn't be bothering you if we hadn't hit a wall. The rescuers went up the trails all day. It's almost night and the temperature is dropping. It's above freezing, but we want to find them."

"Look, lady," Officer Petra said, "We don't believe any of this. Any of what you do. But this woman's half past nuts. We can barely get straight answers out of her. She wanted us to get you. She believes you, why I do not know." His hand swept by as if he were displaying a curiosity. "She wants you up there while we search. Will you come as her friend? We won't put up with any silly shit, mind you." He held a lightly chewed pencil in his hand. "By the way, where were you when the girl disappeared?"

"In the tea room. I think. Give me a time frame and I can tell you where I was."

"While we're here, what did you see?" Detective Loew was actually curious. How strange was that?

Office Petra clearly would have rather chewed off his right arm. "We're not sure how to find them," Petra said. "The regular search methods aren't working. We've ascertained that they were in the park and that they were on horseback. They'd rented horses from the Drovers.

After that we lose them. We found horse prints all over but there were seven other parties of folk on horseback. It's so messed up, it's meaningless."

"Do you have a map?" I asked.

The policeman pulled a fold-up paper map from his pocket. I pushed the mugs out of the way and made space for the map. One of the mugs spilled. A corner of the map landed in a puddle of coffee on the table.

"Let me wipe that up." I reached for a napkin. It wasn't clean. "You really don't believe in what I do, do you?" I asked Loew.

"No," said Detective Loew. "But she does. We're grasping at straws. I don't think you could possibly be right about anything, but our searchers haven't been either."

"I suggest, gentlemen, that you write down what I say. I don't always remember what I see very clearly."

Officer Petra looked down into his notebook so he didn't have to look at me. "Okay," he said, his pencil ready at hand. Detective Loew set his camera phone to film me.

So I pulled up my chair and stared at the map. It wasn't any different than a cup of leaves. I focused to see past the map. I didn't need Laurel there to be connected to her. She'd never left my thoughts since she left the tea room.

The wings were still there. Dark and beating in the sky. There were horses running in terror. And railroad tracks. Then I saw blood dripping from the top of the map into a puddle of water, red slick surface on the top. The puddle reflected the moon and the branch above it. I was on my back looking up at the moon. My head hurt so bad it didn't fit in my skull anymore.

Then I saw Emily, face up on the ground. Not moving.

Panic or prescience? Fear or foresight? Both were possible. But this time I just spilled what I saw in front of these men. I'd never felt so naked in my whole life. I dropped out of the trance and was back in front of the two officers.

"Are you sure?" Petra practically growled at me. "This is bullshit." He meant to slap me in the face with that.

"I'm never sure, sir," I answered him. "All I can do is tell you what I see." My honesty quieted him. Had I claimed my abilities, I'd have proved myself fake. By saying I could be wrong, I left open the possibility of being right. Both men looked at me as if I were a six year old performing a magic trick. They didn't say what they thought, but they didn't think very much of it.

"Okay." Detective Loew asked me, "Marlene, will you come to help this lady stabilize? The lady cop we brought is about to take Laurel in to the bathroom and not come out until the bubbles stop. Laurel's making us all crazy. A friend might help her stay calm."

"Of course," I said. With these buffoons in charge, I couldn't leave Laurel up there alone with them.

The police waited while I found clothes. I thought I was pulled together until I realized I'd put my top on inside out. No help for it.

The police escorted me to the squad car. There wasn't a place for me to sit in front. Sitting in the back, I felt like a felon.

Laurel's house stood circled in news vans. The police men pushed a path ahead for me to walk through reporters. To either side there was a gauntlet of microphones and people yelling out questions. A woman in the blue uniform of a cop opened the door. Laurel sat crumpled in a kitchen chair with a cold cup of coffee in front of her.

"You brought her!" said Laurel.

"You need to understand, Mrs. Worth, she's here as your friend." Detective Loew was trying to set boundaries up. "My sergeant would fry me like bacon if he knew I had a psychic here."

So for several hours, we sat, mostly in silence. There were the sounds of media people. The police kept well-wishers and excitement seekers from the door. Laurel had cried herself out. There wasn't enough energy left in her to drink her coffee. I sat in the silence with her.

When the phone ran it was like a doorbell for a haunted house. The woman officer picked it up first and took the phone out of the room.

Laurel followed her with her eyes, panic welling. The woman officer walked back in, still talking into the phone. "I do think she ought to know. I don't want a reporter telling her."

Laurel stiffened herself as best she could. The woman officer sitting across from her was assessing how much more Laurel could take. The officer spoke and waited. She held the phone against herself to mute the volume. "We think you ought to know," she said. "We've got a forest fire reported up in the hills."

Laurel was shaking too hard to say a thing.

"The rangers say it's localized," said Petra. "They had a storm with lightning earlier. One of the trekkers reported seeing a fire up the hill."

"Where they are? Near the fire?" I asked. I had a flash of the crinkly sound I'd heard in my vision.

"We don't think so," said Officer Petra.

Loew filled in the rest. "We're pretty sure they're not near that. We don't want to keep secrets from you." That was a patent lie but I understood it. Loew told her so he could control where she heard it from. And how it was said. I liked him better for that.

"We'd like to take you up to where the searchers are gathered," he told Laurel. She nodded. The house felt like a box. There were no answers waiting here.

Then Officer Petra pulled me into the other room. I thought he was going to either push or throw me. White rage came off him in sheets. "Why the hell do you pretend you can see the future?" he said.

"I didn't claim I did. I have certain impressions I share with people. Sometimes people find them helpful," I said it in an emotionless voice. No emotion would reach past his anger.

"Don't give me the fine print! This lady doesn't need to be scammed."

"No", I said, "she doesn't. Not by me. Not by you either. For all your search teams and agents, you're guessing too. Not blind guessing. You guess from the best information you've got. Most of the time, you guess right. Except when you don't."

"Are you saying we're incompetent?" His voice dropped to an angry whisper.

I'd provoked him. I hadn't meant to provoke him.

"I'm saying, Officer Petra, you're not infallible. No one is. I didn't come here to scam Laurel. I came to hold her hand while she's scared. She's as much a friend as a client. But she did ask me to look. Sometime what I see is helpful."

"I've never heard of such shit. What do you get out of this?" He shoved his notebook at me. It was as much his exasperation with the situation as anger at me. I turned my head away while he glowered over me.

Detective Loew put his head around the door. "Ah, Petra. Can I show you something?" Petra backed off. We all acted as if someone had belched. We were very busy ignoring Petra's outburst. The detective and officer spoke softly in the hallway. Petra stomped off. Detective Loew came in, pulled out a chair and sat by me. "I'm sorry about that. He used to work the bunko squad. It's touchy for him. He's not open-minded. He thinks you're part of the scam and being paid for it."

I looked down, not in shame but in sorrow. "I'm not. Detective Loew. Believe whatever you want. I'm not."

Detective Loew gave me a gentle shrug, as if to say, "Well, what did you expect?"

He pulled up a more detailed map of the park and its surrounds. "The park has some features that seem to click into what you said. Do you remember what you said?"

"Detective Loew, I told you, I don't always remember," I reminded him. "You did tape me, didn't you?"

"We did," he said. "Will you listen to it with me? I hope you can clarify a few things."

I heard Laurel tiptoe into the bedroom. I prayed she could get some sleep.

Detective Loew shut the door and set up the voice recorder. He spread out the map I'd used as a focus the night before. He clicked the switch. I heard my voice, soft and unfocused. I sounded drugged.

I knew I couldn't control what I saw or what I said. The information poured out of me in a wave. I could hear I was in the focused trance state used for reading.

Here's the bridge." He pointed to the map. "We found a horse that had slid off the trail and fallen. There was a small amount of blood on the rocks nearby. It matches Mr. Worth. There's a mess of tracks, but it looks like the horses ran from there. When we checked with the stable, we found the horses had run home, one of them with a broken saddle on its back. After that it gets weird. There's truck tracks. Some drag marks. A smaller woman's foot prints. Torn bits of a shirt Emily was wearing. We'll show them to Laurel when she wakes up."

"So, what do you want from me?"

"Well, some of this seems to jell with what you said. I'm embarrassed by this but the trackers aren't finding anything else. Would you be willing to go with me into the park and see what you can?"

"Do you believe in me?" I laughed at him.

"I don't know about that," he said. "But I do believe you might help." I nodded assent, and grabbed my jacket. He opened the door for me.

I tiptoed into Laurel's room. Her eyes were open. She lay on the bed curled into a tiny ball. "Laurel," I said, "I'm going to leave for a little while. I'll be back. Sleep if you can. The officers will let you know if anything changes."

She murmured at me and shut her eyes again. Sleep was the best medicine for her at this point. Clearly, she couldn't stagger upright any more with the weight of her loss.

This time I got to ride in the front seat of the cop car. That felt better. Officer Petra stayed behind with Laurel, as I rode off with Detective Loew, up into the hills. I suspected Officer Petra of refusing to ride with a psychic. Just as well. He could keep the news mob off of Laurel until it was over.

What is it about cars that always puts me to sleep? The rhythm of the highway bumps? The sound of air rushing by? Memories of driving with my mom? I drifted off as soon as we were on the highway.

I was standing in a clearing bathed in red-hot light. The wind rushed by in terrible heat and strength. I felt the bat wings fluttering overhead, red too in the light. They swarmed and turned up and out of the clearing. There was a battered truck, once teal, now mostly rust colored, by a cottage in the clearing. My father was at my feet, unconscious. Not my father. Emily's dad. When I looked at my hands again, they were a child's hands with pink glitter nail polish, not my own simple burgundy ovals.

The hair that whipped past my face was not my own brown. It was honey blond. It was Emily's.

I spoke to her over the roar of the fire. "Where are you, Emily? Help us find you?

Can you show me where you are?" I asked her. She might have been speaking, but I couldn't make it out.

But I did hear the kind of music that went with a black and white silent movie. Climactic organ, for the scene where the heroine is in danger. Dum. Da dum. Da dum da dum da dum. Almost like circus music.

The scene switched instantly. I was lying on a railroad track. I could feel the train's vibrations from the rails. I tried to move, to get up, to run. Instead I was tied up fast. Yelling. Screaming. Then I heard small twinkly bells ringing. And the sky blossomed into red flames. I looked into Emily's face in the dream. She seemed dead lying there.

I startled awake. No wonder I dreamed of fire. The stench of smoke was everywhere. We weren't near the flames but the wind carried the smoke over the foot hills. The moon was still up above the trees.

Detective Loew turned his gaze momentarily away from the road to watch me. I could feel his eyes, trying to assess what was going on with me. "Bad dream?" he asked.

"Kind of." I was instantly awake, but still shaking from what I'd seen. "I'm kind of new to this psychic thing," he said, "so I'm just going to plain ask. Did you see something?"

"Ah, you could say that. It was a dream, but I think it was about Emily," I told him.

I described the red sky, the bats, the cabin, the truck and the railroad tracks. Loew shook his head. "There are no train tracks out there," he said. "We've checked." We drove up the rest of the way in silence. We pulled into the ranger station. I got out of the car and turned abruptly. I heard the sound of bells.

On one side of the parking lot there were three llamas with loaded with harnesses and packs. Each llama had a set of bells on its harness. That was weirder than what I'd seen in trance. The llamas were chewing on a patch of dried up grass as the rescue team was being briefed.

The rescue team were a forty-something couple, dressed in hiking clothes and warm jackets. They were physical opposites, He was built like a block of wood, she was a bendable twig. They began to check the rescue gear and

GPS equipment loaded on the llamas. I turned to the detective and asked him. "Are these the search and rescue people?"

"They're other rescuers out there", he said. "They're deployed. This team is trained to go into rougher areas." The woman had a gentle smile and tough hands. She patted the llamas into place as she loaded their packs on. The man was bent over a map with the rangers. Detective Loew brought me over to speak to the woman. She put out her hand to me.

"I'm Karen," she introduced herself. The strange smell off her had to be the llamas.

I shook her hand. "Do you always bring llamas?" I reached out my hand to pat one on the neck. It turned and spat at me. Karen laughed.

"They do that. They're not the best at manners. But they're the best on a rescue team." she said. "Tough, smart, built for mountains. And they let you know if they see anything they don't expect. We always take them for rescue missions." I was still stunned.

"Detective Loew told us you would be coming. By the time they call in us and the llamas, they're willing to do almost anything. They'll even listen to psychics. By then they're half past desperate." I was warmed by Karen's humor. She was confident in what she did and who she was. I envied her.

"I have no idea how much I can help," I said. "I get information and impressions. I don't always know what they mean."

"I'm not a believer," Karen said as she tossed her head from one side to the other. "I don't disbelieve either. You tell me what you saw and we'll take it all in. It's a long way up there, a cold night in the hills, and a fire raging. We take whatever information we get."

"Did you see the footage of my reading?" I asked her. Karen nodded yes. I told her what I remembered, the truck, the cabin, the fire, the wings. "I don't know," I said. "It's just what I saw."

Detective Loew walked fast towards me, map in hand. "They want us up at the next rally point." He led to the car and I followed.

Again, the highway lulled me into a light doze. I heard Loew scream,

"Shit, oh shit! There was a huge bump and then the feeling of the car skidding out of control. That ended as the car landed hard into a tree. I saw what looked like a huge beige dog, terrified by the smoke and leap in front of the cruiser. Not a dog. A doe. We'd glanced off her. The blow skidded the car into a tree. The windshield shattered into starburst pattern where my head had hit. The crumpled deer lay twitching on the ground. Detective Loew was slumped unconscious. He had blood running down his face. I couldn't help him until I got myself out of the car.

I managed to unbuckle myself and get the door open. I slid rather than stepped out of it. I fell on my back, unable to move further. I just lay there, eyes shut until I could collect myself. I looked up. There was red sunrise in the sky and the moon was still up. I looked at the moon through the branches. Then I heard wings. The ravens of the woods, smelling blood, had come for their feast.

The black birds landed softly on the deer. They pecked at her, tearing dead flesh.

It was nature red in tooth and claw. I pulled myself up and started to scream at them, to scare them off to make them go. I found a rock by my hand and threw it. They weren't impressed. They flew off one by one and circled back down. So far, they'd only touched the doe.

Loew was moaning. Even if it was a sound of misery, it was a sound of life.

"Are you okay?" I hollered at him. It was a stupid question. He answered it as if it were.

"Would you define okay for me?" He made a number of grunts and groans, struggling to open the car door. The angle of his shoulder was wrong. Dislocated.

His door was stuck. With his good arm he brought out a wrench from under the seat of the car and smashed the window. From there he could open the door. Something was leaking fluid. Water hopefully rather than gasoline. I saw him reach back in for the radio. He punched at the buttons, talked into it. It was silent. Dead.

I helped pull him from the car. The car didn't burst into flames so the drip was from the broken radiator.

Loew, gestured toward the dead car. "Really sorry about that," he said.

Then he looked hard at me. "You knew this. You knew this was going to happen." He stiffened with his hands clenched in fists.

"I'm sorry." I said. "I saw the ravens. I saw the moon and the fire. I told you I don't know how to interpret what I see. I can promise you I wouldn't have gotten in the car if I knew."

"Well, what good are you?" he asked.

I shrugged. "People still ask me what I see. It seems rude not to answer." I sat back down on a fallen tree, exhausted from getting up. He was beginning to understand how the sight works. I could see it all and not know exactly what would happen. It was like a scavenger hunt for antique curiosities: interesting, but not always useful.

"There are choppers flying all over the area. It can't be long until they see us, even in this overgrowth. Can you move?" he asked me. He held out his hand to pull me up. He wasn't any steadier than I was. He was assessing my condition. Making the triage that would decide our next steps.

"I'm concussed, I think," I said, kneading the back of my neck back into place. "But I'm not seeing double. I seem to be ambulatory. What about you?" I asked him.

"I'm a detective. I'm supposed to bounce off brick walls and swallow bullets," he said ruefully. He rubbed his elbow where it had been bruised. The goose egg bump on his forehead was visibly red and swollen.

"Does that work for you?" I raised one eyebrow. Perhaps too many detective novels.

"Really?" he answered, "Only in the abstract. But for here and now we have a lost kid and she needs what both of us can do for her. Can you walk out?"

His posture told me how hurt he was. "You can't walk," I said assessing his shoulder and leg. "You're not able to hike through the woods."

He made motions to rise off the forest floor. He made a manly effort, but it was hopeless. The noises he made proved me right.

"Look, Detective. I kind of know where she is. I can't tell you where she is, but I can kind of see where she's been."

"Kind of?" he said, confused.

"I see the path where Emily's gone. I need to follow it while I can."

"Foot prints? Broken branches? What?" He was less and less comfortable about this. He wanted a rational answer. But only I could see the thread of energy she's trailing. "I've got to follow the thread. Can you fix the radio?" I asked him.

"I can try." He threw his wrench aside in disgust, but now he had a task that didn't require him walking anywhere. Then he turned and looked hard at me. "The thread?" There was no time to explain. He wasn't going to come with me.

I rose in answer, cursing softly at my twisted side. I stumbled past the dead deer and equally dead car, down the path.

All kinds of smaller animals were fleeing from the fire line. I watched every living thing from birds to coyotes to deer, flushed out in the open to escape the flames. The wind was carrying the flames away from us. I could see the smoke flooding from a rise perhaps 20 miles distant. I followed the path. It was just as well I wasn't driving. The path, bare earth to begin with, had narrowed to the point where the car couldn't have passed. It was maybe a half hour later when I stumbled over what looked first like a deer run. But there were boot prints as well. I followed it up into a tiny clearing, with a rough cabin tucked in between the pines.

There was a rusted-out pickup in the clearing. I went around the cabin and found there was a path that could have accommodated the truck. The back of the truck had a pile of empty beer cans and a gun rack in the front. There was a path up to a solid wood door, but the pathway was half-hidden by piles of dead leaves, and the general detritus of this man's life. This guy was so far out into the woods that he wasn't obliged to take rubbish to a particular spot. So it was everywhere. Broken chairs, broken dishes, a dead battery that had been taken out of a car and left to rust. There was a pile of wood, with an ax left in the tree stump someone used for splitting wood. Lying in the middle of the path was a man, face down with blood over his face. He was filthy even before that. There was a shotgun lying by him. The butt of the gun was bloody. I checked for a pulse. He was out cold. As I walked by the man the smell confirmed all that. His head was oozing blood. But head wounds bleed like that. I knew it was superficial.

The cabin door was wide open. The cabin was not built to take in mountain views. There were no windows in the door, and the other windows were at eye level. They'd let in some air and light but they couldn't be entered or stormed. They reminded me of arrow slits in a castle. Something you could shoot out of.

Over in a corner, Ben was lying unconscious with a pillow under his head and a blanket tucked around him. There was bramble and leaves in his hair. His face was pale gray.

I felt my head spin. I leaned myself up against the wall just in time so I slid down the wall as opposed to falling straight on the floor. As I slid to the floor, I slid into trance.

I was Emily. I was standing over my dad. I was watching both of our horses run pell-mell away from us. My dad was lying by the stone he'd hit his head on when his horse had tossed him to the ground. He was sprawled on the ground unconscious. I ran to him. Patted his face trying to wake him. He didn't move. He didn't twitch. He lay so quiet. I slapped him, trying to wake him. Nothing. I began to punch him. I needed him to get up to take care of me. To be my dad. I was screaming. My own voice scared me. I stopped screaming and the soft noise my dad made was too creepy. I tried to turn him. The noise he made then was even worse. I looked away from him because I couldn't reach him where he'd gone in his pain. I looked up and saw a man watching us. He was utterly silent. I could see the grime on his overalls even at that distance. Something dark and oily.

Maybe motor oil. He hollered down to me.
"Hey girly. Are you okay down there?"

I didn't like the crease lines around his eyes. It wasn't a face I liked. Or could trust. I didn't like his hands either. They were thick slabs of flesh with sausage fingers. But he was help. And my dad was hurt.

The man climbed down off the rise he was on. He reached us and touched my dad's wrist and neck. The man ran his hands over my dad's body. At first it was creepy, but I realized he was looking for wounds. He found blood at dad's knees that hadn't showed through his jeans. "Come on girly. Let's get him back to my cabin. I can help him there." He stood there, question in his voice. He smelled of dirt and beer. It didn't matter. What else could I do? I had to trust him.

"Let me go get my truck. I can get it close enough to him to get him out of here," he

said. This was the only help here. I sat by my father waiting, watching the sky darken.

The man went to get his truck. He dragged my dad into the truck bed, climbed himself into the truck and gestured me in with a sweep of his arm. "Come on girly, let's go take care of your dad."

I didn't like his look at me. It wasn't like Dad's at all. Somehow, he was looking through my jacket and shirt. He smiled at me as if he were looking at lunch. "My name is Eli. Short for Elijah. It's a bible name, my mom told me."

I couldn't imagine him young enough to have a mom. We were bumping down the path in the truck. I couldn't guess how bad it was hurting my dad. He pulled into a clearing with a cabin. He pulled my dad out of the truck as best as he could. I tried to help but my dad was so heavy and limp. Together we got Dad into his living room.

Once Eli got us both in the door, I thought he'd gone for medical supplies. I sat on the floor by my dad. I'd rolled my jacket up and tucked it under his head. Eli stuck his head around the door jam.

"Get you a beer, darling?" He had one in his own hand. No medical supplies, bandages, ice packs.

"I'm eleven. I don't want a freaking beer. I want you to help my dad."

"We can do that. We'll do that. You sure you don't want to party a bit before we do that?"

I knew what that would have meant if he was my age. He was closer in age to my dad. He was nothing like my dad.

"I don't think so. Don't you have a phone? Don't you have a way to call an ambulance?" I looked around desperately for a phone, a computer. Nothing. Just a cabin full of Eli's dirty clothes with animal heads on the wall.

"Well, there ain't no phone service here, girly. I can ride into town tomorrow ...." It was like he was explaining why he didn't have his homework.

"Now!" I screamed at him. "Right now!" There was a boot on the floor by him. I threw it in his face.

"Not your choice, girly," Eli said "You're in my house. My rules. House rules say we party and see where things go." He reached out a hand for me. I backed up. Against the wall. I started to slide along the wall towards the door. There was a stack of magazines that slid into my path. I fumbled over a log in the way. Looked down. It wasn't a log. It was a shotgun.

Dad had taught me to shoot a shotgun, one sunny summer day for fun. We went to a quiet cabin in the woods, set up glass bottles in a row, put on earphones and shot the bottles in a row. This wasn't any different. I took it in my hands and moved the lever, tried to move the trigger. It was too stiff. I grabbed by the barrel and swung it at his head.

I heard bells. It was the oddest sound. It didn't belong in a forest. But there was a delicate ringing in my ears. I thought to myself that I really had been concussed.

I slid back into consciousness. I heard Karen's voice over the ringing. "Hallo the house! Anyone here? Anyone hurt?" Detective Loew moved painfully though the door and down the path. I heard him yell. I heard her response.

Within moments Karen and Rick followed him through the door, checking the unconscious man in the pathway, making the radio calls. Checking Ben's vital signs.

I was Marlene again with Karen standing over me looking down at me. "Uh, how bad a hit on the head did you take?" she asked. She had a glass of water in her hands.

"I may be concussed, but I didn't faint. I saw Emily and her dad. I think I know what happened."

I heard the choppers landing in the clearing. Loew stumbled through the door moments later. "What happened here?" He walked in, stiff and sore with his hands clenched.

"I just saw it," I said quietly.

Detective Loew wasn't happier with me, but he listened quietly. I told him what I'd seen. Ben was here. He was badly hurt but he was still alive and we could do our best by him.

But Emily was running terrified through the woods. I saw her in my own mind. Her blond hair streaming in back running as it the devil might be behind her. Because she'd seen the devil in the flesh.

I grabbed Karen's arm. "Emily's running. She's terrified. The man tried to rape her and she's not going to be likely to trust anyone."

"Will she trust you?" Karen asked me.

"She knows me." I said. "She knows I know her mom." "You're the only person she does know here," Karen said.

Detective Loew added, "She has to be somewhere near the cabin. We'll see probably see her from a chopper. Will you come with me?" Loew asked. "So, there's a face she knows?"

"Of course," I said. Of course, that was before they landed the chopper in the clearing. The noise was deafening as Detective Loew led me under the turning blades, and helped me in.

The helicopter ride was anything but smooth. My upset stomach lurched as it jerked through the woods. And the noise of the propeller ramped my headache into the red zone. We were above the smoke. I saw a thin ribbon of blue running through the forest floor. "There," I said. "There's the stream."

"There's no stream there," Loew said, as he looked at the map. Then he saw it himself. "It's run-off. It's run-off from the storm. The chopper followed the stream along the gully that had been dry before the rain. The search lights were scorched through the sky. I glimpsed a patch of bright pink. A bright pink jacket. A blond-haired girl stunned by the light and the noise. She sped up, but the chopper light was still aimed on her. She collapsed as if she'd been caught, like a doe in the headlights.

Emily's blond hair was a wild nimbus with branches and leaves stuck in. Her jeans were torn. She'd clearly fallen in the mud at some point.

But she was alive. Laurel's baby girl was alive.

They landed the chopper as close to her as possible. Loew helped me out, but he waited by the chopper. I went to her alone. She'd been frightened quite enough.

She took a moment to place me. She was used to me in a long skirt and a scarf, serenely part of the tea room. I was in a borrowed orange jacket, with deep scratches down my face. I could see the wheels in her head, running through. Trying to remember who I was. Then she rushed to me. "Mirella?

Why are you here?"

"Your mom sent me," I said. I put arms around her and she leaned into me. My jacket was wet with the tears running down her face.

"You know those movies," she said. "The black and white silent movies where the girl is tied to the rail road track and some man saves her. He unties her just in time just before the train runs her over. I brought my dad would save me from anything. Anything! He couldn't. He couldn't wake up. He couldn't even walk. He couldn't stop the creepy guy from trying to touch me. It was like the train kept coming closer and closer to me and I was tied up and no one came to save me. He didn't save me. He couldn't save me." Emily's childhood died when her father fell unconscious. As she tried to save her dad. As she had to trust a man who no one should have trusted. As she had to fight to save herself. She wasn't quite a woman yet but she'd had to be fully adult to survive this and help her father survive. Her eyes had the level stare of an adult who's faced the fire and come through.

"You do realize, don't you?" I said. "You saved him."

"I left him. I left him at the man's cabin. I couldn't even wake him." "Yes. But you left your dad where he was safe and we could find him.

He's already down the mountain to the ranger's station. You did that. You did that all by yourself."

She shook her head in disbelief.

I continued, "Did you know that sometimes in the black and white movies, the girl saved herself? Sometimes the girl is her own hero."

Clearly Emily hadn't thought of that. I could see her tuck that thought away for later. Loew lifted her into the chopper and we climbed in after her. At the ranger's station, the medics saw to her scratches and bruises. Her father's wounds would be longer healing. She collapsed into a seat in back by the ambulance as they loaded him in.

That was when another cop car pulled in. It hadn't even stopped when Laurel flung herself out the door towards her child.

Loew stood behind me. "A stream, huh." He waved away the smoke blowing in front of him.

"It's what I saw." I answered. He gave me a flat look, shook his head, and walked towards the rangers' station.

"What good are you?" he turned and said, half pleased, half maddened at me.

I shrugged, "People ask me what I see. I see what I see." I sat on a fallen tree, weary from way too much adventure. "Emily's going home." I said with a glimmer of pride.

"By the way, Detective Loew," I called after him. "No press. No news cameras. No TV interviews. Nothing that mentions me."

"Why? Don't you want the publicity?" He smiled at me. "Wouldn't you like me to talk to your boyfriend about it?"

I smiled back. "Emily and Lauren have had enough. Let them go home and heal." I let the ambulance take me away.

So you can see, I can tell you what I see, but it's not always helpful. And yet, sometimes it's close enough on to matter. Detective Loew didn't put me in his report. But he took my phone number, for when he needs my help again.

Margaret and the Priest

Margaret and the Priest

Bridey sat in front of me, nibbling her sandwich. Bird-like, Bridey's head always tilted on an angle like she was listening to something somewhere else. She came in once a month wearing a purple plaid skirt with a prim white blouse and tweed jacket. She wore a crumpled slouch hat at a slight angle. She regularly asked about her nephew and the bingo numbers. I read her cups and she passed on the good gossip. Bridey was the housekeeper for the priest at St. Philomena's. Father Mallory was a tyrant and bully but she gave him as good as she got. He preached grateful obedience and hellfire. But she ruled the rectory, scrubbing floors in rage and perfection like a sandstorm on a mission. She filled the kitchen with the smells of hot bread and stew and filled his ears with invective any time he tracked in mud.

Bridey told me more than I told her. Bridey treated parish gossip as a spectator sport. It was like watching verbal gladiators sling guilt at each other in a sumo match. She'd lost her love in the war and cared for the priest when she was done caring for her parents. But she knew everything. She didn't just do his laundry. She kept his records and took all his messages when he ducked his calls. She saw everyone who came to the rectory, served them tea or coffee, and then waited behind the door to hear the story. She knew everything. There was little she wouldn't tell.

Today she was between scandalized and titillated. She leaned into me as if to impart a secret. "Old Margaret Ryan died this week. Lord, Father hated that woman. No love lost from her side either. They must have fought for 40 years. Her wake is tonight. They'll be burying her tomorrow."

"What did they fight over?" I asked her.

"Mirella, I don't know how it began. They were blooding each other regularly by the time I arrived 20 years ago." She picked up her tea cup, one pinkie in the air, and sipped delicately.

"Over what?" I asked.

"I don't think they actually fought over things," Bridey said. "They just fought."

"Why didn't one of them leave the parish?" I asked.

"Father wasn't about to. The bishop never said a hard word to him.

It was his home." She put her cup down to nibble a cookie. "But she wouldn't have gone either. Her parents helped lay the church foundation. She always said it was her church, not his."

"What did Father do to her this time?" I asked.

"I think he told her no. She wanted him to put her in charge of the altar guild. The other women would have quit if he had. They hated Margaret that much. He gave the job to Annie. Margaret was so steamed she didn't come to mass for the last three weeks. "

"Was that all, Bridey?"

"Not exactly. Margaret went to the church thrift shop instead and told stories about the last time Father was drunk at the parish picnic. It was true as true, but he wouldn't acknowledge that. He wore his aftershave that he puts on to cover it. God knows who he thinks he's fooling. The other women ran straight to Father to tell him. So, he told Margaret she was a sinful woman and he couldn't give her communion. If she couldn't have communion, she refused to go to church at all. Last Tuesday she had heartburn and pains down her arm. Called the rectory and asked him to come give her unction. He refused to go out that night to give her the sacrament. He said he'd send out the curate, but I know he didn't call the man. By Wednesday morning, she was dead. Margaret didn't get the last rites and he got to have the last word. We're putting her in the ground tomorrow."

"Will you be going?"

She brushed cookie crumbs from her front. "How could I miss it?

Her daughter is bound to have words with Father. I can barely wait. Those Ryans fought with Father for at least three generations now." Bridey bustled off in her tweed jacket, scarf tucked in at her neck, like a child looking forward to a fireworks display.

I shook my head. Father Mallory might be a tough bird, but Bridey was a force I'd bet on. It was a week later when Bridey returned. She told me in a worried tone, "You won't believe it. He's not sleeping."

"How do you know that?" How close were the quarters in the rectory?

"How could I miss it?" Bridey said. "He's rattling around like a dried pea in a pot. He's red-eyed and sore-tailed by the time I bring in his breakfast. He's stopped showering."

"How can you tell that?" I asked.

"Trust me, Mirella, you couldn't miss it. Won't let me wash his cassock either. He's worn it all week, crumpled and smelling like God's own mess. He's not sleeping. And he won't say why. He's nipping into the bottle I'm not supposed to know about." None of that sounded good.

"How did the funeral go?" I asked her.

"It was grand, but he asked three times for a glass of water with baking soda before he was out the door."

"Was the daughter angry?"

"Yes, but she's always angry. It's hard to say at who. She was so mad at her mother it hardly mattered how she felt about Father. But he told me she cheated him on his funeral fee."

"How was that?" I asked.

"She didn't slip anything extra in the envelope." Bridey slung her purse over her arm and rose for the elevator. She didn't quite skip, but she was definitely perked up by the uproar.

Two weeks later she came in with her latest report. It was more serious. She loosened the pin on her hat and put it on the table. "I think he's come to a crossroads, with all that whiskey," she confessed.

"Why is that, Bridey?"

"I've never seen his whiskey bottle at that level. I checked. I heard him talk to himself last night. How to do you fight with yourself out loud? He must be losing something upstairs."

"How did you know?" I hated to ask.

"How could I have missed it?" She waved her hands to describe the chaos. "Screaming at the top of his lungs. 'Get out!', but that wasn't directed at me. God knows who he was talking to. Father didn't know I was behind the door listening. I've got to get back. If I bake something sweet it might soften the evening." She trundled off back to the rectory.

An hour later, Bridey called in again. Her voice was a soft stage whisper. "Father broke down with the bishop. He called the bishop a pencil-headed overstuffed intrusion right over the phone. This morning he fumbled words at the altar. Couldn't get through the consecration. The bishop comes next week. I'm worried for both of them. Father stares off into space, his face screws up and then he looks like he's going to crap himself. And I have to do his laundry, if he'll ever let me in there to go get it. He's in a bad way. Last night he was at the bottle again. But I can't for the life of me think why he'd have poured two glasses instead of one. Surely he's not using both hands."

"Could you hear what he was saying?" I asked.

"Something about 'you can at least drink with me.' I've no idea what he meant. The bishop scheduled a visit at the end of the month. I hope Father's not cracked in two by then."

"Bridey, do you think it's just the alcohol?"

"I don't know. When I cleaned up the next morning, a voice whispered 'Leave my glass alone.' Not a soul in the room. It's a cruel joke if someone wanted to scare him or me. I left the dust where it was and came here. He won't be back until dinner. Do you believe in ghosts, Mirella?"

After three months in the tea room I'd seen one of almost everything, live or dead. How do you say that to a sweet old lady like Bridey?

"Why do you ask?" I said, hoping I could redirect this conversation. "If he's not mad-hatter mad, then what is talking to him? If I'm hearing it, am I mad too?" Bridey wasn't crazy. She could be manipulative, funny, kind at one hand and cruel at the other. But she didn't imagine things because she had no imagination to start with. If she heard something, it was there. "Mirella, you know about these things.

Will you come to the rectory? While he isn't there. Just to see what you can see?"

I never managed to tell Bridey no. Even when I should have. At the end of the day I stopped at the rectory just to see.

We sat in her kitchen, with a cup of tea and some cakes. The pans hung precisely on the wall. The cabinets were a display case. Even the wet dish towel hung with precision from the counter. Bridey reigned in the kitchen. It wasn't the Father's space at all. The parlor served as a community meeting room. His bedroom was almost a monk's cell. Which room would be Father's stronghold? "May I see the study?" I asked.

She took me past the double wooden doors, into a dark curtained room full of dust and books. Bridey turned with her hands out in display. "Well, Mirella, here you are, but I don't know what you'll find." I asked her for a glass of water, to get her out of the room. She scurried out.

I closed my eyes for a moment to focus. Then I heard a small, hard-edged voice.

"And who are you?" It was a woman's voice, but not Bridey's. It had more gravel in it. A smoker's voice. Not a friendly voice. But very clear. "And what are you doing here?" she asked.

I opened my eyes on a small translucent woman sitting primly in the chair across from his desk. She wore a black sheath dress from the fifties, and pearls around her neck. She had a glass of whiskey in her hand. She sipped it.

My eyes bugged slightly but I manage to speak to her. "My name is Marlene." My tea room name wouldn't do here. If I wanted her honesty I had to give my own.

"Little girl, get out of here." I hadn't thought of myself as a child since my mother died. But this woman scared me.

"Who are you?" I asked.

"I'm Margaret. Margaret O'Radigan Ryan. Father did me a wrong and he'll right it or I'll know why." Margaret was a small-boned, delicate woman. She pierced through me with her eyes – hawk eyes, bright and predatory.

"I'm here, Margaret, to help you if I can." "And why would you be thinking I need help?" "Bridey asked me to come."

"That over-prissy step-scrubbing drab. How dare she!" I let that pass.

I'd seen Bridey's spotless floors. I could see what she meant.

"You have noticed that you're dead?" I asked her.

"Well of course. I wouldn't be in his study if I weren't," she replied. I sat in the chair across from her. "Most dead people don't stay here,

you know."

"I haven't a choice," she said. "He refused me the last sacrament. Sad to say for us both, this is purgatory."

"I don't know much about purgatory. Are you here because of your sins?"

"Heavens no. The black-robed bastard refused me my final forgiveness and last rites. I'm here for his."

I was unsure of the theology behind that. I'd never met a ghost who felt their condition as a punishment. Most ghosts I'd run into were just lost or confused. Unless they're having such a good time that they didn't want to move on. But dead or alive, they're just people. Dead or alive, they had free choice. Dead or alive, she could stay in Father's study as long as she wanted. "Is there a reason why he would have done that?"

"Other than the sheer meanness of the man?"

"I won't argue that with you. I've heard some of the stories."

She laughed. The snort shook the drink in her hand. "Well, we fought over the altar guild, but that was just for fun."

"Fun?"

"You get to be older. You take what you can." "What did you do to the man?"

"Other than showing up in his shower every morning?" That explained why Father's hygiene had gone to hell.

"Other than that."

"Well, I sat in the curate's lap in the middle of mass. Only Father could see me. He didn't respond so I sat on the altar, right by the candle sticks. Now that, he responded to." Her face softened a bit. "We fought out of habit. It was just how we were with each other. But I never thought he'd deny me the rites. He knew I was dying. And he wouldn't come."

She wasn't a disappointed parishioner. Her heart had been betrayed. "How long have you been here?" I asked her.

"In the study?" Margaret took out a ghostly cigarette, and lit it. "No, at this church."

She inhaled and elegantly blew smoke to the side. "I was born and baptized in this church. My family has been here at least 80 years, since the beginning of the town."

"So how long has Father been here?"

She tilted her head, as she sorted dates. "It seems that long, but it can't be true. I turned 16 when the bishop sent him here."

"Were you friendly with him then?"

She put her drink down and crossed her arms and her legs. "We were never friends. But he did have a sparkly eye and a very pretty wave in his hair. All the girls noticed."

"And you did too," I continued the thought.

She gave me a wry smile. "I wasn't blind. What can you say about the things you do when you're young? Some of us outgrow being stupid. He was a waste in a cassock though. A man like that ought to be a man, not a priest."

This wasn't a simple grudge match. You can't hate someone with your whole heart unless they've broken your heart.

"What was Father like as a young man?"

She looked as if she'd swallowed something bitter. "A proper good priest. A bit stiff. He said a pretty mass. He wasn't an ass in the confessional back then. Although he became one. I helped with the school program. I came in to tutor kids after school. Sometimes after that he'd walk me home."

"Were you proper too?" I asked.

"Oh, God no," she laughed at me. "There was never a rule I didn't test or a trial I didn't run. It was damned boring to be a girl then."

"What happened then?" I probed.

"I started dating Willy. He was smart looking, but he was an octopus when he thought no one could see. I was pregnant before the end of my junior year."

"What did you do?"

"I did what everyone did back then," she told me. "I dropped out of school and I married the bastard. A lot of good it did me too. But my parents almost died of shame and the priest said it was what I had to do to do make it right."

"Father Mallory?" I asked her to clarify.

"That would be the man," she said. "He wouldn't give me absolution until I did. If my parents felt ashamed about a child on the way, they were furious he could toss me out of the parish. They weren't mad at Father.

This was my problem, my fault, my punishment. I was a bride within a month and a married mother within a half a year."

"That's not so bad," I said.

"It was the end of my dreams. I wanted to go to college. I wanted to go to France and England. I left my baby howling in the bedroom, while I searched the bars for Willie." By now her face was twisted in rage although her voice stayed low.

"So, you resented it," I confirmed.

"I knew it was a sin. And I confessed my rage. The church should help us through heartbreak. I cried tears in front of Father in the confessional. Do you know what he did? He told me to say three 'Hail Marys' and three 'Our Fathers'. And to remember how grateful I should be to have a man who married me in my shame."

"What did you do then?" I asked her.

"Well, I'd already found where Willy hid his whiskey bottle. I took a nip whenever I needed the courage or the strength. And I made my mind up to never trust a priest again."

"But you stayed in the church. That must have been miserable." I shook my head at her courage.

"Where would I have gone?" she shrugged. "Did you still go to confession?"

"Of course I did. I told Father regularly how sorry I was I didn't appreciate my mum enough. And that I'd forgot my morning prayers. I never let him near my heart again." Her face could have scalded milk. "I lost my nerve once. When I was pregnant with my fifth and green sick, I asked his permission to not have the child."

"Abortion wasn't legal, was it?"

"That didn't mean it was never done. I was desperate. He was still the same ass.

• 88

The man was as stiff and unbending as a ramrod. 'Children are a gift from God,' he said. 'Be grateful God has filled your womb again.' How grateful can you be when there's not enough food for the ones already here? And you're unable to fix it for needing to throw up?"

"So, he insisted you had to have the baby."

"Told me it was a sin as black as black and he'd have to condemn me to hell." Her voice quavered. "I did. The babe died of measles and hunger before he was two."

"Are you sorry you had the child?"

"I can't even say. It's so muddled for me. I loved the baby but I knew from the first he wasn't like the others. And the pregnancy broke my health."

"Do you think Father told you the right thing?"

"He always told all of us the right thing. He never said anything against the teachings of the church. It's a shame and a sorrow that the teachings of the church usually broke your head and your heart. And he'd hold you to that track to save your soul whether it broke you or not."

"So, you never spoke to him again?" I shook my head

"It's a tiny place, this parish. You can't ever break that far away." She fiddled with the pearls at her throat.

"One day I went to the tavern to find Willy gone. The priest said Willie left us for my wicked attitude and ungrateful heart. I said the hell with him and the church and God as well. I worked in an office and learned to smoke and swear with the best of them. Slept with my boss for a short bit of time. Drank whenever I could."

"Did you go still to church?"

"I couldn't ask the kids to go and not go with them." "Did Father know?"

"Bits and pieces. Everyone smoked. And he took to drinking with me. He started asking me the oddest questions. Was I happy? Did I know God loved me for my suffering? Did I trust the Lord with heaven and earth? And why is it, I couldn't trust him as God's priest? Did I tell you the man was an idiot?"

"So he knew how you felt."

"He wouldn't say. But he'd noticed that I never told him a thing that mattered to me again. And he couldn't have missed that I was miserable. He wasn't blind *either. He'd have Bridey call me up over some church matter, and she'd shuffle me into this room. He sat for hours trying to get me to say what he wanted to hear. I couldn't trust him. He may have been right. But that kind of cruel can't be right. There wasn't a right decision he made me make, I didn't hate."*

"How many times did he threaten to throw you out of the church?" She shook her head at me. "I lost count sometime after I was thirty.

It couldn't have been more than once a week but it felt like that." "So what was the flap about the altar guild?"

"It isn't like I wanted to do it. I knew it would put everyone in a snit."

"Were you in love with him?"

"What good would that have done?" Her anger confirmed it. Of course she was.

"Do you think he loved you?"

"Don't be thick. He never turned his gaze away from me, and he never looked at another girl the same way." Margaret still had her pride. Even as a ghost.

"Was he your lover?"

"He never touched me. He was an honorable man. And an insufferable idiot. The real fight was if I would let him do the wedding for my daughter and the premarital counseling. I'd rather her talk to Planned Parenthood. It will make more sense in the end. I told him that."

"So he wouldn't come when you were dying?"

"He may have thought it was a trick. A chance to whack at each other one more time."

"Does he hold you here?"

"His sadness does. For being so damn sure, he's damn miserable. For once in my life he can't keep me or bar me. But I'll stay damned if I let him dump his pious poison into my daughter's ear. I'm not angry about the rites. I'm used to his disapproval. I did half of my evil deeds just to tweak his nose. I'm angry that never once, did he choose to be kind for kindness sake. It's a miserable thing to be endlessly right and never kind."

And, I thought, that he was too good a priest to make love to another man's wife.

She faded out of the chair, smoke from her cigarette softly drifting away.

Bridey was, of course, at the door. She'd even put a stool by it. She'd heard me. But she hadn't heard Margaret.

"Bridey, what do you know about Margaret and Father Mallory?" "Not enough to put in a nutshell. They always fought. They drank together although they thought I didn't know. He always yelled at her face but he spoke softly at her back."

"You have Margaret in the study."

Bridey made the sign of the cross. "Preserve me from evil."

"Margaret's not evil," I explained. "But she's heart-broken and hopping mad. Have you seen Father ever bend?" I asked her. "Only to tie shoes."

"Will he speak to me?"

"Only if you're confessing or donating money."

I couldn't quite give the man cash. I was uneasy with what he would do with it. But I could try to make a confession. "Make me an appointment, Bridey. I'm sure I've sinned. Will he do confession in the study?" I asked her.

"He will if the penitent demands."
"Tell him it's necessary."

I had hoped to confess to him his own sins. I hoped to show him his own selfish cold correctness, in someone else's light. It was a good plan. A great plan. But like most plans it simply didn't work the way we thought it would. Bridey made me an appointment in a week. Two days later Father Mallory slid to his final end on a patch of ice on the front stoop. He hit his head on the railing and he was gone before he hit the ground.

If Bridey had enjoyed Margaret's death, she was devastated by the Father's. She hadn't just lost her job and her home. She'd lost the underpinnings of her life. I saw her as I slipped through the church door. She was crumpled into a seat at the second pew, right behind the family. His mother and brother survived the man and stood together with plastic mask-like faces, unable or unwilling to show a loss. Bridey had her hanky in hand and honked her nose almost in time to the hymns. The family had always hated Bridey for running the Father's life. She did so with Father's full permission. But his mother swore that half her messages left with Bridey never reached her son. I knew for a fact that they had, but that wouldn't have made his mother feel much better. I slipped into the church in back to watch the bishop do the eulogy. It was a lovely service, but it was arguable that the bishop left a hell of a lot out or that he simply hadn't known Father Mallory well. His description of the man was almost unrecognizable. "A noble priest whose faith inspired us all. A man who was a true shepherd to his flock. A gentle man who loved the people in his care ...." I had to wonder if the bishop had ever heard him in the confessional. I assumed not. Standing at the altar was Father Brian, the new priest the bishop had brought in. Father Brian still had the rosy cheeks of childhood. There were still creases on his cassock from where he'd unfolded it out of its packaging to put it on.

After the service, I slid through the unlocked rectory doors and wove through the mash of people here to gossip and be fed. Father Mallory's mother was ensconced in the parlor while her other son ran errands and interference. I saw him leaping two steps at a time down the staircase to the kitchen to try to orchestrate the march of hors d'oeuvres, casseroles, coffee and wine. The women of the parish had crammed every surface with pies, a roast turkey, macaroni and cheese, cookies, a lone taco salad, the ubiquitous green bean casserole and an unforgivable bowl of lime Jell- O marshmallow cottage cheese surprise. It left me feeling queasy. Father Brian had been backed into the corner by three women on the altar guild. He didn't have his hands protectively over his head, but I got the feeling that that was only because he was paralyzed in fear. It was clear who was in charge there. I walked past the pantheon of food toward the back door to find Bridey hunched in her small chair looking out the window. The parish women had decided it would be too hard for her to possibly cook. Instead of comforting her with their care, they'd managed to throw Bridey out of her own kitchen with their kindness. Clear silent tears ran down her face.

I didn't try to talk. I put my hand on her cheek, reached for her hand and cried with her.

After we were both too worn to cry more I asked her if we ought to have a cup of tea. "Well, of course." She unfolded herself from the chair and reached for the tea pot and kettle. She looked like she belonged, now that she had a task.

"Will you be wanting sugar?" she asked me. She knew better. But it was the ritual.

"Two lumps please. Is that that lovely black current blend?"

"It is." Her smile popped out. It was faint but present. She swept through the kitchen with the cups and saucers. The steaming teapot came in the second trip. When she poured the two cups, she'd begun to look a bit more like herself.

She looked up at the steps to the parlor. "They don't even want me there. Just as well. I'm going to the doctor next week. I'm hearing things myself."

I thought about Margaret in the study. I felt a crushing need to check. "Bridey, may I go into his study?" I asked.

"It's not like anyone would care. You know the way, don't you?" She settled back into her chair and sighed. She'd lost her expectant bird-like stance. She curved into the shape of her chair in exhaustion.

I opened the dark heavy doors to the parlor. Poked my head in to see if anyone else was there. I half expected Margaret to be there sitting with a drink in her black dress. I was wrong. I was facing Father Mallory, sheet- white and translucent. He jerked up, shocked to see me.

"And why are you here?" he bellowed.

"Actually, the question is, why are you here?" He was dead. He might have been a bully in life, but what could he do to me now? I came into the room and sat down before him.

"This is my space."

"Not for long. There's a spanky new priest upstairs in the parlor. The Bishop brought him in specially for your funeral. Did you miss it?"

I caught the shallow grin that flashed across his face. "The Bishop said the nicest things about me, didn't he?"

"You might have listened to some of the things some other people were saying as well." The smile crumpled into a small pout.

"I've been a good priest. A fine priest. A shepherd and protector ...." He was winding up for his own eulogy.

"Were you protecting Margaret when you refused her last rites?" "I didn't refuse her. I thought I could go in the morning. It was a miserable night and I thought she'd keep." His face dipped in shame. "She didn't, you know."

He began his defense. "I anointed her body. I asked for her soul to reach heaven through whatever purgatory God led her to. And for her to be strong enough for the journey."

"Had you thought that your study might be that purgatory?" "Ah, no. That hadn't crossed my mind. She was such a wicked thing."

"Was she really?"

"You didn't know the woman!"

"I did get to talk to her. Just as I'm talking to you. She had a really hard life."

"No more than most women."

"Mores to the pity. It broke her, you know. Those rigid laws break all kinds of people."

"The Church prescribes proper behavior for a Christian soul. My job is to lead them in that way."

"Your job used to be to lead them. I think you might have another job now." That truly hadn't occurred to him. The man shook his head. "Do you think Margaret was truly damned?" I asked him.

"I used to threaten her with it. Kind of like threatening a child with a spanking you've got no intention to give."

"She didn't know that. And you left her in the end in the dark alone. To be damned by your laziness and indifference." It may be a cruel thing to make a brittle, old rock-of-a-man cry. If I hadn't heard Margaret's agony I might have thought so. But I had. "Did you know she loved you?" I asked. I knew it was another twist of the knife. But I felt like the damage might do him some good.

"Get out!"

"Stop being a black-robed bully. She broke her heart over you time after time after time."

"*Because I was a priest?*"

"*Because you were a cold-hearted, bitter priest with no love or kindness in you. I don't think she'd have jumped your bones.*" He clearly didn't know what that phrase meant, but that might have been just as well. I went on. "*But she wanted your friendship and kindness as part of her life. You left her with a bitter crust of pious correctness. And in the end, you left her to die unforgiven and unforgivable.*"

He crumpled in his seat. His tears rolled down his face. "*She was so lovely. And so quick-stepped. And whip smart. She was like a room full of wild sparrows, darting everywhere. I couldn't help but be drawn. I held my vows. But she always held my heart.*"

I looked up to see Margaret, black dress and all against the wall by the book case.

"*So am I forever damned?*" *she asked him, head tilted in questioning.*

He shook off the tears, embarrassed at her presence. "*You know you don't follow the rules. At all.*"

"*I know,*" *she said.* "*Do you think it's helped either of us overmuch to do so?*" *Her chin pointed out like a precipice.*

He shook his head gently, "*I'm not so sure it has. If you're damned, then perhaps so am I.*"

"*Do you think we're stuck with that?*" *she asked.*

"*If I forgive you,*" *he asked,* "*can you forgive me? It's an awfully small study if we're stuck here for forever.*" *Then he smiled.* "*Do you fancy a walk with me?*" *He rose and stretched out his arm to her.*

She looked at her mostly empty whiskey glass. Put it down. Took his arm. I knew I'd fallen into the shadows for them when he opened the door and they strolled out towards the light.

I opened the study door to leave.

I heard the new priest running down the stairs. "Bridey, they're out of coffee. Did you know what those ladies are like when they run out of coffee?"

"I can only imagine," she smiled as she filled the pot. "Don't you worry, son. We'll get through. Take up that bowl of green Jell-O goo. I don't know why they like it, but they do. It'll keep them quiet trying to figure out what the recipe is. That's a mystery for sure. I'll bring coffee up in five."

The grateful look he gave her told me that Bridey wasn't going anywhere. She was home where she'd always been.

Bridey always took care of the priest.

Grave Matters

Grave Matters

Did you ever investigate ghosts?" Alyx asked me. Alyx was one of the Artemesians, a group of self-proclaimed witches who specialized in healing and moon worship. She came into the tearoom as much a friend as a client. She was not a reader, but she was a brilliant herbalist and a very gifted psychic healer. Blond and willowy, she might have come from Danvers four hundred years ago. She might even have been hanged. Now Alyx was a rising star in her coven.

Alex had the "it-girl" factor. She had the "cool girl" thing going on. When in high school, I was far too emotionally delayed to understand the relationship dance between the girls who fluffed pompoms and went out with the football players. Or their often cruel friendships. There was a witty, catty script to their dialogue, so vaguely cool that I almost didn't notice the cruelties behind the words. I wish I could say I didn't join in because I was better than that. I wasn't. I wanted to belong, like every other backward, awkward wallflower, leaning towards the sunlight of the golden girls. By their lights, I was not worthy.

I was so flattered Alyx had befriended me that I found myself unconsciously mimicking her. It was a terrible shock when I found some of those mincingly cruel comments coming out of my mouth as well. But I felt warm around Alyx, as if I were resting in a pool of sunlight.

If she wanted to go ghost hunting, of course I'd join her. She began by making a list of equipment she thought we'd need.

"Why don't you just talk to the ghosts?" I asked her.

She turned a baneful glance on me. "No one really talks to ghosts, do they?"

"I've talked with ghosts all my life. Or rather they demand to talk to me. But I never went in just to look around."

"You talk with ghosts?" she said scornfully. "How do you codify that?

How can you prove it? It must be done scientifically. You measure the temperature, take pictures, document energy surges, make films. You can prove there are ghosts. It's not like telling someone a tale and hoping they believe you."

Nona had always taught me not to worry about whether people believed me or not. She told me, "You believe yourself and that's plenty and enough. If you saw it, it's there. If you heard it, it's there. You can't prove anything to people who don't believe and you don't need to prove anything to anyone who does." But she also warned me a lot of people would be threatened, and I should keep what I hear to myself until I know how it will be received. I was intrigued that you might actually be able to have proof. Would having proof make speaking to ghosts more legitimate?

"How do you prove you're a healer?" I asked.

"It's simple. If the people you work on get better, you're a healer," she said smugly.

"So why is talking to ghosts different?" I asked, just to burst her bubble.

"It just is. You can't prove you did. If you use the equipment, you can prove what you've accomplished!" She looked down on me scornfully.

I just shook my head. "So where would you go to ghost hunt?" I asked her.

"Don't be silly. You go where there are ghosts!" She gave another smirk.

"What did you have in mind?" I asked.

"Granary Cemetery is right down Tremont Street. They say it's deeply haunted."

"Isn't that like the most public graveyard in all of Boston?" I asked.

Alyx pulled a strand of hair behind her ear. "The sisterhood knows a little trick they use for privacy. We can investigate there all night and no one will be the wiser."

Alyx went home to prep ghost hunting equipment for an evening's exploration. I finished up the day in the tearoom. Rita called me into her office.

"So, do you have plans tonight?" she asked me.

I was embarrassed to tell. "I'm going off ghost hunting with Alyx," I confessed. It seemed childish to say it that way.

•

Rita looked firmly at me. "You watch Alyx," she told me. "She's on the fast track. I'm just not quite sure where she's headed."

I gave her a funny look. Couldn't Rita see how cool Alyx was? "Do you know where I'm headed?" I asked her.

"You're a work in progress, but you'll be a fine reader in your time," she said. "How much do you know about ghost hunting?"

"I know I've always seen ghosts. And sometimes I can speak to them.

Although sometimes they don't seem to see me back."

"That's the difference between a ghost and an apparition," Rita explained. "A ghost is usually a lost or misplaced human soul. You feel like you're talking to a person because you are. They just happen to be dead. Sometimes they've stayed here for one reason or another.

Sometimes they don't know they're dead yet. It's a grace to tell them that if you can do it in a way that's kindly.

"An apparition is anything you see. The psychic world is the Wild West, even here in Boston. Most apparitions are like a recording of something that happened in a particular place and time. It will go through the incident repeatedly and consistently, like a tape recording. The ghosts won't notice or speak to you. My guess is that the memory is strong enough to replay itself over and over but that no one is really present in that memory.

"But there are other apparitions as well. Be careful what you talk to.

When you talk to an entity, it has permission to talk to you. Not everything golden is good." She shook her head gently.

"Why can't Alyx see ghosts?" I asked.

"Healing is about ritual. She's a fine healer. Talking to ghosts is about discernment. It's not the same thing." she explained. "Go have fun."

I ran out the door.

It was a soft fall evening with an enormous moon, yellow as a ripe lemon. I walked down the street, looking for Park Church. I almost missed the sidewalk that led into the graveyard. Alyx called me over. "Right here!"

•

"How could I have missed the turn?" I asked her. I looked around and saw small witch lights at each corner of the graveyard.

"I did a little masking spell. No one will see us. They'll just walk right by, thinking nothing's there."

I had a momentary flash of jealousy over Alyx's abilities. Or maybe over her training. No one had taught me tricks like that. Then again, it was not what we did at the tearoom. The Artemesian sisters practiced what they called gray witchcraft. They did not claim always to be white and insisted they were never really dark. But they practiced the manipulation of the world and things within it. That was something readers did not do in the tearoom. Rita was adamant about that.

Alyx had a knapsack full of gadgets. I shook my head as she started to pull them out of her bag.

"Don't you just talk to ghosts?" I asked her.

"I can't do that," she said. "I don't know anyone who can really do that. I always thought that was a myth. Besides, we need to get proof."

It seemed imprudent to remind her I'd been talking to ghosts since I'd been three.

She pulled out two flashlights and cameras, a notebook, a digital recorder and EMF meter, followed by a collection of candy bars and other junk food. "We need to keep our strength up," she explained. I chose a candy bar and listened to her plan.

Alyx spread her arms in display, over the pile, showing off her available technology. "We can set up equipment all over the cemetery if we wish. It's smaller and that is better, since we can cover it more easily. Do you have anyone you want to focus on?" she asked me.

"I hadn't thought. I didn't know you went hunting for a particular ghost."

"We could. We don't have to. We can focus the equipment on someone specific or we can try to see who is most active."

"Why don't we see who has the most to say?" I asked.

"You think you can get someone to say something?" she taunted me. "We'll see."

•

It was a challenge, pure and simple. She didn't want it to speak to me. Or with us. She wanted it recorded on her machines.

We set up camcorders along the wall and sat waiting for something to happen. Alyx kept checking the equipment, going from one tripod to another, taking readings with her EMF meter. It was a warm enough night that I dozed off.

Something poked me very gently. I thought I woke. But the graveyard was full of people as I opened my eyes. There was a small boy in a tricorn hat and waistcoat.

"Forgive me, milady," he said as he removed his hat. "It seemed you slumber here. Night is swift as shadow. This no place for the quick."

I blinked several times. He didn't go away. "No, I suppose it's not," I replied. "But I wanted to see who was here."

"Look and you shall know," he told me. "The other girl is head blind, is she not?"

"I guess. She does seem to need her equipment."

Alyx was now tinkering with a meter that was presumably not working. She whacked it several times with her hand, in impatience.

"She's waking everyone," he told me. "There are those best left sleeping."

"What is your name?" I asked him.

"Master Patrick. Master Patrick Williams." I shook the shape of his illusive hand.

"Can you tell me what she's doing?" he asked me, pointing to where Alyx was set up in the corner.

I looked over to Alyx. Her face was reflected in the screens of her instruments. She walked from one to the other checking everything, scribbling notes in her notebook by the light of her flashlight. "Alyx!" I called out. "There's a ghost right here!" She stayed hovering over her readings, unable to hear me. She was oblivious to the boy and me.

"She wants to know if ghosts exist," I explained. "She's trying to find scientific proof."

•

"Like Ben Franklin's witchery?"

"Well, as I understand it, Ben Franklin was a scientist along with everything else. He had a lot of equipment that probably looked pretty weird."

Patrick rolled his eyes. "Mr. Franklin was out in a thunderstorm with a key dangling from a kite trying to catch lightning. They say he was a statesman and an author, but he was outright daft."

"A lot of science looks that way if you don't understand it. Alyx is trying to get scientific proof of life after death, I suppose. So no. It's not witchery. It's cameras and measuring equipment."

"What's a camera?" he asked.

"Well, it takes a picture of an image and freezes it in time."

His eyes had glazed over by now. Perhaps all science looks like magic if you don't know what it is.

"Anyway, she wanted to see ghosts."

He started to giggle hysterically. I couldn't help but join him. He went over and put his hand on the meter. Alyx jolted for a moment and began to scribble madly in her book.

"You don't need proof, do you?" He still was bent over laughing. "Never did. But I told her I'd come along."

"Everyone wants to meet you. We don't always get visitors who can see us."

"I would be honored."

"Not everyone actually." he equivocated. "There are some folk you probably should not meet. But I'll introduce the people of quality."

A wispy image of an elder woman climbed out of her grave, as if her hips were still sore and stiff. She stood herself up and curtsied.

Patrick announced her. "This be Goodie Goose."

"The Mother Goose? Elizabeth Goose?" I asked. I'd seen the tombstone.

"Lizzy Goose. I'm snail-paced and a sorry sight but here at your pleasure, child. You'll have to forgive our gentlemen. They argue and tussle every night. They are rebels all, in their own ways."

There was a heated discussion coming from one corner. On a flat tomb-surface, three men played a board game, hardly watching the moves. Instead, their focus was on a conversation so angry they were declaiming over each other.

"John Hancock, Samuel Adams and Alexander Hamilton." Lizzy pointed out the three.

"Do they know what happened? Do they know they're dead?" I asked her. One of them looked up at me. "Well, of course they do. This is a graveyard. To a large extent they remain here to hear what is said about them. At one time, none of them knew whether they would be heroes or hung. It was rather a near thing."

"So, they stay here listening to tour guides?"

It's heady stuff for them," she acknowledged. "They're grander here than they were in life. But they also lived for the fight. Had they not had the revolution, they'd have argued with their neighbors or their church or their second cousins. It's who they were. And don't think that because they were on the same side of the war they agreed with each other. These were never men of peace. They liked nothing better than a huge, messy, irresolvable quarrel. They still love their little nightly squabbles." The ruckus got louder.

Sam Adams pounded his ghostly hand on the stone. "It does not require a majority to prevail, but rather an irate, tireless minority keen on setting brush fires of freedom in the minds of men."

"How do you set a brush fire in the middle of a tea party?" Hamilton smirked at Samuel.

"It accomplished both goals," Samuel grinned. "I soaked their finances throwing tea into the harbor and set alight the fighting fire of our men."

"Hear, hear!" Hancock cheered.

"But how will you do commerce?" Hamilton continued. "No colony will survive at all if they can't trade with each other. You need a strong set of rules agreed upon by everyone so that business can flourish. That takes a central government, a common currency, roads and banks that all work

•

together."

"Are they still making the same arguments?" I asked Lizzy. "As in life, so in death," she said

"It sounds endless," I said as I watched them pontificate at each other.

Lizzy answered me, "It is. It was. It has been. And will be. That's why they're still here."

"Actually, the things they're discussing are still not resolved.

Different states, colonies, still have very different opinions of how much the central government should do, if anything. But we settle it by voting instead of fighting, usually. That's something they gave us."

"They did," Lizzy acknowledged. "They weren't fools. They just loved the fight."

A plainly-tailored man walked near them. He tipped his hat in recognition and they looked up at him. "Are you tyrants still at it?" he said to the three.

Hancock answered, "Rev. Byles, we are not tyrants. We are patriots." "That," the reverend said, "remains to be seen. Which is better, to be ruled by one tyrant three thousand miles away or by three thousand tyrants not one mile away?"

Hancock stared at him levelly. "No one cares for what you say, you Tory son of George!"

"I am not George's son, nor Tory whole, but servant of Christ," Byles returned.

"But you still deny the rights of liberty!" Sam Adams roared at him. Byles tipped his hat and walked away from the three rebels.

I looked in a corner. A beautiful young black woman in a Georgian dress and mob cap sat on a tree stump. She read her words aloud as she wrote.

"Great God, what light'ning flashes from thine eyes? What pow'r withstands if thou indignant rise?

Against thy Zion though her foes may rage."

She didn't look up at us. Her whole focus was on her writing. Byles walked

•

by her, stopped and looked over her shoulder at her writing. She looked up at him in reverence

"Who is she?" I asked Lizzy.

"She's a marvel. Phyllis Wheately. 'a rich jewel in an Ethiope's ear.' Her master taught her to read and write. So she writes poetry, as fine as any in America. Mr. Byles said so after he examined it. Better than mine. Mine are rhymes to put babes to bed."

"Lizzy, people are still putting babies to bed with your poetry." "Really?" she smiled. Perhaps she hadn't known.

"My mother read them to me," I told her.

"Your mother could read?" she said in astonishment. "Most people do now," I confessed. Lizzy looked amazed. "It must be a wonderful age. To all be learned!"

"It's like every age," I said. "Some wonderful things, some terrible messes and some things you just have to get through."

Three shimmering riders on horseback burst through a monument. "Revere, Dawes and Prescott," Lizzy pointed out.

Across the graveyard, I saw a lovely woman in apron and mob cap wave her hankie. "Now you be careful, Willie Dawes, and come home safe to me."

Dawes turned his horse towards her and cried, "I'll be back by midnight, Mehitabel."

Revere grabbed Dawes' reins. "Oh for heaven's sake, Will. Ride. We need to reach Concord by morning."

The three men halted in front of Lizzy. "Madam." They dismounted, removed their hats, and gav her a short bow. Then they rushed through the cemetery to Adams and Hancock. The game was forgotten as all the men spoke in desperate whispers.

"Do they make the ride every night?" I asked.

"Oh, assuredly. Sometimes three and four times a night," Lizzy told me.

"Why?" I asked.

●

"It's their strongest memory. They warned Lexington and Concord that the British troops were on their way. The apparition repeats it over and over because it was the most important moment in their lives."

The ghost of a black man drifted up through the stone erected for the martyrs of Boston Massacre. He walked across the graveyard, neither looking left or right. He seemed unaware of everyone.

"Who is that," I asked.

"Poor Crispus," Lizzy answered me. "Crispus Attucks."

I could hear the man mutter to himself. "Just walkin' through Bunker Hill on a short cut. Tryin' to get back to my ship. Damn all white people yellin' and shootin' at each other. I pushed at someone trying to get away and they had to go and shoot me! Damn all." His specter trudged through the graveyard and evaporated at the fence. Several seconds later, he drifted through the tombstone again and went through his march, like a set piece.

"He's stuck?" I asked Lizzy.

"No one knows, child, but he responds to no one and nothing. I believe this is just his memory. It's sad though."

"Why are you still here, Lizzy?" I wondered what could have held this sensible woman here at her grave.

"I miss my babies," she told me. "I miss my Thomas too. He still wanders through here and I'm waiting for him to be done with this world. When he's done, I'll go home with him. Until then, I watch after other people's babies.

"Babies?" I asked.

"You all are babes. I always enjoyed caring for the young. It's just that the young are a bit older now." She smoothed her skirt with her hands.

There was a rumpus in the back of the yard and one of the stones split open as a man in black robes strutted among the tombstones. A black robed winged creature clung to the man.

Master Patrick grabbed my arm. "You might best leave, mistress. This is not commodious company." The other ghosts evaporated in front of the apparition.

•

"Who is he?" I asked.

"Cotton Mather and his master," Patrick told me. "The thing on his back?" I asked.

"Purely evil," Lizzy answered me. "We keep well out of its reach."

Another man opened a door from his tomb. Like the first man he wore a judge's robe. But the black was a clear galaxy as opposed to the filth hanging on the first judge. Light showed out of his open hand.

"Cotton," the second man bellowed, "you'll not bring that filth in with the rest of us."

"'Sewell, you're deluded. You wanted charity, proof, legal reasoning. Against demons. A court of law is the only place to decide such things and that was our job. Couldn't you smell the devil at Danvers?"

"You're an idiot, Cotton," Sewell answered. "You rail against demons and you wear one like a robe."

Both men turned their attention to Alyx.

Sewell turned towards me. "And why are the living here?" he asked me.

"I was curious," I stuttered. The man put out his arm. It blocked me from Mather's sight. I could see Alyx if I stretched past his protective arm.

Alyx had been watching the meters closely. Apparently, the readings bounced off the chart when the two judges started to rail against each other. She walked steadily towards Mather with her meter extended in her hand. From her face, I could see her amazement. She saw him.

"You're a ghost!" she exclaimed. Her face beamed with wild excitement.

"What if I am?" he said, maintaining his dignity.

"But I'm here to see ghosts. Are you a real ghost?" She waved the meter at him as if to get a better readout.

"You're a witch, like as not," he snarled at her. He reached to the upside-down silver star at her throat. His voice rose to a bellow. "The Maleficum speaks of such deviltry. Do you have a familiar? Do you rut with Satan?"

"I just wanted to see a ghost," she continued simply.

•

"What would you like? Should I rattle my chains? Moan? Appear and disappear?" He was haughty, aloof and handsome in his regal court manners. She reached out to touch him. He pulled himself out of range and stood haughty and mighty as he had always in court.

"I just wanted to see if you were real," she exclaimed.

The ragged demon riding him reached out and touched her hair. It picked a strand up and started to play with it. The wind rattled bushes and trees like castanets.

"Alyx!" I said, anxious to leave. "Let's get out of here!" I ran up to grab her. Sewell blocked me from reaching her. I could see her, the ghost and the demon all together in an unholy trinity.

"Will you teach me?" she said to the pair. "I want to know everything about the afterlife." She looked up to Mather with longing.

I watched Mather smile at her one way as the demon smiled a much crueler smile. "But of course child. We'll teach you."

"Alyx no!" I screamed. "It's not what you think it is. Come on. Come with me. Let's go."

Lizzy and Patrick were on the side screaming "GO!

I ran through, grabbed at Alyx's hand and pulled. She pulled away me and slapped me so hard I fell to the ground.

I rubbed my cheek, feeling the bruise already.

I looked up at her. She was beautiful. Cool. Chic. And a demon like a black rag was draped around her shoulders, stroking her face.

"You can go if you like, wimp. I've found my ghosts. You are such a baby." Alyx dismissed me, the way the cool girls had always dismissed me. It still hurt.

Lizzy grabbed my hand and Patrick stood guard behind.

Lizzy ran with me to the cemetery fence, dragging me along when I stumbled. I flew over it as she released me. "Go!" she shrieked. "Don't look back."

But of course, once I was over the threshold, I did look back. I could see

•

the church, but the cemetery and Alyx were blanketed in thick mist.

I ran down the middle of the street, terrified to be near the bushes or the buildings. When I got home I slammed the door, locked it and shivered over my hot tea in a hot bubble bath.

The next morning, Alyx marched into the tearoom. She looked triumphant. "I thought you'd like to see the tapes and readings." She didn't laugh out loud at me, but I could hear the sneer in her voice. "It's a shame you got scared. I got some great readings after you ran away.

What was wrong with you? I wouldn't have thought you were that kind of a coward. I told the story at the sisterhood and they're still laughing.

Who'd have thought?"

Was there something different about her? A dark cloaked thing clung to her back, close and tight to her skin. But I could see it. Was there a thread of burnished gold around her outline?

Rita stepped out of her office and called to me.

"Sorry, Alyx. Got to go," I said. It was a reprieve. I didn't want to hear Alyx tell me what a baby I was again.

"See you." She dismissed me with a wave and left. Rita opened the door and waited for me to sit.

"What did you do last night?" Rita's eye bore through me.

"We investigated the Granary Graveyard," I said, as quietly as if I hoped she wouldn't hear me. But she did.

She stared at me deeply, investigating, probing. Did she wonder if I had brought back a visitor as well? "You seem to be all right."

"I hope I am. I had help. What was the thing on Cotton Mather?" "You saw old Cotton?" she asked me. "What did you think it was?" "I don't know. It was just nasty. Mean and violent and evil. It gave

Alyx what she wanted, but it felt vile."

"Exactly. That, Marlene, is a demon. And you better not bring one home as a souvenir."

•

"I'm afraid Alyx did. Is there something I can do to help Alyx?" "Did she choose to engage with this thing?" Rita asked. "Actively?" I thought about it. "Yes," I concluded.

"There's a reason I would never have Alyx as a reader at the tea room. Alyx will only learn if she's allowed the dignity of her choices," Rita explained. "She'll find her own way to recover from her mistakes. Or else she won't. But I don't think she'll learn except by experience. What did you do?"

"I chose not to talk to that nasty thing," I said simply. But I'd been helped by the others in the graveyard that meant no harm.

She smiled. And poured another cup of tea.

"Then you can't change her choices. But you may stay," Rita said with finality.

I hadn't realized leaving might be a consequence of the night before. I let go of my breath. "Would you have thrown me out for talking to it?" I asked her.

"In a heartbeat," Rita said.

•

Tea Room Tales by Ellen Anne Eddy

.

What the Parrot Said

.

What the Parrot Said

You couldn't keep anything from Rita. Not with Methuselah around.

Rita owned a blue macaw named Methuselah that lived in the back of the tea room office. She would come in early, lift the cover from his cage, and make kissy noises at him. "Pretty, pretty boyo," she would croon at him. Then she would ask him, "What do you see?" and he repeated that in patter for hours. His day was spent preening in the mirror, spilling his bird food and nibbling at his bell toys. He was a forty inch wide riot of blue, green and yellow feathers. Though his cage took up a quarter of the office, it still seemed like cramped quarters for him.

Methuselah came to her through Sadie, the owner of the tea room before Rita. When Rita bought the building, Methuselah came with it, cage and all.

Thusey, as we called him, had a wide vocal repertoire. He sang several show tunes, said "pretty boyo," and "cracker," "feed me," and "What do you see?" as his most common comments, and whistled several tunes. It added to the tea room ambiance when he learned to imitate the traffic noises below. He also made the elevator noise so precisely, I could never tell the difference. Rita kept him zealously in her office, which I thought was cruel. He clearly liked people, eyeing them through his cage. She would only let him out with the door safely shut. To go into her office, you knocked first to make sure Thusey was safely secured.

When Rita went off to a family wedding, she left me in charge. She stopped at the tea room, dressed in her hound's-tooth coat, floral hat and the ever-present support stockings, to give me marching orders before she left. "Now don't do anything stupid while I'm gone. Don't take any checks or hundred-dollar bills. They don't counterfeit little bills when they can print big ones. Don't let Jamie off easy. Keep on him. He acts like he hates his job here, but it makes him more stable and I promised Maggie to watch after him." I nodded yes to indicate I understood.

"Don't call the police unless it's a physical problem," she said. "They don't get that a metaphysical fight is a fight. If it gets messy, let Maggie handle it. Oh, and whatever you do, don't let Methuselah out of his cage." She pecked me on the cheek and lifted her overstuffed bag on to her shoulder. "Make lots of money," she said, "and have fun." Even at sixty-something she looked like a kid skipping school as she stepped into the elevator.

"We'll be fine!" I hollered back. I wiped my hands on my skirt and began to see that the tea room was in place to open tomorrow. It did look all in place. I picked up fresh muffins. The tea was prepped, all the serviceware was in place. I ducked into the office to calm my nerves for a moment. Methuselah sat in his covered cage.

Rita kept him covered most of the time when we were open. I didn't say it to her, but it struck me as a sad life for a parrot. I grabbed the edge of the sheet and lifted it. He opened one eye speculatively and said, "What do you see? What do you see? What do you see? What do you see?" perfectly in Rita's voice. "Hey, Thusey, What do you see?" I said, in hopes I could get him to talk for me too. But he went into his litany of parrot squawks and squeals. I left the cover off his cage.

"Pretty, pretty, pretty boyo," the parrot crooned. He swung on his cage support in delight.

John and I had let our impossible romance slide into a very pleasant friendship. His interest was strictly in young me, but he enjoyed being my research person, and we still spent evenings together as friends. John called to invite me to dinner. "Do we need anything?" I asked him. He was the resident cook between the two of us.

"No, babe," he said. "Don't go to the store. We're good. We have everything."

"Don't go to the store?" I asked him. I didn't let my disappointment show. The only thing we were really out of was Moose Track ice cream. Moose Track ice cream was a crucial part of my evening wind-down ritual. I decided to go get some anyway. I went to cover Thusey's cage.

"Don't go to the store. Don't go to the store," Thusey repeated. I pulled the drape over his cage and said, "Good night, Thusey." I tried to make the kissy noise Rita always made for him. Thusey gave me a disappointed squawk.

Under his cover I could hear him echoing me, "Good night Thusey.

Good night Thusey. Pretty, pretty boyo."

The grocery store was crammed with people, but only two checkout lines were open. I held my chocolate fudge ice cream, chosen because they were out of Moose Track. Someone bumped into me with the grocery cart. I whirled around at the guy. He looked harmless. And embarrassed. Someone had probably pushed him as well. I smoothed down my annoyance but I snipped at him. "Watch it, would you?"

My bad," he said. He ran his eyes up and down me and smiled. I might be living with John, but no one minds a little appreciation. I gave him a brief smile. Someone bumped my cart sideways. When I turned back to it, my purse was gone. When I turned back to ask the guy what he'd seen, so was he.

That ended my shopping. The manager let me use his phone to call the police. I was waiting on the curb outside when John came to pick me up. I hadn't even enough money to take the subway.

"I thought I told you we didn't need anything?" he said once I'd crawled into the car.

"You didn't. I'm out of Moose Track ice cream."

"Oh," he said. "That stuff will make you sick. Fat too. Why don't you give it up?"

Rage roared red through my face. I said nothing, but I put my hand up as if I were pushing him away. He struggled to remove his foot from his mouth. "Well, it makes me sick and fat. Do you need it?"

This was not an improvement. I let my silence speak for me.

He pulled a five-dollar bill out of his wallet. "Go on. I'll wait for you," he said.

By now my humiliation was complete. But I decided to be humiliated with ice cream rather than without it. I silently grabbed his bill and ran back into the store. When I got back with my purchase, John was looking straight ahead, rather than say anything else wrong. He drove me to his home. We spent an evening in chilly silence, he at his computer, me picking at dinner. I went home before ten to finish the evening, wrapped around my bowl of chocolate fudge with a heating pad draped over my shoulders.

When I got into the tea room the next morning, I went first into the office to feed Thusey. I took off the cover. He began his chatter. "Pretty boyo. That's me! I'm a pretty boyo." He stretched and turned his head sideways. "Don't go to the store, don't go to the store. Awaak. Pretty boyo." I ruffled the feathers on his head. He reached out with his beak. Thusey wasn't above biting people. I pulled my fingers out of the cage.

Then it hit me. "What did you say, Thusey?"

He made the elevator noise, squawked twice and then said, "Don't go to the store, don't go to the store." The parrot twisted his head around to look at me. He cocked his head and blinked. And began the elevator noise again.

It was nonsense of course. All Thusey could do was repeat what he'd heard. Sometimes it sounded like conversation but it was just phrases he knew, strung together.

But, "Don't go to the store?" Whether Thusey understood what he was saying or not, he'd been right. I wished I hadn't gone to the store that night even if it meant no ice cream. The rest of the day would be taken up replacing drivers' license, buying a new phone, then changing card numbers on a number of accounts. I went off to replace credit cards and my license.

I got a call while I was standing in an endless DMV line. It was Maggie. "You gotta come back," she said. "Now." Her voice was edged with panic.

Something wrong? Was there a client who came in looking for me? A fire? An inspector? What? I was searching in my mind for what possibly could have rattled Maggie that badly. Maggie was implacable. I was coming up with a blank when she screamed "For God's sake, Jamie, catch that damned thing." I heard a series of parrot shrieks in the background. "What damned thing?" I asked. Maggie's voice was shaking. "Jamie thought he'd water the parrot while you were gone. He opened the door and the parrot flew straight into his face. That thing is a flying colored rat!"

I heard Jamie in the background. "I'm sorry Aunt Maggie! It scared the crap out of me. I thought it was going to take my eyes out. Claws all out and squawking." His voice was strained into a falsetto.

Maggie said, "You get yourself back right now, Marlene. We don't have anyone in, but I ain't going to touch Thusey, never mind catch him. He's one nasty-ass bird."

I rushed back. When I arrived, Maggie and Jamie were on one side of the room. Thusey was perched on a cornice. He squawked twice, spread his wings out at me and started to croon. "They asked me how I knew, My true love was true." Cole Porter. Rita loved Cole Porter.

Evidently so did Thusey. Jamie and Maggie both sprung at me as I came through the elevator doors.

Jamie was screaming, "It ain't my fault. It just ain't. He flew straight at me."

Maggie was more disgusted. "That bird is just a dirty thing," she said. "If we were at home I'd make it into the dog's dinner. It's nasty." Her face was screwed up in disgust. The parrot stopped singing, and began his patter. "Pretty boy oh. Pretty boyo, pretty, pretty." Followed by more whistling.

"I don't damn think he's pretty," Maggie said with her arms crossed in front of her. Thusey strutted along the cornice above where Maggie was sitting. The bird looked her in the eye and said, "My girdle's too tight.

Lawdy, lawdy that's damn too tight. Damn that spandex. Do they make these things any larger?" It was Maggie's voice out of the parrot's throat. Then there was a splatter of white guano landing next to Maggie's tea cup.

Maggie didn't blush, but you could see the vein beating in her throat. "Nasty! Just nasty!" she said.

"You know he just repeats what he hears?" I asked her.

"I didn't say damn-all about my girdle. I ain't never said nothing about my girdle." I couldn't imagine Maggie had. At least not to Jamie or me. Maggie treasured her dignity and her size was a touchy subject.

But I could see her thinking it. Maggie was of an age where fundamental foundations weren't considered optional. And God knows, they could hurt. She'd never have said it out loud. So how did Methuselah know? Had Maggie said that out loud to herself, maybe in the bathroom?

No. That was nonsense. Thusey's voice dropped. "Moose Tracks!" he said, in my tones. "Moose Tracks!" Jamie and Maggie were confused by that and I left them that way. "Maggie," I said, "why don't you head home. Jamie, I don't know what you'd have done differently. The parrot needed water and you brought it to him. It's not your fault the parrot is an escape artist. Why don't you both stop for a treat at the diner on me?" I tucked some money into her hand. Maggie was still offended. Certainly with the parrot. Maybe with me as well. But both she and Jamie needed to get away fro the parrot desperately, before Jamie was past traumatized and before Maggie wrung its neck. The parrot whistled a tune, then cackled and said "Can I buy a bag? Can I buy a bag?" It was Jamie's voice exact. Maggie grabbed his ear and gave him a pull. "Are you using again, boy?" Jamie shook his head but he hung loose in her grip. He knew that any reaction on his part would make it much worse.

"No ma'am I ain't." Jamie squeaked.

I stepped in. Maggie tended to lose it on the subject of drugs. "Maggie," I said, "I don't think he is."

"We going straight to the clinic to find out," Maggie said. This was something Maggie did regularly to Jamie and resistance was futile. He shuffled out behind her, rubbing his ear.

Now, how did you catch a parrot? I hadn't a clue. I called up John. "John, I need you over here. The parrot got loose."

"A parrot?" He asked. "What parrot?"

"You know the parrot in Rita's office?" I asked him. "It's that parrot."

"I always thought it was stuffed," he said. I hoped he was joking. "And did you think you were hearing a recording of bird noises?" I heard my voice rise. I was desperately hoping his sweet and stupid act was an act. I wasn't going to let him get away with it.

"I never thought about the sounds. I just kind of tuned them out." Then he asked me, "What do you want me to do?" This response was supposed to get him off the hook. Not a chance. Not in this.

"Get yourself over here and help me figure out how to catch him. And bring a ladder." I was trying to think if we owned a ladder. Neither of us were handy with repairs.

That was followed by John's groan. "Really?" I imagined him rolling his eyes and holding up his hands, like he'd been captured by lunatics.

"Tell me you're joking," he was pleading.

"I will, when you show up with the ladder," I said. I hung up on him.

I went out into the tea room. Thusey sat on the cornice, humming "Smoke gets in your eyes," rocking back and forth with his eyes shut. His eyes opened wide. He said in his own voice, "Don't want to go home.

Don't want to go home. Pretty, pretty, pretty." Then in Rita's voice I heard him say, "Don't you bite me, you bad bird."
I looked up at Thusey and decided to discuss it with him. "Thusey," I said, "I don't care what you want. It's not safe for you to be loose. You've got to get back in your cage."

"Cracker, cracker, cracker," he answered me. I was reduced to this. I was reasoning with the parrot.

I heard the elevator rise and open. I heard a series of bumps and whacks within it which meant it wasn't a parrot noise. John emerged with a battered ladder that I didn't recognize.

"It came from the janitor's closet. I liberated it," he said. This time I rolled my eyes. John's gypsy childhood had left him with some finely- honed locksmith skills and an ambivalence about ownership. I feared he would decide to take something important from someone. This ladder wasn't it, but you never knew.

He looked around. "So where is this parrot?" he said. As he turned, Thusey swooped up from behind him, knocking him off balance. John and the ladder clattered to the ground.

"No way," he said as he untangled himself from the ladder. He turned towards me, betrayed. "I'm a good friend, Marlene, but this is past my pay grade. No way am I dealing with that parrot."

The parrot settled gently on the lamp fixture. In John's voice Thusey said "Walk through the park and see where the boys are tonight. Sweet meat." It sounded just like John. I always wondered if John was interested in boys and girls. But that was just grotty.

It sounded just like John.

We both looked up at Thusey, appalled.
"What boys?" I wheeled in on him.

He did his best innocent look. "I don't know what you're talking about."

"Methuselah does," I said. "What boys?" There was no safe answer.

He chewed the inside of his cheek.

Thusey hung off the lamp fixture, singing, "Give me land, lots of land under starry sky above ...." I grabbed a tea cup from a table and threw it at the parrot. He squawked and levitated enough for me to miss him.

John and I tried to speak while we were cleaning up the broken tea cup and splattered tea. John explained. "I didn't. I wouldn't. I just watched them. I did see them but I wouldn't have approached them. never talked to them."

"But you wanted to, didn't you?"

"I'm not exactly dead yet. But no. I didn't. I thought about it. And then I thought about you."

I wasn't buying that. But we had a parrot to catch.

We made three mad scrambles up the steps only to find Thusey landed on the opposite side of the room. It was hopeless. Then Thusey relieved himself with white flush of liquid. John's head was splattered in white bird shit. We both slumped across from each other at a table only to have Thusey land on the chair back between us. As we both lunged at the bird, we slammed heads together as he flew up overhead. We both saw stars.

When we untangled from each other, Thusey was strolling on the floor towards the elevator. "Got to see the captain. Got to see the captain," he said. John attacked the parrot, only to find himself headlong on the tile floor. John looked up at me dazed. "This isn't working," he said. The parrot perched on the door jamb above him.

Thusey started to sing again. "When the lovely dream dies, smoke gets in your ..."

"Ah, no," I said. "It's not working." I sank down to the table with my head in my hands.

John slumped into the chair next to me. "Do you think he can find his way into his cage?" John asked. We went into the office and found Thusey's crackers. I laid down a trail of them from the middle of the room into the bird's cage. "He ought to follow that." John looked confident. I had some doubts.

"Do you think he'll go into the cage?" John asked.

"He might," I said. "We can try it. We don't have a lot to lose here." We left the building, securing the elevator door so Methuselah wouldn't be waiting for the first elevator down in the morning.

I thrashed around, unable to sleep. When I did sleep, my dreams were vivid and violent. I stood in the tea room, wearing a summer skirt and sandals. I heard a series of squawks behind me and turned to find Thusey behind me. My mother yelled at me, "Don't touch that bird. It's filthy." I ran from Thusey. He spread his wings, swooped over my head and landed in front of me. He lunged at my head in a halo of blue feathers and talons. His claws grabbed me by the shoulders as he began to sing "When We Begin the Beguine."

I woke screaming. Jane woke, panicked by my cries. "Shush, shush, you're okay," she said. "It's just a bird. It's a damn large bird, but you can handle it. When is Rita coming home?"

"Three days," I groaned.

I called up John. "Look … we need some help here. Can you find me a bird expert?"

John could find anything on the internet. He could find sunshine in a blizzard. He planted himself in front of the computer screen and started to type. I pulled on clothes and left for the tea room. I had to get there before anyone else let Thusey out of the building. When I arrived, it was secure. Thusey wasn't in the cage or near it, but he'd eaten all the crackers I'd laid out. I made up two paper signs that said, "Elevator out of order" and taped them to the upstairs and downstairs elevator doors. I called everyone with an appointment and canceled their readings. I got most of them. I couldn't reach the wedding party coming in for a reading in an hour.

Thusey was on a chairback in direct morning sun. He chattered, "Pretty boyo, pretty boy, cracker? For me?"

"Cracker for Thusey," I said. I laid a row of crackers on the table in front of him. Each one closer to me. He ate one, and stretched for the next one. I grabbed for him. He squawked, beat his wings in the air, snatched the middle cracker and flew to the light fixture. He swung on the light, squawking.

Since Thusey had proved uncatchable. I decided to treat him as a sort of rain forest decoration. I'd filled his bowl in his cage with seeds, but he went nowhere near it.

Instead, when the wedding party arrived, he stood on the mantel piece, reflected in the mirror. The bride, her mother and the maid of honor arrived on time. They'd all had their hair and nails done as a group. Then they arranged to have a reading together for fun.

They arrived in a giggling trio. They had matching Stepford-wife similarity but it did make them appear as a unit for the wedding. The similarities stopped there. The bride had a bruised look of exhaustion that her delicate complexion couldn't hide. She kept twirling her engagement ring on her finger, as if to examine the engagement itself. Her smile was one step from a grimace. The bridesmaid seemed more mature. They might have been best friends in college, but you could feel the competition off both of them. The bridesmaid was taller, leaner and much more refined. Her frosty smile created distance rather than warmth. These girls must have competed for everything: boys, grades, social standing, all while they were dressed as Barbie twins. This wedding could be an end game in that competition. I was unsure who had won and who had lost. They might be confused about that too.

The bride's mother missed all of that because she was in competition with her daughter. Was her daughter prettier than her? Smarter? Sexier? God help the child if she was. Was the groom richer than the girl's father?

I did not look forward to reading for them. But I could entertain them. That would be enough.

Methuselah flew over the table to the curtain rod above them. He squawked twice and started his litany "Pretty boy, pretty boyo." He turned, preened his feathers and let out a series of whistles and squawks. Then he said clearly in the bride's voice, "Mother. He's my boyfriend.

Why can't you leave him alone?" There was a black look between the two of them.

The mother looked at me. "What a funny bird. What kind of bird is he?" She twisted back to look at him.

"He's a macaw. He's pretty, isn't he?" I said, to defuse her rising outrage.

"He's something," she said. She pursed her lips. Her daughter sat with her lip pouted like a child, in a full sulk.

"Let me get your tea and sandwiches," I gushed on. "I have a lovely cucumber spread and some artisan bread. Would you like a cup of Darjeeling tea?" I scooted out into the kitchen, hoping Methuselah would follow me. He did not. Instead I heard him whistling. Then I heard the bride say, "He only liked you first because you're easy." Only it wasn't the bride. It was Methuselah. When I came back into the room, the mom was standing between the two girls, arms stretched between them trying to stop a cat fight. "You think I'm easy?" The maid of honor's nostrils flared as she drew in a breath. That was when Methuselah said. "She's always been a thief. She's always been a thief," copying the bridesmaid's voice.

"Ladies, please sit down," I pleaded. Their more lady-like qualities eroded in the light of Methuselah's revelations. "Ladies, ladies, would you like me to read for you?" I tried to bring them back to themselves. The bridesmaid grabbed her purse, turned her head away from them both and flounced out of the room. The daughter and mother stared daggers at each other. "Why did you go after him, Mom? He's my guy. Why do you have to take everything I have?" Her mom looked away out the window.

Then Methuselah spread his wings and flew over their table so close I was afraid his claws would catch in the girl's hair. "What's in your pocket? What's in your pocket? Squawk!"

The mother's eyes popped. "You didn't. Not again. Not after all that therapy."

"No, no, no Mom. No. I don't do that anymore. I haven't shoplifted since I was sixteen. How could you even ask me?" She fled the room. The mother glared at me. "Do you know how highly this tea room is recommended? Can you imagine what this story will do to your reputation? You've ruined her special day. Ruined. You'll be hearing from my lawyers." She gathered her dignity and her purse and stomped out in her Jimmy Chu shoes.

In all I was glad they were gone. People offer to sue you a whole lot more than they actually do. If it hadn't have been true, it wouldn't have bothered them. I hated the kind of creative lying I would have had to do to make up a reading they'd like. But how did Methuselah know?

Whether or not the person heard or saw Methuselah, they tended to take his comment as if it came from the person he was imitating. It was as if Methuselah wasn't there.

When Major Willis came in for the UFO reports for the Air force, Carolyn always gave him the report. He loathed the process, but Carolyn flirted and fussed over him, and that got him through it. They sat together when Methuselah settled onto the light fixture behind them.

When Willis turned his head towards me, Methuselah sang out in Carolyn's voice, "I don't know. I don't care. I'm not wearing underwear." Willis froze, disbelieving his ears. Carolyn froze too, in embarrassment. "Excuse me," she said. She skittered out of the tea room to the bathroom. I found her there in tears. "I can't go back out," she said.

I looked back into the tea room. Willis was gone. "I don't think you'll have to. Why don't you go home?"

"Will you deal with this parrot?" She wasn't asking. She was begging. "I'm working on it. I'm working on it," I told her.

After we got everyone out the door, John called me with some information. "Prin and Son's Aerie are the best local shop," he said. "They're located walking distance from the tea room." I shut down the tea room with a sign at the door saying "Closed for Illness". By now it wasn't a lie. We were all sick of Thusey. No one was reading for clients as long as Thusey was loose. I walked briskly to the store. The sign over the door said "The Aerie, Prin and Son". The window displayed a dozen bird cages, hung in columns, containing budgies, parakeets, and a toucan. On one side, a red and blue macaw spoke to me. "Welcome to our store.

Welcome to our store." Did all macaws do this?

"Good afternoon," I said. I walked inside. I ducked through a maze of hanging cages. The man who greeted me wore a crisp suit, a dapper red tie and a tidily trimmed fringe of gray hair. He was, perhaps, in his late fifties, an old school Bostonian. "Good afternoon, dear lady! Welcome to our store. How can I help you today?" This man was the source of the voice the macaw in front used.

"Are you Prin?" I asked him. I looked up at this precise rail-thin man. "Indeed I am. Don Prin. I'm the 'and son' on the sign. Our family has run the Aerie for three generations." He hooked his thumbs into his belt loops and grinned broadly.

"I need help with a bird I'm babysitting. My boss' macaw got loose. We can't get him back into his cage." I was babbling by now and I knew it. I went on. "Methuselah is blue and green, but he looks like that bird." I pointed to the red and blue bird in the window.

"You say his name is Methuselah? And he's a blue and green macaw?" he asked. His eyes grew wide.

"I guess. I'm from the French Tea Room on Tremont. Rita is my boss. Methuselah is her pet."

"Methuselah! My father and I always wondered what happened to him. I'm so glad to hear Methuselah is still with us." He smiled and clasped his hand together.

"You know him? How could you know him?" I was perplexed. "I fancy I know all of the macaws in Boston. A macaw is an expensive and rare bird. They live around 100 years with good care. We see perhaps 2-3 come through for sale per year. We not only sell them. We serve as a major information source for owners. My father facilitated Methuselah's sale when I was in school. But I worked here then. I used to clean Methuselah's cage."

"Where did Methuselah come from?" I asked him.

"A sea captain brought him in for sale. The man was a salt dog. He ran a tramp steamer. We run a quality establishment, but we serve all bird people and their feathered friends. Captain Roche was a tough old bird, as they say. But he lost his ship berth, and was unable to keep Methuselah. My father arranged to sell Methuselah to a woman named Sally? Sarah? It must have been 25 years ago ..."

"Could you mean Sadie? Sadie sold the tea room to Rita several years ago. Methuselah came with it," I said.

"Yes, of course, Sadie," he confirmed. "I have to ask. Are you having problems with Methuselah? Other than getting him back into his cage?"

"Why do you ask?" I said. The man was playing with me past his politeness. I sensed a story behind it.

"Methuselah was always a bit different," he said. "Unique, I might say."

"In what way?" I asked. He was going to make me work for this. Prin spoke more softly, as it if were confidential. "Most macaws will repeat what they hear. Methuselah does too. But his hearing is a bit keener than most birds." Prin nodded. "Methuselah hears what people are thinking."

I sat down hard. "That would explain a great deal."

"Has he been causing trouble? My father always speculated he would be a hard bird to place. We worried about Methuselah. Methuselah's a beautiful and incredibly valuable bird. But he does bring out the worst in people. We feared an owner might misunderstand and either harm or neglect him in some way."

"That may happen yet. We had a bridal party reading that ended in a fist fight. Over what Methuselah said."

"That's the usual effect," said Prin. He gave me a knowing smile. "That's why we felt it was such good fortune to find him a home in a psychic reading establishment. We thought he might fit in better there.

We knew we couldn't place him in a home with children. He can't edit what he says, you know."

I asked him, "Did Methuselah do that when he was at your shop?"

Prim explained it. "I believe he's always done that. The captain mentioned it. It started several fights on-board. Methuselah says what he hears. Unfortunately, he hears everyone's deepest thoughts. As far as I know, he doesn't necessarily see the truth. He just hears what they're saying in their head. You need a cup of tea." He turned over the closed sign, locked the door and led me to a kitchen in back. Within minutes I held a steaming cup of tea, trying to take it all in.

"So how do we shut Thusey up?" I asked him.
"It's quite simple." he said. "You cover his cage."

Well, duh, I thought. "He's out of his cage!" I'd hit my limit with this self-important little man.

"Well, that is a problem," he acknowledged. "Can you darken the room?"

"The tea room is dark at night." I said. "We can draw the blinds down. But how can we track him in the dark?"

"It doesn't have to be pitch black. It just needs to be dark. He quiets down when it's dark. Do you have a butterfly net?" Prin asked.

"He's not a butterfly!"

"He's not," Prin said briskly. "But it will do the job. Would you like to borrow one?"

I had visions of chasing Thusey through the tea room this time with a ladder and a butterfly net. I didn't have the courage. Or the strength.

"Can't you come help us?" I pleaded with him. I clutched my arms.

He shook his head. Then he said "I guess it's time to go see the old boy again. I'll get my net and some bird treats."

Within minutes we'd walked back to the tea room. We went up the stairs so as not to let Methuselah into the elevator. Prin restrained me. "Quiet. This is up to him. Do you have his cage? Is it open?"

Tea Room Tales by Ellen Anne Eddy

"It's been open for days in hopes he'd climb in it." I said in despair. "I could have told you that wasn't going to happen," he said. "Bring it closer to the table. At my feet," he said. I placed the cage within range.

Prin felt his way through the dark to a table and sat down. I could hear Methuselah flap his wings. Prin brought out his bag of bird treats and spread them on the table. He pulled out an amber bottle and three glasses. He filled them, and handed me one. He put one in front of the empty chair beside him. He placed the butterfly net within reach.

"Now," he said, "let's just wait and see." He put his hand on my arm. I had this overwhelming urge to get up. To chase the bird. In fairness, by this time, to take a shot at him.

Prin smiled. "If nothing else, Methuselah loves to party." Prin whistled softly under his breath.

I heard Methuselah whistling back. The parrot ended with a series of squawks and shrieks. Then, in Prin's precise voice, Methuselah said, "How is your boyfriend? How is your boyfriend?"

If I was shocked, Prin was not. "He's just fine, Methuselah. It's nice to see you too." There was no anger in Prin's voice. Just polite conversation. "Cracker, Methuselah? Would you like a cracker?"

"Cracker, cracker, cracker," the bird answered back. But he came no closer. Instead Methuselah started to sing again. "Birds do it. Bees do it. Even educated fleas do it."

Prin joined in with him. "Let's do it. Let's fall in love." They sang in duet. Methuselah landed on the back of a chair two tables back. There was another series of squaws.

Prin started up the next song. "I get no kick from champagne. Mere alcohol doesn't thrill me at all."

And Methuselah blended in with him. "So, tell me why should it be true, That I get a kick out of you."

By now they were both at top volume. Prin sipped at his drink. I did too. If we were going to drink with a parrot in the dark, I wasn't going to be left out.

• 130

Methuselah took a step to the next closer chair back. Prin started into another melody.

"It's friendship, friendship, just a perfect blendship ..." Methuselah had stepped to the chair next to Prin. Prin gently moved the extra glass of whiskey within the bird's reach.

Methuselah bobbed his head into the glass. After a mighty swig he started up, "Let's misbehave." He stepped off the chair back onto the table and began to eat the crackers. I was frozen in space. Methuselah took up most of the table standing on it. Prin reached out with the gentlest hands and stroked the bird. Methuselah rubbed into his hand. But still Prin didn't try to grab the bird. Instead he pushed Methuselah's glass into reach again. Methuselah gulped quite a bit before he knocked the glass over. Prin continued to pet him. Methuselah, eyes half shut, soaked up the affection. Within minutes Prin turned the bird upside down in two hands and slid Methuselah into his cage. "Pretty boyo, pretty boyo," Methuselah said. Then he passed out.

"You are at that," said Prin. He hadn't needed the butterfly net.

I turned up the lights and we carried his cage back to the office together.

"Do you think you can handle it from here?" he asked me.

"I think so. Will he be okay in the morning?" I peered into the cage, hoping we hadn't poisoned the bird. He was unmoving.

"Methuselah has always had quite a capacity for liquor. He didn't get that much. I watered the bottle before I packed it. He should be okay." He drew the cover over the bird.

"Have you gotten him drunk before?" I asked, appalled.

"I didn't. But the Captain told me he had a sip of whiskey with the bird every night. Methuselah is basically an old reprobate. I think he misses his drinking buddy."

"You just talked to him."

"I could never tell what Methuselah really knew," Prin confessed. "But he'd quiet down if you'd acknowledge what he said and treated it as conversation. It was dodgy when Methuselah outed me about my boyfriend in front of my dad, but we both got over it. You have to understand, Methuselah doesn't tell the truth, necessarily. He tells what people are thinking. Sometimes that's more truth than people can bear. But it's never his fault. He's basically a living echo."

"What do I owe you?" I asked. By my reckoning, I owed this guy my shorts if he wanted them.

"No, no," he said, as he spread his hands apart. "It was nice to see an old friend. You will let me come visit him from time to time?"

"You'll have to ask Rita." I told him. "But I think she would. She's coming home tomorrow."

I closed up the tea room and went home to sleep the sleep of the exhausted and the just. When I got into the tea room, Rita was already at her desk with a steaming cup of tea. Methuselah's cage was uncovered and open. He sat on a pile of her books. I thought it would be fine until he said in my voice, "Catch him! Catch him! Oh shit."

You couldn't keep anything from Rita.

The Eyes Have It

The Eyes Have It

I pulled off my winter coat, unwound my scarf and walked into the tea room to find the room crammed. I'd been away for a couple of weeks and had been out of touch. There were people waiting for readings at every table. Carolyn and Jamie were dashing out with tea on trays, busy as fleas on a fat lady.

I stopped Carolyn at the kitchen door. "Carolyn, are we giving away free money today?" I asked her.

"Almost. We have a guest reader," she said.
"Have you ever heard of Cloe Canton?" she asked me.

How could I have not? Cloe was originally from Boston but had coast to coast fame by now, after certain powers in Washington and Hollywood had started to consult her. She had her own TV show called Sight and a talk radio show that went on every Saturday night syndicated. Of course, I'd seen pictures of her.

"How did we get her here?" I watched her reading for a customer.

Her gestures swept across the whole table. I thought the client would have to duck.

"Rita knows her from when they were both beginning readers. Cloe was in the area taping and Rita asked her if she could drop in. It was Cloe's idea to read for everyone."

Jamie rushed by us bearing another tray of tea remains. "So, is anyone else reading?" I asked Carolyn.

"I'm not. I'm not competing with that. Maggie just refused to come in. Said she has her own clients and she doesn't need any worshipers."

"Is Rita reading?" I asked.

"Rita's out getting more muffins. We've run out three times today."

That was out of character. Rita wasn't exactly competitive, but she was always first. The tea room was a benign dictatorship. "Okay," I took the information in.

A large overblown woman with dark wild hair pushed her way through the isle between the tables. She focused on me for a moment.

"'And this is?" Chloe asked Carolyn, staring at me.

"Marlene. We call her Mirella. One of our young and up-and-coming readers," Carolyn answered for me.

I reached my hand out to the woman. She brushed past me towards the back room. I decided not to make anything of that. Maybe she needed the bathroom that badly.

"Is that Cloe?" I asked Carolyn. "I'm afraid so."

"Really powerful readers tend to develop into characters as they age.

Rita was one, but she was never exactly unpleasant. Rita was just very sure of herself.

This woman seemed not to notice there was anyone else in the room but herself. It appeared that everyone else was a prop in a play called Cloe the Magnificent. Need I say I thought the play was dull?

"Is she really that good a reader, Carolyn?" I couldn't imagine. "She's terrifying. But astonishing. I've never seen anyone that electric. They say she's never wrong."

"No one is never wrong," I muttered.

The elevator door opened to Rita with her arms full of three boxes of muffins. "I got every flavor except ear wax, I think," Rita said.

"Good." Carolyn grabbed the boxes from her. Rita sat at a table, overwhelmed from the heat and the rush.

"Well," Rita said as she hugged me. "Good to have you back!" "What is going on?" I asked.

"Cloe was in town and we both saw it as a nice little promotion.

She'll be reading here for the next week." Rita smiled her fiat smile and nodded. That meant that no matter what the rest of us thought of it, Rita had decided that this what she would do.

"How do you know her?" I asked.

"We started as readers together. When we were around your age." "In Boston?"

"Where else?" Rita unwrapped her winter wear.

"Isn't she a bit full of herself?" I asked. Unasked was the question why this nasty woman was in the tea room with us.

Rita answered me without my asking. "Cloe was always a presence. I never needed the limelight like she did. Will you help us, while she's here?" For Rita, this was almost asking my permission.

"Reading, or serving tea?" I had visions of myself scrubbing dishes in the back.

"Both, of course. Your clients will always want you." I was less sure of that. But I agreed.

I went back into the kitchen and put more tea water on. As I sat down, I looked for a moment at my watch.

There was an eye in my watch face staring straight at me. It blinked for a moment and then panned the room from right to left. Then I blinked and it was nothing but a simple watch face.

I shook my head. I had to be over-tired. I loaded up a tray full of tea and muffins and went out to feed the crowd.

After the tea room had closed, there was an informal gathering outside Rita's office. Rita, Cloe, Carolyn and I sat at a table to wind down. But really it was an unofficial meeting with Cloe so the rest of us knew where we stood.

Cloe was larger than life. Her hair stood out in a black cloud down to her shoulders. Fat short fingers were divided by rings. She favored moonstones, agates and opals. Around her neck she wore an eye of Rom with a piece of blue faience in the center pupil. Her outfit was a cashmere black loose top over tight black leggings. She might have been ludicrous if she hadn't been the most famous reader in America

In contrast, Rita was much quieter in dress. But you could see they were out of the same decade, the same school, so to speak. Rita wore warn plum tones, and she fancied skirts. Her hair was piled into a crown of braids. They smiled at each other over tea. They were friends, but it was clear that there was a competition going on as well. Were they frenemies? Who was more famous? Cloe, clearly.

But Rita had made a comfortable life as a psychic and was highly regarded in our community. The things Cloe was famous for were things Rita would have never deigned to do. A number of the readers skirted scandal, even in these everything-goes days.

I went to close the door to Rita's office. Methuselah had been left up and awake. "Aye, aye! Aye, aye, captain!" he squawked. I gently drew the drape over his cage.

Rita introduced us. "This is my dear friend Cloe, perhaps one of the most psychic women I know!" She gave the lady a small sideways hug and smiled at her.

Cloe looked out and gave us the on-stage smile one might expect

from her.

"What a pleasure to be in your lovely tea room, dears. Rita and I started out together in a tea room like this, oh, it must have been at least forty years ago. Do you remember?"

"How can I forget?" Rita mused.

"It's so relaxing and renewing to work again with young able minds. Usually I'm around people who are psychically cauliflowers. Your abilities are a wonderful tonic for me after my sojourn in the wilderness. Rita has asked me to evaluate any of you who wish further training and instruction in your gift. I know you are professionals, but you are still young and developing. Rita has trained all of you, but she'd like me to offer guidance and training to you while I'm resting here."

Rita smiled broadly at us. There was an unspoken request here, that I certainly didn't understand. As young readers, we had learned from other more experienced psychics in the room. But this woman was an outsider. Past her very polite show manners was a waft of a lazy indolence and an abrupt rudeness, towards those of us who were clearly lower creatures. And the sensitivity of a three-day-old ham sandwich. Even if I could learn from her, I'm not sure I'd want to.

But Rita pushed the matter. "Why don't we set up a time where you can read for Cloe, show her what you've got. And when she can read for you and evaluate your skills?" It wasn't exactly a request. Carolyn and I grudgingly allowed we could do that. Time was scheduled in the early hours where we would read for Cloe, supervised. And she would read unsupervised for us.

I trudged to the elevator and looked down at the buttons. For a moment, the up, down, close and open buttons were all fluttering eyes of different colors and sizes. One blinked at me, another stared past me, another seemed to focus on my nose. I closed my eyes for a moment, just to clear my head. When I opened my eyes, there were nothing but regulation elevator controls on the wall. I went home to bed.

Before I turned out the light I looked down to see eyeballs on my finger nails.

"Enough!" I cried out. I put the lights out and went to bed.

I met Carolyn at the door to the tea room in the morning. "Did you sleep well?" she asked me.

"Not exactly," I said. "I had a strange disturbance last night that kept popping through."

She looked at me conspiratorially. "Did you see what I saw?" "What?" I asked.

"Eyes. Eyes everywhere."

The clouds had gathered darkly and there was a sprinkling of fresh snow on a crust left by the weather several days before. It had been a knee-high snow fall, melted slightly and frozen over. The first flakes swirled softly around us as we climbed over frozen snow mounds.

We entered the tea room, already crammed. Rita was bringing back dirty cups on a silver tray. "Thank God you're here. Get out there and take tea orders. Everyone is waiting for Cloe to read for them."

Curiously enough, Maggie still wasn't there. But the room had thirty women, of all walks of life, waiting for Cloe. As I walked by her table, serving people, I heard her patter.

"Now you know I'm always right, dear. Within a three, three days, three months, three years. No. Dry your eyes. This is a good thing for you. This is your liberation." Cloe's arms were wide, the woman was shaking with sobs. "It's really for the best you know," Cloe continued.

The woman was devastated. But the Magnificent Cloe had spoken. The woman tipped Cloe in silence and slunk out the door, terrified of her future, ashamed of her response.

Cloe went on to the next table, and the next, and the next.

There wasn't time to ask Rita. We bustled tea tray after tea tray until the lunch crowd ended at about one thirty. At two the deluge burgeoned again, filling the room with more women.

The snow was thickening. We hadn't paid attention. But a radio announcement came on suggesting that people leave work early to avoid being caught by the storm. By four the room was empty, but the storm was blowing snow in deeper drifts across the commons. I looked down to watch the very few drivers brave enough to try the streets. I could see the headlights as they swerved and slid in a dangerous waltz that was, at least, slow. No one was going anywhere.

Cloe was at her table, head in her hands, exhausted. Carolyn and I were too, from waiting tables all day. Rita was still relatively chipper, but she'd spent the day ringing up what had to have been a pretty good take for the tea room's restaurant side.

The final indignity was when the lights flickered out, signaling an assault to the city's electrical towers. Traveling in thigh-deep snow was hazard enough, never mind in Stygian darkness. None of us were going anywhere.

Actually, we were prepared for sleepovers. We had several cots in the back room, folded up in case we had visitors stranded. Rita's office contained several chairs that converted to beds in case she stayed late or napped. We had candles. The heat was unaffected by electricity, although the wind swept past cracks in the windows, adding to the night's chill. We emptied our bags into the center of the table to see what we'd be eating for supper. Two oranges, a ham sandwich, a bag of peanuts, a roll of mints, a Snickers bar and the leftover daily muffins would just have to do. Rita carefully cut the ham sandwich and the Snickers bar into pieces while I lit the stove with a match to heat up tea water. Soon we were sitting around the larger round table, enjoying what there was of our repast.

Rita sipped at her tea. "This is perfect," she said. "Cloe, I was hoping you could read for our girls and let them read for you." The candles flickered from the blasts of wind the windows didn't quite stop, but there was enough light to see tea leaves.

Cloe sat as if she were a lioness among dogs. "Of course," she answered, condescendingly. We were all aware who Cloe read for regularly. She was the first lady of the American psychic community, consultant to the first lady of the White House, and a half-dozen stars. But here we were, stuck in a storm, and Rita had asked.

Cloe handed her almost empty cup to Carolyn. Carolyn twisted a strand of hair around her face as she peered into the cup. "Eyes," Carolyn whispered. "You are always looking. Always seeking." Carolyn pulled out the chopstick she used to tie her hair into a bun and pointed at a circle of eyes around the rim of the cup. "You are always looking. But you are always observed yourself. They know you. They'll tell." Carolyn collapsed at that point. The reading had taken her outside herself as if someone else were speaking. If it had disturbed Cloe, she didn't let it show. Cloe sat in her chair as if it were a throne.

Carolyn turned her cup upside down and turned it around three times. She handed it to Cloe.

"I see you are a water creature." Carolyn's face didn't move. She seemed a mask in ivory as Cloe read for her. "You've been a wanderer for many lifetimes. But you need water. You crave salt water. Fresh is of no use to you. People are foreign to you.

"There's a man in your life but he's not your passion. You are his, though. Don't run from him. In the end, he will save you.

"Fear the moon. Fear betrayal. Don't go to the beach alone, although I can see you crave it like you might air." At this point Carolyn's face twitched, blinking her eyes as if she'd held her position past as long as she could.

"Have you a question for me?" Cloe asked.

"Is there such a thing as forgiveness?" Carolyn asked in a whisper. "For you, no. Don't ask them. Your enemies have been waiting for

you. They will give you no quarter."

Carolyn eyes looked bruised in the candlelight. Her face was full of longing for something forever gone. Cloe put her cup back on the saucer, signaling the reading's end.

"And Marlene?" Rita requested.

Cloe picked up my cup and stared into it. "The Hand!" she exclaimed, startling me. I felt suddenly like I had eyes on me. I looked up to see the eye of Horus glittering at Cloe's throat.

Cloe continued. "Theresa!" she exclaimed. She dropped the cup. It fell to the floor and shattered.

Cloe looked like she might faint. Rita put an arm around her. "Yes. I thought you'd remember." Rita soothed her friend and sent me out for another round of tea for us all.

This was the ugly edge of reading. Usually Rita had fostered an environment where we were taught to be responsible about what we saw and what we said. This kind of reading was much different. There was a no-holds-barred quality to it that made my stomach spasm. The readings were guaranteed to terrify us, to dig at the past in a way that was destructive. To whip us into some protective and violent defensive response. And something in my past was all of that for Cloe, who was staring at me like I was a rattlesnake. It was my turn to read. Rita handed me Cloe's cup. Cloe snatched it out of my hands, spilling my tea across the table.

Rita asked her, "Do you want Marlene to read for you?"

Cloe shuddered and shook her head. The lioness now looked like a cowed dog. But she handed me the cup back.

I lifted her cup and started to read. "Eyes swirling above you. They accuse you. Nasty old fraud. You have no gift. You only see through a trick. You're like someone searching the trash for truth. And your eyes see what you do. You have no secrets here. Or power. You're an evil old fraud."

I saw the eyes in her cup moved, pointing back at her. She had a circle of them around her head. Somehow my humanity drained out of me and I cruelly played with her extra eyes. I reached out with my mind and grabbed one of them. I flicked it with my finger and it spun mindlessly. Cloe screamed.

I caught myself, feeling like a cruel cat poised over a mouse. I flicked it to the floor with my finger, and stomped on it. Then the wave of cruelty left me.

"Stop that!" Rita commanded me, her hand up freezing my inner motion.

Rita put a hand on Cloe's shoulder. "You'll have to turn the eyes off, Cloe. It's unsettling for her and she can see them." Cloe moaned.

"The eyes?" I asked. "They're real?" I saw them flicker and shut down with a small audible pop.

Cloe stumbled up from the table and fled to the bathroom.

"She always read that way," Rita told me. "She learned a spell where she set eyes on her clients and then she could see anything and everything about them."

"She's that powerful?" I asked, stunned.

"Shush, child!" Rita scolded me. "Not here." Cloe returned to the table, white-faced in the candlelight. Rita put her arms around Cloe softly and rocked her. Cloe sobbed. I went off to wash dishes and find my cot.

As I drifted to sleep, I felt Nona sit on my cot, her frown like a waiting thunderstorm. "Are you pleased with yourself?" she asked in her most acid tones.

"What? What did I do?" I asked, still confused by the night, the readings, and the storm.

"You hurt a frightened and confused old lady for your fun." "Cloe?" I was having to rethink who this woman really was. "What do you think you did?" Nona asked me.

"I read for her." I answered simply.

"You know better than that. You exposed Cloe. Power like that rots people from the head on down. She's been losing focus and the ability to hold her shields for years. Rita brought her here, partially to evaluate her and partially to give her a safe place to rest. What do you think you added to tonight's proceedings?"

I had no decent answer so I didn't try to make one.

I reached into my pocket for comfort and felt my hand charm.

Tonight, it represented Nona's disapproval as well as her love. "Does Cloe know you?" I asked Nona.

"Of course, she does. I trained her."

"Nona, I don't know your name. I always called you Nona." "Theresa, cara mia," she said. "For you, I am always your Nona."

Screams woke me. Cloe was in her cot, unable to wake from a hideous dream as Rita stood over her. "They see me! They see me," Cloe shrieked, half awake. A wave of power shoved me against the wall.

"Stop that, Cloe," Rita said. "No one here will hurt you." "But I can see them. They're all coming for me."

I watched as Rita concentrated and sang slowly. "There'll be blue birds over the white cliffs of Dover ..." Soft as a lullaby because that's what it was. Cloe clung to her and then slowly softened, slumping back into the cot. "Bring me a basin of warm water and a towel," Rita demanded, soft but firm.

I watched her bathe Cloe's face, covered with sweat in the chill room, like a mother would a frightened child with a fever.

The snow plows broke through by late morning. Electricity came on shortly after that. Rita's call brought Cloe's daughter, a woman twice my age with the same wild eyes and dark hair. They whispered together in Rita's office and the woman led her mother out to the car.

"Rita, did I do this to her? I've never read like that before. It was like we were run by something that fed on pain."

"Because you were. But it wasn't entirely your fault. Chloe is the reader she is because of the bargain she made when we were young. She asked for eyes to see. She got them."

"A bargain with who?" I asked. But I'd guessed. I already knew about the dark things that helped readers sometimes.

"She thought we were attacking her. But she's totally crazy." "Yes, Marlene, she is. That was the part of the bargain she didn't understand." Rita put her arm around me as we went took the elevator down to finally go home.

Gypsy Curse

Gypsy Curse

"Hey, babe. I need you to come to my sister's wedding." Life with my boyfriend, John, was like assisting on stage with an illusionist. He pulled unexpected bits of his life out like a magician with silk handkerchiefs. I didn't think he had any family. He'd told me he was an orphan. It was something I thought we shared.

"You have a sister?" I stood still, in shock.

I didn't know a whole lot about John's past. He didn't share his childhood much. I could tell you which toothpaste he used, how he liked his coffee, and what his favorite music was. I was less clear about his history. John told me several stories that didn't quite match. That was okay. I'm Irish and Italian. Even a false story brings in some truth in its telling. But that breaks down fast when you are dating your storyteller.

John was good company, but he was never my lover. Physically he held me in reserve.

Sometimes he felt like a space alien.

"Zia is my half-sister, Marlene," he explained. "She's older than me. We weren't raised together. Her name is Kezia." He gave me that adhesive smile that meant he intended to win his way here. "Anyway, I ran into her at the market. She's getting married. She'd like me there. I'm her only brother and her dad's gone. She'd like me to walk her down the aisle."

Well, that was reasonable enough. I could see that. "Okay. When's the wedding?"

He coughed. "Two weeks from today."

That was not reasonable. A bomb went off in my head. "What? Do I get to meet her first? Do you know the groom? Do we have the day off?

You can't plan for a wedding in two weeks!"

John sputtered. His face broadcast that this was removed something so reasonable I couldn't possibly object.

I rolled on with questions. "What am I going to wear? What are you going to wear? Why haven't we seen her before?" I finally let him get a word in.

"I told you, Marlene, we got raised by separate branches of the family. My mom married another man before my father. She had Zia. When she married my Dad, Mom argued with my grandparents and my grandparents took Zia from her."

"Why would they do that?" I asked him.

He balanced his head from side to side, showing me he couldn't make sense of it either. "Religious reasons mostly."

"Catholic vs. Protestant? Jewish vs. Christian? Buddhist? I've never known you to attend any kind of church." My look dared him to tell the truth for once.

"It's not something you'd have heard of. Trust me. The family didn't approve of mixed marriages." He put his arm around me and kissed my nose. That momentarily stopped my questions. If nothing else it led to other things that didn't involve speech.

"So, when do I get to meet her?" I tried to pull him back on track. "Soon," he said. "I'll call her and we'll set up a time."

"Is she nice?" I tried to envision him as a slightly older girl. Black hair? Girlish? It wasn't working.

"She's my sister." He threw his hands wide as if that explained everything. "I really don't know her that well. But she's family and she's asked this of me. I need you to do this with me. Okay?"

"So," I said bargained, "do I need a special dress?"

"Do you ever!" he said with a laugh. "Something wild and glitzy.

Formal. You want a long dress, with crystals or rhinestones. Maybe with a slit."

My look stopped him. I was appalled. I let him pick out my tea room clothes, but this sounded like Las Vegas working girls go prom. My gag reflex kicked in.

I wondered if he had some dress-up fetish we'd not yet dealt with. "Yeah, I know it's not your taste. But my family will expect you to dress like that." He looked like he'd swallowed flat beer. "Your sister will?" I didn't believe him.

"The whole family will."

"I thought she didn't have a family?" I said, spinning in confusion. "She lives with my grandfather's people. They'll all be there. They'll

expect you to bling a bit." He inspected me, as if dressing me. I almost wished he was undressing me.

"You're paying for it. I wouldn't wear something like that to a worm wrestle."

"In blue? You know you always look gorgeous in blue." It was his best shot. Blue made my eyes shine.

Flattery got him somewhere, but I wasn't completely convinced. The search for my dress became his special project. He dragged me past several dress shops to look at sapphire blue dresses, featuring too much poof and crystals. He was insistent. He planned on a white tux, himself. It was as if we were getting married. Only in blue.

Three nights from the wedding, his family invited us to a dinner, so I could meet the bride. We arrived at a Hungarian restaurant. Our waiter whisked us back to a private table.

The only person there was Kezia.

She had John's olive skin and dark hair. Her hips worked her tight black skirt and her top showed more skin than I was comfortable with. She had gold earrings and a chain of gold dangled between her beasts. "Ion!" she squealed. She air-kissed him on both cheeks. As she reached up to hug him, her top revealed her belly button.

"Zia!" He was already blushing pink. But he accepted her kisses and folded her into a hug.

Then he stepped behind me to present me. "This is Marlene."

In a fluid movement, she reached and wrapped her hand around mine. I felt the sharp points of her lacquered nails. She fixed her eyes on me, searching. This was not exactly an introduction. Sweat dripped under my arms. John looked away as if it wasn't happening.

"Your wife?" she asked John.

"Who marries nowadays?" John said. He blushed again when he remembered why his sister needed him.

"Marlene's my friend," John back-pedaled. "We've been together for almost two years."

"That, John," she waved her hand in my direction, "is not a friend." Her nostrils flared as she raised her head. She wasn't confused, perplexed or even opposed to our relationship. She was disgusted. She covered it with a thin smile.

She dropped her gaze from my eyes, picked up the menus, and handed one to each of us. We chatted blandly about the weather. We ordered dinner. Then John proved himself rat bastard of the universe by leaving me alone with her. "I need to check something," he said. "You two girls can chat and get to know each other."

She waited until he was out of earshot. Her eyes narrowed. "Are you his lover?" she hissed at me.

I let a soft smile answer for me. "How does that concern you?" I asked her in return. This was more than religious differences. It was as if I were a leper.

"No brother of mine would willingly live with a gadji," she declared. "You're unclean." She sniffed at me.

I'd had a shower. My hair was still damp and smelled of shampoo. I wasn't putting up with this. I sputtered, objecting to the judgment.

She went on, "All gadji are unclean." She leaned into me. I backed away from her.

"Let's back this up a moment," I said. "What is a gadji?"

"You are," she sneered. "Anyone who isn't a traveler is a gadji."

"I've gone with my mother to Canada and Ohio when I was a girl," I said. Somehow this was not the right answer.

"A traveler. One of the Rom." She lifted her head in pride, and arrogance.

The penny dropped. "You're a gypsy? John is a gypsy? I thought his parents just wandered around the country doing psychic readings."

"My mother married a gadji after my father died. That was Ion's father. My grandparents took me to live with them so I'd have a good upbringing." Her mouth dipped and her hands fell to her side. This woman looked like a pole dancer and acted like a school marm. Nothing I could say was right.

"So," she asked me, "when did you put him under a curse?" "Excuse me?" I couldn't follow what she'd said. It was too weird. "He wouldn't stay with you unless you tricked him. Or forced him.

Did you bind him to you with a spider's web? Or your hair? Or did you lie to him about a baby in your tummy?"

"Excuse me?" I couldn't get anything else out of my mouth. "I'm sorry Zia, but I wouldn't know how."

"So why is Ion with you, gadji?" she asked. "And don't call me Zia.

My name is Kezia. Don't call Ion John. It's not his name."

"It's how he introduced himself to me." I wasn't sure why John had picked me. He was a good-looking guy and I'm not especially pretty. But I wouldn't give her that. I was too humiliated that I didn't know his real name. "We complement each other. We're friends. We make good company for each other."

"But you didn't marry him." That was an accusation, as well as a statement of fact.

"He didn't ask. It's not quite like that," I said.

"Only a whore would permit anyone but her husband to touch her hand or kiss her cheek." Okay. The knives were out. She'd called me a whore.

I was out of patience. I felt my eyebrows raise in appraisal. "I get that this is how your family operates, Kezia, but John's a bit more up to date than that."

"Because you bound him to you!" she accused me.

"Uh, no. We like each other's company. It's not much more complicated than that." Maybe it should be, I thought. But it wasn't.

"But you're a reader. A gadji reader." Her look was pure disgust. "Yes, I'm a reader. I see the future, sometimes. I don't mess with people's love lives or dance naked under the moon with a knife in my teeth. I just read cards and tea cups for folk."

"Ah!" she said. "I know your kind." She slipped a knife out of her belt. She made a cut in the center of her palm and spat into her hand. She reached out and grabbed my hand with her bleeding one. "So, gadji. I curse you back. I curse your blood. I curse your breath. I curse your head. I curse your heart. Until you release my brother from your curse, I curse you." She ripped the scarf off my neck with her bloodied hand.

I rose out of my chair and backed out of the door. I didn't turn my back on her. I bumped into John, returning from the bathroom. He looked from Kezia to me. He stood between us, as a buffer between us.

"Are we going home now?" he asked, puzzled. He knew it was bad, even if he didn't know the details. As John turned, he bumped into the waiter bringing our food. The tray crashed to the ground splattering chicken and spätzle across the floor. In the middle of the clatter, I ran out the door.

John found me afterwards on a bench across from where he'd parked the car.

"Did you know she'd do this?" I accused him.

'Not exactly. She's a bit over-protective," he said.

"I see that. Did you know she thinks I'm unclean?" That had really frosted my bacon.

"That's just gadji in general," he tried to explain. "She thinks they're all unclean."

"Do you?" I accused him.

"I'm half Rom," he answered. "I'm also half gadji. What do you think? I love you." He sat by me and tried to put his arm around me. I flinched from him.

"What does she want?" I asked him.

"She wants me back in the Romani community. I can't do that with a gadji wife. Less with a gadji girlfriend. The family has doubts about me. They'll never accept you. So she's decided to scare you."

"She's good at that, you know!" I said in a harsh whisper. "If nothing else, the bloody curse trick is a health issue."

He shrugged. "It's complicated. Zia hates who I am, but she can't let me go."

"She cursed me." I yelled at him. "Who does that kind of thing?" "She was just blowing off steam. She's over-dramatic. She's a drama

queen. Don't think about it." He tried putting his arm around me again. This time I let him.

He walked me over to the car, opened the door and helped me in, the picture of courtesy.

He got into his own seat. Turned the key. We heard a series of clicks and then nothing.

"Do we have gas?" I asked him.

"Just filled it," John said. But his eye brows raised.

"Did you leave the lights on?" I asked him. I wanted a rational answer too.

"It's still light out." It was.

"Why won't it start?" I asked. By now I was officially nervous.

"It just won't," he said. He stomped out of the car and put the hood up to look at the engine. I didn't say anything. We were both upset enough. No need to ratchet it into a full-blown fight.

Two hours later, the motor service arrived. They towed the car to the dealership for a new starter and lent us a car to get around in. Driving home I asked him, "Is this how curses work?"

"Don't be silly," he said. "Starters break. It happens." He put his hand under my chin and tipped my face up to kiss me. "Let it go," he repeated. "She plays at being a gypsy. But it's an act. I don't think she could curse her way out of a brown paper bag." By then we crumbled into bed, exhausted by the drama.

I startled awake from my dream at three am. I was at the church dressed as a bride. A creased old man brushed into me on his way into the chapel. He was wearing an oxygen mask. His eyes glowed green, like a dog's at night. He opened his worn jacket to reach for a hunter's knife in his belt. His chest itself was already sliced open. I could see his heart beat. He raised the knife up at me. I reached for the pressure point on his arm to disable his grip. He should have let go of the blade. But

I couldn't stop him.

When I looked up into his face, he had changed. This was a much younger man, wearing the old man's features. He drew the knife. But the blade reached past me, and cut across John's throat as he stood beside me. John fell to the floor. The young man spat on John's shoes. Then he pointed to his own chest with pride. He crowed at the sun, "I am king! King! Born king!"

That was when I woke. I clumped into the bathroom and took a handful of aspirin. I lay back in bed, but it was useless. All I could do was roll from side to side, remembering those eyes. All the men in my dream had the same green eyes. Just like John's.

By morning I held my coffee cup shivering from cold. My family didn't use knives when they disagreed. And no one ever cursed anyone. They might curse at you but they'd never curse you.

I called up John. "Are you still going to help with her wedding? "I asked him.

"I dunno," he shrugged. "I'm not sure she wants me to. I'll give her a call and see if she's feeling better."

"In case you're interested, John, I'm not. I'm not going to her wedding." I crossed my arms in self-protection.

With that I sauntered out of our building. The rain was pouring off roofs and gutters. A car barreled through a puddle, and splashed me past up my knees. "There are no such things as curses," I said to myself.

I walked across the commons. Two boys ran in front of me, and caught my eye. A third boy bumped into me from the side. "Excuse me?" I said, embarrassed and angry all at once. I glared at them and marched on through the rain.

As I walked into the tea room, I patted my pocket for my cell phone.

It was gone.

Rita was already there setting up the tea service. "You might want to wipe yourself off," she said. "Did you fall into a mud puddle?"

"Something like that," I said. "I got splashed by a car. And some boys stole my phone."

"Ragamuffins," Rita sighed. "Did you know them?" "Not from Adam," I said in disgust.

"See if you can get off the mud spots before they set. Call the police and report your phone in a moment." She sent me off to the bathroom to sponge myself.

From the bathroom I hollered, "Rita, do you know any gypsies?" "Of course. There's a large gypsy colony in Boston. Why?" When

Rita answered the question with a question, the answer was complicated. "Is there are reason we don't have gypsies in the tea room?" It was

true. We had one of everything else, but no gypsies.

"Several, actually. Mostly because they don't like being around us. Almost snippy about it, if you know what I mean. And they don't read the way we do. They're quite easily offended. They tend to be high maintenance. Where did you run into gypsies?"

"I met John's sister. I always thought he looked like a gypsy. I never believed he was one. Turns out he is." If I'd expected Rita to be shocked, she wasn't.

"What did his sister do?" Rita asked me.

"She said I'd cursed John to get him to stay with me. Then she cursed me in return."

Rita waved her hand and laughed. "Don't think about it." "You don't think it's real? How do you not think about it?" She looked more serious. "No one knows how real curses are,

Marlene. But it never helps to brood. You'll talk yourself into curses everywhere, if you start thinking that way. If you don't believe. it can't touch you."

"This lady cut her palm and grabbed me with her bleeding hand.

Our car broke down right after that. The kids stole my phone. And I got drenched coming to work." By now I had a list.

"If you think it's real, you make it real," Rita explained. "Do you want to do that?"

I heard the kettle whistle coming from the kitchen. I ran in and grabbed the handle to pull it off the burner. It seared my hand through the pot holder.

"Rita?" I howled in pain. She came in and saw me holding my hand out like a wounded paw.

"Stop that," she demanded. "You can't put faith in curses. And run some cold water on that hand."

Later, John called, suitably humbled. "I am unredeemable scum. My sister is crazy unredeemable scum. I get that," he acknowledged. "Can I take you out to eat tonight?

It sounded like it might be an apology. "Okay," I said. "But it will cost you. La Belle Paine?" I suggested as an elegant restaurant.

"Seven pm," he answered me, without a whimper.

The restaurant was walking distance from the tea room. I strolled down the parkway in a sea of umbrellas and turned down the tiny alley, where it was located. It was crammed with people. But I could see John at a window table. Right next to him was Kezia, and the man who stabbed John in my dreams.

I wasn't afraid for John. I was furious with him. I ran. Rage overtook me and I ran, home through the streets, as a thunderstorm cracked the first lightning flashes. Random drops skidded down my face. Then the rain escalated into a flood stream of water from the sky and a river of water flushed up through the sewer. My shoes weren't made for flood waters. The straps strained against my feet, too large and too small at the same time.

How could John betray me that way? Had Kezia betrayed him? Who was her knife-toting suitor?

John was the only one with answers, and I couldn't bear to be in a room with him, never mind ask questions.

But I had to speak to him sometime. I reached his door, put in my key. The door pushed in without me turning the lock. He was standing at the window, back turned towards me with a wine glass in his hand. He turned, gestured to another full glass waiting on the table for me.

"How could you!" I screamed, slamming my purse into a chair. His face was so sad. It stopped my rage.

"They're family, Marlene," he said. "But that doesn't mean they mean they're nice or well-intentioned."

"Could we use the word 'assholes'?" I suggested.

"I could see why you might need to," he acknowledged. "Was the man there Zia's fiancé?" I asked him.

"He's our cousin, Raef. But he's also her intended." This was the simple explanation. Like explaining a world war as an argument over personal insults. This wasn't working for me.

"Did you know her fiancé was in my dream last night? He had a knife. In the dream, he cut your throat." I told him. I shook thinking about it. "Would he do that?"

"Probably," John acknowledged. "I would in his shoes."

"What? He doesn't think you'd marry your sister, does he?" This was only getting weirder.

"It's something my family does sometimes," John said. "Mother was gypsy royalty. My grandfather is the gypsy king, the Rom Baro of the Campania. When Mom left the family, they say she broke my grandfather's heart."

"Is Zia's fiancé family too?" I asked.

"Some kind of second cousin. But he's not in the succession. Zia is, but she's a girl. She can't ever lead. I'm a bastard by their lights. Raef has all kinds of substance issues. Zia will marry him because she's been told to. The family will accept them if they have to."

That was all too fast without enough explanation. I already knew we'd come to the land of rabbit hole rules.

"Your grandfather?" I asked him.

"Is the old king." John told me. "Grandfather wants this all settled before he dies. And he's dying soon." I couldn't tell if John was sad about it or not. His face was unreadable stone.

I asked him. "Does Zia want you to come back and be the new family king?"

"Gypsies are hard on their royalty. Zia may want Raef off the hotspot," John explained. "She loves him. Gods know why. Grandfather probably would like options. I'm one of the options."

"Does Raef want to be king?"

John nodded in confirmation. Then he gave me a smirk. "But it doesn't matter. We don't any of us care much what Raef wants. He's done too many drugs to have a vote. He'll make a wretched king. But Grandfather won't have another choice for his successor, if I don't return."

"Then this really isn't about Zia's wedding, is it? Zia's wants to bring you back into the family for family politics." I finally understood.

"She has to, Marlene. If she wants to discredit me, she has to show them why I'm discredited. If she wants to escape the burden, she'll have to give it to someone else and I'm closest. Either way, she wants me involved. If I'm not, there will always be doubts about Raef and me both."

"Do you want this? To be Gypsy king?" It all seemed so unlike him.

He was so self-effacing. So quiet. I couldn't imagine him in charge of anything more serious than lunch.

"It's got its advantages," he mused. "Everyone kisses your hand or your ass. And they bring you money. No. They've got more rules than Plymouth colony in the 1600s. Actually, the Rom Baro of the Campania is mostly the person the police talk to first whenever there's trouble. I hate being in charge. Everyone blames you for everything." He shook his head as if he were shaking off the responsibility.

"Do we have to be involved in this? Zia is like a pit bull with gold earrings. She scares me. Green." I was more than scared. My hands balled into fists at the thought of Zia spitting and bleeding on me. John could go off with the raggle-taggle gypsios. I surely wasn't going to.

"Zia would be proud she'd scared you. She plays gypsy witch when she's frightened. But she's not all bad. She's just old fashioned, like my mom's parents."

"That's old fashioned?" I was appalled.

"It's certainly old school," he explained. He spoke with the soft tones used to coax wild animals. That was probably smart.

"Are there gypsy witches?" By now I felt a need to know.

"Gods, no," he said. "Could we just treat this as if she's farted in public?"

"It was a bit more than that. Did you miss the fact she got a knife out?" He shook his head as if that were just what they always did.

"Can you let it go?" he begged me.

"Forgiven isn't forgotten, John. I'm not going through that again." "For me. Can you put it aside for me?" He was pleading. I hated it

when he pled for something. It made me feel I owed him.

"So, do I have to make this okay somehow?" I asked him. "She needs to apologize to me."

"I'm not sure you can. And I'm not sure she will," he said. "We can keep contact to a minimum. I'll walk her down the aisle, hand her to her new husband, wish her luck and duck if she throws something. They'll see what a reprobate I am. The family will accept Raef and Zia as the best possible king and queen."

"How do you get to be a reprobate?" I asked him.

"I'm living outside the community, seeing a gadji girl I didn't marry." He had the good grace to color when he said that.

"Which is why you need me at the wedding," I said. Rage rose up in a red line starting at my throat and blotching my face. I was his ace out of the hole. I was his get-out-of-jail-free card. If he was with me, the family would leave him alone.

"I was hoping," he countered, "that you'd miss that." His voice was very soft.

"While they all point at me and hiss?" I threw back at him. "It wouldn't be that bad." He shook his head softly.

"Close enough for jazz," I was winding up again. "Close enough that I want no part of it. No. I'm not doing this with you. No. No. No. No."

"It's a family ob. When it's over, it's over.

"Do I have to call you Ion? Kezia said that was your real name." How does someone lie to their lover about their name?"

"John is my real name," he said. "I changed it legally." At least, it made our life a bit less of a lie.

I unbent a bit. "You don't think I put a spell on you?" "You're not a spell caster," he said.

"I'm glad you know that." I posed with my hands on his chest, more than mock angry.

"But I wouldn't know if you had," he said. I raised the newspaper and hit him lightly in warning.

"You're a topnotch psychic. Zia's not. That's partially why she's jealous."

"Jealous? Does she read for people?" I asked, surprised.

"Like my mom did. My dad did her research. We searched through their papers and trash. She told them what they want to hear. The rubes loved her." All of a sudden, I understood John's passion for internet research. My gut twisted.

"Do you think I read that way?" I asked him.

"Uh, no. At least you don't always tell them what they want to hear.

I've heard you tell people they're going to die," he acknowledged. "Only if it's true. If it's true, it's true. And only if it's helpful.

Sometimes you have pull things into the light," I shot back at him. Then I asked, "Do you believe in what I do?" I put my hand on his heart. It was, in a way, a lie detector. I could feel the beating of his heart shift.

It was a delicate question. I knew at some level he didn't. But he dodged delicately. "I believe in you." He kissed me on the cheek. Still not on the lips. There was something in the limits I didn't yet understand.

That night I dreamed Kezia and I were sitting side by side in the commons on a park bench. Her voice spilled over me like a waterfall, raging noise with no words. She grabbed my wrist again with her nails extended. I glared at her. When she turned to release my hand, she found her hand held immovable, not by my hand but by my mind. I gave her an appraising glance as she examined her wrist for wounds. I smiled, showing my teeth.

I woke and drowned that dream as best I could, in hot shower water and coffee.

I went off to the tea room. John called me.

"Um, I've got another favor to ask of you," he said. "No," I said.

He let go, aware of the edge in my tone. "No?" It was almost a mocking echo.

"No. If it has to do with Zia, no. What does she want?" I said. I heard my voice rise.

"She wants to talk to you again." He was pleading. This mattered to him. Damn. I'd have rather gone down a snake hole.

"Hell, no!" I said. Insanity is infectious. Zia and John's whole family were all insane. Batshit. Barking. Crazy as flamingos under a full moon. I could feel my stomach lurch at the thought of Zia's presence.

"I don't think Zia will curse you again," John tried to soothe me. "She knows she was out of line. Zia does drama like Raef does drugs. She won't try that again."

"What does she want?" I asked him. "She needs a good psychic."

"Oh my God! She has a whole gypsy community. And she needs me to read her leaves? I don't think so, John." His face took on a little boy pout. I thought about hitting him. It was like hitting a puppy.

"Okay," I capitulated. "But she comes here. In public. Where my friends are. And if she's not happy, she tells you, not me. I don't want to hear anything from her except maybe, thank you." I wondered if those limits would keep me safe enough.

"I'll try to explain that to her," he said. "Don't try. Do it. This is not a request."

"Okay." He'd won what he wanted. He'd give me that.

The next day Zia sauntered in to the tea room in a skirt so short I thought I'd see panties. Or fur. I sat her down and brought us both a cup of tea. She was frigidly dismissive with Rita as she walked in. We were frostily polite with each other. She drank tea staring off into space. She handed the empty cup to me.

I didn't trust her but that didn't mean I needed to be cruel. What could she do in front of the whole tea room? "How can I help you?" I kept my tone light and professional.

"John says you have real sight. Not like gypsies." From her that might have been an apology.

"I thought gypsies were all psychic." My statement was a question.

She knew that.

"Not always," she said. "Not so much. We don't read for each other.

We're too close. But we don't always see with the gift. We say what we think people want to hear. At least I do." Her head hung. This was not an easy admission.

I stared into her cup. I'd decided to give her precise professionalism.

I see you in a dress covered with roses. It's at the handle of your cup. It's very soon. Your groom stands nearby. He has his hands out to you. He'll need your help There's a woman at your wedding with a knife in her hand. She would cut your ties apart if she could. She might try to cut you. I'd watch her. I see a pair of eyes watching you. They're kind eyes, that wish you well. And I see people dancing. I see an old man in bed.

He's so tired. But he loves you. He's dying." I almost didn't say that. But I knew she needed to know.

"Yes," she nodded. "That's pretty much what is going on. Although I can't think who wants to knife me. Do you know who?"

I shook my head. "Someone with a K or a C in their name. I see two crowns intertwined with something dripping from one of them." I went on. Then unbidden, I saw John in her cup. Not with me. But holding a man the way he might hold a lover.

"But do you see a curse?" She asked me.

"I don't see curses. I don't do curses, Zia. I don't know how to undo curses."

She stared at me as if I were an idiot child and changed tactics. "So how did you meet John?" she asked. Somehow the ice between us had melted some. I let her in a bit.

"I met John two years ago at a party. I'd been hired to read cards. He was one of the waiters. John told me your mother had died when he was young, He said his family traveled with a carnival, but I didn't know you were gypsies."

"He's pretty much turned his back on us," Zia said. "Do you love him?" she asked me.

"We're fond of each other," I said.

"Does he love you?" Again, the real answer was much more complicated, but not something she'd understand.

"He looks after me. Helps me do research and promotion. Makes a mean omelet."

"I didn't mean to curse you." She looked down at her high heeled shoes.

"Yes, you did." I laughed at her lightly. "You thought I'd hurt your baby brother. You meant to have my guts for garters." I tilted my head in denial. "I'm glad you care about him."

A soft nod yes. "About my mom?" Zia asked.

"Are you worried about what she'd think about your wedding if she were alive?"

"Mama lived such a different life. I'm not sure why she left the Campania. She thought we were hidebound and old fashioned. I don't think she'd like me being a gypsy bride. Maybe she would like me to marry a gadji who'd let me be freer," she said.

Maybe Zia might want that too, I thought.

"Are there a lot of rules for gypsies?" I asked her.

Zia laughed at me. "You have no idea. Most gypsy girls never kiss a man before they marry."

"Have you?" I asked her.

"Of course not." She was appalled at the thought. "But I did do something scandalous. I went to school."

"That's a scandal?" I was more shocked by that.

"That's a big scandal," Zia explained. "A gypsy girl is supposed to cook, clean and be gorgeous. Me, I loved math."

"Mathematics Queen of the Vacuum Cleaner isn't much of a career," I said.

"It's not." She shrugged. "But it's who we are." Her face was sad.

Whoever's dream this was, it wasn't hers. "Is it who you are?" I asked her.

"I'm Romani. It's who I will be." She shrugged again. The past that reached out for John already bound Zia in tradition and rules. She hated it too.

As she left, Rita came over and put an arm around my shoulders. "That is why we don't have gypsies in the tea room."

"She's not that bad, Rita. She's got a bad case of wedding stress." I was beginning to think John and I might survive. I read for most of the afternoon and closed up the tea room.

On the way home, I found Kezia parked on a bench in the commons. She sat with her hands jammed in her pockets, her purse as a shield. If she was embarrassed, so was I. Hadn't she been satisfied with the reading? This was John's doing.

Then I noticed the tears rolling down her cheeks. If this was about John, I could kill him later. "I'm listening," I said.

She shook her head no. "This is not for me. I need you to come with me." She said. "The Rom Baro, my grandfather, is on his death bed."

I shook my head no. "Does he want to see me? Did he ask to see me?"

"He demanded it. He's stubborn and he's old and he's dying. But he needs help."

"Demanding my help doesn't always get you my help," I said frostily. "Grandfather said to bring you to the Campania." She explained,

"As the king, he wants to lift our mother's curse before my marriage."

I put effort into not yelling. "I can't lift a gypsy curse! I'm not a gypsy." I didn't want to get in a car with Zia. Certainly, I didn't want her mother in my head, Or her grandfather, no matter how sick he was. I wasn't sure I'd leave the Campania alive.

"Will you try?" she said. "My sight isn't strong enough. And I'm too close.

When I told Grandfather about my reading, he asked me to ask you."

My face blanked out along with my brain. I had no clue. "Let me ask my boss. Rita might know about curses," I offered.

"Grandfather knows Rita." She said, "But they have bad blood between them from a long way back. This is a gypsy mess. You're living with a gypsy. You can find a gypsy way to help us."

That explained her earlier attitude with Rita. But I didn't know about curses. I didn't know about gypsies. And these people played with knives.

"There's nobody else we can ask," Zia sighed. "Anyone in the Campania is too close. And has too much to lose. Look for us. Please."

As little as I liked the idea, her eyes were narrowed in fear and her hands shook. Zia threatened to curse people but she was afraid she herself would live under a curse.

"Okay," I said, regretting it already. "But no cursing, no spitting, no name calling. No knives."

"From me, no," Zia promised. "Grandfather, I can't answer for. But he's too sick to do much." She stood as an older town car pulled up to the curb. "Will you come?" she asked. She opened the door for me. I sat in the car and she sat next to me in the back. A dark young man with black curls looked back at her. "Raef," she said, "Take us to the

Campania." We drove off out of the city. I hoped to God this wasn't a kidnapping.

I touched Nona's charm in my pocket. If these people meant to kill me, I was already dead.

Raef must have been psychic. He read my mind. His smile was a knife in itself. "No harm to you, missy. If you are John's woman, you stand under our protection."

I didn't point out that I belonged not to John but to myself. Even by John's definition.

We drove through parts of Boston I'd never seen, to the edge of the city. We went down alleys and cow paths.

"Do Romani really curse people?" I asked her. "Did your mother?" "My grandparents always said she did. Mother cursed them for

taking me from her."

"Do you think your mother put a spell on John's dad?" I asked. "To make him stay with her?" It's what Zia had accused me of.

She shook his head. "I was pretty little then. I really don't remember.

But he wasn't a Romani. Momma might have."

Sometimes what I offer people as a reader is the truth. I'm not always a fan of the truth. If a polite lie gets everyone through in one piece, I'm not above a falsehood. I believe in embroidered stories as an art form. But there was an ugly reality here that needed light and air. As a disinfectant.

"Your grandfather needs to understand. I see what I see," I told her. "Sometimes people find what I see helpful. But if he doesn't, he can't blame for it."

"He's too old to hurt anyone. He wants to break my mother's ill wish before it ruins my life too," she said.

We came to a clearing by the road. A dozen disheveled RVs stood in a crooked line.

An old woman greeted us as we drove up. Zia led me though a path of stepping stones that avoided the mud puddles.

"Zia, where were you?" the older woman's voice whined. Graying black hair streamed down her back, unlike Zia's braided crown. "He's asking for you, Zia."

"I'm home now, Mati." The old woman showed us into the RV. The Rom Baro of the Campania lay on the built-in bed. His breath was labored. He had an oxygen mask strapped to his face. Was it the lighting that made his face look blue?

"Is that her?" he barked. He might be old. He might be sick. He was still in charge. I was damned if he'd be rude.

"My name is Marlene. I know your grandson." I stood as tall as royalty. I'd make my own dignity if I had to.

"I know who you are. I know what you are." He warmed up for the tirade. A series of coughs stopped him.

"Before we go there, Rom Baro, yes, I'm a gadji and yes, John didn't marry me. And no, I didn't put a curse on him. Was there anything else you wanted to ask?" I'd hit the old man when he was down. But this guy had already taken a verbal swung at me. I needed to hold my space.

"Is she real, Zia?" he asked his granddaughter.

"She has real sight. Stronger than anyone here," she answered him. "I'm in the room," I said. "Was there something you wanted to ask me?" I kept my tone imperious. This old man wasn't going to bully me.

"Zia, and Drina, leave," he thundered. Zia and her grandmother crept out through the door.

"You see the future?" he asked me. Softer. "Sometimes," I replied.

"You see the past?" His eyes peered into mine, cold sea green. "They're not that different, Rom Baro. The past makes up the present. So I see them both. Sometimes it bleeds into the future as well. But I can't control my sight and I won't try. I won't make something up for you."

He laughed softly, a guttural choking sound. "Good," he said. "I think you can help us."

"This is an odd way to ask for help." I didn't have to do this. But there could be a favor in the offering, if this went right. We were bartering.

"I'm an old man," he shrugged. "I don't ask so good." It was almost an apology.

"You don't," I said. "But let's pass that by. What do you need me to look at?"

He was a sick old man. Was it worth battering a sick old man? He was too hurt not to help. But I wasn't going to give my help for free. My price was his honesty. I stood silent, waiting for him to decide whether he would tell me or not.

"My daughter, Rachel, Ion's mother," he started. "Yes?"

"She cursed us. Before she left, she cursed my wife and I."

"Why would she do that?" I asked. I waited for him to tell me what I already knew.

"She was a bad seed. A wild girl." He shook his head. I wondered how long he'd been telling himself that.

"You took her child," It needed to be acknowledged. "Anyone will fight to keep their child."

"My daughter went with a gadji. The child would have been corrupted." That made sense for his world. Not for mine.

"Was she corrupted?" My sarcasm had to show a bit at this point. I wasn't sure a life of misogyny and patriarchy was an improvement.

"We don't live outside our own kind," he explained. "Your world is full of filth. Why is Ion with you?"

"You'd need to ask him," I said. Right now I was asking that myself. "Why are you with him?" he asked me. Did he understand love?

Relationships? Friendships with benefits? Would he understand our odd friendship where touch was just too hard? How do you tell an old man that your relationship with his grandchild was just your friend?

I didn't try.

"Can you see my Rachel? Can you help me talk with her?" he asked

me.

"I can try." I pulled a chair by his bed, shook out my shoulders and took a deep breath.

"I see a dark-haired girl running to you. I see her wedding day, dressed in a huge pink princess dress. Her daughter, Zia, nursing at her breast. I see her husband, lurching towards her, drunk. He puts his hands around her neck, first she thinks it's passion, but it's not. It's an assault. Tears. Rachel kneeling in front of you, begging to be released from the marriage. Your refusal. You telling her, 'You're married. You need to obey. Go back and be a good wife. He'll be a better husband if you're a good wife.' You turn your back on her tears.

"I see Rachel's husband breaking the door. Grabbing her throat.

Shaking her. I hear the baby wail in the background. He tightens his hands around her neck. She reaches with her mind through his chest, grabs his heart and squeezes. He falls dead." I took a breath.

The old man groaned. He really hadn't known.

"I thought she killed him. I didn't know how," he acknowledged. "Or why."

"You would have if you listened to her." I would not let the man off the hook easily. This had cost Rachel everything.

I pulled out of the trance for a moment. "What did you do to Rachel?" I asked him.

"I tried to bring her home," he said flatly.

"To care for her?" I said hoping for some human response here. "Her husband almost killed her." I pounded it at him. This was his fault. This old man would either look at his actions now alive or forever after his death.

"I didn't know." His voice was waveringly soft.

"You should have." I repeated. "You really should have."

"I see you break through the hotel door. You grab the baby. But you're afraid of your daughter. I see her screaming at him. Clawing your face. I see her mouth shape her screams. I see you push past your daughter, running with the baby. Did you love your daughter?" I asked him.

No words from the old man. Tears down his face. "Did you try to help her?" I continued. "Were you afraid of her gift?"

"Most of our women, they play at curses," he explained. "Rachel had the sight. She had power. But she chose bad things, vile things."

"Gadji things? Worse than a murderous husband? Worse than your condemnation? Worse than the theft of her child? Is a good gypsy girl supposed to stand still and smile when her husband tries to murder her?"

I felt a tap on my wrist. There was the shadow of a dark-haired woman by my side. Rachel, his daughter, had come to see him die.

"Do you want to speak to him, Rachel?" I asked her. She shook her head sadly, "He's pathetic."

"He is," I agreed. "But he's your dad."

I watched Rachel put her rage aside. She pulled a strand of energy from me. She held his wrinkled hand in her ghostly one. She flared like a lamp so he could see her. "Why didn't you protect me, Tatta?" she asked him.

"You were supposed to be a good girl. A Gypsy girl. Your husband would have been king after me. You would have been the camp queen, honored, loved." This was his dream for her. Her nightmare.

"By my husband? The man you chose for me?" I felt her give off a torrent of images of what had passed between her and her first husband. I knew the Rom Baro could see them as well, from his flinch. "That, Tatta, is not love."

There was a commotion of cars and doors outside. At that point, the camper door burst open. John stood there. Instead of his neat khakis, he wore a loose shirt and vest. Rough denim jacket and jeans. A hat I'd never seen before. A gold hoop in his ear where he usually wore a stud.

Beside him stood a beautiful man perhaps a couple years younger trailing in his wake. I recognized Jude, his friend who also waitered with him at the parties.

"Grandfather," John said. "We've never met." John pulled up a chair and sat by the bed. There was a swagger in John I'd never seen before.

The old man turned his face to the wall, unable to face his grandchild. His face turned a darker blue. "Get that abomination out of here!" His oxygen mask muffled his scream.

Rachel was still on his bed. Visible to everyone. "Ion!" She held out her arms to him. John backed away from her, unsure of the ghostly image.

"Do you want my son, Tatta?" Rachel asked the old man in bitter tones.

Rachel shook her head at her father. "Look at him, Tatta. John's half gadji. It might be better that he is. He bonds with men, not women. He is our blood. But I didn't raise him to be a gypsy. I couldn't bear to. For one thing, I taught him not to hit girls. He'd be lost running the Campania. This girl," she gestured at me, "is a good soul. But she'd make a dreadful gypsy queen."

"Ion," she said, touching his face with her ghostly hand, "Do you want to be king? It's your right. Do you want to be Gypsy? Would you want the responsibility and the crown, if it means hiding your love from everyone?

Would you want the responsibility and the crown?"

John shook his head no. "I'm sorry. No. It's not in my heart. I don't like travel. I don't understand your customs. The clothing and the music is cool, but I hope I'm not that much of an asshole. If I wanted to be a gypsy, I would have come here years ago. Grandfather, when you threw out my mother, you threw me out too. I'm here, Tatta, so you can see who I am. You can dress me up as a Rom. But I'm my father's son."

The older woman entered the trailer with Zia and Raef.

"Drina," the old man demanded his wife's attention. "What kind of gypsy do you think Ion would be?"

They all stared at John, unhappy with him in every regard. John was dark, handsome, mysterious, charismatic and gay. He would never be a real gypsy.

Drina spoke. "Old man, get over Ion's choices. We already have an answer. This is Raef and Zia's turn. They'll do fine."

Rachel asked, "Tatta, what do you think of Zia?"

"She's magnificent," he said. "Too headstrong. But a real gypsy. She has a gypsy heart."

The grandmother asked him. "Would Zia make a good gypsy king?"

Zia gasped, the wind taken out of her sail. "What!" It had never crossed her mind.

The grandmother put her arm around her. "If you weren't a girl, would you make the right decisions? Keep the Campania safe? No one wants Raef to make decisions. Sorry Raef, it's not your strength. That's nothing new. Men don't have our control or sensibility. We let them play at power. We clean up their messes. The larger decisions are ours. Raef would be king, but Zia, you would run the camp. Keep the traditions alive. Set the rules we live by. It's how it's always been. The Rom Baro holds court. But the queen holds the Rom Baro."

"So why did you condemn my mother?" Zia asked. It was an accusation rather than a question.

"I made the decisions," Drina said sadly. She looked away from Rachel and

Zia's eyes. "That doesn't always mean I was right." Drina reached out her hand to Rachel. Rachel wasn't ready for forgiveness yet.

The grandmother said, "This is how most marriages work. Raef isn't that bad. He can't have responsibility. But the camp loves him. Let him wear the crown. Let them kiss his hand. In the end, Zia will be a spectacular gypsy queen."

The Rom Baro touched Rachel's ghostly hand. "Did you curse me?" he asked her. He gripped his sheets with spotted old hands.

"Was I angry at you?" she answered. "You gave me to a wolf. You left me as a bone for him to chew. You wouldn't help me. You wouldn't even watch or listen to me. I saved myself. And then you stole my child." The words were daggers. She'd thrown them true. He lay mortally wounded by what she said.

"Did you curse me?" the Rom Baro asked again.

"You're my Tatta," said Rachel. "I raged, I cried, I killed a man. I ran.

I cursed about you. But I never cursed you." She sat on his bed, a ghost against the white sheet.

"Do you forgive me?" he asked her, one tear down his seamed cheek. "Did you do something you would like to be forgiven for?" She wasn't going to let him go without the words. You can't forgive a harm that isn't claimed.

I left the camper. They needed privacy. When Zia, Drina and John left the RV, they sent me back in. Rachel was sitting at the Rom Baro's bed, holding his hand. Raef was standing uncomfortably by the bedside.

"Raef," Rachel said, "Do you love my daughter?

Raef's eyes went soft. "Like dew. Like moonlight. Like my own heart."

"Enough to change?" she asked him.

That was less simple. "What? What do you want me to change?" "You're a wild gypsy boy. She treasures that. But you are cursed. The curse is in your blood."

"I knew it!" said the Rom Baro. He raised his head off his pillow. "It's not me, Tatta. I didn't curse him. It's hereditary. He can't control the drugs and drink because of who he is and who he comes from. You remember his father. Stink-eyed drunk every morning by 10 am. I can help with that if Marlene joins me."

"Can you change that?" I was stunned. I'd never heard of that kind of psychic healing.

"With your help," she said. I nodded assent.

She slid into my body. Using my hands, she put hers around Raef's. Raef grimaced as if my hands were barbed wire. Within a few moments he was in agony. But he wouldn't pull away. He held himself stock still against the pain. "For Zia," he moaned. "For my Zia."

Raef's wrist went hot. Then red. A dotted line of wounds, like pearls, opened around his wrists. Then the wounds started to drip black drops from his wrist onto the bedspread. There was a wave of shadow flowing down from his face to his wrist. Gobs of black goo dripped out of his wrist where we held him. He fell backward onto the bed, passed out. The black goo sizzled, congealed and evaporated.

I slumped back. Rachel was almost transparent. The healing had drained us both.

The Rom Baro was terrified. The whites of his eyes popped out of his face. "Could you always do that, Rachael?" he asked.

"You never asked." She smiled. "You wouldn't have been comfortable. But the drugs and drink won't hold him hostage any more. I'd like my daughter to marry a man she can trust as well as love."

Rachel pulled at her father's hand. "Come, Tatta, you're done here. Come with me. It's time to fiddle by the campfire." His breath stopped and I watched them fade together. I slid back into darkness.

When I woke I was outside the trailer, lying in John's lap. He stroked my hair. "Why did you do that?" he asked, and shook me. "Didn't you know it was dangerous?"

"It was your mom. I didn't think she would hurt me. Besides, it was a wedding present for Zia."

"Do you know why I called you Mirella?" he whispered to me. I shook my head no.

"It's the Rom word for 'Marvel'" He brushed my forehead with his lips.

"Don't." I said. "Don't play at being my love." John smiled at the sound. "You do know I care about you?" "Okay. Maybe. But do you love me?"

"There are so many kinds of love," he tried to explain. "But that kind of love is simply a disguise. Don't try."

He shook his head sadly. "It's not you. I wanted to love women. Men are so much more ...."

"Male? Interesting? Compelling?"

"I really can't help how I feel. I did try. You will never know how hard I tried."

"It's not enough. It's not nearly enough," I said bitterly.

When Zia walked John and I to the car, she asked, "Will you come to my wedding?"

"Are you going to curse me again," I asked her. "That was really just for effect," she confessed. "It was very effective," I told her.

"I'd just like my brother there, and he needs you to be there," she
said.

"Was this marriage your choice? Was it arranged?" I asked.

"It will work about as well as what gadji do," she explained. "Raef's a
good boy. He'll make a good provider for me. I'll be safe."

I hoped that was true. "Do you want Raef to be king?" I asked her. It sounded like such a fine destiny. To be married to the king. To be the camp queen. I knew better.

"I'm scared for him," Zia acknowledged. "Raef may not strong enough."

"Is he strong enough to be your husband?" I asked. "I'm strong enough to be his wife," she replied.

"That's not much of an endorsement. Is it what you want to do?" I shook my head. If I could rescue her from this, I would. But she was not looking for rescue.

"It's what we do," she explained. "I let Mati and Tatta choose for me.

They know me best. So, will you be at my wedding?" she asked again. I reached for her hand. This time she held mine gently as a friend.

"Of course," I said. By now, knives aside, I'd come to see her as a sister under the skin. Of course I'd be at her wedding.

That night I dreamed that Rachel and my Nona were holding hands, dancing in a circle in the moonlight to wild fiddle music. They whirled around a campfire, full of joy, full of life.

I let John buy me a ludicrous gown. I could always wear it for Halloween if I wanted to go as a stripper.

Zia's wedding was at a pretty church off in Watertown. I got there around an hour early to help her get ready. When I arrived, three girls fussed at her makeup and hair. Drina leaned over the ironing board, pressing her veil. I tucked a pretty lace handkerchief into Zia's hand.

"What is this?" she asked me.

I smiled at her. "It's a tradition from my family. It's one of my Nona's handkerchiefs. For tears of joy. And I brought flowers for your hair." I unwrapped a bunch of grape hyacinth I'd brought from my garden. Zia smiled wanly. The girl behind her primping Zia's hair pulled at a lock as Zia winced. "Do you want me to tuck these in?" I asked her. The other girl sniffed and walked off.

"Was she really trying to mess your hair up?" I asked Zia.

Zia waved her hand in dismissal. "It's complicated. She had an engagement with my Raef that fell through."

That had to be awkward. "Oh. So why is she your maid of honor?" "She's my cousin once removed on one side and three times removed on the other," she answered me. "You always have family as your bridal party, if you can."

"Even if they're into sabotage?" It was more than I could do. But Zia was to be Queen of the Campania. Which meant she had to be above petty tiffs and small slights. She was no longer just a girl or even a grown woman. She was the family's figurehead.

"It's not that bad," Zia said as she patted a stray strand. "Get the hair spray and comb it over. It should be fine. Tatta was hoping Ion would come home. We still hope that Ion will someday come home."

"But he can't come home with a gadji man, can he?" I asked." "Maybe with a gadji woman like you." It was a huge acknowledgment

and I smiled in acceptance. "Tatta said if I cursed you you'd be frightened and leave him. And Ion would come back to the family."

I almost broke out laughing. Zia was too serious to take that in, and this was her day. "Oh, Zia. You don't know the Irish or the Italian. I might leave him because I'm mad at him or unhappy or just feeling a need for something different. I don't ever leave anything because I'm frightened."

"Are you that brave?" She raised an eyebrow.

"I'm that stupid. I have a thing in my head that says I can't let myself be scared. Pissed, tired, upset, yes. Afraid, no."

"Are you really able to stop me from moving with your mind?" she asked quizzically.

I had thought I just dreamed that. Evidently not. "Why would I do that, Zia?"

She let that one sit. I let her. Strength doesn't need much demonstration. Power needs no explanation.

"Do you think he'd come back to us?" she said.

"You'll have to ask him, Zia. I really don't know. But you're right. John and I are not married for a reason. There's a lot that's right about John and I. There's a lot that needs to wait and be seen."

"Would you let him go, if he wanted to?" she asked me.

"I wouldn't have any way to keep him. He's not a zoo animal. I'm not a keeper."

"You are so gadji!" It had stopped being an insult in Zia's mouth. "Yes," I said grandly, "but good though."

"Do you think my mother has cursed me?" she asked me. "Do you want me to look, Zia?"

She nodded visibly, tears stopping speech. I took off the necklace John had given me.

"Sit quietly with me," I asked her. I took her hand and looked into the mirrored surface.

The first thing I saw was a pair of eyes. Deep beautiful eyes, bright green, slanted up into laughter. Full of her love. Rachel smiled at her beautiful daughter and faded in front of me.

"There's no curse there, Zia. There's pain and betrayal and loss, and a lot of harsh words, But she never cursed them. She left to survive. She had no way back. But she never stopped loving you or your grandparents. Even with they failed her. Even when they kept you from her."

I thought of my own mother. I might have disappointed her. Made her unhappy. Pinned her to a child she didn't want. But she'd never have cursed me. Or left me to live under a curse.

Drina spun into the room and placed the ironed veil over Zia's head. "My beauty!" she said, patting Zia's cheek. Zia winced. I pulled out a hyacinth and anchored it into her circlet. We both stared into the mirror and approved. I placed the others in her crown in small clusters.

There was a soft knock at the door. "Zia," John said. "Are you ready?" He was elegant in his white suit. He held out his arm.

"Yes," she said. "I am now."

I straightened her circlet and tucked in a strand of escaped hair.

John steadied his sister and I watched him walk her down the aisle to her groom. To the open door of her life.

A Spell on You

A Spell on You

My friend Alyx and I sat in the tea room watching Michael Havel, the new astrologer, read for Carolyn. His charisma was thicker than his aftershave. Michael specialized in intricate astrological charts. But he put effort into being eye candy. He wore his shirt half buttoned. His skin glowed a soft tobacco brown. His hands danced as he talked.

We watched him read for Carolyn. "That's why you're destined to meet the love of your life very soon." He gave her a fresh-pressed smile. He almost touched her face, hesitated, and laid his hand back on the table. "The stars say it's your time to meet a mysterious man. Dark. Full of passion and insight."

He went on in that vein for some while. This was not a reading. He was hitting on her. His eyes glowed. That itself shredded his believability. He reached again to touch her hand.

She didn't quite pull it back, but you could see her twitch at the contact.

I wouldn't have been so offended by it if I hadn't seen him run through this act with two other clients.

Alyx rolled her eyes. Alyx was a witch adept at the Artemesian Temple. She didn't read so much as she did healings for people. Recently it seemed her gifts had expanded past anyone's expectations. She was a rising star within her coven. She pressed her lips together in a grimace. "Marlene. Is there anyone out there in the world who believes that kind of shit? Who is he kidding?"

I wasn't entirely certain where Alyx's orientation lay. Certainly, I never saw her in the company of men. "Evidently there are."

I looked Michael up and down, not believing what he was doing. I'd been reading in the tea room myself for a couple of years. I thought I'd seen it all. But I'd never quite seen something like this. "Look at her." Alyx pointed towards Michael's table. Carolyn was focused on Michael, sandal dangling half off her foot, curling her hair around her finger.

Carolyn flirted by reflex. It didn't mean much. She interacted that way with any man in her presence.

Both Alyx and Carolyn were infinitely cooler than I was. Carolyn for her indifference to her male worshippers, and Alyx for her complete superiority and security. Alyx was so sure of herself that it erased the part of my head that knew when she was wrong.

Carolyn came and joined us at the table. "Did you hear him, Marlene?" Carolyn giggled. Her eyebrows arched.

"More than I wished to," I said. "Did you really ask for a reading from him? I heard him go through the same spiel three times this week."

Carolyn nodded her head slightly. "I wanted to see if it was universal.

He gave Mrs. Bartle exactly that kind of reading, too."

Mrs. Bartle was past sixty and had a permanently red nose. It seemed positively cruel to tease her.

"The list goes on," Carolyn continued. "Sue, and Jean, and Billy and Rita ..."

"He did that to Billy?" I asked. My eyes went wide and Alyx laughed so hard she choked.

"He did an 'I'm-your-lost-little-boy presentation.' I couldn't believe it!"

Carolyn wrinkled her nose as if she smelled something rank. Billy

was a dignified older gentleman who preferred the company of gentlemen.

Alyx grimaced, "It's disgusting. He needs to be taught a lesson."

"It's not the flirting I mind," Carolyn shook her head. "That kind of manipulation gives readers a bad name. He thought he could roll me straight into bed."

"He couldn't do that anyway? Come on, Carolyn, I thought you were into that," Alyx snickered. "But it does damage credibility. So do you want to stop him?"

I gave them a wry smile. "I already spoke to him. I told him it was tacky to treat the tea room as a dating pool. Do you know what he said to me?"

"What?" Alyx gave us an exaggerated eye roll.

"That all we poor white ladies needed was his extra special touch to bloom into hothouse flowers. And then he gave me that deep, soulful stare like I was a lamb chop. And smiled. I'm still trying to wash it off."

"I would think so," Alyx agreed.

I speculated. "So, how to we stop him, short of putting a sock in his mouth or just heaving his ass out of the tea room?"

Alyx looked at me as if I were yet to evolve. "Nothing so crude. We can change his attitude."

I imagined a crowd of Artemesian sisters dropping him on his head into a dumpster. Actually, I liked the thought. "So," I asked. "How would we do that?"

"We can do a little ritual to remind him of consequences." Alyx stirred her tea cup.

I explored the idea. "It wouldn't hurt him, would it?"

"No. If he behaves himself, it won't affect him at all. If he acts out, it will give him back three times whatever he puts out to the world," Alyx explained. "If we let him continue he's going to hurt all kinds of people. He's not just dumb. He's dangerous."

That was true. Sleeping with your reader worked like sleeping with your shrink. It eroded the borders between you and a client that everyone needed for safety's sake. Manipulating a reading to make that happen pretty much shredded your reputation for honesty.

Carolyn nodded her agreement.

"Come with me," Alyx said. "I'll show you." Alyx walked out like an Amazon off to war, and Carolyn flipped her hair and followed. I let them persuade me.

Alyx brought us to her study. She had decorated her sanctum with ritual objects: daggers, a staff, a sword, a chalice. Piles of books lay everywhere. Bunches of herbs hung on pegs. A mortar and pestle sat on the counter.

The huge book that lay open on the book stand was not a Bible. I briefly felt a pang of jealousy. The tea room had taught me to read. But this was magic.

Alyx left the center of the room clear, cushioned with rush mats. She motioned for us to sit. She joined us in a minute with a bowl of herbed water and a towel. I smelled lavender and something else. I remembered the scent from somewhere. I couldn't recognize it.

She answered my quizzical expression. "Hyssop. It's cleansing." We dipped our hands in the water and dried them on the towel.

Alyx piled a small brazier with wood and pine needles and brought it to the center. She wrote Michael's name on a scrap of paper. "Focus," she directed us. "Close your eyes and direct your attention to Michael Havel. Bring him into the light. Make him aware. Make him responsible.

Change his heart. Make it honest. Make it kind. Give him the ability to take responsibility. Give him a conscience. Give him qualms. Whatever he gives out, may he receive trifold. Whatever good. Whatever bad.

Whatever truth. Whatever falsity."

Alyx nodded at us and we repeated after her as she'd told us. "Whatever. Whatever. Whatever. Three times more. Whatever he does returns to him in three."

Then Alyx drew an image for illuminating light on the scrap of paper, light that would reveal truth. Carolyn drew an ear with a shield over it, removing the ability to hear falsehood.

What would I do? If I could change this man, what would I do? I drew his heart open and beating, able to take and give real love. Alyx got out a bottle of rubber cement and sealed our drawings and our wishes to his name.

And dropped the paper into the fire. The stench from the rubber cement was nauseating. It smoked for a second and then burst into flame. In moments, the paper burned to ash.

I thought I saw something float out of the brazier from the corner of my eye. A spark trailed from the smoke. As it turned and flew towards me, it wore a face with malevolent look. It stared back at me for a moment and then pinged off the wall, through the window. The flash burned against my eyelids when I shut my eyes. When I opened my eyes again, I was sure I'd imagined it all. But I shivered. It reminded me of the demon in the graveyard.

"That's it?" Carolyn asked. Carolyn reached out and touched the cooling ash. It crumbled to nothing.

Alyx nodded. "Bound to work." She rubbed her hands in satisfaction. I thought I saw a black shadow flutter over her shoulders. "His attitude will shift. He will have new gifts from us. He will have a new attitude. He won't want to manipulate women that way again. He'll be a changed man." Alyx smiled, pleased with herself and the evening's work.

Michael wasn't at the tea room the next day, or the day after that.

We didn't see him for at least a week.

That afternoon, we heard a thundering herd on the staircase. When the door opened, Michael staggered out. He wove into the room, off balance. He held onto a corner of the wall as if he was trying to straighten the room out. His eyes focused unevenly. They sat dull as stones in his head. Michael stumbled into Jamie.

Then his pursuers arrived. Old ladies in hats and scarves, with huge junk jewelry pins, waving their canes and bumping each other's walkers. I knew some of them as his clients; a historian I knew who worked in the Art Museum, some old women who took their walk on the commons daily, a sweet old Bristol lady in her eighties. We were pushed out of the center of the room as they circled around him.

"Mine. All mine," the historian was screaming. From the street below I heard a lady screaming, "Michael, I need you," from a crowd of other blue-haired heads. The old woman with a magazine stand had followed him with the mob. She reached out for his shirt. It tore.

"No! No! He has to read for me first." The woman with the red hat pushed herself closer to him. Michael moaned, not in pleasure but in terror.

The elevator arrived. Madam Marie, the voodoo priestess, strutted out of it. She stared at Michael speculatively. "I would not have believed it if I hadn't seen it. Boy, you got them jumping into your pants." She grinned like a hungry jack o'lantern.

I wasn't sure she wasn't going to mob him too.

Jamie pulled away from Michael, who tumbled on the floor.

Maggie walked over and gave him a dark look with her hands on her hips. "What you ladies looking for?" She turned to Michael. "Whatever you dipped yourself in, boy, you need to start selling it." When Michael turned away, Maggie reached to pinch his bottom. Then Maggie stopped as if she'd just caught herself just in time.

Michael moaned. "You're not funny. This isn't funny."

Carolyn peeked around the corner at the mob. "Sorry, Michael. It's funny."

"No, it's not funny." Michael started laughing. He continued until it sounded like a bark. He couldn't stop the noise coming from his throat.

I edged closer to him. I sniffed at him. I pulled him into a corner. He didn't smell of either grass or alcohol, so it wasn't a chemical issue. "Michael," I asked him, "what did you do?"

"I didn't do anything. You all did it. You white girls, you're all witches. All those ladies are after me. They chased me from the subway.

It's a spell of some kind. White witches. Can't trust white witches." He had his hands up, repelling the women in self-defense.

I wished I could tell him that wasn't true. But it was. We'd cast a spell and it had worked.

I pulled Michael's arm and cleared a path to the kitchen through the biddy parade. "Michael, you need to understand something. If we did, we wanted to show you that your behavior was unacceptable."

He pulled away from my grasp. He was not capable of understanding now. His eyes lit up, but not with understanding or consciousness.

In each pupil. I saw the same malevolent spark that flew out of the brazier during the ritual with Alyx. The spark had burned away his intelligence, personality, and awareness. If it hadn't consumed him entirely.

Rita poked her head out of her office.

"Michael, come on in and talk with me." Rita sounded genial, but she wore her stiff there's-trouble face.

Methuselah the parrot chanted in back. "Michael, we need you!" followed by his lone moan, "White witches got me."

"Stop that, Thusey," Rita thundered.

Rita surged out of the office. "Ladies, I'm so sorry. Michael is indisposed today. The spirits are not aligned. If you'd like to make an appointment?"

"White witches," Michael muttered.

Maggie and I pulled at Michael's jacket to get him up before he fell down.

Michael tore loose from our grasp and staggered away from us down the stairs without waiting for the elevator. "They got me. They got me. White witches ..." His voice echoed up the staircase.

Rita stood between the women and the exit. "Ladies, please. We'll give you a free session next week on an appointment. Our special treat. Come sign up for your appointments."

Carolyn slid behind the desk and started to sort out the calendar for them. I looked out the window to see a fresh mob of old ladies chasing Michael across the commons.

Alyx, Carolyn and I had focused a ritual on Michael. The ritual didn't just give Michael qualms. Three times more of what he was putting out had made him into a demented chick magnet, at least for the older biddies, exuding paranoia, extreme sexual magnetism, and panic.

Something was past wrong.

Rita walked back to her office. "In here! Now!" Rita commanded me.

"Do you know what that's about?" she said. Her look might have boiled milk. I heard Methuselah chanting, "White witches! White witches!"

"What did you do?" she asked me. Each word was a tight little kernel of rage.

"Michael was messing with the clients. He flirted with them. He tried to manipulate them." I tried to explain it to her.

"True." She looked sideways at me, face full of rage. "And why was that your problem?"

"It's unethical," I told her, standing on my highest moral ground. "He gives us all a bad name."

She shook her head at my stupidity. "It's theater. There is a certain kind of lady who just wants to dance the flirtation dance. She's not looking for a liaison. She doesn't want it to go further than verbiage and titillation. You're not of an age to want that kind of attention yet, but you may be some day. That's what he does. Yes, some ladies might get confused, but it's a show, and he knows it's a show. What did you do?"

"Alyx and Carolyn and I did a ritual to turn his behavior back on him. To give him qualms. We sent what he does back at him in triad form."

"What made you think you had the right?" Her face had gone from pink to magenta.

"He was doing something tacky," I insisted. "And disrespectful to those women."

"What he did was flirt with women, some of whom were bamboozled by him. It's not like he didn't take no for an answer. He specialized in taking no for an answer, with a wistful flirting smile. Just to make some older women happier with themselves. So, for that, you saw fit to torment him. You set something on him that's made the women rip him apart so they can each get a piece. It's driven him literally crazy. This is your fault," she said. "Go. Fix it."

She shut the door in my face. Fix it? How?

I ran to get Alyx on the phone. "Alyx, we need your help. Michael came in. He's unbalanced. He's got old women chasing after him like yellow dog dingo. He thinks he's bewitched. He yelled up and down the staircase that white witches put a spell on him."

I heard her intake breath on the phone.

"Well," Alyx answered, "Then he's right, isn't he? I wouldn't have thought he was that perceptive. Very good. Excellent, in fact."

• 186

My blood ran cold. Alyx had no compassion at all. Or sense of responsibility.

"Can't we do something for him?" I asked her again. "He's being assaulted by mobs of old ladies."

Alyx exhaled deeply, exasperated. "Listen, he's where he is because he chose to be there. If he behaved like a decent human being, this would never have happened. You wanted him changed. He's changed. There's nothing we can do. This is in response to his own actions. Let it work its way out. He'll be fine in a day or two." She hung up on me

Alyx didn't see Michael's condition as her problem. I hung up, slowly.

I'd fought against an evil. I used all the force and power available to me to right a wrong. I flung myself headlong into an attack. And it felt for all the world as if I'd fallen into a mud puddle in the process, taking Michael along with me. I'd personally dragged him into the mud.

I hadn't known what might have happened. I didn't know what the consequences would be. But I had set it into motion, even if I hadn't been alone or even in charge. The three-fold response would eat at Michael, until he was destroyed.

Alyx didn't care to fix it. Carolyn was out having her hair done. I went back to Rita's office. I knocked quietly on her door. "Come in," her voice thundered through.

I opened the door.

"Well." She looked at me like I had dog poop on my shoe. Spiritually I did.

"I can't fix it, Rita. I don't know how. I don't know who to ask. Alyx suggested this. It was her idea, her ritual. But she won't help me."

"That's Alyx. So, what are you going to do?" She had her arms crossed, waiting.

I looked up at her, helpless. "I don't know. Which is why I'm asking for help. To undo harm I've done."

I'd said it. I claimed myself responsible for the spell. Even if it wasn't all my fault, it was my responsibility. And I had no answers, no cures. Just the raw knowledge of damage done.

"Rita, help me to undo this. What do I do?" I sat across from her, hands up in supplication, tears down my face.

Rita wasn't giving out amnesty of any kind. "You intended to hold him responsible for his actions. Now you need to be responsible for your own. Whatever rules you make other people live by, you'll march to yourself. So what would be the opposite of your ritual?"

I thought about what we'd done. We imposed our ethical judgment over his behavior. What was the opposite of that?

I flailed for a while. It wasn't a simple question. "It wouldn't do just to send a card, would it?" I said helplessly.

Rita looked like she really was going to hit me.

I tried again. "I held him accountable for my standards for my reasons. Would it work to put intention into protecting and healing him in spite of what he's done?"

The more I held him accountable to my standards, the guiltier I became.

"Good." She showed me her teeth. It was not a smile. "You're getting to the root of it. Find three kindnesses. Kindnesses that will matter to him, never mind you. Imagine them. Make them real in your head.

Intend them for him. Make them happen." "Like a prayer?" I asked her.

"Exactly like a prayer. You can go light a candle for him as a start." I blinked, remembering Rita's long lectures about gypsy candle rip-

offs. "I thought only gypsies lit candles."

"Only gypsies charge to light candles. A burning candle is an extension of your will. You've set your destructive will in motion. The reason to pray is because there's nothing else you can do. You let it loose. You can't put it back. You might as well go ask Daddy to fix the toy you broke."

"Why aren't you yelling at Alyx and Carolyn?" I knew I couldn't shove the blame off onto them, but it wasn't entirely my fault.

"Carolyn's next. Alyx isn't my problem. She belongs to the sisterhood, and they will know about this after I call the motherhouse. You two are. Go."

Rita dismissed me.

We normally used the cathedral as a source for holy water and salt. I'd never been there to pray. I hadn't been raised in a church. I found the candle stand, put in a quarter and lit one of the wicks. The flame took a moment to catch.

I heard Nona's voice in the back of my head. "I don't care what anyone else does, Cara. Only you. You are the only one who can fix what you've done."

As the match flared, I saw the spark again risen out of it, malevolent, evil, waiting for someone's intention. It hovered over the flame, staring at me.

"Leave Michael alone," I demanded.

"Did you change your mind?" The demon spark smiled at me. I couldn't follow it with my eyes. The silky voice made me muddle-headed. I shook it off.

"Yes! I was wrong. I had no right." If I could command this thing to hurt him, surely, I could command it to stop.

"You don't understand, do you?" It shook its head at me, as if I were an idiot child. "I'm not here because you're right or wrong. I'm here because you willed me. I have nothing to do with right or wrong. You requested something of me. I did exactly what you asked. Michael has all kinds of qualms now. You owe me."

"I'm asking you to stop. Stop bothering him," I demanded. "You can't change your mind. That would be a whole other transaction. You still owe me for this one." It swept around my head in an arc. "You requested a favor of me. You were supposed to pay me with his fear and pain. Now what can you offer me? It's usually a life for a life. Do you have a dog? A boyfriend? An extra child?"

I shuddered. Had we really offered Michael to this thing? I guess we had. I couldn't put someone else in this place. "My own. I offer my own fear and pain. Whatever I requested for Michael, do it me."

"Why?" It looked curious. I'd done something unexpected. Its eyes widened in arousal. "Because I can't set you on anyone else. I'll fight you. I'll have to. But I won't send you on to someone else. If you're going to attack anyone, then it should be me."

"Not Carolyn? Not Alyx?" The demon spark gave me an appraising look.

"I don't have the right. I can't choose someone else's penalty. Only my own."

"You asked for a triad response, you know." It was teasing me. Trying to scare me. It was working.

"I know." I was sick at heart.

"Oh goody!" It chortled with lascivious glee. "Then," the spark spoke as it swirled close to my eye, "we'll begin. I'll be waiting for you."

The flame guttered and went out. The spark flew off into the black dome of the church. I sat alone in the dark.

I lit another candle. It flared so brightly that the fire shot up the tapestry next to it on the wall.

I tore at the tapestry, trying to get it down to the fireproof stone floor. I stomped the ashes on the floor, trying to extinguish the blaze. Sparks circled my head, my shoulders. Somehow, my sleeve dragged into the flame and caught fire.

I dropped and rolled on the tiles. My wool coat smelled like burned hair.

I was shaking. The tapestry itself had burned out on cold stone. I

breathed hard, sitting on the floor.

After I got myself up, the wall began to shake. I held on to the pew to keep my balance. The floor buckled under me.

As I headed for the back door, the St. Mary statue crashed off her pedestal. The statue shattered at my feet, with her hand broken off, pointing at the door. I didn't know if I was being expelled or guided. I fled.

I pushed the heavy back doors of the cathedral open, and ran to the street.

Before I hit the sidewalk, there was a skuzzy street person walking up to me with his grocery cart.

"Lady," he said, "lady, can't you help me? Please, can't you help me?"

He stank. I picked up my pace and ignored him. He followed in my wake, anyway.

I reached the edge of the commons. I walked into the trees, only to find a small maple wrapping its branches around me in an embrace. As I struggled loose, I felt my skin rip under sharp branches.

Five teen boys, black and proud, stood at the corner. Their jackets declared them part of the Kings of Creation. The tallest of them spoke to me. "Hey, pretty mama. You smell good." They laughed and started for me.

I turned, knocked down the homeless man as I tried to escape. His cart slowed them for a minute. I would never feel safe in that park, ever again.

I streamed down the sidewalk and skittered in to a nicely dressed business man. "My, you clean up pretty. How much?"

"How much for what?"

Oh God, that what. I was between the gang and the business man. I tore my arm from his grasp. As I ran into the street, I heard a screech.

Bright lights and deep darkness.

When I woke I realized that the cab had bumped into me, even after having hit the brakes. Blinded by the headlights, I heard the driver say, "Hold on."

As my eyes slid shut again, the spark was waiting for me in the darkness.

The ER doctor looked me over, declared me shocked, and bandaged up my arm and leg. He wanted me to stay overnight.

I looked at the orderly who kept following my eyes.

Jane was waiting for me at in the lobby. She clung to me, and petted my head as if I was a child. Normally we never touched each other.

We walked into our apartment. Jane had called my friend John, who was waiting for us. Jane left us in the living room while she went to get my bed ready for me.

John turned and blocked the door. "Marlene, I'm so glad you're okay!" He swept me into his arms and tried to cover me with kisses. It was like he was trying to eat my face.

I threw up on him. Screaming for Jane to throw him out, I locked myself in the bathroom.

I heard them both yelling and crashing furniture. They weren't fighting about me, but over me. I shivered at the thought.

John gave up and left, and Jane let me sleep.

In the morning, I was still carrying a bag of sloshing emotions, fear and rage with a touch of panic in my gut. I pushed it down. I knew where this was from. I didn't have to give it control over me. I thought about rubbing myself with onion or garlic or something else that smelled bad, before I went out again.

I spent a day or two in bed, letting my bruises heal.

Several days later, I swathed myself with a big scarf and sunglasses to go out. Things seemed to be settling down. A group of pigeons circled me in flight as if they might come in for a landing, but at least nobody human chased me.

I stopped at Michael's door and left a package of his favorite cookies and ginger beer for him, anonymously.

I went to the psychic fair that weekend with some business cards for the tea room, with Michael's name circled. I passed them out through the crowd.

I went to the cathedral and lit another candle for him. The walls didn't rumble. There was a new tapestry above the candle stand. The flame I lit just glowed against the darkness as candles do.

Two days later, I walked into the tea room. I passed by Maggie's table.

She patted the seat of the chair to invite me to sit. Her eyes were deep set and sad.

"So, you know?" I asked her.

"I always know, child. What did you think you were doing?" You never hid anything from Maggie.

"He wasn't honest with those women. It was wrong," I tried to explain.

"As wrong as setting demons on him?" I blanched at the look she shot me.

"Child, you made a bad enemy and a worse friend." She pulled out her small bottle of holy water and poured it into my hands.

It startled me. It was Maggie's way of saying I'd walked into something evil. She used holy water like hand sanitizer.

I left Maggie's table to see Michael standing in front of an older woman, reading her chart. I could smell his aftershave across the room. He made his moves, the touches, the smiles, the innuendos.

But I watched her instead. When he reached to pat her hand, her cheeks pinked a bit. Her smile was hesitant and mildly shocked. She preened just a little. She walked out of the tea room with a lighter step and a lighter heart.

He'd touched a part of her that at her age was past love, past romance, past attraction. She still wanted those things to be part of her life, and for a moment, they were.

After he finished his reading, I brought him tea and a plate of cookies as a peace offering. "Are you feeling better?" I asked him.

"I'm golden," he said. "You know, for a white lady, you're not such a white witch."

"I'm not a witch at all," I told him. Technically I wasn't. I didn't belong to a coven. Did that make a difference? Perhaps not.

"If you throw spells at someone, what does that make you?" He looked down at me from his height.

"Stupid, I would guess. You knew?" I was stunned.

"I could see you," he said. "That fire elemental showed me everything. You, Alyx, Carolyn and the fire spell. After I saw what it was, I could shake it off. But you need to deal with that temper of yours before you do someone a damage." He gave me that smarmy smile. It was just who he was.

"I'm terribly sorry," I said. The words were inadequate.

"You really are, you know. If you were jealous ..." He gave me an appraising look as if he were considering me.

My distaste must have showed in my face. "Ah, no. I'm fine," I said. I didn't want his attentions. But I did want his forgiveness. So, I asked, "Do you forgive me?"

He looked at me as if I were a puppy chewing his shoe. Then he looked past me as if I weren't there.

He turned to Rita. "Is my next appointment here?" He went off to wash his hands as the lady came up anxiously to his table and sat down.

You can't change someone's nature. Not his. Not mine.

I could at least understand that my code of decency didn't necessarily coincide with his. I believed in honesty except where honesty breaks people. He in kindness. They sound like they might be inclusive, but not always. Honesty cost some things kindness couldn't pay for.

Kindness demanded some things honesty couldn't offer. Perhaps it's a good thing that not everyone frames the truth the same way.

Rita called Michael over. "You've got another reading."

He was at the tea room to stay. He popped a breath mint and stood to greet the next client.

I went to vacuum the tea room floor. I flipped the switch and began to sweep it back and forth over the rug. The vacuum handle was hotter than usual. Something odd was happening with the dust and crumbs.

They swirled around my feet, coating my legs. As I looked down to see sparks clinging to my hem, I fled to the kitchen for water.

Black Paw

Black Paw

"I had the worst dream," Bridey said. She was staring into her cup while I was contemplating her leaves. "I was lying in my bed and I thought I saw a black paw through the doorway. Just the paw. It was pure black. I lay back down and tried to go to sleep. I shut my eyes and I heard running in the hallway. Not people. Animal feet. Galloping."

Bridey sat in front of me, her weekly appointment. As usual, she told me more than I told her. "I've been watching a program called 'The Power of Dreams.' There's a man who explains people's dreams to them. He comes on every Friday night and three celebrities join him and bring three dreams each. He says he's not psychic, that he's a Jungian. But he always knows just what their dreams mean. They show his interview with the celebrities right after they have their dreams and he interprets them. He's almost always right. So can you do that?" She dumped a pile of notebooks full of dreams and sketches that she'd scribbled in the few moments when she'd woken at night. She opened the first book and pointed to a wild scribble in pencil.

"It means something important, doesn't it?" she asked for the fifth time. "I dreamed I was inside a cloud and the rain started to fall ..."

Bridey was always overly excitable. Even in her late sixties she had the energy to work as the housekeeper for the local priest, and she kept herself completely appraised of the latest psychic fads on the speculation channel. The Power of Dreams Show was latest in a series she'd become obsessed with.

"The person who knows best if something is important to you, Bridey, is you," I repeated for the fourth time, wearily. "Lots of people have wild dreams. Sometimes dreams tell us something, but sometimes it's just your brain sifting through your day to button it down. Have you been sleeping poorly?"

"Well, no, except for the need to get up two or three times to skip to the loo."

"Are you still drinking coffee after dinner?" I asked her. "Well," she said, "only a wee cup. Or two. But then I have the wildest dreams."

There had been some wild storms last night. I can see how that might have disturbed her sleep.

"Did your dream leave you frightened? Nervous?" I probed at her. "No, but I felt there was something other than the good Father and me in the house. Like something was creeping around the corners."

That could have been a concern. The church itself was a magnet for homeless and helpless people as well as less savory sorts looking for an easy mark. It was also a big enough structure that someone could easily hide in it. And in the spiritual realm, lost and frightened dead people sometimes congregate around churches, hoping for help.

"Have you told Father? Bill, the sexton?" I asked her.

"They both looked at me as if I were daft. But they both went around to see that all the windows were locked and that we didn't have a window smashed. I followed them around just to be sure."

Of course, she did. Bridey always made sure for herself.

Ever since we'd had a ghost in the previous priest's study, Bridey had sought out every paranormal experience she could. Now that she was interested in dreams, she was convinced every dream was a portent of something to come.

"Bridey, this is not something I'm trained for. I just don't know that much about it. I'm delighted to read your cup for you."

She finally allowed me to go back to reading her cup while she demolished her muffin.

"I see you with a broom and dust flying," I told her. "I see flowers in the garden."

"Likely enough," she said. "Spring cleaning."

"A spot of money gone unexpectedly." A sprinkling of round tea leaves, heading off the rim of her cup. "You'll meet someone with a T in their name. And remove mice. Live, not dead."

"God, I hope not," she said fervently. "Hate mice. I can't get Father Brian to clean up after himself, no matter what I do. If he goes into my kitchen, there's a trail of crumbs that would summon the rat god himself."

I stopped reading for her there. But I had a flash as I placed her tea cup upside down to show I was finished. I saw black panthers stalking in an abstract jungle of green.

"But what does my dream mean?"

I wasn't likely to get her off of that without an answer. But, of course, I didn't have one.

"I think you'll know before I do, Bridey. Sometimes you simply have to wait and find out."

She slipped some bills on my table, donned her jacket and headed back to the rectory. Within an hour she'd called me back.

"You won't believe it, Mirella!" she shouted into the phone. "The mice you told me about. They're directly in the middle of the kitchen floor. But you were wrong about them being live. They're dead as door nails."

"I never said I was always right," I acknowledged. "You're more right than wrong," she crowed

"You didn't put down mice traps, did you?" I asked. "Rid Rat?" "No, I did not use Rid Rat. Something battered them to a fare-thee-

well, but I don't think it's poison."

"Will Father take them to the trash for you?" I had this horrid feeling she might want me to help dispose of bodies.

"Ah no, I may hate them but I know what to do with them. We had a burial at sea. Vavoosh!" With that, I assumed they'd been flushed to the great beyond.

"So," she continued, "what does it mean when animals start dying in your kitchen?"

"Bridey, not everything means something! Even Freud said sometimes a cigar is just a cigar."

"Was he one of the new councilmen?" she asked me. Bridey also had a deep interest in city politics.

"No, Bridey. Look. Sometimes people have dreams. Most of the time it's just a strategy your mind uses to process your life. It's all information and none of it bad."

"You have bad dreams sometimes," she reminded me.

I don't know how she knew. It wasn't something I would have told her.

"Not very often, Bridey. Most of the time when I dream it's something my unconscious knows before I do. But I wouldn't worry about it. You haven't seen any movies lately that scared you, did you?"

"Does Bride of the Ape King count?" she asked. I suspected her of twitting me.

"Bridey, anyone would have bad dreams for weeks trying to process Bride of the Ape King. Isn't that the movie where the ape people hang the protagonist in the end?"

"Well, yes," she acknowledged.

"You know you have indigestion if you eat popcorn." Her indigestion was a thing of legend.

"What's a movie without popcorn?"

"Give it a rest," I told her, exasperated. "I bet you can't even remember the dream in two weeks." It was a sucker bet. Bridey never forgot anything. But by now I had to get off the phone and she'd have held me on all day if she could.

The next time Bridey came in she was glowing. "My dream life is becoming richer and more complex. I can feel my spiritual gifts growing with it," she declared.

"How so?" I asked.

"I was lying asleep last night and I heard a scratching, like paws on the window sill. I opened the window and there was nothing there. I went back to bed. I was sure I dreamed the noise. But as I drifted off, something sat on my chest. It was terribly heavy and it made a rumbling noise. When I woke in the morning, the window was wide open. And there were damp paw marks on my desk."

Even for Bridey this was a bit over the top. "How big?" I asked her. "The paws were paw sized," she said. "But the thing itself felt like twenty pounds on my chest. It's coming. Every night it's coming closer." "What does your inner voice say?" I asked, going with it. "Is it afraid?"

"Maybe I should be," Bridey mused. "But I'm not." "Were there claw marks with the paws?" I asked her. "No. Why do you ask?"

"Just wondering," I told her.

Paws with claws would have meant an animal with claws that didn't retract, like a dog. Paws without claws would mean something else. I didn't share that with her, though. Bridey was wound up enough that I didn't want her wound any tighter.

Bridey didn't have a great sense of discernment. She enjoyed the drama of things and blew situations all out of proportion. That was what frightened me most for her. She ran into situations where angels feared to tread and dragged everyone around her in with her.

It worried me enough that I popped my head into Rita's office and spoke with her.

"How much do you know about bad dreams?" I asked her.

She laughed raucously. "What everyone knows! People go nuts, literally nuts, if they don't dream. Even bad dreams are an improvement over not dreaming at all. If you don't dream you develop sleep psychosis. Do we have someone who's in that particular nut house?"

"Bridey," I answered.

"Well, as long as it's Bridey. Going nuts isn't going to be a really long walk for her, is it? Is this in response to a new TV show?"

Bridey had involved us with the Paranormalizers show team earlier.

We'd had to rescue her friend from the demon the Paranormalizers brought with them.

"Of course, it is," I answered her. "Should I be worried? She's talking about something that sat on her chest in the dream."

Rita whistled. "Actually, that's not good. Psychic investigators talk about a particular spirit called the night hag. It's a creature that sits on your chest and makes it hard to move or even breathe. I've never experienced it, but I've spoken to people who have. There's some argument as to whether it's a ghost or a demon. It happens in a dream state where the victim can neither wake from nor control the dream. It's like psychic sleep apnea, but it's supposedly terrifying. I've heard it argued that the sleep hag could strangle people in their sleep, rob them of their breath and leave them dead."

"It's Bridey. She's bound to exaggerate," I said. "Should I be worried?"

"Keep an eye on it. If it escalates, we'll talk to an expert on poltergeists."

It probably was too much popcorn too late at night after a too scary movie. And Bridey had added too and too and too and ended up with the night hag sitting on her chest. It wasn't likely that the night hag was really there, but I liked the old lady and I felt responsible. If she didn't hang around the tea room, she might not think in those terms.

"How does this become about a poltergeist?" I asked. "Don't they throw pots, pans and dishes?"

"A poltergeist is an angry ghost who can move physical matter. That's much rarer than you think. You've run into ones who can move small things. Move a paper. Make the wind blow. Shut a door. This is a ghost that can crush the life out of someone."

Methuselah, Rita's parrot slid one eye open and said "Eye of the cat.

Eye of the cat. Blackspaw!" several times in Bridey's voice. "Shut up, Methuselah!" Rita and I shouted in unison.

Sometimes that worked, but not today. He kept repeating himself. "Eye of the cat. Eye of the cat."

I was beginning to get the picture. No, this wasn't ordinary. "Who's your expert?"

"She's a psychiatrist I know," Rita told me. "She's made a study of poltergeists. She was haunted by one when she was a teen herself. I'll call her and let her know we may need her."

Bridey was waiting for me at my table when I got in the next day. She bore two deep scratches down her arm. "I remember the wind blowing the curtain, and falling asleep. When I woke there was a smear of blood on the sheets from the scratches." The scratches were around five to six inches long and fairly deep. They had to have hurt. Bridey had no clue how it happened.

Rita and I concurred that it was another physical phenomenon and that we ought to run it by an expert. Rita made a phone call and we ended up with an appointment with Dr. Cynthia Ver Nouth, psychiatrist and spirit guide.

The tea room never officially practiced psychology. But the lines were never that neatly drawn. We did have people with psychiatric problems.

But the tea room was about spiritual answers rather than scientific or social ones, although we had some people who were interested in the scientific measurement of phenomena. To me it sounded like measuring color as numeric light waves. You could do it, but why?

Bridey and I walked to the doctor's office and rang the doorbell. Dr. Ver Nouth opened the door of her brownstone down Newbury Street. She should have been tall, but her shoulders were bent too much. She wore her graying hair in an unkempt bob and a cardigan sweater with her woolen plaid skirt. She stared at us through her shaggy bangs, looking like an aging school girl. But her manner was confident. "You may call me Dr. Thia," she told us. "It's short for Cynthia."

I'd come along with Bridey to provide emotional support, but also to make sure she didn't get lost along the way or decide not to show. I didn't plan to stay. I was surprised not to find a fainting couch. Instead there was a room of comfy chairs and some soothing floral art on the wall.

"Which of you is Bridey?" the doctor asked.

Bridey waved her arm that wasn't clutching a pile of journals. "That would be me, Dr. Thia," Bridey said. "I'm so excited. Do you do dream work?"

Bridey obviously hoped this was the place for her current obsession to bloom.

As Bridey settled in, I took that as my cue to leave. "I should be off on my errands, Bridey." I walked out the door, presumably to go off to the library. But Bridey had worn off on me. Partly out of worry and partially out of curiosity I stayed for a minute or two and listened through the door. I lost my inhibitions and stooped down to look through the keyhole.

"We look at dreams, of course," Dr. Thia was explaining. "But we often find that people who are experiencing physical psychic phenomena are victims of intense rage. Do you find yourself angry often?"

Dr. Thia smiled in a way to indicate she'd gotten in charge of her rage. "I used to suffer from a poltergeist. What I came to understand was that my anger would have its way one way or another. Once I recognized it as my own, I could channel it in much better directions. You know, anger is neutral. It's neither good nor bad. It's simply energy. Your energy is blocked and it's being used against you, by your own mind. You experience shame and self-blame for feeling a simple, natural emotion.

Once we acknowledge that, the phenomena will stop." "My dreams?" Bridey asked.

"Are they violent? Disturbing?" Dr. Thia probed.

"Unsettling," Bridey finished. "As if there's something new in the world I don't know about. I keep seeing a black paw coming through the window."

"Anger is always unsettling," Dr. Thia said. "So, who are you angry with?"

"Well, the good Father I work for at St. Philomena makes me livid when he tracks mud through the house," Bridey admitted. "And I'm furious when Ann Rasish takes over the Altar Guild meeting."

"That's a good start." Dr. Thia latched on and went with the flow. "He's your father? At your age? No wonder you're experiencing unbearable rage. We need to let that out somehow."

"He's not my father," Bridey corrected. "He's the Father. He's the priest of our parish."

"You're Catholic?" Dr. Thia peered at her, as if she were a specimen in a jar. "No wonder you're a victim of unbearable guilt."

At that point, I got a hold of myself and tiptoed out through the front door. Instead of going toward the library, I headed to my appointment with Father Brian at St. Philomena.

He was waiting for me in his parlor.

"Good afternoon, Father," I said as I went through the door.

He led me to one of the overstuffed chairs. I noticed the older wallpaper in the room, a riot of wild jungle plants in blue-greens.

"Father," I asked him, "have you noticed a change in Bridey?" "Good heavens, yes. She's such a vital woman, even at her age. But she's started looking into every corner. She's a formidable house cleaner. She's a formidable person. But she's started to follow me around as if she's checking on me."

"She's always done that with her priests," I reminded him. "Well, yes. My mom was a lot easier to fool." He chuckled at the thought.

"I'm sure that's true. Do you know a reason why she might feel that way? As though someone was trying to fool her?" I asked him.

He blushed crimson. Guilty as charged. "I'm afraid I might. Please don't tell on me."

"Father, what did you do?" I had visions of a new hobby, something that included potting soil or mud or plaster of Paris.

"She's going to kill me," he moaned. "I just couldn't leave them in the street. You can't tell on me."

"I can't promise that, Father. Bridey's my friend."

He held out his hand to stop me. Then he motioned me to his closet.

He opened the door. I smelled faint urine and cat box. There was a cardboard box with small mewing forms in it. And a mother cat. All but one of them pure black. The other was a male gray tiger.

"Momma Cat had been in the alley behind the church. She kept rubbing my ankles. My mom kept cats. I knew she was pregnant. I brought her in."

"Why didn't you tell Bridey?" I asked him.

Ruefully, he rubbed the back of his head. "Have you ever heard her talk about black cats?"

"Not specifically." Then I remembered. "And if you see a black cat, that's the devil itself waiting for your soul." Another direct quote from The Power of Dreams.

"Father, have you noticed that you're supposed to be in charge here?" I asked him.

"You know Bridey," he said. "How in charge do you think I really am?"

Just then, Bridey burst through the parlor door. "Mirella! What are you doing here? I left after that lady wanted me to howl and tear phone books. I have my moments when I'm annoyed, but I don't need howling lessons. What am I smelling in that closet?"

Bridey pushed past me, past Father. She peered into the closet. "Well," she said, putting her hand out for the cat to smell. A pink tongue washed her thumb. "Poor momma," Bridey said, "You're hungry, aren't you?"

She bustled out of the parlor and returned with a plate of shaved beef. "There you are, momma. A girl has to keep her strength up."

Father looked at me, nonplussed.

"It's Bridey," I said, shrugging. "You might as well just have told her.

She has a million prejudices about everything but they disappear the moment someone is hungry or in need. What are their names, Father Brian?"

"Mickey and Minnie," he said, embarrassed. "I haven't named the tiger kitten."

I smiled. "Bridey, I think we found your mice killers."

Bridey picked up one of the kittens that rubbed and suckled at her thumb. The other was chasing her apron tie. "I told you dreams were real." And she shook her finger at me.

I picked up the gray tiger. He climbed up my arms to my shoulder and nestled under my chin.

"He's yours now," Bridey said.

"I guess so," I acknowledged. For a moment, it was as if he'd mewed into my mind. "His name is Echo," I said as he climbed to the top of my head, purring madly.

Voodoo You

Voodoo You

Most of our clients were middle-aged Bostonian women on their lunch breaks or out of the house for the day. They wanted a time in their week that was all about them. But not all of them. A fair number of them worked as psychic practitioners themselves. In the same way you wouldn't do your own psychotherapy or your own tooth extraction, you didn't do your own reading. For about the same reasons.

Not everyone was mainstream either. Lest we get around to religious name calling, the tea room was an endless alternative faith convention. We also had Sisters of Ishtar, Artemesians, White Mountain Brethren, Druids, Sisters of Ra, Wiccans, and a group of Eastern disciples who practiced levitation. We discouraged the faux vampires, not because they were vampires, but because they were posers, and predatory. We did welcome the Zoroastrians until they left a ritual mess we could not contain or clean up. These groups were zealous, insular and sometimes scary. But they kept themselves separated in their xenophobia. The tea room was not a place of worship. Instead it served all kinds of psychics as a point of connection. We all understood that whatever trouble you had stopped at the tea room elevator door.

You didn't always know who you were talking to. I didn't know who the tall angular woman was when I first met her. Dark skin gleamed against her white dress. She tied her hair in a white cloth with odd folds in it that looked more like a cross between a turban and crown than a head wrap. Her blackness was a blazing shadow. But it brought your attention to her presence without focusing on her face. She might have been thirty, or sixty. Her eyes were much older.

I was sitting at Maggie's table when Madam Marie arrived. Her presence was so unsettling, that everyone turned their head either away or towards her as she walked through them. I asked Maggie who she was.

"That is Madam Marie. She be the head Mambo in Boston." "Mambo?" I asked.

"Voodoo Queen," Maggie answered me. "Madam Marie ain't her name.

The scarf she wear, that's the seven-fold tignon scarf all voodoo queens wear. You better not wear one like it unless you are one of them." Maggie gave Marie a wide berth, although they acknowledged each other in brief nods.

Madam Marie beckoned me to her table. "They say you be Mirella." She appraised me. Like her, I didn't use my real name in this place "What you see for me?" Her lips pressed in a grim line. Eyes wide open. Her smile was warm but not her eyes. She had a reptilian quality that made her exotic. Like a serpent, there was no malice in it. Only flawlessly polite instinct and observation. She wasn't American. Likely she wasn't legal. That hardly mattered in the tea room. Her voice had a tropical overlay mixed in. The snake bracelet she wore might have meant anything or nothing. The small leather bag at her neck told me more. It was a gris-gris, a voodoo charm.

I peered into her cup. I saw nothing at the handle. The leaves clinging to the rim told me that her life was made of people who came to her as she came to me. I described them as I saw them one by one: the bent woman in pain, the woman with a sick child, the lost boy who lived with her now, off the streets. The list swelled. She was a warm rock in the cold world these people inhabited. She kept them warm. She kept them safe.

A clump of leaves fell out of her cup onto the saucer. "Something is leaving your life. It's been a burden. It will leave within a six." She knew the custom. It was easier for a reader to get a number than to know what that number meant. Six hours, six days, six weeks, six months. It was useless as a measure of time, but sometimes the number held significance as a location or identifier.

Where the clump of leaves had been, I saw a smattering of small dots. "When that leaves, a nice bit of money will follow. I see a party." There was some kind of wild dance, erotic but in no way about romance. "I see you open the gate for a young woman. I don't think she can go through it." The girl was falling backward from the opening. "Someone with an R in their name is angry and she'll turn on you. Renae, Rachel?"

"Richell," she answered. "You think?"

I nodded. "There's a storm over her, but it may splash over on you as well. She won't tell you the truth either way." Her lips pressed together again as if she were thinking that over. I saw a wild group of people dancing not as couples but as rhythm itself. She swayed in the center, snake wrapped around her like a caress.

"You dance, I see. There's a man with a C in his name. He holds a knife. Don't trust him."

"You know I don't," she said. Then she gave me a wide grin. There was one gap between her teeth. She clapped her hands once. Very demonstrative for her. She must have been pleased. She tilted her head and slipped me a twenty. "For you. For sight."

She rose gracefully. Her stance was flexible but full of power. She had endured probably everything. She was almost living stone. "I see you again." She patted the table with her hand.

As she left, the air went out of the room. I felt the vacuum as she got into the elevator.

Maggie explained to me that the dance wasn't a social event.

Madame Marie led the ancient ritual as a priestess. She served the gentler Petra loa spirits who specialized in healing. I had read her cup. I didn't fear her. I knew her. Not her real name, which she might not ever give to me. But I'd read her cups enough to know her life looked much like my own. It was a series of people coming to her for help of one kind or another. I came to understand and like the voodoo women from Haiti.

They were straightforward and honest. If you were, they responded in kind. I wouldn't, however, go out of my way to cross any of them.

After Madam Marie, I had three giggly school girls in identical jeans waiting as my next clients. Since they shared jeans, tops, and cell phones, they were a unit of a sort. The only difference between their cups was the name of the boy. And in one case, it was the same boy.

The next Saturday I saw the swirl of white skirts that meant Madam Marie was here. Madam Marie had whisked in the door with a woman and a four-year-old girl in tow. The woman and her child were in bright tops and summer skirts, but they had the same unbending posture and dignity. Both women wanted to be read separately. They sat at a table across the room from where I read, and came up one by one.

Madam Marie came first. She brought her empty tea cup in hand on its saucer. She sat it down in front of me

"Did you get your windfall?" I asked. My earlier accuracy made her more talkative.

"But of course, Cher. What you seen now?" She patted the table and pushed the cup towards me.

I held it up close to read. It was still warm. "Wind whirling around you, but you are centered," I said.

"Folk coming in for the weekend. We dance," she told me.

By now I knew that was a euphemism for a ritual of some kind. I didn't much care to know about that. But I could see it coming.

"You have guests everywhere," I noted. "They've come from everywhere. There's a man from the south. He's riding a storm in towards you." He was literally straddling a black tea leaf cloud with lightning coming off it. "Martin? Marvin? I can't tell if he's bringing trouble or if he is the trouble."

"Martin. I thought he was coming as a peace gesture." Marie tapped the table with her lacquered finger tips. I wouldn't much want to be Martin this weekend.

"Not so much." I answered. "You watch him. I don't think he means you well."

"You know it, Cher." "I see a snake."

"He my friend. Don't you worry about him." Her smile was almost cozy.

"He rides on your shoulders." The snake in her cup was draped over her.

"Yes, he do." I wondered if this was literal or metaphysical. Did she have a real snake?

"There's a woman coming to you with a gift. Be careful of it. She's asking for more than she's offering you."

"What you think?" she asked me.

There were coins falling from the woman's hands out of reach. "It will cost you in ways you can't know or count. Someone with a 'V' in their name."

I could see her tick off names in her head. "Vom, or Van or Vam, maybe?"

I asked her.

"Maybe," she answered.

"There's a new baby. A little girl."

"My grandniece. Her mother bring her up north for a blessing."

Then I rattled through the flow of people in her cup, waiting for her help. It was charted water. The people came and went. Her consistency was her care for them.

"They're coming next weekend?" I asked. I could tell because all the chaos was in the middle of her cup, not the bottom or the rim.

"I be busy," she said. She smiled again and folded her hands on the table.

"I didn't get your name," I risked the question. It was a test for both of us.

"Madam Marie," she said. She smiled at me. No hand shake. Either that or her name would be a loss of respect and I knew it. She'd given me her title. That was a gift of respect and trust. "You read for my niece there. Yvonne." She waved the girl over to the table.

"She's not your sister?"

"No. My sister's girl. She at the crossroads."

The women changed places. Yvonne was a less-sure copy of Madam Marie. Her bright clothes were a disguise. Where Madam Marie took up the whole room, Yvonne was a small shadow in the corner. Her smile was soft, but not her eyes. She might have been eighteen or twenty-five. You couldn't tell.

I took her cup from her. Everything was clumped at the bottom. There was a tornado shape swirling out from the biggest leaf pile. The clump scattered loose and spattered the bottom of her cup. "You're in a state of change."

She gave me a dead blank stare. This woman wasn't going to give me any clues. Not a problem. The energy shivered off her.

"You're here for the ritual." I could see from her face I wasn't supposed to know about that. Too bad. I did. "You haven't seen your aunt in years. But you love her very much."

One tear. Just resting in the corner of her eye.

"I see a bird soaring above the chaos. There's a way out if you'll take it. It will take courage." I didn't tell her about the other bird next to it, falling out of the sky. "I do think you'll be moving, though. You came without your husband's permission."

"He not my husband," she acknowledged, "but yes."

There was a haziness that formed around her, a bubble in space and time. That happened sometimes with strong psychics. They made their own privacy, even in the bustle of the tea room. It invisibly encompassed us both. I watched as smoke swirled around her. It settled around her head, coming out from her ear. It wound like mist and circled her face. The smoke shifted. It moved like a snake, slowly and sinuously. On one side, I saw a crude mouth form. Then eyes and a nose. It spoke not to her, but to me.

"She mine. She born to be mine. She know what she got to do. She always known what to do, but she stubborn. But she know what you got to do." Then it was speaking to her. But I could see and hear it. "It's that time. You don't deny me. It's that time," the shape whispered.

Too shaken to keep my balance. I grasped the back of my chair for support. The smoke drifted away. The bubble evaporated. I was left staring at Yvonne.

"Does your aunt know?" I couldn't pretend I hadn't seen it. She knew I had.

"She say that my guide. You gotta do whatever your guide tell you." "Is that what the ritual is for?" I asked her.

Her head turned away from me, refusing to tell. But I knew already.

It was her initiation. It was the beginning of her life as a priestess.

I had a working knowledge of most kinds of spiritual mysticism, but here I was out of my depth. Most psychics will let spirits affect them only for short periods of time, if at all. Voodoo rituals served their loas and invited the loas to ride the worshipers in their passions. I liked Madam Marie personally. But even temporary possession terrified me. You couldn't always know what you had let in. I shivered as I pulled in my scarf around my shoulders.

Her aunt rose from her table across the room, with the child in hand. "Yvonne, you get done. We got to go shopping." Madam Marie smiled broadly. "I told you she be good." She handed me twenty for her niece as well. Yvonne wasn't done. There was something she wanted to say, needed to say. Madam Marie wasn't going to let her.

I reached across the table and pushed the plate of cookies towards the child. "Who is this?" I asked.

"This be Nicole." The child had been examining her shoes. The cookies had drawn her eyes to mine. She reached out to touch the energy around me, not physically but with the energy she already owned. It set off an internal sparkler. It was, in its own way, a smile between us.

"May she have a cookie?" I asked.

"Not every day," Madam Marie said. "This day special." The child did a double-handed cookie grab.

They marched to the elevator together, trailing cookie crumbs.

What had I seen? The tea room was its own twilight zone. But the tea room was a place where ordinary walls didn't conceal much. The womb-like red decor gave people a primal sense of safety. That was illusionary. In the tea room secrets stood out in the open. Everyone lied. But the lies bought you nothing. Mostly they underlined whatever was truly true. Lying worked about as well as a cat covering up on linoleum.

Every so often people brought in impressions of their past that were so strong you could see them. Sometimes the future vibrated for them so hard you could see it coming. Whatever I saw off the niece was real time, right now. And insistent.

The week passed from one day to another, from one reading to another. Most clients came once a week or two on their day off. I was finishing with the kindergarten teacher who always came in on Saturday afternoon when I saw Yvonne in the mirror. No child or Madam Marie in tow.

Yvonne sat down and waited for me, her legs crossed, one leg swinging. But not in nonchalance. There was a dark bruise on her throat. Sorrow, shame, rage and panic rose off her in waves. One of the girls had served her tea. She'd drunk most of it. I sat down across from her. "How can I help?" I asked her.

"You read for me." Her eyes and her voice were flattened, as if she'd been pressed against the floor. Maybe she had been.

"Of course," I answered.

She handed me her cup. I didn't even have time to start to read it. The smoke wafted up around her and formed the spectral snake that rested around her shoulders. It spoke again. It was talking to her, but it shot a glance at me that acknowledged I could hear it too. "She do what I say, because I say it. She be safe. Her child be safe."

Most people who have guides aren't afraid of them. Yvonne was so terrified of this being that the cords of her neck stood out like rope. The guide twisted and wound around her neck and shoulders. She flinched at its touch. It turned its focus back on her.

"Madam Marie been mine since she years younger than you. It be your turn. I make you safe. I make Nicolle safe." Its voice was oily smooth.

The word "safe" seemed to have acquired new and terrifying meanings. Safe from the Neanderthal who had hurt her? Safe spiritually? Safe from what the snake would do if she didn't follow orders? Safe from Madam Marie's anger? Safe from what?

There was a clatter from the kitchen. Someone had dropped a pot. It brought us all back to the reality of the room.

But she knew I'd seen it. She knew I'd been shown. That was permission. She could tell me.

"My aunt, she a great priestess."

"Yes," I said. "We all know that. She's a good leader. Her people love her."

"She say I be like her. She want me when I was twelve to live with her. To learn from her. I love her but she scare me. Her gods scare me. I ran."

Well they might, I thought. I was scared past breath. "What does she want you to do?" I asked her

"It not her," Yvonne explained. "It her guide. He say I've got to give up my man, the one I ran away with."

"Maybe that might be a good idea. At least for a while. If you're away, you may see it all more clearly." The bruise at her throat offended me. I wanted her away from this jerk.

"My guide say I have to kill him. Stab him in the heart." Well, that, I thought, wasn't going to bring clarity. Or was it a metaphysical request? If it were literal, it brought the possibility of other, much worse problems. Like a life sentence in prison. Or the internal moral decay that happens to people who have the misfortune of killing someone.

I looked at her aghast. "He wants you to what?"

What answered was not the girl but the snake. "One man less. And an evil man at that."

"You can't do that." I was talking to Yvonne but I was talking to the snake as well. It couldn't possibly ask that of her. "You can't ask that of her. If they catch her afterwards the court will execute her."

The snake wound gently down her arm. It reached across the table towards me. It held me with gold eyes. "Who are you to say?" it asked. I couldn't move under its gaze. "You all die sometime. She die. You too. Someday." There was an implicit threat in that.

Yvonne was so mortified she might have been naked. I'd seen more than she wanted to show to anyone. She clutched at a leather bag at her neck.

"I got to go," she said as she turned to flee.

She didn't even wait for the elevator. She bolted down the stairs, unsteady on her heels. I knew she wasn't running from me.

And there it was. Would a guide or a guard take a person to their destruction? I'd never asked the question. Who were we all talking to? Trusting? Leaning on? What said their druthers had anything to offer to her advantage? That their goals were for the benefit us puny humans?

I opened the windows. The air felt foul inside and out. I went down to the corner for fresh flowers, to clear the room. I can't say that worked.

Madam Marie never brought Yvonne to the tea room again. Would the girl run to back to her man? Stab him over breakfast? Make him a very special coffee with herbs? Ask her aunt for a favor? Turn to another young man to fight for her, over her?

Or did she walk in Madam Marie's shoes? Madam Marie would have welcomed her. She was Madam Marie's choice. All of Yvonne's options were tainted. In the end she didn't choose. It might have been better if she had.

I found a picture of her in the newspaper, several months later. "Young woman slain by boyfriend." There she was, in an old school picture. A smile full of promise that ended in a hateful love. Knifed in her bed. She might have done better to kill him first.

Madam Marie came in, serene and strong, week after week. Nicole came to be in her care, and she often came in with her niece's child in tow. Nicole had three fat braids with rubber ball bands on the ends, white shoes and sweet pastel dresses. She didn't speak much to me. But her sight was evident from the first. We had crayons and cookies out for her and she usually waited for Madam Marie in the kitchen.

Today Madam Marie came through the elevator, sternly holding Nicole's hand. Madam Marie brought her directly to my table. She sat at my table and grabbed my hand. Like a friend in pain. Maggie slipped back in to the kitchen with the child in search of cookies. Madam Marie spoke to me privately.

"Nicole good. She good as gold. But she scared bad," she said. "We keep her safe, everybody keep her safe. But she scared out her mind. She peed the bed last night." Nicole was too grown-up for that unless something was physically wrong or her fear was overwhelming.

Madam Marie was a voodoo witch. She was a personal icon of terror. But Nicole never had any reason to fear her aunt. Nicole was more than her ward. Nicole was her baby. Madam Marie would never let anything dangerous, near the child. Although I don't know we shared the same definition of dangerous. Madam Marie's protection was strong and able to defend the child.

So, if Nicole was scared, we needed to know where that was coming from. Nicole saw more than shadows. Madam Marie had her own ways of knowing, but she'd want confirmation. It takes a village to raise a psychic child.

Of course, we weren't sure if Nicole was seeing something past, present or now. But it was an adult matter. Nicole not only needed help but she might also need help just to tell us what she was seeing

I went back into the kitchen. Maggie had found her cookies and milk. Nicole had done her duty by them. I brought in a pad of paper and some crayons. I sat. She touched the edge of my energy. I brushed hers, gently, in greeting.

"Would you draw for me, Nicole? Your Gran tells me you are the best artist." Nicole was not our first or last child client. I knew enough to have the sixty-four-color crayon box with all the flesh colors.

It was a safe request. She grabbed a crayon and began. Her tongue poked out in concentration as she drew. She drew the house with windows like great eyes. She drew herself and Madam Marie in front on the porch with a dog at their feet. She seemed not to hear me. She certainly didn't look at me. But she picked up a black crayon and began what was a scribble over the house. She picked up the red crayon. Made an oval. The oval became an eye. Then over it all she drew arms and legs that made the scribble into a huge black man with the eyes inside him.

I sat back. When she wanted me to join in, she'd give me a sign. Her face glowed red in anger. More anger than fear.

I let her lead me there. "Is that someone I know?"

"That not someone. That be something." Nicole pushed her upper lip forward in intense concentration.

"It doesn't look happy. Is it bad?" I asked. "Kind of," she said.

"Is it someone you know? Is it just a monster or is it a person with bad things inside?"

"Monster comes and goes. He isn't a nice person either." She narrowed her eyes. She hated this thing.

"Have you seen him?" I asked. I was trying to figure out if this was spiritual or physical. Not that that made much of a difference.

"He around. I see him sometime." Her eyes focused back on her picture as she surrounded the house with red flowers.

"Do you see him when he's not there?" I was still trying to assess the risk.

"Sometimes." The grass she was drawing turned into a faster, harder scribble.

"Did you see him last night?" I asked.

"He with Gran in the temple clearing outside. With the other people. They was all dancing and clapping and beating the drums. He was near the bathroom. I needed to tinkle but I sure wasn't gonna until he was gone." She wrinkled her nose as if she smelled something bad.

I asked, "Did Madam Marie see him?"

"She don't see the monster. She just see the man. She don't hear him. He talk to me at night."

"Do you hear him out loud or inside your head?"

"Out loud. And inside," she said. Not just a home invasion. He was intruding into psychic space. Something spiritual was breaching their defenses.

"Does he talk just to you?" I probed gently.

"He yell so loud, he talking to everyone." Her face echoed a face I'd seen Madam Marie make when she was angry. "But Gran won't listen." She shook her head in disapproval.

"But you do." I said.

Such a serious little face. With burdens no child should bear. "Can you tell me what he's like?" I asked.

"He big. He make big messes. And he tried to hurt Veve." Clearly that was beyond forgiveness.

"Who is Veve?" I asked.

"My dog." Nicole pointed to a brown circle with four legs, a head and a tail. Clearly Veve.

"How did that happen? I asked."

"Veve didn't want him to come into the house. She barked at him.

She bit him too. He kicked at her after that." "Is she going to be okay?"

"Veve didn't let him get near her. Gran say Veve is a guardian." "Do you know the man?"

"He say he my daddy. Gran say he ain't. But when he come to the house it's not just him. He have that cloud inside him. That angry cloud pick him up and make him do things. It shake him up and down." The drawing of Nicole was turned to look at the monster. Madam Marie's image seemed to be focused on something else.

"Is this your house?" I touched the drawing, feeling energy in the crayon strokes.

"Gran's house. But I stay there too." She drew in more pink flowers by the edge of the sidewalk.

"Do you like staying at your Gran's house?" I asked.

"The house be just fine. Don't like being outside it though." "Because of the monster?" She nodded in answer.

"You love your Gran?"

Nicole gave me a serious nod.

"She loves you," I confirmed for her. A smile spread across Nicole's face. "Does Gran look after you?"

Three big nods. "Always. Best as she can."

I thanked Nicole, refilled the milk glass and walked back outside with Madam Marie. Maggie took over in the kitchen.

"Madam Marie, Is there a new man around in your family. Or your congregation?"

"There always be people come and go. Now family, we stay pretty much the same."

"Someone you haven't seen in a while?"

"All kinds of new people come up north. Oh, God." She was thinking of someone specific. Madam Marie was not normally demonstrative, but she was clearly shaken. "In my congregation?"

Madam Marie was a voodoo priestess and the morality was somewhat different from mainstream. The loas, the voodoo spirits, were complicated and amoral. They protected Madam Marie and anyone in her household. But that didn't mean that they might not use someone cruelly.

"I'm not sure of anything, but there's a man who Nicole says has a cloud inside him," I said

Madam Marie ran through names. Cousins, uncles, step brothers, people from her temple. She shook her head. "No one I know for sure. Not necessarily my congregation. Could be one of Bocor Claude's people. They service the Rada spirits. They always at odds with me and mine."

"Whoever it is, Veve doesn't like him. She tried to bite him." Madam Marie smiled at me.

"Veve be my best babysitter. And my guardian. She bite more than one fool who got too close. But I still not sure." Madam Marie shook her head.

I told her to keep Nicole close and to ask the women in the community to watch as well. It didn't mean what Nicole had seen hadn't happened. Or that it wouldn't. Vision is elastic. It stretches time. The past and the future are often indistinguishable from each other.

Sometimes you didn't know until you let it play out.

After Madam Marie and Nicole left, I went into the kitchen for a cup of tea. The tea kettle was at an odd angle. I grabbed the handle, and I burned myself on the boiler. Pain flared through my hand. It wasn't serious. Just angry red. Tight and very tender. When one of my clients went to touch my hand later that afternoon, I could feel it before she reached my skin. It was prescient pain. I felt it before her touch. And yelped. It was a wound that gave me an awareness of what was to come.

I thought of Nicole with her sensitivities. I wondered if there was a wound that made her aware of things before they came to be. I thought of her mother who died. Of the violence between her mother and her mother's man. Of the isolation of a little girl left with an older relative.

Of course, there was a wound.

It was Saturday when Nicole rushed in, Madam Marie in tow.

Another child might have hugged my knees. Nicole brushed the edge of my energy and I let it glow around hers. Madam Marie caught up to us.

"Do you need me to read, Madam Marie? I asked her.

"Is there a way to read for Nicole?" she said. "She not drink tea." "I have something that might help," I offered. I had a collection of polished beach stones in a sand box, in one corner of the room. It was a place where clients built and rebuilt their future hopes in the sand. I took Nicole's hand in mine and brought her over to the sand box.

I took a pretty black and white agate and placed it in the center. "This is you, Nicole." She nodded. I took a larger piece of slate and placed it in her hand, "This is your Gran. Where do you want her?"

Nicole put her Gran right by her. Then she drew lines in the sand with her finger, round and round in concentric circles. "Are you in your house" I asked.

"Nope." She shook her head so her braids swung from side to side. "That's our fence." She began to scribble in the sand. There was the man with the monster inside. She drew Veve, barking at the man. Then she smoothed the sand out from the circles. Nothing was threatening from outside. The man was gone. She had made it safe. She topped the image with one cloud with the sun shining past it.

I plucked up the black and white stone. I placed it in the child's hand.

"That for me?" She asked.

"That is you." I answered. "You are the only one who gets to decide for you. Your Gran will help while you're young, but no one chooses for you but you. You keep your stone in your pocket. It may tell you things."

She shook the stone in her hand. She held it up to her ear. "It's not saying anything."

"It will if you need it to. Or maybe it will help you say something." Nicole tucked it carefully into a pocket. Then she skipped off to the kitchen where she knew we kept the cookies.

Madam Marie sat down and grabbed my hand. "I tell you something I not supposed to tell you."

I was mildly shocked. Madam Marie was known for not sharing secrets.

"You know about my serpent friend."

"I know he's your loa and that he's part of you." "You know too much for a white lady."

"I'm part Irish," I told her. "I'm not that white."

She smiled as if to say that didn't count. "There be other loas." Madam Marie was trying to explain something to me. I let her. I thought I knew where this was going. I was wrong.

"Loas don't change," Madam Marie said. "They be forever. They be your friend forever. They trick you forever. They be your darkest enemy, a knife in the night. But they don't change. They follow your line."

"Your blood-line?" I asked.

"Sometimes blood. Sometimes people you choose. Sometimes the people who choose you."

"Is Nicole going to be Ayida's?"

I knew Dumballa was the loa represented by serpents and that Ayida was his consort. It was a good guess that Ayida was the loa Madam Marie served. I'd consistently seen snake imagery in her cup.

"Someday," Madam Marie acknowledged. "If Nicole choose. Her mother couldn't bear the choice. You can't do this if you weak."

"Nicole isn't weak," I said.

"No, but she young. It too early. Way too early to know." Madam Marie shook her head from side to side.

"Is she part of the rituals?" I asked.

"She just be old enough to watch from the circle. She watch us dance and feast. She don't need to see anything that scare her."

"But she has," I said. "She's seen something that terrified her." We both looked over to the child who was too solemn and too silent for her age.

"This man with a beast inside, is he her father?" I asked.

"He be her sperm donor. He got Yvonne pregnant, and two other girls at the same time. He ain't much of a father. But her blood is his blood. The thing that owns him, want to own her. He part of Monsieur Claude's group." I knew Monsieur Claude's people followed the Rada loa, the ones who specialized in revenge and destruction.

"Is he the man who murdered her mother?" I asked.

"That be another fool. Yvonne never had much luck. She wouldn't choose. She just run from one thing to run away to another. Other things chose for her." Marie shut her eyes and shook her head slowly.

"Can the loas choose? Without permission?" I asked.

"They strong. Petra loas very strong. Her father belongs to the loa, Baron Cemetery. The baron will come out of the graveyard hunting her. He terrible strong."

I asked it out loud. "Is Nicole being stalked?"

"She being courted," Madam Marie explained. "Our gods, they don't just take us. They court us. We come to love them. We come to need their love. We do whatever they ask. We serve them. Some are kinder than others."

Everything I knew about Baron Cemetery, the loa master of graves, was dark magic. "Nicole saw a dark entity in her father. Is that her father himself? Or does the loa take him over?" I asked."

"That the problem with the dark ones. They take you. There ain't much of you left."

"How far does this go back?" I asked her. "All the way to Africa," Madam Marie said.

"The relationship with the loas as well?" I asked. "It all be part."

I said, "Do you think Nicole is seeing past or future?"

Madam Marie scratched her head and tucked in her turban that had wound itself loose. "I think she be seeing both. Mostly she sees what's now."

"I thought you were going to tell me you had a real snake," I said, mostly to relieve the tension between us.

"But of course, Cher. Who you think I'm dancing with?" Her smile cracked open, she slapped her leg and gave me a real laugh. I wasn't sure whether she was teasing me or not.

Most religious beliefs have their dark corners. In most cases, I don't want to know. If you think as a Christian, you have no dark side, remember that you drink your god's blood and eat his flesh. Not every dark or hard thing is evil.

Madam Marie was getting ready to leave the tea room when I saw a wild-eyed black man slide into the tea room. He saw Madam Marie across the room. His clothes smelled of vomit, stale cigarette smoke and rum.

He pointed at her across the room. His face was a mask of rage. "You can't run from me. I find you. I find my child."

Will was working Rita's books in the office. He pushed outside the office door. "You can't do that in here, sir. You'll have to leave. I'll call the police on you," he said. Will's face was a mask of a reasonable man. Speaking reasonably. He had his phone in his hand. Will was not a brave soul, but he was protective. Will stood in the doorway, unsure what he could do but determined none of us would be harmed.

This man wasn't going to listen to reason. I reached him first. I grabbed one arm. Will put his phone down and grabbed the other one. The man went limp in our hands. It was hard to hold the man up. He felt like dead weight. "Out. Now." I yanked him by his arm and headed him toward the elevator. He smelled like a dumpster. He struggled in my grip and then I watched as his head fell back and rocked from side to side. His slack mouth took on a vile smile, evil and dark. His eyes lit from behind. He might be drunk, but the thing inside him was in control. He smelled something more like a dead thing. He didn't move but I felt a vacuum form around him

The man was a shell. Squatting inside him was that black scribbled monster with red eyes that Nicole had drawn for me. The baron, the black loa of the cemetery. There was a ragged shadow spreading across his chest. The shadow deepened into a pool. The center of it cracked open and the smell changed to graveyard mud and burnt ashes. Nicole was standing behind Madam Marie's skirt.

Then a shadow stepped out of his chest. A man-form made of ash and smoke formed from the shadow. He wore a formal top hat and tails, but daubed in mud and dusted in ashes. The shadow man smiled a feral smile, and tipped his hat to Madam Marie and to Nicole. I felt my shielding engage around me without having thought about it.

The man had gone limp since the Baron's spirit came out of it. Will dropped his arm and started to punch in numbers. I let wretch fall where he was. The only sign of life out of him was a low whining sound.

Madam Marie stepped towards the slumped-over drunk. "You found her. Now you go. You not much of a father if what you bring her is your hate." Then she turned to the shadow. "You!" Her face was twisted hate. Her hands contracted to claws. "You think you can force my child? With her people standing by?" Her eyes rolled back into her head, though her body stood stiffly as if was a plank. From Madam Marie's mouth a pale golden serpent slithered, on to the floor. It grew as it wound its way down her body until it almost filled the room. It coiled carefully, waiting.

The battle was not between Madam Marie nor this man. Her loa serpent, Aiyda and the Baron crackled in the space between them, for those who could see. The loas circled each other like prize fighters, like jungle cats. The snake coiled and then struck at him. The baron danced away from it, knife in hand. The tail of the snake whipped behind him. It wrapped around his ankle. He slashed it and the tail convulsed in pain.

Nicole pushed past me. She stood between her father and Madam Marie, directly in front of the fighting loa. Everything stopped. She raised her head. "This is for me? You fight over me?" Nicole said. She'd seen men fight over women in her Gran's house. She knew it was that kind of fight. The man might win, but that was not what defined what happened next. The men fought. But the woman chose who she went home with after. Nicole's eyes were glassy and her skin ashen. There was a force drawing her toward the Baron. But the snake pulled her as well. She flashed the Baron a look of pure hate. The snake slithered around her feet protectively. She was there to choose. But not all the choices were equally good. Nicole clutched her pebble in her hand. She would make her own decision.

We all made sure that she could. I saw my energy flow from me into her as a green cloud around the child's. I felt Madam Marie radiate her red glow through the girl. Then Maggie, standing to the side, joined her energy glowing blue against Madam Marie's red and my own green. The child was bathed in circling color. Soaking up strength from all around her, it flowed into her and emerged into a blinding white beam shooting out her eyes and her mouth.

Her words were for her father, his Baron Loa. She spoke with a grown woman's voice. "You want me to choose? I'll choose! You ain't my father. You ain't my kin. And you ain't any part of me." Everything stopped. Nicole reached her hand down to the serpent who shrank in size to a snake a child could bear on her shoulders. Slowly the serpent wound up her arm and twisted gently around her neck. The light show was over. She was a little girl again. She reached back for Madam Marie's hand.

I could hear Will talking with the 911 operator. "168 North Tremont. We have a man unconscious." I thought to myself, how do you tell the emergency line that you have unconscious possession victim? I had no clue, which is why I left it to Will. He hated psychic situations, but for real life emergencies, Will was flawless.

That was when the elevator cranked into motion. Rita walked into the room eyes wide and mouth open. "Mirella, what is going on here? This place smells like a trashcan." I pointed to the man on the floor. Rita lifted her eyes across the room to see Madam Marie and Nicole. "Madam Marie, with all respect..." Actually, respect was absent from Rita's voice. It was a sound like leaking battery acid. Quiet but deadly.

The man lay where he fell, crumpled as if he were kicked. Marie motioned with her hands as if she were wiping the mess away.

Maggie stepped between, and reached for Rita's arm. "Little thing happened. We took care of it. Tell you later." That was code for 'This is a damn-all mess but it's over. We'll fill you in as soon as we can."

Madam Marie grabbed Nicole and walked past him to the elevator. I thought I heard the sound of a snake looping in the dust on the floor. It slid in ripples between him and his child. He seemed to shrink. The graveyard and ash pit smell lifted a bit. I turned away from him, not wanting to watch. The police arrived. They assessed the man twisting on the floor and made the way clear for the EMT's. Medics strapped him to the gurney as he shook and moaned. Rita glowered over the proceedings.

After they got him down the elevator, the sun flooded through the windows where it had been sullenly gray. I opened the windows and let the breeze clean the room.

Was I wounded too? My mother and I lived so alone. I had no real sense of myself then. I'd scrabbled through school to find that school didn't count or change anything. I still wasn't sure of who I was. I had my wounds as well. I saw, through my wounds.

Next week I found Madam Marie and Nicole at the tea room, sitting with Rita. Rita wore her crown of braids. Madam Marie, the seven- pointed scarf that declared her the reigning Voodoo queen. They'd made a detente over tea and muffins, two queens at a peace conference. I saw Madam Marie slip a small wad of bills into Rita's hand. "We sorry for all that mess last week."

Nicole ran to me and pulled at my skirt. "You got my cookies?" she asked.

"You know I do." I waved her into the kitchen. I could see the small hazy golden snake draped around Nicole's shoulders.

Rita was getting up so I could read for Madam Marie. She followed the child into the kitchen. I heard milk poured and the child's happy patter.

Madam Marie grimaced as I sat. "I need to say sorry to you as well. Didn't mean to bring that trash anywhere. But you stand with me and with Nicole, like a friend. That make you my friend. You need something I got, it yours." I shuddered inwardly to think of what that might be. And was grateful.

"It wasn't your fault," I said. "It wasn't your mess. It just followed behind you." It really wasn't. You can't be called accountable for the evil that stalks you. Only the evil you do.

Then I remembered Maggie right in the middle of it, shoulder to shoulder with the Voodoo queen. "Is Maggie your friend as well?"

"We might as well be," Madam Marie admitted. "We know each other since Eden. She just worried I'm goin' to hell. But she a strong light."

Madam Marie nodded towards the child as I sat down. "Dumballa be a good loa. He teach her love and how to care for people. She too young. But it who she is."

Madam Marie sat at her table and nibbled on her muffin. I raised her cup to read.

Gifted

Gifted

Carolyn took my arm as we went into the gallery. We'd left the tea room early to check out the Cambridge Gallery Walk. The Friday night gallery scene was a movable feast where people wandered from building to building, from one exhibit to the next. This exhibit, though, was the one Carolyn had insisted we see. Hung on the wall was a collection of portraits that were singularly different. The portraits were recognizable individuals. But each one had an animal quality to it, as if the artist had caught the person in some kind of fairy tale transformation, Sometimes, it was a look in the eyes, sometimes the angle of the ears, sometimes something about their carriage. It was as if the artist peeked inside and allowed a little of the animal nature in the person to expose itself, just a bit.

Carolyn walked me over to a canvas that looked oddly familiar. I knew that pale, almost green hair. It was clearly Carolyn. But her lips had the plumpness of an angelfish's mouth. And her legs melded into a muscular length.

"Carolyn? Is that you?" I asked, giggling.

A deep, liquid voice came in from behind. "Carolyn, I'm so glad you could be here. Are you pleased with your portrait?"

Carolyn blushed from her pale roots to her nose. "Delighted, actually."

Carolyn reached down and she hugged the woman, who was in a wheelchair.

She was not old. But her face wore the creases of constant pain and physical limits. Her hair was a short-bristled ruff of gray wire on edge. Her eyes flitted from blue-gray to blue-purple with aqua edges. She looked small in the chair, crumpled. But her face was vividly alive, as if you could see the synapses of her mind processing the things around her.

"Verena Randolph," Carolyn said, "I'd like you to meet Marlene, my friend from the tea room." As I touched Verena's hand, I felt toned muscles that had been kept strong in spite of the woman's disability.

"Carolyn has told me about the tea room. I don't leave my studio often, but it sounds fascinating. And you, Marlene, are charming. Could I ask you to pose for me at some time?" She looked me up and down in a way that was not sexual but was a complete appraisal.

I was flattered. "Why would you want to paint me?"

"I see something in you," Verena said. "Would you be willing to explore that with me?"

I looked around the room at the other paintings in the exhibition. The images were all clothed, but incredibly revealing. It was as if she'd peeled layers away from these people to reveal something underneath their public masks, not in a cruel way, but in a way, that left no room for polite deception.

"You are so gifted! I wish I could see in your head. I wish I were that talented," I blurted out.

"No, you don't, child." She shook her head. "You wouldn't want what it costs."

I realized her painting represented her vision, clear as my own and night and day different. I still wanted to see what she saw. Perhaps I could get a glimpse of how it worked as she painted me. "Yes," I said. "I'd be happy to model for you."

I never was the kind of person anyone would want to use as a model.

I'm plain, pleasantly ordinary. A dark-haired girl with a slightly curved frame. Good enough features, but nothing special to draw the eye. I knew it. I'd gone through high school and college watching other girls turn heads. But people did not turn their heads to look at me.

So, what would Verena see, this woman who saw bears and panthers, snakes and bees and pandas within the faces of her models? We think of animals as cute, but these were anything but.

Some of the images were charming. Others were not. The animism was unsettling because it emerged from a surface that was smooth and predictable to make an image of the wild under-layer in these people, an expression of uncomfortable truth about who these people were. What would she see in me?

We made a date, and I found myself a week later standing at her studio door.

She let me into a room so cluttered that pictures propped up other pictures across the floor. The studio was in the top floor of a warehouse with skylights. An oriental carved screen partitioned her living space away from her painting. For all the clutter, there was a pathway made for the wheel chair she had used at the reception, although she greeted me at the door with a cane. She moved slowly, checking her weight and position with each step to make sure she was not pushing her body past its limits.

"Come in," she said gaily. She motioned me towards a small breakfast table, full of croissants and two glasses of ice tea.

"Sometimes I do portraits as paid commissions," she said. "Mostly I paint people who interest me, and I need to explore their imagery. Either way, that takes their consent. Do I have yours?" she asked cautiously. "You may find that having someone paint you can be an invasive process."

"I'm actually curious," I confessed. "You know what Carolyn and I do for a living, don't you?"

"You read fortunes, don't you?" she returned.

"I have a feeling that what you do isn't really different from what we do," I said thoughtfully. "Only you aren't looking at past and future.

You're looking at current personal character."

"I thought you might understand. Good!" she said. "I don't often work with people who understand the process well."

"I was surprised you'd want to paint me. I'm not very photogenic." "You mean people don't notice you much, don't you?" she asked me. "Well, yes," I acknowledged. "I always thought I was kind of ordinary."

Verena broke out laughing. "You know better than that! Please! That's a deflection on your part. I wondered if you did it on purpose. You're very good at generating a sign over your head that says, 'Don't look here. Nothing to see.'"

I took a moment to take that in. "I guess I do that."

"Mind you," Verena said, "I think that's brilliant on your part. It saves you from dealing with people's jealousy and their fear. It's limiting to be ordinary. But sometimes it's freeing to appear ordinary."

"Are you ordinary?" I asked her.

"What would that look like?" She turned her head, looking askance at me. "There are no ordinary people. Normal is a setting on the dryer. Sometimes we hide and sometimes we shine, but none of us were ever made to be ordinary."

"Did you study to be a painter?" I asked her. She must have, I thought. She was so skilled.

She pulled out one tube of paint after another, picking a palate as I might have picked a bouquet of flowers. "Marlene, don't be silly. There's no one who could have taught me what I do. Is there anything you could have studied that would have made your gift work better or differently?"

I shook my head.

"I thought not," she said. "It's the vision you have, and the way you express that vision. If I'd been a singer I might sing, or if I'd been a storyteller, I'd tell stories. As it is, I'm a painter, so it all comes out in the paint. It's an exploration for the subject as well as for me. I paint well because I cheated. I practiced. I painted poorly until I learned how to do it better. If I didn't paint, I'd feel as if I was seeing the emperor's back end while everyone else was admiring his trousers. I'd feel as though I'd seen my dad dress up as Santa and told no one. The paintings are the way I acknowledge a significant part of what I see. Does your gift work that way?"

"Sometimes," I acknowledged. "Mostly when I'm reading for people, I see the periphery of their lives. The things that fill their days. I believe what you see is who they are. Did you always paint?"

"No, child. I used to hurt." She was talking, but her attention was on her brush and paint preparation.

I thought she was being facetious. But her face was so serious. I asked the question politeness would have had me not ask. "What happened to you?"

"An accident." Verena rubbed her back at a spot near her hip. "I fell down the stairs. It damaged my back and lower limbs badly. I was young and resilient, so it really didn't make a big difference at the time. But as I grew,

• 236

the damage grew greater. I found I was falling a lot. I went to a physical trainer who explained it to me. I wasn't hurt because I was falling. I was falling because I was still hurt."

"What do you do for that? Can they fix you? Do surgery? Give you better meds?" It seemed impossible there wasn't a decent medical answer for something so simple as a fall.

"Who says any of those things might fix me? That isn't always how healing works. They tried all of that. They did their best." She rubbed the spot again and stretched lightly. Her face relaxed a bit as if the pain had backed down a bit.

Now she posed me in a chair. She gently took my chin in her hand and tilted my face to the sky. I froze as best I could into place, waiting for her to start. Her focus centered strictly on the blank canvas on her easel. She mixed a soft brown, grabbed a small round tipped brush and swept across the surface arcing in odd shapes.

"Most folk find it disorienting to watch me paint," she said. "I'll show you everything when I'm done, but I work in layers and it feels tedious for people sometimes. You might want to wait to see it when it's all finished."

I wasn't entirely sure that was strictly for my benefit, but I was willing to work with her in the ways that worked best for her.

After that, I relaxed into the process. I let my mind wander. As my mind wandered I thought of floating. Flying. Sitting in trees under the moon. I was propped in place in such a way that I drifted off at some point. When I woke, she'd sat in the chair opposite to me, fresh ice tea in front of both of us.

"I'm embarrassed," I said. "When did I fall asleep?" I stretched, stiff from sleeping in the chair.

"Don't be," she told me. "People find modeling exhausting. You lasted better than most."

"So, did you study art? Was this what you wanted to do?" I tried to image her in art class with teachers over her shoulder, guiding her work. I couldn't imagine them understanding what she saw.

"Heavens, no, child. I was going to be a forest ranger. I was studying forestry and animal rehab. But my body wasn't up to the task."

"So, what happened?" I probed.

Verena sighed deeply. "I got so far. Took a header down a flight of stairs. Spent a long time in bed." She took another sip of her tea.

"That must have been awful!" I exclaimed.

"Most things are mixed blessings," she answered me. "The blessings usually have a sour rind you have to get through. The curses usually have a shiny spot that's sweet and creamy. Nothing is really all one thing or another."

"Did your injury stop you?"

"Yes and no. It stopped me from living a life in the woods. My legs weren't stable enough for the trails. And my back was too fragile. But what it really did was set me free. I bought paint and canvas and painted."

Every so often someone turns you on your head and shows you the world upside down. It's as if you were looking at leaves and turned them upside down only to find a butterfly. It's neither good nor bad, but it's deeply unsettling. We expect way too much from expectation. I looked at Verena, trying to figure out how being crippled for life had set her free.

"If you can't do one thing, the energy that drives you, still beckons you. Sooner or later the broken thing that you cannot do becomes something different that you have to do. The river refuses to be dammed. Whatever your gift is, it will find a way."

"Will you show me my painting?" I asked her.

"Not yet. It would be better if you can wait a little longer. Next time, maybe. We've got the bones of the painting in. Now it's time for the details." Verena threw a tarp over the picture, and showed me to the door.

The sidewalks were wet with a storm that was still passing through. I got into my car, started the engine in the light rain, pulled onto the highway.

For just a flash I saw Nona in the rear view mirror. "Don't be afraid, cara mia." Nona smiled gently at me. "You'll be okay."

I looked away from the mirror, only to be rammed by the car behind.

It was a while before the pain receded enough for me to be conscious. I woke in a hospital bed with my head wrapped, feeling four times its original size. I'd been scraped and bruised. My brain had bumped itself on the inside of my skull. I tried to open my eyes. Nothing. Total darkness. I put my hands up to my eyes and felt the bandages.

Someone grabbed my hands gently and stopped me.

"No." The nurse held my hands not in comfort but in restraint. "Take it easy here. Don't touch your face.

Jane was there in the chair waiting for me. "You okay?" She reached to touch my forehead. I could feel her fingers before she made contact and I flinched.

"As compared to what?" I said. "Not so much. I feel like I got rammed by a car."

"That's only because you were. You are always the toughest girl I know. It's a good thing you don't arm wrestle," When Jane tried to be funny I knew it was bad. She was a font of disinformation.

"The doctor will be here in no time" the nurse said. "He'll tell you what is going on." The nurse spoon-fed me Jell-O and soup until I refused to swallow any more. Then I fell asleep to the thump of my pulse against my brainpan. Whatever drug they were giving me wasn't good enough.

I was awake the next morning when the doctor walked through on his rounds. He sounded like a socially disconnected Frazier Thomas from Garfield Goose. He had answers to my questions, but none of them told me anything.

"Well, we really don't know what we've got here yet. You've suffered a brain trauma, and it's way too early to speculate as to how bad that is. Right now, we want you quiet and healing with as little stress as possible. Some of the glass from the broken window got into your eyes. Again, we did our best to repair things, but we just don't know enough to say what happens next, except that we'd like you to be our guest for a while and let people serve you hand and foot. How does that sound?"

I didn't have words for it. Health insurance for a psychic is nonexistent. Instead of calming me, his words made me feel as though I'd been linked up to a live electric wire that was being blinked on and off, randomly. The pain was breathtaking. I didn't even hear his footsteps leaving.

Several days later, the doctor discharged me, insisting how lucky I was. "Nothing really bad on your MRI. A small amount of swelling. I'm sure it hurts like a firefight, but you'll be back to yourself in a week or two. We won't know about your eyes for several weeks. We'll write you several prescriptions and have you follow-up in my office in a week."

I was discharged with instructions to lie flat and let the ceiling spin until I felt better.

The driver of the car who hit me was responsibility itself. He gave a statement to the police that put him solidly at fault and his insurance company was gracious about my hospital bills and needs in the hopes that I wouldn't sue them for more later.

After the whirl of my life at the tea room, it was incredibly odd to be lying in bed. Maggie called on her church to set up help for me. I had a stream of the sweetest old ladies who sat with me, and brought in cold drinks and warm soup. They set up the TV so I could listen to an endless series of soap operas and detective dramas. But my attention was limited and the laugh track was almost an edged weapon. I felt so far from the tea room and from myself.

But that was entirely just as well because I couldn't have read tea leaves even if my eyes had been working. When I sat up, the pain almost made me black out. It was hard enough to get to the bathroom. Even the effort of straining to pee increased my headache. I would stagger back to lie down, hoping the pain would drift down from a level eight to a six. I learned to Braille my way to the bathroom. Six steps down the corridor and on the left. Three steps to the stool. Toilet paper on the right.

I started listening to books on tape. What worked best were the Victorian novels I'd read as a child. I knew how they ended. Like old friends sitting around my bed, they never distressed me with unexpected endings. If I drifted off, they would be there when I awoke.

Rita and Maggie came to visit. "Now don't you worry," Rita said. "I lit a candle for you at the cathedral. Your clients miss you, but you are the only one they want to have read for them. They'll be there for you when you're better."

Maggie hugged me as tightly as she could without hurting me. "Don't you mind, child. This will pass." Maggie marked a wet sign of the cross on my forehead. Holy water, surely. "To keep off the raff," she said. "Don't you try to take on any more station wagons or SUV's in a fight again."

"I won't, Maggie. I promise." I wasn't up for taking on anything tougher than my pillow.

"Are my friends taking good care of you?" she asked. "I feel like I have fifteen new moms," I told her. "Good!" Maggie answered. "You do."

Did I image an energy rush as she hugged me? Or had it just been her body warmth?

Neither of them talked to me about coming back. It wasn't that they didn't want me there. They just knew I was stuck in my bed until it was over.

The days sat on a rubber band that stretched further and further during the afternoon. Right now, I was starring in a major drama, roughly titled Poor Blind Marlene. It was true, but it wasn't helping me out in any way. I took my meds on time, desperate for recovery to arrive. I lay disconnected from the pain, but still trapped in it, hoping the day would finally wrap itself up and be over. I imagined a life where I stumbled helplessly blind through every interaction of every day. I tried to count blessings. I didn't have to use more than one hand to do that.

I began to sneak extra meds, hoping for the best of booby prizes, pain-free sleep. The home nurse caught me, of course, when I ran out too soon for their calculations. She said some hard things about addictive process and some stupid things about just toughing it out. Maggie's friends began to tightly count out my pills that had become a lifeline. It wasn't ever enough. The pills edged the agony but never stopped it. It was no longer a surprise. It was background noise.

Maggie came to visit, surrounded by a whiff of flowers and talcum powder.

"You want me to read for you?" she asked.

It sounded ludicrous. I was blind. My life as I knew it was over. "Maggie, I don't know. I'm stuck here until I'm not stuck here. How long is that?"

"How about we pretend that stuck ends at some time or another. Of course, we both know the whole history of the world is set in concrete, but let's pretend that something could change." Having acknowledged my depression, she pushed me to walk for a moment outside of that dank place inside myself. By now my misery felt normal, but misery is a cold couch.

"I see you sleeping a lot," Maggie said. "Pay attention to your dreams. Someone's trying to talk to you. There are three masks at your feet. Each one of them is going to be like different eyes. Try them all on. They all fit. They'll all show you different things. but there's one you'll like best. I see you painting a wall with broad strokes. I see you with a child in your arms, dancing. I see you take the mask off, and throw it to the winds. I see you flying." She let go of my wrist to show I was finished. I shook my head as she left.

But that night my dream time became wild. I didn't dream of my mother or Nona. I woke screaming. I made Jane punch in Maggie's number

She answered on the tenth ring, still muzzy from sleep. "Why did you ask about my dreams?" I yelled at her.

Maggie groped for a way to say it. "Sometimes dreams take us forward and backward in time and sometimes they give us a different perspective on things."

"I hate dreaming," I said. "I wake up and I'm so angry, my hands are clenched. I bit the inside of my mouth tonight." I was furious.

"What did you dream?" Maggie asked me.

"I dreamed I woke up and it was still black everywhere, like it is now that I'm blind. I was trying to go to work and leave my apartment and all I could do was crawl because I couldn't see where I was going and what I was doing. And I bumped into people. They kept saying, 'What's wrong with you. Are you blind?' "And I said 'yes.'"

"One by one, they said, 'Well, watch where you're going,' as though I was sighted. I walked into a post. I fell over one of the people as I was trying to walk. Everyone expected me to be like everyone else. As though I could see. Only I can't."

"Do you feel you're trapped and can't go anywhere?" Maggie asked. "I'm blind, damn it. How am I supposed to go anywhere?"

My hands were clenched and my body and voice were both shaking.

Maggie just let me spew it out at her.

I did know better. I'd watched blind people travel cross country, teach school, be lawyers, do art, all sorts of things, even in my own small experience. I knew full well that my blindness wasn't my biggest disability. My disability was all tucked in between my ears while I starred in the stage show of Poor Blind Marlene.

It wasn't my eyes. It was the rage of a broken dream. I could know all of that. And still be crippled by my rage, and by the unfairness of it all.

Maggie's voice soothed me back to my bed. "Go back to sleep, Marlene. Don't stop dreaming. The dreams are the best road you got right now. You want to go somewhere else, you gotta dream the journey first."

I knew she was right, which only made me madder. I hung up on her.

I didn't sleep for the rest of the night. When I could smell the coffee that told me morning had come, Jane put food beside me, all things I could pick up and stick into my mouth. Cheese sticks. A pastry. A cup of coffee for myself. Then she left me with my meds and my tray.

I drifted off in the heat of the sunshine.

In my dream, I was still blind and lying in bed. But I was a child. My friend Terri, who was stone blind without her glasses, had come to visit me. It was the summer we broke her glasses trying to fly from the top of the hay loft. Thank God, the barn floor was covered with deep hay. I hadn't seen her since we were nine. The summer after that, she died of meningitis. It was so fast. She was just gone.

In the dream, she was sitting near my bed. When I woke up she startled me and I knocked over my breakfast tray. As I apologized, she laughed at me the way she always laughed. It sounded like a cough, small and contained but full of mischief. I knew her instantly.

"Terri, is that you?" I put my hand out, trying to locate her.

"I missed you, Marlene." She sat next to me. I could feel her thigh warm against my own.

"I missed you, too," I said. "How can you be here?"

"I always was. I always am," she told me. "You just didn't know where to look."

"I can't look." I told her. "I'm ... I'm blind."

"Oh, for heaven's sake," Terri giggled. "Like that matters. I'm over here. Come towards me."

I leaned towards her voice, knocking a glass down. She reached the bed. She fell on it, almost landing on me.

"For heaven's sake, don't fall on me," I cried. "Why are you in bed?" Terri asked.

"I've been hurt. I'm recovering from surgery."

Terri's clever hands found me and ran up my arms to my face. My face was too sore. I screamed.

"Owww! That hurts," I wailed. "Didn't mean to hurt you."

I made an oof noise as Terri settled on to the bed. "Why are you here?" I demanded of her.

"I heard you felt poorly. I thought I'd come in and tell you a story." I stopped being Poor Blind Marlene for a moment. I was nine year old Marlene, listening to Terri who couldn't see very well, either, tell me a story.

"I was sitting on the porch and I heard a boy bird singing," Terri began.

"Are you sure it wasn't a girl?" I teased. "He was too loud to be a girl," Terri said.

"You're loud and you're a girl," I answered her.

"But I'm not a bird. He sang for me. He said, 'Tiwerr, tierrererr,' fine and high and over my head. I could feel him fly over me. He batted his wings along the edge of the porch. My Gran said he made a bed for his love in the porch eaves. Every morning I heard the two of them sing to each other. He'd sing tiwerr, tiwerr, tiwerr, and she'd sing right back at him. Tierrererr. We put yarn bits out on the porch where they could find them. They'd be gone in a day or two. Gran said the birds had a nest with red and yellow yarn, just the thing for a good bird's nest.

One day, instead of hearing tiwerr, we heard peeps instead. Those two robins were so busy they couldn't fly straight. The babies were peeping and their parents went hunting for worms, and grubs and seeds. Gran got out the garden hose and watered the area under the porch special so they could find more worms there. Just like it had rained. And the babies kept peeping. It was crazy out there with the noise. Then two weeks later, it stopped. Gran said the babies had fledged, just flown up *and out of the nest."*

In my dream we spent the whole day making the birds a nest. She and I put it out on the porch so the birds could see it and maybe use it. She kissed my forehead and I heard her walk down the stairs. I woke to a sound outside the window. Twitte Twirre. The birds continued to sing to me through the afternoon.

The doctors peeled off my bandages. I could see light and dark, but no real specific shapes. He put fresh bandages on, shaking his head. "Too early, still. We need to wait and see."

I waited. Unable to see. Furious with the dark.

Carolyn came to visit. She brought me a basket of sea shells. "These are straight from the ocean. Nothing is as healing as the ocean. You can hear the water in the shells." She held up a conch to my ear. I could hear the soft roar of something like water. My mind knew it was the pulse in my head, but my imagination felt myself drifting out in the surf, in warm sunlight, washed in the waves.

I drifted off as she left and woke cradling the shell, feeling the glass-like inside and the rough external shell.

I'd waited almost two weeks. My bumps and bruises had quieted into simple sore spots. But my brain bruise was still an agony. It came and went in waves. It was unrelenting. Finally, the pain hit a point where it was past intrusive, or agonizing, or compelling, or overwhelming. I found myself talking about it with a friend on the phone and realized how exquisitely boring my pain was. Simply boring. Horrid, agonizing, dull, limiting, and above everything else the most boring thing I'd ever endured.

And I still couldn't see. My bandages cushioned my mind as well as my eyes.

I still needed massive amounts of sleep, and the meds they fed me reinforced that.

I dreamed constantly, odd scenarios different from my Nona dreams or the stress dreams of ordinary life. I began to dream in color. I drifted through shades of blue and green dawn into aqua and gold and morph towards lilac in pulsing amorphous shapes. I began to notice colored shapes that formed when people were in the room with me. Jane's was green with odd brown corners. Maggie's was deep blue and reminded me of a sea of open umbrellas. Rita's was like a fleur de lys in deepest red purple, nothing like the flaming red that followed Jamie or the turquoise shot with green that floated around Carolyn.

The doctor unwrapped my eyes again. Light streamed through the gauze as he peeled away the layers. It hurt. I found myself blinking back tears against the light. But it was a reprieve. I would not be blind.

The next step was a room always half-lit and dark glasses. The light made my eyes ache in their sockets. But I could see darks and lights, and shapes.

Light became easier. I got used to my shades. I began to see details. Rita brought me a coloring book and art pencils. I still needed to rest most of the day. But I found the time when I colored was a time when the pain receded, in the path of something else to do. It was odd to color with shades on, but I took the colors as I saw them through my dark glasses

Rita's coloring book became a godsend. I spent my good hours coloring in the shapes. The pencils came with a color wheel printed on the box for reference. There were flower shapes and mandalas. Mostly it was an exercise of adding color to texture. At first I worked in natural colors, adding only what the rational eye would expect to see. But after a while I started playing with color in other ways. What would it look like if everything in the world was blue? Or gray? Or brown? Or shades of yellow? I knew a small amount of color theory, and started to make rules for myself, one per page about the colors I would use. Sometimes only colors of the same family but in shades and tones. Sometimes I took colors across from each other. Or worked only with colors next to each other. Or I would pick three colors at random and make them work somehow. The process stretched into a series of color exercises as opposed to coloring time.

I dreamed I was sitting in a chair on the lawn in the moonlight.

Three birds flew down from the branches, each with a mask in her beak. The raven bore a black mask with indigo feathers and a tear down the cheek. "So sad," she warbled. She dropped the mask into my lap. It had ribbons on either side. I held it up and looked through it. Everything was beautiful, but dark and a mysterious blue. And everything was motionless. It was a frozen mask of death. I let it flutter to the ground.

A golden bird dropped a mask of bright oranges and yellows and pinks. It was sunlight. It was held on with a clover chain. I looked through it. It was warmth and joy, but without responsibility. And I could see there were things obscured by this mask too. Instead of seeing things frozen in time, I could only see things growing in space. I couldn't find rest in that mask. It was the energy of childhood, and I was not a child. I held it back up by the chain and the bird grabbed it in her beak and took it with her to the top of the trees.

The third bird was a snow owl. She swooped overhead and dropped her mask at my feet. I reached down. It had illuminated eyes of diamonds and snow crystals that augmented what I saw in the darkness. I slipped it on and my vision was electrified by color and light I'd never seen before. Instead of ties, it melded around my head and fitted onto my ears. I became an owl in the wearing of it.

I waved to her in acknowledgment. This was my mask. How I would see my world. She swept down again and whoo-whooed at me from the branch above. I found myself reflecting her sounds back to her. Both of us whoo-whooed at the moon.

Jane came into my room bearing lunch. Somehow her face was wreathed in a golden glow that ended in a bright red border with odd streaks of green. "You won't believe the next travel route I'll be taking. Thailand! Can you imagine?" While she was talking, her face pulsed in the strangest colors.

"Jane, by some chance did you eat something that didn't agree with you?" I asked her. What else could account for that odd yellow and red coloration over her face?

"What?" she said. "Why would you say that?" She shrugged to show me she was fine.

"Your face is yellow and red," I told her.

She reached up and wiped her forehead over her hand. The colors rippled across her arm as she did so.

"I don't know why, and I bet it's not easy, but you are definitely red and yellow," I chided her.

I heard her pick up the phone to call the doctor when she left the room. Within the next couple days there were several more tests. Another scan. Nothing changed in the results.

Except that the nurses and doctors all were in color too. One of the nurse pulsed blue and purple except for the beginning of a flush pink at her upper stomach. Was she pregnant? The doctor looked a different shade of blue, more aqua. But he had black ridges that came up his back. He walked as if his back was in agony. Were the black ridges his pain?

What was I seeing? I wisely chose not to tell the nurses or doctors that I was seeing colors that couldn't be there.

When Rita came to visit me, I watched her come in glowing bands of plum and orange, colors that glared even through my dark glasses.

"Rita, I hate to say this, but why are you purple and orange?" I asked her.

She looked down at her blue dress. Thought for a moment. "Oh!" she exclaimed. "I didn't know you saw auras."

"What's an aura?" I hadn't heard the word before.

"It's a color field," Rita explained. "People throw off energy all the time. Some folks see it as color. It's called an aura."

"I didn't see them before, Rita. This is new. I thought it meant I was really hurt." The tears I'd been holding back threatened to seep out of my eyes.

Rita hugged me. "No, no, child. It's much more normal than that. I don't see auras, but some of our readers do. Maggie does. You should ask her about it. What else do you see?"

"The kid downstairs is purple and brown around the face. I think he's on drugs." I started to tick off the list. "The doctor has a black streak down his back and his sides are bright blue. I didn't think he'd turned into a smurf. Jane is gold and red."

"Well, of course Jane is," Rita explained. "She has a deep interest in travel and she's basically a happy person."

"Is that what I'm seeing?" I asked.

"Sort of. It sounds like it. Most people who see auras consider it background noise. Every so often they'll see something that's glaringly obvious. For heaven's sake, if it's that blatant, pay attention. It's something you need to know. But people generate color constantly. It will tell you more about mood and health, than about personality or path.

The colors actually have meanings, so you might want to look them up." "I think this happened when I was coloring. I started noticing colors outside the coloring book." I patted the coloring book.

Rita's smile was filled with reassurance. "You were paying attention.

I'll bet it's always been there. You just had other things that you were focused on."

Somewhat relieved, I relaxed into a new awareness. I had John download a chart of aura color meanings. As I met new people, I watched them turn from scarlet to orange to gold in conversations, and I came to understand that I was seeing the very energy around them. It was not a consistent phenomenon. Instead, it seemed to be a real-time status report.

You would think we were built with all the parts we need, and just enough of those. But it's not true. We're built with all kinds of spare parts, available as we need them. Particularly when you get over the idea that you have to use something a particular way to make it effective. If a part of your life blocks that path, another less used pathway opens in response. Our gifts are often a path opened in response to an end, a death, a harm, an impassible fear, a dead end. The spare parts of our lives help us build the new paths out of our lost past to our new self.

My head began to swim less, focus more, hurt less. I was able to read a little. Watch TV for an hour at a time. I was up and out for small periods of time. I decided to make a visit to Verena.

I adjusted my dark glasses, and felt rather than saw the doorbell button. The glasses still felt strange, but I was grateful I didn't need a white cane as well. Verena met me at the studio door and we both limped to her sitting area. She perched in her chair and I sat stiffly to avoid straining my back, but it was good to see her.

"I wondered where you'd been," she said. "I should have called and checked." She turned her head at an angle, as if to inspect me from a different direction. Waves of silver and indigo lapped the edges of her face, showing enlightened giving and a deep spirituality, edged with a crust of brown which I knew was an indication of agony.

"I wasn't well enough for conversation or company," I told her. I stared at the pictures hung randomly up and about the studio. I asked her what I wanted to know. "Why do you paint people as animals?"

"I paint what I see, child. Doesn't everyone? Art is only partially skill. All art begins as vision."

I recognized her picture of me on the easel. It was well in process by now. It was me, but there was an owl formed around the edge of my face and my eyes were the eyes of an owl. There was a part of me that suddenly was looking for a way out of the room, not in anger or disappointment or even panic, but just because I could feel the need to fly high and wide over trees, over forest, over the moon. It shook me physically. It made me want desperately to take flight. I could feel wings I really didn't have trying to flutter.

I got it. She'd painted the physical part of our souls. "This wasn't always what you saw, was it?" I asked.

"No." She offered me her hand and the connection gave me the view through her eyes. I glimpsed up at the mirror across from her and saw a beautiful serpent, dark blue and silver scales with a turquoise mouth. I should have been terrified, but I knew this was not about what she would do. It was how she saw the world. She saw her world through the unblinking eyes of a serpent that was focused on souls. "Is this a gift?" I asked her.

"Everything is a gift if you look at it the right way." She waved her hand to wave away the thought. "We are the product of everything that happens to us, and those happenings make us who we are. It's a gift. The gift isn't so much the production of one thing or another. The gift is the ability to see things in different ways. But I doubt people would want it if they knew the cost. I don't think I would have chosen mine if I did. Even knowing what I know now. Although I can't imagine my life without it."

"You didn't fall, did you?" I asked with perfect clarity. I already knew.

I saw her dangling in a woman's arms, a small child at the top of the stairs. The woman shook her and Verena slipped from the woman's hands, tumbling down those stairs to the floor far below. It made every injury afterwards much more perilous. And inevitable.

My face must have given me away. Or perhaps Verena could see what I saw. Or guess. She knew that I knew.

"Don't you blame her?" I blurted out.

Verena blinked softly. As if to clarify her view. "Well, it was her fault, but I really think she did the best she could. My mother was much confused by the solitary nature and extreme demands of motherhood.

She didn't do very well at it."

I gasped. Verena had understated the issue in a way that shocked my core.

"Her actions hardly matter at this point. All that does matter is what I choose to do now. No one would ask for my gift," Verena continued. "No one would do something like that actually on purpose to create my gift, I believe. But it's mine. I choose to illuminate the world as I find it."

My mouth was still open. I closed it purposely, leaving words behind that would not ever make any difference. Verena had left shame and blame behind her, to walk boldly with her sight. "So, this was your response to the pain?"

"There are closed doors child, but there are no accidents. There's only what is. If you look around there is always an open door and a dream worth keeping. Someone has to show people who they are." She smiled up at me. Her acceptance of all of it, damage, betrayal and gift ere tied into each other and complete.

I tried to place my own injury on a similar trajectory. "Will my injury mean I'll take up painting? Will I change?" I asked her. It seemed silly to ask. I had no talent for art.

"I doubt you'll paint. But you've already begun to change. I don't believe in accidents. Your vision is a gift you've been given. But you have to respond to a gift to receive it. The only way you can lose it is if you pretend it out of existence. Or freeze in inertia Somehow I don't see you doing that."

She kept stroking the painting with her brush, one corner and then another. In a short while, she stopped and wiped her hands. "There," she said. She turned the canvas so I could see myself. I was a blue owl caught in flight across the sky. "Now you're ready," she told me. "Go fly."

Ms. Guided

Ms. Guided

The tea room was crammed from the Summer season touristas. As Boston swelled with tourists, the tea room swelled with travelers wanting the experience of a Boston tea leaf reading. Fourth of July brought back- to-back readings, for all of us, day after day.

After a while it seemed like I was floating in a trance.

"You will meet a stranger. Five is your lucky number. Be careful with your car. The storm is coming." I heard myself pump out reading after reading after reading until I simply didn't know what I was saying anymore.

It wasn't uncommon to lose myself in trance. It wasn't uncommon not to remember what I'd said to one person or another. The clients blurred, and since they weren't regulars, I really never did get to know this stream of strangers. I'd stagger from one table to another and tell people what I saw.

But that could wear out quickly. And today it did. I couldn't see a thing in the cups except tea leaves.

Was it exhaustion? Vision of all kinds has limits. I can see farther than you, perhaps, but at some point, there is a horizon line I can't see past either. And there is another point where I simply need to close my eyes altogether.

There was a time before the tea room when I was a college student who sometimes read tea leaves for her friends. As a hobby, I could open and shut that door at will. Now I was a professional psychic. It had become my job. Every day, all day, I was open to both to the psychic world and to psychic attack. I had a door in my head propped open that might have been better sometimes locked. Sometimes that door sensibly slammed shut on its own.

What can a reader do then? Presuming she's decided not to just simply quit? Most psychic readers depend somewhat on cold reading. It's the practice of taking minute information in the client's physical presence and using that information to know more about them.

I sat at a slender older woman's table. That slight tremor of the hand, is it fear or illness? Or exhaustion? "You've been under terrible strain lately," I told her. Here, eyes went wide.

"I see you've been separated from someone you loved. I know you hurt horribly now, but you will come to see this as a grace and a new beginning." I could see the indentation where her ring used to be. A woman might much easier remove her ring if her spouse leaves her rather than dies. One is a clean grief that can take time. The other is an amputation that has to be speedy to be survived. So that tan line and indentation on her finger means she has been abandoned and needed to make a swift change by removing her ring. Was it an improvement for her? He had to be a special ass to have treated her that way. She gasped as I finished and slipped two twenty-dollar bills in my hand.

Cold reading is very effective. If you're a little wrong, your client tells you. They shake their heads or look at you oddly. Then you nod, change it, and pretend that's exactly what you said in the first place. It's astonishing how much they want to remember you as being correct. The client will forget your first guess.

Cold reading is considered disreputable, but there is another side to that. A reader is asked to tell you what they see. Physical observation is part of what you see. Often other people would not see those clues any more than images in a tea cup. There is an art to collecting, curating and sharing those insights. Added to precognition, cold reading makes a tea leaf reader spectacularly effective. It's simply good observation. It's not exactly like you were caught raiding through people's trash cans before you read for them.

I was good at both cold reading and precognition. My psychology training had included a class in micro expressions that was very helpful.

No one hides their emotions that well, unless they mean to. Unless they are practiced and skilled liars whose lives depend on deep cover and deception. Then you have to ask why. What is the difference between a serial killer and an undercover cop? The differences are mostly in motive. At bottom, the ability to present an image that simply isn't so, is survival. And in practice, identical. The serial killer and the man sent to catch him are perilously close in their abilities and skills. The only difference between them is not the how, the where, or when, but the why. Which really only can be reached psychically.

Somehow, we readers all ignored the very relevant piece of Ms. Manners that suggested it was none of our business. After all, clients asked us to look for them. "Tell me my future. Tell me what's holding me back. Tell me the terrible fear I feel is my imagination. Tell me the thing I dream for most is almost here." And we did.

But how does the psychic gift work? Where does the information come from? If it were simple mind reading, it would mean your clients already know the information they're looking for. I've found that's only occasionally true.

If you buy that we are spiritual creatures, there is a spiritual world we also live on. The spiritual plain is more transparent than our daily world. It contains a whole network of information on a psychic plane that is vast and deeply confusing. Most people develop helpers to search that plain.

Entities on the astral plain don't wear name tags. Nor are they obliged to show you who or what they really are. They can and will disguise themselves. They can and will lie to you for endless reasons. Again, they may be benign help, they may be real help geared towards their goals. They may offer nothing but misinformation to your detriment. And no amount of vision will make you sure what you are looking at.

I sat at the table with a thirties-something couple. They were childless, charming, clearly rising stars. It was unusual to read a man and wife together except at a party. Men don't come for readings. But these two were from somewhere urban and cliquish and wanted the reading experience as part of their trip to Boston. She clung to him slightly. He had his eyes everywhere except on her.

So, I faced this couple absolutely blank, unable to pick up anything except that they had tea in their cups. As I sat there staring into her cup, I heard a voice over my shoulder.

"Do you need some help?" It was a savvy woman's voice, sophisticated, knowledgeable. I thought it might be laughing at me but it didn't literally. It just seemed to imply that my problem was small and silly if I only knew the answer. More to the point, it sounded like an older, smarter me. I closed my eyes to listen to her better.

I was so tired. My mind was so blank. I surrendered.

The voice continued in my ear. "They're not married yet." I looked over at hands. No rings. "Read them separately. It's essential."

I opened my eyes. "I really need to read you separately," I said. "It's just what we do." I motioned the young man over to my table and sat down to read his cup. I was still blank. I shut my eyes and let my new guide take over. Her voice sounded like I might when I was older and surer of myself. I followed her voice and the images she fed me.

"You are a self-made man." He nodded. There were a half dozen business sites in his cup. In each, he stood tall with his hand open, talking to someone and taking coins from them, while his other hand was behind his back. In each pose, his hidden hand held a weapon. There was a rim of coins around the cup edge. And a black crow at the bottom. By the handle was a shovel and a grave.

I got it. A confidence man. Possibly a murderer. Someone who was not what he seemed to be. Someone who at least killed people's dreams if not their souls. I flinched inwardly, but my guide continued. "Your businesses will flourish, but you need to know when to get out of them." No kidding. He needed to know when to run from the police.

He never said a word to me. He listened as if I were complimenting him on his excellent taste or talents. He pressed money in my hand, gave me a short bow and sat back at the other table as I read for his fiancé. He seemed pleased with my reading.

Again, I let the internal voice lead. I finished up and went to another table and sat with her cup in my hands. "You love him so much," my guide said. "Keep watch. He's not who you think he is. He's not who you want him to be. He will show you if you stay quiet. Then you can decide if that's what you want."

"He's my soul. My destiny," she gasped.

"Be careful of that," my guide said. "Or he may become that." "He's my true love," she continued, lost in her own fantasy.

I wanted to shake her loose for her own safety. This man would destroy all kinds of people in his path. It shouldn't start with a sweet woman just out of her teens, heartsick in love with him.

My guide continued. "Follow your heart. Your friends and family can't make decisions for you. Don't let them."

Then I broke loose from my guide and spoke. "If he scares you, when he scares you, flee. He's not who you think he is."

She stumbled from my table. "That's not a very nice thing to say," she mumbled in complaint.

My guide upbraided me. "What did you do? You didn't need to scare her!"

"I did," I insisted to my guide. "She needed to know. This man is false straight through."

"Much good it will do telling her," my guide snipped at me. I watched the couple stomp out of the tea room, furious at my honesty.

Rita arrived at my to my table shortly thereafter. "What are you doing?" she demanded.

"My readings," I said, knowing nothing could make what I did okay. "You enraged both of them, him by being banal, her by scaring her

spitless. What were you thinking, Marlene?"

Why was I unwilling to tell Rita I was listening to another voice? It was a voice that sounded just like me. That's an excuse. I knew perfectly well that the voice was something separate from myself.

I didn't want to subject this new voice to Rita's supervision. I needed it a bit too badly at the time. I needed a shortcut, an easier way. And I needed to be consistently right.

I nodded acceptance of Rita's assessment of my reading. She stomped back into her office. I could face her rage over bad form before I could for allowing an entity she wouldn't approve of.

The next day, the woman was back at the tea room, alone. "I need to know more!" she begged me.

Again, her cup held nothing I could read. I opened a door in my mind and my guide came through, silky and shiny, smooth in delivery and sounding almost like me.

"What do you need to know?" she asked the girl.

"Does he love me as much as I love him?" she asked first.

"This is not a person who love is all that important to. He's much more interested in other things. He's very interested in appearances.

Having you there supplies a certain appearance, and he very much wants that."

The girl blanched. "He doesn't love me?"

My guide continued, "It really isn't important to him. But it is to you. What do you want to do about that?" I felt my guide pointing to shapes in the tea cup with my hands, smiling with my face.

She burst into tears, sobbing into her hands. My guide repeated herself from the day before. "Don't let anyone tell you how to feel or what to do. Follow your heart."

That meant a whole new different thing today than it had yesterday.

Before the girl left, she'd changed her travel arrangements and was leaving before her man could know she was gone. Onto a new life where what she wanted was possible. Considering what we'd all seen of her man, perhaps that was better.

Rita had no problems with a client in tears. We saw clients cry on a regular basis. What she hadn't seen from me before was a client enraged. Just plain emotionally devastated was acceptable. I didn't tell Rita that I had not read for the girl. My guide had.

If I'd been able to see at all, I simply would have screamed at her to get out while she could. But I couldn't. And my much more urbane guide had arranged to get her out without the drama or potential danger. It was slick. It was graceful. Best of all, it got the job done.

I sat at the next table by a sweet fifties-something woman from Bedford who wanted to know whether her daughter would bring her grandchildren soon. I didn't have a clue, so my guide stepped in.

"Within a four, I'm sure." My guide patted her hand as tears seeped out of the woman's eyes. "That's either four months or four years. Both a girl and a boy. But keep the lines of communication open and don't push or she may restrict your time with them. In between there's a neighbor child, name begins with an M. Mary? Marion? Maybe Megan. She needs an extra grandmother. Go buy some cookies and befriend her. She'll need you." The woman left still crying but with a beatific smile on her face.

From then on, I listened for my guide, for that silky voice that knew how to negotiate muddy water and handle sticky surfaces. Who could fill the gaps when I couldn't. Sometimes I let her bring me the information I needed. Sometimes I let her handle whole readings. I relied on her more and more. She quietly took up a bigger and bigger place in my head. And I took it as gospel that she was a helper, honest, correct and kind, when my own abilities failed.

Woof

Woof

"My dogs are scared." Sandy's hand was shaking a bit as she picked up her tea cup. "Actually, my dogs are acting crazy." It might have been from cold, because the frost had settled the night before. But I didn't think it was. Sandy's skin was the color of beach sand, except for the raw red at her cheeks from the wind and cold. Her eyes were a light clear gray and her hair was three shades lighter than straw. She wore a rough pair of jeans, riding boots and a beige plaid shirt. Her usual pink aura was flaring red and brown, a signal of anger and distress.

Sandy's family had in the past bred race dogs. In another time, her father might have been master of the hunt for some British lord. Their kennel was famous for unbeatable greyhounds. Recently at her parent's death, she sold the farmstead and rented a small farmhouse near the Berkshire Hills, large enough for the six remaining dogs.

Most of the tea room people kept pets of some kind. But they weren't exactly pets. They tended to be either animal companions, partners of some kind, or avatars, an animal image of themselves. Rita kept a parrot named Methuselah who was psychic too, and would blurt out private things about people in the room that no parrot should have known. Maggie had a sweet hunting hound called Molly with one blue eye and one brown eye. Maggie claimed one eye was for what was here in the physical world and one eye was for looking around corners. Madam Marie kept a number of boas and other snakes in honor of her snake spirit guide. People without animals are often cut off from their own physicality and their spirituality. We are only large animals too, and we lose part of ourselves if when we lose the bond. I lived with a smoky gray cat named Echo who was surely more attentive and any lover I'd ever had.

Sandy's dogs were the center of her life. "What are the dogs doing?" I asked.

"They were up all-night pacing and whining. They can't sleep so I can't sleep. Did I tell you Cash has started to have seizures?" Cash was her oldest male. His health was always fragile.

"The others are just nervous and twitchy. They're not sleeping," she said as she pursed her her lips. That was past odd. Greyhounds sleep over half the day if you let them." I took her cup in one hand with my chopstick in the other. There was a huge cloud over the handle of cup, half way down from the rim. An owl was over the top right at the handle of her cup. And there were eyes peeking through the tea leaves, all around the edge.

"Trouble of some kind, Sandy, right at home. You're being constantly watched by someone. There's an owl overhead. In Indian symbolism would mean either danger or death."

"Then it's a good thing I'm not Indian," she said. "There's no one out there to watch me. I'm at least five miles away from a bottle of milk or a neighbor. There's just me and the dogs," she said. "But," she nodded with me, "I'll have my eyes open."

"I see hands reaching out to you, help from all sorts of different places." I read through the rest of her cup. It showed mostly her dogs and the farm. Small birds flying through the edges. That meant people visiting. But there was a storm cloud over the cup handle. Something had disturbed their quiet lives deeply. I didn't think it was over.

Sandy rose ramrod straight from years of riding English saddle, and gave me what might have been a tip of the hat if she'd been male and wearing one.

The hairs were up on the back of my neck. I couldn't see what was coming but I felt the electricity around her. My skin at the back of my neck itched against my sweater. I scribbled my home number on a piece of paper and tucked it into her hand. "Don't hesitate to call if I can help." I almost never offered that. But she left me really worried.

"Will do," she said and took the elevator down.

I counted Sandy more friend than client. We both had lost parents.

She knew I missed the freedom of country space and had invited me several times the small farm house she'd rented. It had felt like going home.

It was three in the morning several days later when I took her call. "Hello?" It was hard enough lift the phone, never mind speak through the right end of it. I couldn't connect her sounds to meanings. "What did you see ...?" It was Sandy, terrified and angry. I'd never heard her like this. "Did you tell me what you saw? You've got to tell me."

I always told people what I saw although I sometimes didn't elaborate. And it wouldn't help at this point to discuss it. "What happened?" I asked her.

She dropped the phone. I heard it clatter to the floor. A moment later she said, "Sorry about that. I'm really klutzy tonight. I'm at the vet." Had one of the dogs fallen ill? I wondered. Her normally stolid voice was full of panic.

"My dogs got into a fight. Three of them are pretty badly mauled." That was followed by dead silence. Because it was almost unthinkable.

I knew enough about greyhounds to know how unlikely that was.

Greyhounds didn't all get along, but they didn't normally fight. They just weren't wired that way. They were purposely bred not to be aggressive. "Okay," I said, "From the beginning."

"I turned the dogs out, left them to do their business. I heard them running and some barking and then I heard growls. Cash yelped, as if he were hurt. I ran to a lump of dogs in the yard savaging each other. I opened the gate and Harpo streamed straight in past me. He had blood running down his chest. I ran down the stairs to the yard where the other dogs were weaving in and out at each other. Billy was on the edges of all that. I grabbed Billy to the side, got a lead on him and tied him to a fence. Rogue and Ruby were circling each other with bristled backs, growling like wolves. There was blood down Ruby's neck where her ear was torn. She'd gotten a bite out of his haunch as well. I stepped between the two of them. If I hadn't had thick gloves I would be having stitches right now too. Rogue did his best to bite me. I wouldn't have ever thought it of him. I had to hit him to stop him." She started to sob. "Sadie had a torn ear. Cash and Billy hid behind the tool shed. I leashed them to different parts of the fence. When I got them inside, Harpo's chest was covered in blood, but none of it seemed to be his. We're here at the vets because Sadie, Rogue, and Ruby needed stitches. But I don't like the other dogs out there alone. Would you go out and see to them?'

"What do you think is there?" I asked.

"I don't know, but I've never had dogs do this. It was like an evil wind got into them."

"Can I get in? Is anything locked?" I'd been to her farm for a gentle fall day of riding and picking apples. It was unimaginable to think of her turn out as a blood-soaked fight pit.

"No. Gates are latched. Nothing really locked. Would you could go heck?"

A half hour later I drove past her pasture into the front driveway. I walked into the house. Three needle nosed hounds lifted heads from beds. Billy came over and greeted me by rubbing his nose on me. Cash looked up in acknowledgment, too exhausted to rise. Harpo, was in his crate with the door open, whining. I put my hand in for him to sniff. He backed to the far edge of the crate.

I checked food bowls and opened the freezer. As I had guessed, there were frozen shank bones, the ultimate dog pacifier. I passed those out. "There," I said. The dogs were completely absorbed in chewing. I slid outside the back to look at the turn out.

The ground was hard frozen. I could smell blood, shit and urine, all products of a dog fight. There was a trail of droplets up the back steps. I got a bowl of soapy water and a rag so that Sandy wouldn't deal with it in the morning. I rolled up the sleeves of my winter jacket and pulled my scarf around tighter.

I could hear the raspy screeches of a barn owl, as I scrubbed the stairs. At one point he took off, drifting on giant wings. I felt the owl spirit in myself stir, wishing I could fly with him. As I was quieter, I became more aware of night noises. Soft wind. A small chitter. Small creatures. Maybe rabbits or chipmunks.

I heard a muffled sound from the nearby woods. Someone was beating a drum. Not a large drum. Not a large sound. But it was persistently rhythmic. I went through the different night birds I knew that might make that sound. Nothing I could think of sounded like a drum in the night.

I wiped up the last of the blood, and flooded the steps with water to wash away the soap. I went in and found Harpo, Billy and Cash asleep with their bones under their paws. I went out with pet salt to make sure the steps didn't ice over. When I looked up the moon was half risen over the trees. It was hugely round. The drum beat started up again. I went through the back gate and walked in to the moonlit wood.

I followed the path, mostly covered with frosted leaves. The first dusting of snow still laced over dead branches and bramble. Most of the trees had gone bare. My boots felt unsteady under uneven ground. I walked around ten minutes hearing the drumming consistently ahead of me. I got out my cell phone and tried to call Sandy. There was no phone service in the woods.

I lost my footing over a patch of ice and slid, landing on one knee.

Out of the dark something swished over my head. Dark and enormous, it hissed, furious at me. Wings thundered up into the sky. I'd startled the owl in his hunting and he startled me. I wandered further.

I passed a clearing with logs that Sandy had set as a campfire. The circle of the moon was reflected in the slick iced puddle. Sitting on one of the logs was a young Native American boy, perhaps twelve years old. He wore only trousers and moccasins, with a necklace made of shells and teeth. His song echoed the beat of his drum. The owl rested on a branch over his head.

His song wasn't in English. I understood it instinctively, anyway. "Wolf, wolf, wolf, wolf, wolf. All wolves. My wolves. My pack. My wolves." He seemed not to see me. He began to elongate the o sounds in the word so that it took on a rooing quality. "Wooooolf."

I heard a branch break behind me. Now he shifted to the space behind me. But the child was a grown man. Same face, but muscular and tall. His blue-black hair hung loose around his shoulders. His smile was a showing of teeth. I smelled rancid grease in his hair. The man's nut- brown skin erupted with red swollen spots. He blazed strange warmth against the cold. He'd left the drum in the clearing and instead, his hand held a knife casually, as if to show it to me. He reached out and touched my forehead with it, not an attack but an acknowledgment. I didn't move. I couldn't. Hot sweat poured off my frozen skin.

"Wolf," he said, this time in English.

"I am not a wolf." I acknowledged myself human, not a spirit crossed between being a wolf and a god.

"No. No wolf." His voice had gone from deadly serious to a soft cackling. He shook his head. "Wolf," he said with his hands on his chest in explanation. It was a declaration of pride and power.

"You are the wolf," I acknowledged.

Sharp cold wind circled us. In the mist that rose around us, I saw the green glitter of eyes. I made out the shapes of a pack of wolves from gray to white. His body stretched like molten plastic and slumped from his human form. He drew up his hands and knees until they were short and under his hunched body. His mouth was a snarl of teeth. His pelt was coal black, with silver edging on his ears. There was a ridge of bristled hair down his back. I held myself motionless, but my heart was pounding. I thought I was scared of him as a man. Was this a threat display? Was he going to rush me? I thought of all the dog manners Sandy had tried to teach me. Don't run. Don't turn. Don't look in his eyes. I knew if I ran, he would chase me. So, the safest thing was to freeze in place and keep my breath steady. He was unlikely to attack me unless I ran. Or challenged him. Or reminded him how hungry he was. If he stormed after me, his pack would too. I purposefully looked away from his face as I put my hand out for him to smell me. Palm side up below chin height. All active displays of dog respect. He crept up slower to sniff my hand. I felt steaming breath on my palm.

Something rustled down the pathway. Billy the brindle greyhound, skittered up the path through the leaves. Sandy had told me that Billy knew how to open the gate to the wood path. Billy had gotten out and followed me. The wolf and I watched as Billy picked his way gently through the night woods. Billy was focused on me and the lead wolf. He didn't respond at all to the pack.

"Not wolf," I said, raising my chin. I'd claimed Billy as mine. "Part wolf." Well, that was true. As a dog, Billy was part wolf. The wolf head tilted slightly.

"Leave. Leave wolves to wolves."

I turned back to find the man, not a boy or wolf, farther away from me. His dark hair curtained half his face. Billy distracted me by putting his head into my outstretched hand. I looked away and back. There was a gust of wind that blew leaves into whirlwinds. I put my arm over my head to protect my eyes from the dust. Billy leaned into me for protection. The wind railed around us for a moment. And then stopped, leaving the forest silent. The mist and the pack evaporated. I saw a lone wolf shape, running into the night.

The clearing was cold and empty. No drum sound. No fire. Only the moon remained, shining overhead. Three owl feathers stood upright in places in the frozen grass. I gathered them up and put them in my pocket.

Billy and I walked carefully home, alert to every sound. But the woods seemed empty. The walk to the house was shorter than the walk from it. As I entered the warmth and light of the house, I heard an odd drumming of a different sort. Cash was lying on the floor shaking, with his eyes rolled up in his head. His feet were banging against the wall, his head battering the floor. Then the shaking stopped and he started to twitch in his seizure. His body was running an invisible race as he lay here. It was a doggy nightmare that Cash couldn't wake himself from. I tried putting a hand on him to soothe him. He snapped at me with his eyes shut. Harpo barked hysterically behind me, trying to get me to do something, anything.

I finally remembered seizure protocol. Make them safe. Make yourself safe. Get the sight-seers out. I placed a perimeter of rolled up blankets between Cash and the wall. Because there was nothing else to do for him but to wait, I backed away. Harpo was howling by now, and Billy was backed into a corner behind the couch. "Out," I said to the two of them, opened the gate, and they fled out the door.

I went back and watched Cash come out of his fit. He stopped shaking. Then he began to pant heavily for around a minute. His eyes finally slid open. He lay exhausted.

I pulled his water bowl over to him. He was back with us. He stood shakily on his legs, trying to figure out where he was.

I opened the door for the other dogs, waiting at the screen. After a lot of exploratory sniffing, they lay down with a pile of dog biscuits each.

I sat down to the phone to ask John to find anyone who knew more about Indian spirits than I.

Sandy called me at dawn. Sadie was out of surgery. Rogue and Ruby, sporting vet wrapped bandages, were ready to come home.

"I don't think so, Sandy. Not a good idea yet." I told her as gently as I can. "You've got a real problem here. Cash had another seizure but he seems to be OK. But there's something going on I don't understand. Do you have a place where you could board your dogs?"

Jacob, her neighbor did. He was a gentleman farmer who played at raising vegetables on the weekend and worked on Wall Street professionally. His wife offered a warm space in the barn.

I had a pot of coffee hot and ready when Sandy came through the door. We sat down to steaming cups at the table.

"An Indian?" she said. She clearly didn't believe me. I didn't believe

me.

"An Indian." I gave an ambivalent nod.

"There are no Indians here. No Indian people left." Sandy said. "I didn't say it was a person." I shrugged.

"Was it a ghost?" She asked as her eyes went wider.

"Ghosts don't turn into animals. Not usually. And they usually don't have small pox." I answered. I warmed my hands around my cup.

"Small pox?" Sandy yelped. Her eye's bugged out just a bit." "I'm not sure, but he had raw-red bumps that looked like a skin

infection. Maybe small pox, maybe chicken pox. They were equally deadly for Indians," I said.

"Tell me it's a joke." She sipped her coffee and gave me a desperate wink.

"I wish, I wish I wish," I said, shaking my head no.

Her calm broke. She leaned forward, hands pressed against the table. She wasn't frightened. She was furious. "What do I DO?" she asked me. Who was I to say? She had a mystical Indian spirit summoning wolves around her camp fire. I'd already called Rita and Maggie. Neither had a clue. I took a few minutes to search online for a local listing for New England shamans. Reasonably enough, there was no listing. I was waiting for John to find me a source.

We got the dogs ready to transport. They were each fitted into a harness and a coat. She'd taken Rogue and Ruby straight to the farm from the vet. Sadie was still at the clinic. The vet wanted her there for observation. The hatchback was large enough for two dogs at a time. She transported Cash and Harpo next. The big dogs made the leap into the cargo hold in one bound. Cash was worn-looking but he was mobile. I was to take Billy. When Billy came to through the door, I had his lead ready to secure him. He had a moment of panic. He bolted past me instead. He slammed through the gate and the door banged open. He was at a full run. "Billy!"

Sandy screamed. Come back here." I'm not sure he could have heard her. Billy in his racing days clocked forty-five miles an hour on the track. Age hadn't slowed him that much. We both bolted after him, but in the woods, he was as invisible as a deer. His gold brindle coat blended perfectly with the brush. Within seconds he was out of sight.

Sandy barked orders at me. "Do you remember where the wood ends, by the road in back?" she asked. I did.

"Drive there. Now. Get out and start walking the path back to here. He may run for the path." She threw a leash around my neck. I'd need it if I found him. She was already on her phone. The greyhound group within the area had a search team that regularly looked for lost dogs. She was spitting out directions at them as she shooed me toward the car.

I drove around the forest edge to the end of the path. There was a gate there as well, that led into the woods. I walked the path slowly, watching the sky go pink and then brighten to a light blue gray, scanning the brush for the dog, listening for the sound of breaking branches, crackling ice and twigs. Nothing. By the clearing I was met by three other greyhound people Sandy had called for help, trampling the woods hunting for Billy. They walked through the woods rather than down the path. I turned and walked with them in a grid against the brush. Billy was nowhere. In the silent dawn, I went back to the house and began to pack up dog beds, and dog food for the other dogs. By then the rescue team was warming themselves over coffee. They'd tramped the woods through to the border to no avail.

Mary, who led the group, started to ask me about what Billy was like and what he'd do. I turned to Sandy. I had no idea.

"Is he a shy?" she asked. "A spook? Has he run away before? Is he wearing a coat? Do you walk him on a particular path? Has he eaten?" All of that went into their records for the next wave of searchers who would be there in two hours. They walked the grid one more time before they took a break. Still nothing. The freeze made it critical. Greyhounds can't survive in the cold.

We drove the dogs over two miles to the neighbor's farm. His wife helped us get the dogs into stalls.

"You stay here for a day or two and let me figure some things out." I told

Sandy.

John called me. "I've made a phone call to the closest Indian tribe, the Pequots. I called and made and appointment with Dr. Swift, who is their top anthropologist."

I thanked John, got in the car and drove to the reservation. When I arrived at the museum there, I asked for Doctor Swift.

I didn't tell the woman at the desk I had a wolf spirit I was trying to eal with in the back forty. I said I was curious about the history of the land in that area. I didn't exactly need a historic doctorate. I needed a shaman who could speak to wolves.

"Yes," the woman typing at the desk told me without looking up at me. "Dr. Swift is expecting you." I found myself ushered into a book- crammed room. A craggy, thick-waisted woman with close cropped gray hair focused on her computer screen. Her skin was copper brown and wrinkled like a paper bag. She might have been 60. She wore a plain black knit shirt and jeans. Her only Indian adornment was a necklace of cowrie shells. And one silver feather earring.

Without looking at me or turning she asked, "Are you going back to college?" It was almost an accusation. Then her head swiveled to face me.

I was more than a bit taken back. "At some time. I hope."

"Was your great-great-grandfather Arapaho? Navaho? Chippewa?" she said. She swiveled her chair around looking directly at me. "No?" She said. "Then why are you here? I can't cure your cancer. I can't help you see your spirit guide. I can't bring you to the sacred buffalo. Why are you here?" She was not smiling. She was showing her teeth.

"I am so sorry," I backed up, "to disturb you. I was hoping I could ask if there were Indian history connected with a farm my friend is staying at. We wondered if it might be an Indian grave yard."

"We've been here for thousands of years. Go throw a stone any direction and you'll hit an Indian graveyard. We're buried all over the place." She turned her chair back to her computer as if she were dismissing me. "I can show you the local white graveyard if you want."

"I meant no disrespect."

"You're not here for a college course? You are not a historian?" She asked. "Or an anthropologist? Or a social worker?"

"No", I confessed, "except by accident. I'm a tea leaf reader." "Do you want me to show you how to call down the power of the

moon? How to collect moss for menstrual blood? How to cook and kill a weasel?" She was laughing at me. Responding in kind wouldn't buy me anything.

"Ah, no. I want to know how to talk to an Indian Spirit.

Respectfully."

"You didn't try just screaming into the woods?"

"I didn't think it would help. Although it crossed my mind." I answered her.

She turned back towards me. "'Don't want to learn the mysteries?

Find your totem the Great Brown Bear?"

"Not so much. I want to make peace with a spirit that's on my friend's farm."

I placed the three owl feathers in front of her.

That opened her eyes wider. She started a deep belly laugh. "OK, white lady. We regularly get white ladies who want to play

Indian. It's like teaching a pig to dance. So tell me a story. Where are the feathers from?"

I started with Sandy's phone call. The dog attack. The walk in the wood. And the angry spirit that turned from boy to man to wolf and back again.

She listened without looking at me. She waited until I was done, raised one eyebrow and gave me a hard smile.

"What did you do after you got back to the house?"

"One of the dogs had a seizure. I took care of him. I waited for Sandy to come back. We got the dogs there into the car and out of there. Except for one dog that ran away. We're still trying to find him. We took her animals to another place to stay. But I can't help but think Sandy or I really made something mad. If I have, I don't even know how to make amends."

"Is this woman stupid enough to think she owns this land?" "Actually she's renting."

"So she needn't stay there."

"No. And I can't imagine her wanting to. She just wants to get her stuff, find her dog and leave." Then I spoke my own question. "Why didn't the spirit hurt me? Why didn't he hurt Billy?"

"Did you mean the man harm?"

"I actually don't think there's any way I could do him harm." I thought of the wolf/man with knives that turned to teeth.

"You'd be wrong about that" she said. "You said he was covered in red boils."

"Is that a past memory of small pox? Is he a ghost?"

"You know about that? It's not history, Marlene. That's now. Right now. Does your friend need to go back to the house?

"We've got to find the lost dog. Sandy will need to pack and move. I was hoping I could apologize enough to make it safe for her to do that."

She nodded, either with understanding or grudging approval. It was hard to know which. "You need to know this is not a person. This is not a ghost. It's not exactly an Indian spirit. It's a spirit of the land there. It projects itself as a wolf, an owl or as the wind, but that is not its nature.

That is its disguise."

"Why did it show me the boils on his arm?" I asked her.

"The land is sick. He's furious because the land is sick and all of his existence is there. He is the land. He's been defiled. And he cannot leave."

"Can I fix this?" I studied her face anxiously.

"Don't be silly, child. Congress couldn't fix this. The town council wouldn't be bothered to fix this. Wall Street won't try, although they should. Twenty-five medicine men in a row chanting from now to next Tuesday couldn't fix this. But good intention goes a long way. You're stupid as shit, but that's just Wôpáyuw people in general."

In spite of the fact that she was insulting, I liked her. Everything she thought just bubbled directly out of her mouth. She had some hard notions about white people, but it wasn't personal. It certainly wasn't directed at me.

"Is this about something toxic on the land." I asked her. "You're not as stupid as most white people, I guess." she said to

herself.

"Can we report it? Help clean it? Call in an agency?"

"All that's been done. It didn't do much then. I don't think it will do a thing now. Do you wish to make apologies?"

"I want my friend and her animals safe. She wasn't trying to do any harm."

Her eyebrows gathered in. "Actually, neither was he, I think. But tell me this. Is this who you are? What you do? Forgive me, but you're not much of a warrior."

"I'm not one. Mostly I just see glimpses of things and try to understand. If I can put it right, I do. Most things correct themselves if we can see what's going on.

She raised her eyebrows. "So you are a person of power?"

"I'm a person who sees further than most people. Sometimes. Mostly it's scary as shit. I don't know that that's power." I felt especially dumb trying to explain the reading gift to this woman.

"Do you have a teacher?" she asked.

"Everyone in the tea room teaches me a little," I said.

She rolled her eyes. "White people really are stupid. But I think I can get you through this."

She began to pack up things and place them in a worn knapsack: a small drum, a turtle rattle, a bundle of cloth that smelled of dry earth and hay, and a bundle of sage. She got out a pouch of tobacco and made another cloth bundle with that.

"Okay, Wôpáyuw, are, you ready to go talk to an elemental?"

"My name is Mirella." I tried to give just my tea room name. I didn't know how to take this very sure, very angry woman.

"No it's not." She wasn't going to let me get away with that.

"I was born Marlene." I admitted. "What does Wôpáyuw mean?" "It means white girl. You better call me Liz. It's going to be a long

night." And she held her hand out to me. "Are you the tribe shaman?" I asked.

"We don't have shamans. We have elders. I have a PhD from Brown in anthropology, just so I can chase out the over-curious college crowd.

White people can't be Indian. Any more than we can really be white." She shook her head in disgust

I thought about what her PhD had cost her in time and effort and did the math. She'd come to this through a gauntlet of prejudice against her sex as well as her tribe. She had traveled through all the professional traps, pitfalls and barriers to be Dr. Swift.

"Actually," she answered the question I didn't ask, "My tribe would have let me lead, centuries ago. Our men only lead in war time. Women led in peace." With that she put on a beige parka and snow boots.

"Are you dressed for a cold night?" she asked me. I'd come directly from Sandy's farm, but I'd raided her winter wear. She looked approvingly at my extra thick gloves and the hideous but warm hat with braids coming off it.

"Should Sandy know?" I asked her.

"Let her know after we're done," she said. "I'm not sure how this will work out."

"By the way, what is an elemental?" I asked. I really hadn't run into the term before.

"It's a nature spirit. Remember that old saying about not messing with Mother Nature? You don't mess with elementals."

"Would this thing hurt you?"

Liz answered, "It can, if it's mad enough, tear up the territory in fifty- mile swaths. If it hurts you and I, it's just an accidental afterthought."

"Why are you helping me? I know you don't like white people." "You are not who I'm helping. The land has cried out in pain and I

will do what I can."

It was just before twilight when we pulled past Sandy's paddock. The dog searchers had gone. There was a note on the door that Sandy was settling in the other dogs and would be back to look for Billy again in a little while. I showed Liz where the dogs had fought. I asked her, "Did I do something wrong when I cleaned the steps?"

"That wouldn't make a difference one way or another. At this point the spirit is not just mad. It's not just angry. It's crazed. Sometimes it loses its reason. And it drives other things mad in its path."

I asked Liz if she knew anything about the history of the farm. "Was there some kind of massacre here or something else bad?"

"Not that I know of in olden days, she said. "No particular tribe claimed that land but they probably fought over it. They fought over everywhere. But the farm has been involved in a lawsuit about dumping. The old farmer rented out a chunk of the area near the woods as a military dump site after World War II. It was so remote that no one thought it would be a problem. No one knows exactly what went into it but there have been a lot of cancer deaths in the nearby towns. For sure, half the motor pool waste ended up there. We know there's motor oil all over it. There was some speculation about experimental chemicals as well. There's been several court actions but the local governments have stalled any action. No one wants the bill or the blame." I showed Liz the path and the campfire. I kept looking for a brindle dog as we shuffled through the brush. There was no sign of Billy.

Liz brought a small drum along with her. She settled by the camp circle, shaved some kindling and lit a match. Unlike Sandy and I, Liz had a lifetime of practice at fires. First it smoked, then it flared. She added bigger twigs and then a couple of logs. She threw the bundle of sage on the pyre.

The smoke stung my eyes and the sudden heat made me dizzy. I sat for a while and listened to her tap her drum and chant tunelessly. My eyes slid shut and I was asleep.

I was on my side. I sensed that the wolf was there over me. Watching me. Sniffing me. I could feel its hot breath. It smelled dog-like but also like something rotting. I rolled over onto my back. Now the wolf was across the sky as a cloud over us. The old woman kept up her chant. I slid deeper into sleep. Then I jerked awake to see the Indian boy speaking with Liz. Billy was by the fire with them. The Indian was feeding Billy dried meat out of a pouch.

"She's an idiot, grandfather, but she can't help being white." Liz said.

He snorted in agreement. "Why did she risk coming back here?" He slipped another morsel to Billy.

"She did it for her friend. And for the dogs. They're worried sick about this boy." She scratched Billy's ears. "And they wouldn't leave him here. They're not that kind of white folk. This girl wants them to be able to leave in safety. She knew they had offended you. She wanted to apologize. Why did you attack her?"

"Had nothing to do with her. I touched her forehead with my knife so she'd know I could have killed her had I wanted to. But this striped dog is an animal of great courage. He knew what I was and that I was there. And he refused to let her face me alone. Not all wolves have the heart of a wolf. He does. When I called him to run with us, he did. But he misses his people. He needs to be home." He smiled at Billy's warm grin. Billy leaned up against the boy.

I was awake enough. Liz heard me and beckoned me to rise and come near the fire. Billy danced over to me and leaned into me. I grabbed his harness, almost by instinct. I did an awkward bow in front of the Indian boy. Liz handed me a bundle of tobacco. "For you, elder," I said, as she had taught me. As I handed it to him, he slid into the older man, with a smile on his face that was no longer cruel. I looked away, speaking to him in respect as Liz had shown me. "I am terribly sorry we troubled you." Then I laid the three owl feathers in his hand.

He peeled back a part of my mind. I was held in place in the vision. He showed me the dumping ground the farm had used for the last fifty years. There was the usual farm trash, tires and kitchen waste, broken down fencing and household junk. But there was a slick puddle of what looked like motor oil seeping through the soil. He showed me drainage pipes not far from the woods. I could feel his repulsion, and the internal sickening creeping through his body. "You did not do this yourself," the Indian said. "Your friend did not do this. But your kind does."

"Does this harm you, elder?"

"It would harm a stone." He laughed at me sadly.

"My friend, with the horses and dogs, she meant you no harm. She simply wants to leave without her animals being further hurt."

There was something about the way he was holding himself. Some of the pain and the madness had drained off. I felt nerveless. I sunk down to the logs again and drifted into sleep like deep clouds.

The moon was high and thin when Liz shook me awake. Sandy was standing over me, Billy's harness in her hand. She'd stumbled through the night and found Liz, Billy and I by the fire.

Who was the boy, I saw?" she asked.

"What boy?" I said, but I was pretty sure I knew.

Sandy described him. "He was about eight or nine. He was in jeans and a parka. I tried to talk to him but he ran past me and whacked me in the ass."

Liz nodded. "Counting coup. He'll feel much better for having counted coup."

"Which includes whacking my ass? "Sandy said. "Actually", I said, "I think it does."

"Are you hurt or is it just your dignity?" Liz asked her. "Dignity mostly. Is that our Indian?" Sandy asked.

Liz said, "Not exactly. But I believe you'll find all this sorted out after this."

"How did you find Billy?" Sandy asked me. He was leaning into her as she was rubbing him all over, ask if to check for wounds or frostbite. Actually, the elemental had kept him quite safe.

"He found us." I said, simplifying it. I could tell her the full story when we were out of the cold. The fire was nothing but cooling coals. I thought I heard owl wings overhead.

"Come now." Liz said as she pulled me to my feet." We've done what we can."

I rolled my back muscles to pull myself together. I was stiff from sleeping on the ground. We hiked past the house and I drove Liz back to the center where her car was. Sandy loaded Billy into the hatchback and drove off to the neighbor's farm.

"He's mollified," Liz said. "He's still in pain but he knows it'snot the fault of the people who are there now. He's a bit embarrassed. He hates it when the madness takes him. Your friend should be able to leavewithout repercussion."

I hadn't the words to thank her. I stumbled through my gratitude. "You're a stupid white lady. I was afraid you'd make it worse." Then she said. "There's much to be said for a good heart." She handed me the three owl feathers."

"For Sandy?" I asked her.

"For you, Wôpáyuw. Should you ever have a need." I was so stunned I forgot to ask Liz what she meant. Or what it might buy me. I drove her back to the center and her car. She walked silently even on pavement.

Sandy found another farm near the woods with room for her dogs. Sadie snuffled in the soft dirt floor of the barn. The other dogs licked wounds and slept, the storm over. When Sandy moved to another farm nearby, there were no sleepless nights or drums in the dark.

Sometimes Sandy told me she thought she saw the shadow of a black wolf following her at a distance when she walked dogs through woods. "It's weird you know." Sandy told me. "I can see it but it never comes really close. And the dogs aren't afraid. If they're not scared, I'm not either."

Sandy didn't know what it meant. But I did. That wasn't a threat. It was an honor guard. For the wolves had taken Billy as their own. Billy was walking with his pack.

The Princess in the Tower

The Princess in the Tower

The bird woman was perhaps in her 70's. I saw her daily, seated by the pond in Boston Gardens. She'd sit at the bench with a stone wall behind it. She'd cast a circle of breadcrumbs like snow around her on the flagstones in front. The pigeons pecked and shoved each other in competition for their breakfast. Then one by one they rose, turned with the wind and circled overhead. The birds looked like leaves in the wind, rising rather than falling. Pigeons soared over her on her bench in formation, like miniature planes, and would land one by one back down to the circle of crumbs.

She was plain but beautifully groomed. Her hair was a crown of steel- gray braids piled up into an elaborate bun. Her skin was still a soft peach, even with its wrinkles. Her tooled leather purse and her lacquered cane were almost one of a kind art pieces. Her coat was tailored cashmere. She wore sensible lace-up shoes, that were terribly expensive but old-lady ugly. She never spoke to anyone. But we often passed each other walking through the Commons. She'd unbend to glance at me and nod crisply. I would nod back. As winter days started to soften into spring, we passed each other more often in the park. Occasionally we would smile at each other in the exchange of nods. Once when I was walking by she signaled me to stop. Then she pointed upward to the birds above her. As I paused, she told me, "It's the cardinals. They're mating. I don't want them disturbed." She shushed me, one finger to her lips.

I tiptoed past her. I didn't want them disturbed either.

We never would have had a conversation if I hadn't sprained my ankle. I jogged past her bench and heard my joint pop as my muscles stretched past where they belonged. I fell like a stone on dried sod.

I heard delicate footsteps, as if she herself was a bird. She was leaning over me. "Good heavens, child, are you all right?" she said in a crisp voice. She was someone used to giving orders.

"I will be, I'm sure," I muttered. I was still a bit stunned. My ankle throbbed, an impressive purple already.

She helped me to her bench. Then she tapped a button on a security device at her throat. It was three or four minutes before a man in his later fifties came rushing down the path towards her. "Are you all right, Mrs. Pierce? I'd have been here sooner, Ma'am, if I hadn't had trouble parking. Is everything okay?"

"I'm perfectly fine, Alfred, but my friend is not," she said.

"No, no, no. Please don't put yourself out for me," I said. "I'll just call my roommate and she'll get me home." Alfred already had an arm around me, pulling me up.

"Can she do that immediately?" she said. She steadied me on the other side.

"Ah, probably not," I acknowledged. Jane's flight wasn't due in until afternoon. It might well take an hour or two to get here from the airport. It wasn't like I didn't need the help or like Jane would get to me immediately.

"Then what good is that?" said my rescuer. "Alfred, help her in the car." He grabbed one arm and placed on the bench. Alfred tucked me into the front of an early 1970s Bentley. The bird woman took her seat in the back. "Let me introduce myself," She said. "My name is Mildred Pierce. This is Alfred, my driver." When Alfred tipped his hat in acknowledgment, I could see the port wine birthmark that stained his face by his left eye.

"My name is Marlene," I said, as the car bobbled up the cobblestone road.

So, I allowed them to kidnap me. Twenty minutes later I was sitting in her parlor with my foot iced and elevated. Alfred had made tea for us both. We were staring at each other over steaming tea cups.

"I'm the last of the Bostonian Pierces since my brother-in-law died," she said. Her Beam Street brownstone was in impeccable Victoriana taste. There were curio cabinets full of china and softly faded oriental rugs on the floor. There was a mild musty smell, like the room needed dusting.

Books were on every surface. A print of Audubon's *Night Heron* hung over her couch. "We ladies need to look after each other. Forgive me," she said. "I don't use this room often. I don't entertain as much as I used to."

Mildred should have been old and stodgy but she wasn't. She was clearly having too much fun. "How long have you been bird watching?" I asked her.

"Since I was three, I believe. My nanny took me out to the common or garden to see the birds every day. I might have gotten older, but they're still hungry. Poor things haven't anything much to eat in the winter. Of course, they like bread crumbs in the summer too, so I stop and bring them their lunch." I nodded my approval. "Of course, I don't just feed them. I keep a birding journal and I photo them on good days." She patted her pocket and pulled out a small digital camera.

"That's a neat camera," I said. I was wondering how someone her age had learned to use it.

"My grandnephew, Neville, got a more sophisticated one for his birthday, and he gave me this. It's perfect for my purposes," She said. "It even has a zoom. Would you like to see my pictures?" She turned the camera on and the screen was filled with shot after shot, not only of her pigeons, but of most of the birds in Boston. She had photographed the secret life of birds. She must have spent most of her time waiting and watching them. In response, the birds had showed her everything.

"And how is that ankle?" she asked me.

I looked down at my swollen foot. "Properly chilled, I believe. Thank you for coming to my rescue."

It was an hour later when the Jane rang her bell. Alfred and Jane helped me totter to the car. I went home to another ice pack and a handful of aspirin.

After that I often stopped to talk to Mildred at the park. Sometimes a gangly dark-haired boy joined her taking pictures. Neville, her grandnephew, had the serious self-importance of a twelve-year-old. He kept up a steady patter of camera advice, which she clearly but kindly ignored. He had a more sophisticated camera. But he didn't have her eye. He mostly shot selfies for Instagram. Her photos were an astonishing window into the world of birds.

I started to bring her a coffee when I bought one for myself. We chatted regularly, mostly about the birds but somewhat about our lives. She was mildly scandalized that I read tea leaves. But it was clear she thought a little scandal would be fun. I found her witty and wry, unlike anyone her age I'd ever met. She told me about her girlhood.

"I was so sheltered," she said. "My parents made most of my life decisions. I attended finishing school, instead of a proper college. I'd wanted to be a scientist. When I told my parents that, Mother took me shopping for more gowns. She was always trying to seduce me with fashion. My father bought me a new hunter."

"A hunter?" I asked. I had visions of a guy stalking the commons with a rifle.

"A beautiful dappled grey mare called Mary Gray. Of course, I called her Mary." Her eyes smiled at the memory. "She could almost fly."

"I can't see you hunting," I said. Mildred so loved nature. I had trouble imagining her squishing a bug.

"Hunting back then wasn't about hunting. There was a fox we were chasing, and what happened to the beast was truly dreadful. But we ladies went to ride our horses through the wood, and chat with young gentlemen. I believe that was what my father had in mind. After I refused to marry the man he wanted me to, I never got to go out. My father refused to let me out of the house. He particularly banned museum visits and teas. Too many educated women I might talk with. He always said education ruined a girl for life."

I shook my head. "He sounds like a martinet."

Mildred smiled. "He was like everyone's father at that time.

Controlled and controlling. It didn't work well for his health or his business decisions. It's not surprising it didn't work for me either. He liked me best in the tower. It was like he'd stored me away for safekeeping."

So much of her life had rushed by while she sat, locked in her father's tower. In one way, she was used to that. She would live in the tower within herself, even now when she could leave her father's tower at will. Her habits had made it her cell.

"But that led me to my birds," she said. "You can see the brownstone sits near the Charles River and my room made a perfect observation post. I've surveyed the birds watching them come and go. I could observe their lives, even when I couldn't live my own. I've watched generations mate, nest and fly. You know they come back to the same nesting place each year. The birds are my family. They're certainly more fun than Neville."

She pointed up to a camera in her curio case. "This was my first camera." It was a battered old brownie, sitting on her shelf, kept like a childhood toy, too precious to give up, even if you don't intend to use it again.

I thought about her controlling father. Surely, he wouldn't have bought her a camera. I'm not sure Mildred ever handled money as a girl. "Where did you get it?"

"It was a gift." She smiled her secret smile. And poured more tea.

We still weren't out of frost, but spring showed signs that it might come around. At least the snow was gone. As we sat on her bench, I thought I saw a young man across the park watching us. He stood stock still, too far away to get a look at. All his attention focused on Mildred, on that bench. Although he carried an older box camera on a tripod, he didn't take pictures or fiddle with his camera. He wore a lightweight gray suit with a vest, no coat, and a fedora.

He made me nervous. At first, I thought it might be Neville playing dress up. But the man was too old for that. And Neville would have died of embarrassment, before he dressed like that. This man was maybe in his early twenties. He was almost as thin as his tripod.

I wasn't worried for myself, but I was concerned that someone might be stalking Mildred. It did look that way. He came closer day by day. He didn't slink around or try to hide. But she never acknowledged him, even when she saw me staring straight at him. He stood perhaps thirty yards away, above us on the bridge. I didn't want to alarm her. But I decided to stop to his game.

I excused myself from Mildred and walked up over the bridge in his general direction. He casually walked past me. He was wearing that odd suit, and hat, with his camera and tripod over his shoulder. I whirled around and followed him. As I walked towards him he was receding, not in motion, just in space. I couldn't get close. Mildred wasn't on her bench anymore. She'd gone home early because of the rain. As I looked around for her I saw him back up on the stone bridge above me. The mist came up thick from the river. When I got to the bridge he was gone.

The next day was light rain and wind. I went through the park to the coffee stand. On my way back, I saw the same hat bobbing in front of me in the mist. He effortlessly sped up. He was still walking but further in front of me. As I came behind him I was losing ground. He faded in and out of the mist. He went past the bridge wall and I lost him. I began to limp. When I past the wall, I saw him standing behind me. As I whirled around, there was a series of blinding flashes from his camera. As I stood there, he picked up the tripod and whirled it around his head like a baseball bat. He slammed me with it. I felt it go through me but there was no contact. An energy wave slid into me, through me, out of me. Then he and his camera were gone.

I followed the path back to the tea room. I slipped off my rain coat and looked in the mirror to tidy my frizzed hair.

"Rita," I asked, "Is the commons haunted?"

Rita laughed at me. "Okay. Who'd you see? The Hessian soldier? The fishwife? People see them all the time. Benjamin Franklin too."

"Have you?" I asked her outright.

"Well, not all of them," she acknowledged. "The fishwife chased me once through the commons. But I personally think the Hessian is a joke. Franklin didn't hang out in this area of Boston, even in his day. I doubt he's here now."

"I'm not joking," I said. "I'm serious. I saw a photographer ghost."
"Photographer like the paparazzi?" Rita asked me.

"No. More like Ansel Adams, a 1940s shutterbug. He hit me with his camera. It swished right through me. I wasn't hurt but I am offended. I'm usually good at dealing with ghosts." The whole episode did make me feel incompetent.

"Ah, that," Rita said, "to my knowledge, is new. Where did you see him?"

"Over by the bridge wall. He was stalking this old lady." I bit my lip in contemplation.

"Well," Rita said, "Who is the lady in question?"

"Mildred Pierce, the older woman who rescued me when I sprained my ankle."

"One of those Pierces?" Rita gave me a sharp look. "Don't mess with the Boston Brahmins. They're a whole other class and they offend easily." Rita shook her head.

"She's a friend," I said.

"They don't keep ordinary people as friends," Rita said. "And the Old Bostonian families tend to deal with nuisances pretty harshly. Don't make yourself into one. As for the Commons, watch yourself. The Commons is old. No one knows what all is out there."

The next day, the sun was wan but present. I sat with Mildred an hour before the tea room opened, and watched her birds with her. The photographer stared at us from the bridge again. He held my gaze. I couldn't help but stare.

Mildred followed my eyes. But she couldn't see him. "What are you looking at, child?"

I would not frighten her. I wouldn't let anyone frighten her. "Thought I saw a blue bird," I said.

Mildred was, in her own way, helplessly trusting. But she wasn't dumb. "What is it really?"

"Just a guy taking pictures." "Of what?" she asked.

"Hard to know." I could guess. Should I tell her, she had a stalker? I had to know who he was and what he was doing. First, I asked

Alfred. Alfred never saw the man. "I watch her all the time she's out, you know. Poor old lady. Anyone could take advantage. I make sure I know of everyone who approaches her," he said. "But don't tell on me. She hates fuss." I believed him.

The next time the photographer appeared, I decided to confront him. I said nothing to her. I made my goodbyes and walked off as if I were off to the tea room. But I circled back to where he was. Again, he led me in a chase. I followed him around the park until I was out of breath and flung myself on a bench to catch up. When I looked up, he was sitting next to me. "Well, this has been embarrassing, hasn't it?" he said. He shook his head ruefully.

"Do you usually hit people with your tripod?" I asked him. "I really never hit anyone before. You scared me."

"I scared you," I laughed. "You're a ghost. You're supposed to be professionally scary."

"You scared me because you see me. No one ever sees me," he said in a monotone voice.

"You don't have to worry about that. I also see rainbows and sunshine, but only when they're there."

"You're not afraid of me?" A tear rolled down his ghostly cheek. I'd let him down. If you can't be seen as a ghost, it has to be discouraging.

I tried to explain to him, "Ghosts are just people who happen to be dead. Most people are kindly. Most ghosts are too, unless they're angry or scared. Like people. So when I see ghosts, I see people like everyone else." "You're sort of different." He was beginning to get this.

"Not so you need to worry about me. I see you. But I'm not going to do something to you. No exorcisms, no Bible verses, no holy water. Not if you don't bother people."

"I'm so sorry," he said, almost like a reflex. Something he said all the time because it was expected of him, whether he'd done anything wrong or not.

I laughed. "Well, if you're apologizing, I'll have to do so too. I was afraid you were stalking Mildred. She's a dear friend of mine."

"Miss Downing," he corrected me.

"Was that her name before her marriage?" I asked him. "It was her name when I knew her," he said sadly.

"Is she a friend of yours as well?" I asked.

He hung his head and nodded yes at the same time.

"She doesn't see you, does she?" I asked him. That was the fount of this pain.

"No," he said firmly. "It was long ago. I don't know if she would want to see me. But I've seen her walk through the gardens, and I've watched for her. She has such a lovely face."

It was odd for this twenty-something man to be smitten with an eighty-year-old lady. But he was a ghost. It had been a long time since anyone had worn a fedora like his. She had been twenty something herself at one point, I reminded myself.

"Your name is?" I asked him.

"Reuben Levi," he said, looking away from me. He looked down on the ground. "Miss Downing is a terribly practical girl," he said. "She won't see a ghost. She won't see me. I've tried that several times. It's embarrassing." He hung his head. "It's too depressing."

I could see how that would work. "Are you looking after her?" I asked him.

"Always," he said, and his smile was the last part of him to disappear.

I knew then I didn't have to worry about Reuben.

But I'd begun to worry about Mildred. There were a couple of rainy wet days where she skipped the park. It was sensible but it was not something she did often. When she came back she had a light cough. It didn't seem to clear anything for her and it didn't go away. She sat more on her bench and moved less among the birds.

One wet day when she was missing, I took her coffee to her house, just to check on her. Alfred led me up to the study. She was there in a window seat, with her camera, quietly shooting some wrens in their private moments. She looked up at me.

"Oh, my goodness!" She said. "I didn't send you chasing after me, did I?"

"I missed your smiling face. And I already had bought you coffee." I handed her the lukewarm cup.

"Bless you, child." It might be lukewarm and it might be bitter. But it was a love gift, and she knew it.

She walked me to the couch and we sat together, her sipping the cooling liquid.

"When did you learn to be a photographer?" I asked her.

"Am I a photographer?" she asked me. "It's a hobby, not my job." "But you're good at it," I said.

"Oh, I learned years ago." She said. "My parents hired a man to take photos of us for my brother's wedding. He was kind enough to give me his old brownie camera and show me how to use it."

"How is it you've kept up with the technology?" I asked her. I was awed at the fact that she'd taken so well to a digital camera.

"It's all good, as Neville says. It's so nice not to wait to develop film anymore. Neville showed me a computer program where you put in the picture and push a button, and your picture is perfect. Well, almost perfect. I love not running out of film." She patted her little camera. It pulled in its lens and shut itself down.

"But you still keep the brownie?" I asked her.

"It was a gift. It was part of a magic spring," she said. "I was 17. I was supposed to marry in a year or two. They selected my cousin Wilfred for me. It didn't matter that he smoked cigars and drank fish style. The marriage would have protected our money on both sides. It's a shame I loathed him."

"Did you?" I was mildly scandalized. I suspected her parents were

too.

"I'm afraid so. I couldn't have spent more than two uninterrupted hours with him, never mind a lifetime, without letting him know what I thought of him. My dear, I'm not a lady. At least not by my mother's definition." Her feet didn't quite reach the floor from her seat. She swung them as if she were a child.

"So, he's the man you left at the altar?" I asked.

"I had to leave him somewhere," she said. "That seemed to work about as well as anywhere else I could think of. That was the summer we had a photographer take portraits of everyone as part of my brother's nuptials. The photographer was so quiet. And so kind. He posed my mother so her beauty mark and double chin weren't obvious. It wasn't easy. He took all morning to get the shot right."

"Did your mother know how good he was?" I asked her.

"She'd have noticed if he were bad at it." She said. "Mother wasn't perceptive about the lower classes."

"So, he took your picture too, Mildred?"

"For a whole afternoon, it seemed." Her cheeks took on a pink I hadn't seen in her for a while. "He posed me here and there, with a fan, with my shawl, with my terrier. He had the loveliest hands. They were soft and languid, like a girl's. But large. His every motion was considered." She'd gone languid herself. Her eyes were soft and dreamy.

"Did you fall in love with him?" I gave her a sly smile.

"Don't be silly child." She snapped back to her sensible self. "As if that would have mattered? He was a workman doing a job for us." She waved off the notion with her hand.

"It would matter, now-a-days." I picked her fan up off the table and pointed it at her hand.

"Then wasn't now," she said with bitter formality. "But you liked him?" I pushed at her.

She sighed deeply "I met him in the park, day after day. He gave me a camera and I wandered the park with him, taking pictures. We watched the birds while I fed them. I'd outgrown my nanny by years, but she went out with me as a chaperon. She didn't even try to keep up with us. She understood. She never said a thing. Not to me or to my mother."

"Do you know what happened to him." I asked her.

"Not for sure. Mildred sighed again. "He delivered our photos, and I wasn't allowed to go out for a while. I lost track. I figured he moved away. People moved a lot after the war."

"Was the photographer why you wouldn't marry your cousin?"

"I could never have married Rubin, child. He was an immigrant. He was from the Baltics. He came over right before the war."

"Did that stop you?" I asked her.

"That and the fact that my father threatened to cut me off from the family forever. I could face being poor. But I couldn't lose my mother.

She would do what my father requested. But his mother wouldn't accept me either. I wasn't Jewish. We both would have lost our families."

"How did your father know?"

"Families were different then," Mildred said. "Your father always knew everything. Servants everywhere and nothing ever private or secret. My father claimed it was for our protection. He just liked being in control."

I packed myself off and went through the park to the tea room. I stopped to sit by Rubin on her bench.

"Mildred was so in love with you," I said, looking closely at his beautiful hands.

"I know," he said miserably.

"Were you? In love with her?" I asked it tentatively. There was already so much pain between them.

He shrugged. "It was a dream. It wasn't possible. I wore a dapper suit and carried a camera. That made me look respectable, but I wasn't wealthy. I just looked acceptable to my clientele. Besides, she was a good Protestant girl. My mother would have died if I'd brought home a girl who wasn't Jewish. Mildred didn't even speak Yiddish. Her father threw me down the front stairs when I brought over the photos and asked his permission to court Mildred. One way or the other, the only way we could stay together was by losing all the family we both had. I read about the bans published in the paper, when she was to marry her cousin. I didn't come to the park again. I missed it. I missed her. But I had no future with her. If we'd been true to each other, we'd have betrayed everyone we loved."

"How old were you?" I asked.

"Nineteen," he said. He didn't look much older than nineteen now.

He must have died awfully young. "When did you die?" I needed to know the rest of the story.

"A year later," he said. "I went to fight in the war with all the other boys. I was in France at the time. I stood at the wrong spot under a bomber."

"Why are you waiting for her?" I knew the answer. I just wanted him to claim it.

"What else could I possibly do? I held my faith. I honored my parents. I lost her and nothing was right again in my life. I couldn't do anything then. I can watch over her now." His love had transformed over time from Eros to Agape. From passion to deep concern. It cost him a world of hurt but it was breathtakingly beautiful.

I told him her secret. "Did you know they shut her up in the tower?" Her family was beginning to make me ill.

"Literally? Like Rapunzel?" He shook his head at a modern fairy tale gone too real.

"Pretty much," I told him. "She spent years in the family tower, drawing and photo'ing the birds."

"I didn't know," he said. There was sad finality to that.

"She married years later," I told him. "But not to the cousin. She left him standing at the altar. She was waiting on you."

He shook a bit. He faded as the tears started to roll down his cheeks again. He left me, sitting on the bench alone as the mist rolled over me.

Mildred didn't get better. She came to the park on warm days, but her visits were less frequent. I took to visiting her once a week. I came in to find her, not in her study or in the window seat, but tucked in bed.

"This is undignified," she grumbled. "I hate it. I had a light-headed moment. Alfred called the doctor. The doctor is an ace-class bully. He told me I could rest at home or in the hospital. My choice. So here I am. Are the robins out in the park yet? And are you feeding my birds?"

"Your birds are fine. As for the robins, I saw three. Two males and a female up on the eves under the folly. The males are fighting it out as to who gets the girl," I gave my report. She clapped her hands at the news.

Mildred drifted to sleep after that.

That night I dreamed of Nona's long hair tangling with mine as we lay on the bed. "Are you lonely, Nona? I asked her. "Momma's always lonely." Nona hugged me. "I'm never lonely, Cara. I have you." Our hair twisted as it grew into a stout rope.

It spilled out the window, falli to the ground. Mildred was standing by the window. Nona looked at her and said, "You have to leave. You have to fly away, little bird. This is not a nest. It's a tomb." Mildred climbed out the window and began to climb down our twisted hair. She clung to the rope, unable to fly, unable to climb, unable to let go.

I came the next day. I didn't stay long. Mildred was weaker and I knew she needed rest. Alfred stopped me at the door.

"I'm glad you come to see her." His red face was shiny with sweat. He made a much better chauffeur than a nurse, and he knew it. He was well out of his comfort zone.

"She's a treasure." I told him "I've missed her at the park." "She's a lonely soul." He said.

"Well, that too. How long have you worked for her?" I asked.

He wiped his damp forehead. "It seems like forever," he told me. "Can I make you tea?" he asked.

We sat in the kitchen with a pot between us and two cups. It was then I noticed how similar he was to Mildred. His cheeks were different, but his eyes were much like hers. And, for a mechanic, he had lovely long hands. I had a notion.

"Alfred, are you a relative of the family?" It was a close shot. He flinched. I didn't want to hurt him but I needed to know. "Are you Mildred's son?"

"I'm not supposed to tell anyone that," he said with his eyes cast down at his shoes.

"Alfred, I don't think anyone who could be hurt by that is still alive.

You are a good son. You take good care of her."

"That I know," he said with more dignity. "They didn't let her raise me. They took me from her when I was born. Everyone said my birthmark was a sign that God was angry with me or with her or with both of us. I grew up in the home of a cousin in Chicago, until I was old enough to understand my position. When I was in my teens, they brought me to the house to be a servant. It's my home, as much as anyone else's. I don't think anyone knows, except Mrs. Pierce."

"You don't call her Mom? Mother? Mildred?" I knew as I said it none of those forms of address would be permitted.

She wouldn't mind. But no one else understood," he said. He shook his head as if it weighed too much. "It was sad, but we had rules then. We all had our place. No one would have hired me with this." He pointed to the birthmark on his face. "Her brother promised me a home, if I told no one."

Mildred did more than take pictures with her beautiful photographer. The family tried to marry her off appropriately to a cousin who would have been discreet about her problem if not unpleasant, and she'd refused. She bore her baby in her prison cell, the top tower of her family's home.

When I visited again I was greeted by Neville, with earbuds stuck in his ears. "Neville, I want to see your grand aunt," I hollered trying to be heard over the sounds in his ear. A businesslike forty-year-old woman in a classic grey suit came in the room carrying a clipboard.

"Who are you?" It was not just a question. It was an indictment. "I'm a friend of Mildred's. I came in to check on her." I could feel

her eyes up and down my clothes. I did not pass muster.

"She's far too ill for company," she snipped at me. "You'll have to come back later." I was shooed out the door within seconds.

I went around the block and landed at the servant's entry. Albert was polishing the car. "Marlene! Mrs. Pierce will be so glad to see you," he said as he put down his polishing cloth.

"I just got booted out the front door," I told him.

"Oh, that would be Judith. She's Neville's mother. She's taking an inventory of Mrs. Pierce's gee-gaws.

"She looked like a cross between auctioneer and undertaker," I exclaimed.

"Yep. That's Judith. She wouldn't let you in?" he asked. "Well that's silly." He opened the servant's entry to the kitchen where he'd taken me before.

"Judith will be in the study a while, I expect. But if we go up the back stairs, she'll never know you're there." He led me up the narrow corridors.

Mildred was in bed but clear-headed and awake.

"Mildred," I said, "I don't mean to alarm you, but Neville's mom is inventorying your stuff."

"I suggested it," Mildred said. "It got her out of my room. I couldn't stand another moment of her nursing me." She gave me a slick smile. "She asked me how we were today. I don't think she has a mouse in her pocket. I surely don't."

""What do your doctors say?" It couldn't be good. She looked too gray for it to be good.

"Mostly, they told me to pack my bags and get ready to go to God.

They wanted me in the hospital for tests and trials and all kinds of nonsense. I sent them out the door. The hospice nurse comes in regularly." She was clearly more chipper about hospice than hospitals.

"Oh, Mildred!" I was heart sick. But she didn't sound like she had a case of depression. It sounded like the end of a journey.

"Don't you dare be sad for me!" she said in mock anger. "I want out of here. And I'm going to get to go. I will miss you, child."

"Not until you're gone," I said. I would not grieve for her before her death. That was coming soon enough. Then I asked, "Is Albert going to be okay?" She looked at me like I shouldn't know anything about Albert.

"Have you set him up so he'll have what he needs? He is your son, isn't he?"

She was too sick for a belly laugh. But she tried. "Oh, that. You're a sharp cookie. I knew you'd figure it out. Isn't he a good boy?"

"He's a lovely man. And he loves you so much."

"I never handled wills or legal matters. My brother made the decisions and told me where to sign." She may have been bullied. But she was sheltered too. She had no idea how wrong a will could go.

"I don't think that will work this time," I told her. "Just in case. You can't leave him without a home. He's as sheltered as you are." Or as caged, I thought.

"Either way, he needs to be provided for. Give me your lawyer's name and I'll make an appointmentfor him to visit you. You can confirm that your will says what you want. Do you want me there?"

"That would be nice," she said. "I don't always understand what they're saying. I wish I were a bird," she said. "I wish I could just fly away."

"Don't we all," I said as I tucked her in for her nap.

The law firm, Gasper and Phillips, sent the younger Phillips, a man in his early sixties. He was buttoned into his suit but there was no guarantee he would stay that way. The buttons were straining across his stomach.

Albert brought chairs up to her room and Phillips and I sat around her bed.

Mr. Phillips said, "I don't know why you want to review this, Mildred. Your brother set this up with the firm 5 years ago. We do have your signature on the will."

"I'm an old lady," Mildred started. I don't always remember things. I'd just like to be sure. I don't need you to read it to me. It's legal gobbley gook. I need a synopsis of what it says."

"I do have those figures on paper," he said. He pulled out a sheet from his folder. "There's an endowment to the Protestant Church of Boston, Boston College, and to the Boston Art Museum."

"I see," she said. I could tell from her face that all of that was news. "Then things are divided evenly between Judith and Neville Anders,

and your cousin Patience Long.

"I see. Is there anything in there about my staff?" she asked. "Your staff?" The lawyer looked confused.

"Albert," she said.

"Albert? Who is Albert?" Phillips had no idea who that was.

"Albert Browning, Mr. Phillips. I think we'll need to rearrange a few things here. Get out your pen and write this down. How much money do I have?"

I sat quietly in the room. I was there to make sure no one ran roughshod over her. But Mildred held her own. Phillips said he would bring the documents for her to sign, and I whisked him out the door.

Two days later I found Rubin on the bench again. "Come with me," I said. I have something you should see." You can't grab a ghost by the arm. But I made as if I were going to, just to make my point.

He grumbled a bit at me. But he let my gesture work. He followed after me. "It's about Mildred," I said. "It's important." He followed me in ghostly fashion, to her home. When we arrived, he started downstairs to the servant's entry. "Don't be silly," I said. "No one but me can see you. But I think she might."

"Is she that ill?" he asked with closed eyes.

"Yes. I think so. But she's not sad about it. She needs to know someone's waiting for her." I rang the bell. Alfred let me in through the door without noticing Rubin at my heels. We climbed up to her room. I put my head around the door jamb to check before we walked in.

She looked more faded than before. When I touched her cheek to wake her, her skin felt papery, like parchment. She opened her eyes first on me and focused across the room.

"I brought you a photographer," I said softly. "He wants to take your picture." Her eyes widened. She recognized him. Her coming death permitted her to see him.

"Mr. Levi," she said.

"Miss Downing," he said in answer. "I hear you have need of a photographer." He took off his hat and placed it on the table.

"I do," she said. "Come sit down by me and we can discuss my portrait."

He sat on her bed, her hand in his.

Downstairs both Judith and the lawyer were in a screaming match. "What do you mean she changed her will?" Judith's voice cut through walls and ceilings.

Mr. Phillips said, "She's of sound mind. This is her decision. It will hold in court, although you're welcome to try. She made a number of very sensible changes. She gave money to the Audubon Society, and to a battered women's shelter. She said that they were doing work that changed people's lives. She was inspiring on the subject."

"And her chauffeur Albert gets everything remaining?" Judith's voice went up two or three notes higher.

"Not everything. You, and Neville after you, will have a nice two million dollars. As will Patience. The rest goes to her Albert."

"She must have been tricked by him." Judith's reality had just taken a left turn she couldn't follow.

"I don't believe so," said Mr. Phillips. "She told me an interesting story out of her early womanhood. In the will, she called him her son, Alfred."

"What!" Judith screamed. "Mildred never had children. She just lived up in her stupid tower."

There was more yelling and stamping of feet. Someone slammed a door hard enough you could feel it through the walls. I heard Alfred's footsteps approaching. "Mrs. Pierce," he said.

"Stop that, Albert. That's play acting. I'm too old for play acting.

What did I ask you to call me?"

"Mother?" This was going to take Albert some time to get used to. "Alfred, I'm ashamed in ways that I can't say. But I've called you mine now. I should have done it fifty five years ago but I was a coward. If they give you trouble, the lawyer has suggested we do some genetic testing immediately. He has it all arranged."

Rubin's eyes were wide. There was his son. A kind good man who had cared for the woman they both loved all of their days.

"He's mine?" Rubin asked her.

Mildred nodded. "He's a hidden gem," she said. "He has your hands, you know."

Mildred said, to Albert, "I loved your father with my whole heart.

They wouldn't let me marry him. I've loved you as well. They wouldn't let me claim you. I wish we'd lived in a world where the differences mattered less." She sighed deeply. She closed her eyes.

She faded into Reuben's arms. Her breathing stopped. Albert was crying as he ran down to call for the medics. There was no point. Mildred was gone and so glad to be going. She had gone to be with her love.

If a nice Jewish ghost were in love with a beautiful Protestant ghost, there was no one who could say anything about it now. I saw Rubin take her hand and they walked together through the window.

I looked out the window to see two small birds soaring together in the sky.

I went back to the park to Mildred's bench and scattered a handful of bread crumbs in a circle around it. The birds fluttered down to be fed.

Tea Room Tales by Ellen Anne Eddy

Tea for Two

Tea for Two

Silvy sat at the table with me over our muffins. Silvy had almost been my college roommate. An argument about overdue library books and chaos levels belayed that, but it never stopped our friendship. Instead, we'd been left-over loser girls who made our own fun together, lost for no dates and far too uncool to party much. One winter evening Silvy had made tea and read my leaves for me.

I was amazed. Charmed. Compelled. It was so cool. Eventually she taught me to read. Once a week at least, we stared into each other's cups, not that we needed too. We already knew everything about each other's lives. The options at school were so limited. More homework. An occasional guy to flirt with in class. The full expurgation of the impossible crush.

Silvy's business degree had brought her an up and coming spot in a design firm for women's sport gear. She didn't look more fashionable in an on-the-town way, but she looked more together. Some of the baby fat had gone out of her face. Her dark blond hair was arranged into a French twist. Gone were the sweats and the colored sneakers. In their place was an elegant draped top and tight jeans with spike heel shoes. She looked grown up. Corporate in a place where fashion was corporate. Such big changes for her in less than a year's time. Did she have a few gray hairs?

Her aura bloomed around her, red and purple, ambition and common sense mixed.

I had evolved from dark sweats and jeans into a retro hippie top and broomstick skirt, my hair up in a bun pinned by two chopsticks, dangling earrings like small wind chimes in my ears. My sandals were Earth shoe clones. I still wore Nona's hand charm at my throat. Neither of us mentioned the shaded glasses I needed to wear after the accident.

The differences between us had widened the gap farther than I was comfortable with. But she was still my Silvy.

I read for her first. "You're moving," I said. "I see boxes everywhere. It's somewhere sunny. I see you with a new cat. Your home is in turmoil.

There's a new man in your life with a name that starts with C. Charles? Cummings? He's very good for you.

"You're going to grow a garden. I know you hate dirt. But I see you with roses all around your doorway.

"Beware of those pumps. I see you lying on the ground with a twisted ankle. Can't tell if that's past or present."

I placed her upside-down cup on the napkin, showing that I had finished. She shook her head in mild disbelief.

"Well, the sprained ankle already happened. The move too. I'm being placed in San Diego. You can't imagine how beautiful it is! Sun every day, and palm trees and parrots living loose in the park. It's a dream."

"What about the guy?"

"No guy yet. Our company profile is almost all women except at the very top. Too much work, not enough men there to find. But you're right about the roses. The house I bought is circled in them. They bloom all year and it's amazing to walk through them. Did get a kitten. His name is Captain. So. Hand your cup over and it's your turn."

I twisted my upside-down cup on the napkin and handed to her. She squinted as if she'd seen something that hurt her eyes. "Marlene, what have you been doing? There's a UFO in your cup. There's a guy with a knife. And a doll with teeth! Did you really go into a gypsy camp? And why is there a snake in your cup?"

I laughed out loud. "Silvy, it's a long story." And I poured her more tea as I told her everything.

Author
Ellen Anne Eddy

Ms. Eddy has spent over thirty years teaching fiber art to the quilt community all over America. Her books, *Thread Magic*, and *Thread Magic Garden*, have been seminal to the Art Quilt Movement.

The stories in these books are from her early years in Boston. They are works of fiction and imagination, but they have their roots in the time she spent there.Ms. Eddy currently resides in Galesburg, Illinois with her husband, Donald Bowers, and her cats and dog. She sews, quilts, writes and dreams up crazy stories, just as she always has.

Want More Tales of the Tea Room?

What would you do if you could see the future? If you were psychic? Could you read the future? Help order people's lives? Keep them safer? Win the lottery? Change the world? Or would you discover that foreknowledge changes nothing. What would you risk? What would you try? What would you do?

Marlene finds herself working in a tea room, where she is confronted with witches, psychics, artists, Voodoo practitioners, scammers, and genuine. Can she embrace them as people, and still hold on to herself?

How do you help people truly different from yourself? How do you put the differences aside?

Follow Marlene's stories as she transforms from a college student to one of the most powerful psychics in her community. Can she negotiate the future? Unravel the past? And find her own future in the world of sight?

Book 1: Tea Room Tales	Book 2: The Inverted Cup	Book 3: The World in Reflection